Green Lord's Guardian

L. J. Hutton

ISBN 13: 9781791928261

Published by Wylfheort Books 2016

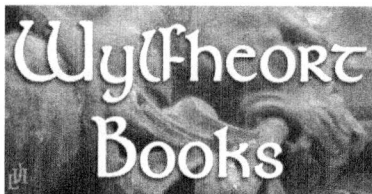

Acknowledgments

Mary Ward has continued to provide food for thought with discussions on Old English poetry, which led to some moment of inspiration for this book, and which have provided some much needed intellectual stimulation.

Also thanks to Kev Robinson for running a cracking course on crime writing some years back. Check out Crime Writing Solutions and his writing for some good background on how the police work. (Any mistakes are mine, not his!)

Thanks to Ann Farr for ongoing moral support.

And of course to my husband for putting up with me being in a different world for large chunks of a day. He's also the arch-pedant who double-checks my work for those 'dyslexic finger' moments that spell-checkers just don't get, and walks our lovely lurchers when I just need to get 'one more paragraph' down.

Our lovely Minnie was curled up on the sofa providing silent support for most of this project with the other two, but is sadly now gone, but her place has been replaced by Dirk – who has no idea what his mom does when she's tapping away, but is good at making me stop when it's time to feed him.

Thank you every one of you!

Chapter 1

Monday - Wednesday

DI Bill Scathlock woke up and roundly cursed the Thompson brothers as he'd done for the last seven mornings. There wasn't a part of him which wasn't sore, and a good deal which actively hurt. He eased himself gingerly into a sitting position, and then forced himself to bend his legs to put his feet on the floor. His only consolation was that the Thompsons were in a worse state than he was.

He'd been in the car with Clive from Traffic, as good a driver as you could get, but who would have thought the Thompsons would have done something so indescribably stupid as to do a hand-brake turn on the M5? Let alone in a knackered van that would roll, not spin! As he padded through to the shower and let the hot water do its best to relieve the overnight corpselike feelings, Bill went over the scene yet again. How Clive had torn off the motorway at junction five, picked Bill up from the car that had brought him from Worcester police station, and then shot back onto the M5 again. The Thompsons were a part of a large, settled family of ex-Travellers and the bane of many officers' existence. They would steal anything which wasn't nailed down, but normally their crimes were of the petty variety – heartbreaking for their victims but not easily solved, nor a high priority if truth be told. But this time they'd done something Bill could really nail them for. A security guard had got badly hurt in an attempted factory break-in in Bromsgrove, and a sharp-eyed witness had taken the licence-plate of the villains' van. And so had begun the pursuit.

By pure chance Bill had been in the station when the calls had started to come in, but he'd known that number plate without checking, and where it was heading! Determined to be there when the pair got their comeuppance, Bill had joined the chase, and now he was suffering for it. He was glad that the shower had steamed up the mirrors. That way he didn't have to see how bad he looked. The bits he could see had every shade of purple, blue and green a bruise could produce. Thank God he'd been in the front where the airbag had protected him. Had Clive had his normal partner with him, Bill would have been in the back and probably dead now. It was a measure of Clive's skill that when Bertie Thompson had pulled his daft stunt – apparently intending to nip back to the slip-road at junction seven which he was just passing – that Clive had managed to spin the big BMW so that the Transit van only went up over the back of the car. They'd still had to be cut out, though.

Now the Thompsons were lying in Worcester Royal looking like something out of a bad comedy sketch, bandaged to the eyeballs and with bits in traction, and Bill was off work for the next few weeks. He'd protested about that. The fortnight he'd been signed off as sick leave he couldn't do much about, but his superintendent had added another two onto that.

"Bill, you've had a major accident," Williams had insisted. "On top of that you've got leave backed up from since God knows when, not to mention the time you still need to take from the overtime you did on the last big case. There's no way I can pay you for it all, some will have to be taken as time in lieu."

Bill had grumbled as best he could when he was lying on a hospital bed with his ribs strapped up and nurses present, but Williams had been immovable.

"You've got cracked ribs from the seat belt. They're not going to heal overnight! So you'd have to be on light duties anyway. And I'm not having you prowling round the station, sticking your nose into everything you can find because you're bored. Take the damned leave!"

And so Bill was now at home, and he was already bored stiff.

He put on a soft tracksuit as the kindest thing for his battered bits, and made his way carefully to the kitchen. It wasn't a big flat, just one of everything – lounge, bedroom, bathroom and kitchen – but it was in the lower ground floor of a huge old house, and so the rooms were spacious and high-ceilinged. In pride of place in the kitchen was an expensive Italian coffee machine, which was soon gurgling happily to itself with the first brew of the day.

Rustling noises, and a groan from the direction of the large squashy sofa, alerted Bill to the fact that his overnight guest was surfacing.

"Is that coffee I can smell?" a disembodied voice asked, soon followed by the bleary eyes and tousled hair of Morag Duncan.

"Hot and strong and coming up any minute," Bill confirmed.

Morag sat up, pulling the duvet around her. "Jeez, how much did we drink last night?"

"You mean, how much did *you* drink last night! I'm on the painkillers, remember? You arrived with a takeaway curry and two bottles of red. I did my bit with the curry, but there's two empty bottles in my recycling which never went near my lips."

"Christ! No wonder I've a mouth like a parrot's crotch!"

Bill brought her over two Alka-Seltzers fizzing vigorously in the bottom of a glass of water. "Down the hatch!"

Morag gulped the mixture back as soon as it was dissolved, wincing as she did so. "Bill, you're a saint, you know that? How come some woman's never snapped you up?"

He chuckled as he came back with a steaming mug-full each. "I know, if I was a woman you'd snap me up."

Morag managed a wry grin. "Can't help it if my hormones have me batting for the home team, can I?"

It was a long-standing joke between them of the sort good friends have. They'd known one another since Bill was a DS and Morag one of his DCs. Now Morag had taken a sideways move into the admin' side of the police, working alongside the civilian members of the team, but if Bill had a major case ongoing he would still ask for Morag to be his Statement Reader. She had never lost her keen eye for detail, even if she'd found the actual operations side of things had become unbearable – tough enough for any female officer, but to be gay as well just gave the misogynists amongst her colleagues another stick to beat her with.

"Oh shite!" she suddenly exclaimed, the residue of her Scottish accent creeping out in her anxiety. "What time is it?"

Bill put a hand on her shoulder to stop her trying to leap up. "Calm down! It's Monday but you're not on duty, remember?" He couldn't help laughing at the expression of relief which crossed Morag's face as she subsided into the comfort of the sofa's cushions again. "You daft bat, even you don't get that tanked-up when there's work the next day!"

She cast a baleful eye his way. "It's come damned close a few times in the last couple of months."

Bill had heard Morag's confessions last night. Of how her wife, Jackie had thrown a tanrum of massive proportions right in the middle of a nasty case where

4

different members of a family were telling conflicting versions of how two children had died. No-one liked these sorts of cases. They left a bad taste in the mouth of even the most hardened officers. Getting through one was tough enough without your personal life imploding on you, and Morag had Bill's sympathy. She too had taken a few days leave to try and get herself straightened out, and now Bill was glad he'd made her stay rather than pouring her into a taxi to go home. They both needed the company.

By Wednesday morning she was still there, albeit with a trip home to get fresh clothes in between, saying that she felt that she and Jackie needed some time out from one another. The sofa was big enough to be a substitute bed, and after the number of stakeouts they'd shared in the past, they were hardly shy of being in such close proximity with one another for a few days. On Tuesday they'd neither felt like driving and had walked up the riverside path to Grimley and had a pub meal, then strolled back, taking time to sit and stare whenever Bill found himself wincing too much. It was good therapy for him – just enough exercise to stop him from stiffening into immobility without overdoing anything. As Wednesday morning drew on bright and sunny they were contemplating walking into town and taking a trip on the train. Bill had a much-loved classic Mini tucked away, but it wasn't the car for him to be driving at the moment, and Morag's tiny and elderly Micra was equally as cramped for someone of Bill's height and bulk.

Morag wandered back into the lounge towelling her hair dry and noticed that the French windows were open. The joy of this flat was that it had a glorious view across the River Severn to the racecourse on the other side, and being the basement one, had easy access out to the lawned garden which sloped steeply down to the riverbank itself – which was why it had been a main room in the old house despite being downstairs. Wandering out onto the small veranda, she draped the towel over the rail and drew in a deep breath of the fresh air. So much better than her city centre flat!

Bill was down by the gate watching the kids from the local private school rowing on the river, mug in hand. He'd always loved sports and was drawn to most kinds, but was more of a participant than a TV watcher. However he still got huge enjoyment out of watching pretty much any sport if he could be there in person – hence his absorption with the school sports. Unfortunately, as a player, he'd finally realized that rugby was no longer the game for him, and that getting trampled on a weekly basis got tougher as the years went by. As yet he hadn't seemed to find another sport which suited his build and temperament, although Morag couldn't quite imagine him in one of the slinky skiffs he was now watching so intently. His only other concession to having turned forty this year was that he now drank decaff for most of the day, but Morag sometimes thought he'd be lost without a mug in one hand or the other.

The first lot of rowers had now disappeared from sight and yet Bill was clearly still engrossed. Suddenly there came the sound of distant shouting and the odd cheer, and Morag then realized that it must be some sort of rowing contest. Lots of smaller children appeared through the gaps in the riverside trees, paddling the small individual skiff for all they were worth, and the noise was that of proud parents egging their offspring on.

She was about to go back in with her towel when she caught sight of something on the opposite bank. A small boy had clearly got fed up with being left behind by his more able competitors and had nudged his little skiff into the far bank where there was a bit of a sandy shelf. He threw down his paddle in disgust and, having plonked the front end of the skiff on the bank high enough for it not to be washed away. The way he then stopped and began rubbing what was clearly bad cramp in his leg revised Morag's opinion, and he was turning to limp up the bank when two men appeared.

To Morag's horror they grabbed him by the arms and began towing him up the steep slope. His yells of distress, apparent to her by her view of him turning back to call out, were being drowned out by the parental cheering.

"Bill!" she screamed, seeing that he had turned his back on the river and was walking back towards her. "Over there, Bill! The kid! Someone's taking the kid!"

Bill took it in in a glance, dropped the coffee mug unheeded on the grass, and ran hobbling back to the bottom of the garden and out onto the bank. Morag shut the French window more forcefully than she might have, grabbed Bill's keys which were on the coffee table and her own mobile, and slamming the back door behind her, ran out after him, dialing straight through to the main police station as she did so. She gave the answering clerk short shrift and got through to a sergeant who must have been new.

"Someone's just grabbed a little boy on the banks of the Severn," she said tersely. "No it's not his parents, yes he is struggling, and I'm former DC Morag Duncan, so don't tell me I don't know what I'm seeing! They're dragging him north across the racecourse, not towards the main entrance or the rowing club. DI Bill Scathlock is with me." She hoped like mad that Bill's name might ring bells, and mercifully it did. By the time she'd reached Bill there was a promise of a response coming, but more surprisingly Bill had managed to attract the attention of the support boat for the rowers, and it was coming in to the small landing stage on the other side of the riverside path to the garden. Before it had made full contact, Bill had scrambled aboard and Morag had to make a leap not to be left behind.

"Get me across the river!" Bill snapped authoritatively. "There, where that skiff is!" The boat's pilot took in the abandoned canoe, but before she could argue Bill added, "Someone just grabbed the kid from that boat!"

"Who are you?" the pilot blurted.

"DI Scathlock and this is DC Duncan. Off duty!" Bill growled.

The pilot turned white and shot the small boat across the river at speed, not worrying about soaking those onboard.

"Thank God they won't have been able to get a car close!" Bill said over his shoulder to Morag with more than a little relief. "We'd have no chance at all of catching the bastards if they'd been nearer the cathedral and the road!"

Instead, the spot they were heading for was backed by the full width of Worcester racecourse, and was nearly half way along its considerable length. Before the boat had fully come to a halt at the sandy shelf, Bill was out of it and pounding up the bank. A concrete slope put in for the regular fishermen made his ascent all the easier, and before Morag was even out of the boat he was lost to sight.

Puffing up the slope, Morag instantly realized that there was no way she was going to catch up with Bill to assist him. It might be a few years since Bill had played rugby, but he had certainly kept fit, and the burst of speed he was putting on now in spite of his pain reminded her of watching him making tries for the police team years ago. If the kidnappers thought they were going to get away without a chase they were in for a nasty surprise! As it was, the two men were dragging the boy across the open grass, but had their hands full with him. For such a small child he was putting up a spirited struggle, kicking the men when they tried to put him over their shoulders, and lashing out at their legs when they swung him between them.

Suddenly Morag heard the sound of sirens. Stopping and dialing back to the station, she managed to get a message through to the cars as to which end of the racecourse the kidnappers were heading for. Not for the main gates and the small public car park beside them, but to the north end of the racecourse and the much less used gate out onto Waterworks Road. As she panted along in Bill's wake, she caught a glimpse of a flashing blue light in the distance and knew that help had arrived.

Unfortunately, so had the two men. They now veered to their right, and Morag knew they'd be trying for the other small gate onto Pitchcroft Lane. Ahead of her, Bill had gained ground on them because of their sudden turn, and was closing fast. Whatever the pair were expecting it wasn't Bill's flying tackle. The one went down with Bill on top of his legs, and Morag heard Bill's yelp of pain as his ribs took another hit.

Normally Bill was remarkably restrained over any use of violence, but in his present state he was short on patience. As the man he'd brought down tried to rise and shake him off, Bill head-butted him hard, scrambled half to his feet and grabbed the ankle of the other man, who was turning to run with the boy. Staying low, Bill waited until the man did as he'd anticipated and tried to kick back at Bill, at which point he toppled the man by the simple expedient of lifting his leg even higher, using his own leg muscles to push upwards with. As the man crashed to the ground, Morag was close enough to grab the boy, then discourage the man from further struggles by kicking him in the balls.

As Bill staggered to his feet, they could see four officers streaming in from the north end of the racecourse towards them.

"You! Stay still!" Bill growled at them as he hugged his sore ribs. "You're under arrest!"

9

Yet before Bill could begin to formally caution them, the two men crabbed sideways away from him and, hanging on to one another, struggled into a stumbling run.

"Oh you are fucking joking!" Bill groaned.

However Morag just nodded in the direction of the main gates, and Bill saw that now there were more officers coming in that way too, and he sank down onto one knee in relief.

"Bleedin' Hell, Bill, can't you keep outta trouble for five minutes?" panted one of the first four uniformed men, as they hammered past them in hot pursuit of the kidnappers, who had now turned towards the river in their desperation.

Someone could be heard yelling into a radio calling for someone to head them off along Grandstand Road, and Bill and Morag were able to turn their attention to the boy.

"It's okay, you're safe now," Morag reassured him, holding him close.

Now that they could see him properly, it occurred to them that he was probably older than he looked. From his height and build he'd barely seemed old enough to be going to a senior school, but Bill didn't think the juniors from the linked school up the road were allowed to row on the river. However it seemed more likely that he was of an age to make the first year of the senior school, even if he still had a lot of growing to do.

At the moment Bill was struggling not to swear with the pain, but he managed to force some calm into his voice as he asked,

"What's your name, son?"

The lad looked at him and then to Morag with eyes so pale they were almost colourless, and seemed to reflect the watery grey sky. His hair was dark to the point of being a true black, but his skin was also remarkably pale, with visibly high cheekbones which gave him an exotic appearance, and Bill belatedly wondered if he might be one of the foreign children at the school. There was certainly something about him which didn't quite fit with the idea of him being one of the local kids.

"You do understand me, don't you?" Bill added, and was rewarded with a nervous nod. He breathed a sigh of relief. Thank heavens for that! It was always hard to know how hard to push a child for information when they might be badly shocked. Overcoming a language barrier would have made it near impossible. "I'm a policeman. Do you know what that means? I'm a detective from the police station here in Worcester." Again he got a nod. "Good, so you understand that you're safe now? Whoever those men were, they won't harm you now. So can you tell me what your name is so that we can tell the school you've been found? Are your mum and dad here today?"

The boy shook his head.

"Who looks after you, sweetheart?" Morag asked, hoping that he might respond better to her than to Bill. "Don't you worry about DI Scathlock, here. He's a funny colour because he's been in an accident. It's just bruises. He's quite normal underneath."

Too late, Bill remembered how he'd looked in the mirror this morning, and blessed the fact that for the first time since the accident he'd actually been able to face having a shave. With the stubble coming through the techni-coloured blotches he'd looked like Bill Sykes out of *Oliver Twist*! Enough to scare any kid half to death, let alone one who'd had such a nasty fright.

"Does it hurt?" the boy suddenly asked, pointing to a particularly livid bruise on Bill's left cheek.

"Like mad!" Bill answered truthfully, but managed a lopsided smile too.

The boy regarded him with the gravity of one far older than his years, as if thinking of what to say. "I am Tapio

Törni," he said out of the blue, and held out his hand for Bill to shake.

"Pleased to meet you, Tapio," Bill returned solemnly, carefully shaking the small hand which disappeared into his huge paw. "We'd better get you back to the school. They'll be worried."

The three of them began walking back down the racecourse, and had just reached the car-park when a patrol car screeched in, and a harassed woman leapt out and then seemed to buckle at the knees when she saw Tapio was all right.

"Oh thank God!" she gasped.

"It's all right, Miss Flanagan," Tapio said with remarkable calm. "I was rescued by this policeman."

"*You're* a policeman?" she gulped, taking in Bill's battered state.

"DI Bill Scathlock," Bill confirmed. "Off duty."

"He is," declared the police officer who'd climbed out of the passenger side to join her. "He's just a bit battered because he was in a crash after a high-speed chase last week." Then couldn't resist adding, "God knows what the Super's going to say about this – he's supposed to be on sick leave!"

"Oye! You leave Williams out of this," Bill protested with a roll of his eyes. "I'll deal with him when I have to."

However the teacher was waving a shaking hand in his general direction. "But ...but ...I don't understand. How did you get involved then?"

Bill pointed back to the river. "I live over there. My friend DC Duncan, here, was visiting me and we were watching the rowing from my garden. She saw Tapio being taken because she was higher up the bank than me."

The teacher turned and grasped Morag's hand. "I can't begin to thank you enough! What we'd have done if he'd gone I don't know. We're not ...we don't have ...we're not trained for *this*! I don't think we've ever had a kidnapping from the school in over four hundred years!"

"Well you haven't now," Bill told her firmly. "He's fine, but why don't we get him back to the school where he can have a hot drink and recover from his fright?"

"I'll walk, sir," volunteered the constable. "Tom can then drive you four all together to the school."

"Good lad," Bill approved as he hobbled to the car and eased himself into the front seat. "You'll have to excuse me hogging the best seat, Miss Flanagan, but I don't think my ribs will take me folding up to get into the back!"

Chapter 2

Wednesday

Morag got into the car behind Bill, put Tapio in the middle, and the teacher got in on the other, and the car pulled away with its occupants sitting in relieved silence, until Tapio said earnestly,

"Are you all right, Miss? I can feel you shaking."

"Yes, I'm fine," Miss Flanagan said, but with little conviction. "We were all just so shocked when we got the call from the police to say ...to say..."

Bill looked at her in the vanity mirror above him and saw her swallow convulsively. She was right, British teachers weren't taught what to do in the case of a child being kidnapped for the simple reason it didn't happen here – or at least not out here in the sleepier counties. Maybe in London with the children of diplomats, or the like, but not here. And he could just imagine the chaos such a thing would cause at any school – private or state – never mind the legal implications of the school standing in *loco parentis* and failing. No wonder she was looking rattled to the soles of her rather nice Italian-looking shoes.

"Not something you got in the teacher training course, eh?" Bill said to her, turning in his seat and giving her an encouraging smile. "If this makes you feel any better, there are specially trained people in the police who deal with abductions." He was very careful not to say the word 'kidnappings' in front of the boy, because it came with such a raft of emotive connotations, and he didn't want to scare the lad more than he was already. "Had things not been sorted so fast you wouldn't have been left to the tender mercies of us lot – we'd have called in the big guns pronto! And they're *very* good at what they do. That's why they don't talk much in public about what they do. They don't want the opposition to know just what they can do, but take it from me, they're the folks you want holding your hand every inch of the way, and they don't give up."

Miss Flanagan managed a watery smile for him, as she took in what he was trying to say to calm the riot of imagined outcomes which were racing through her mind. However, they were already pulling up outside of the school, which occupied several rather splendid Georgian former townhouses, and another pale and anxious teacher hurried them to the head's office. The name plate declared him to be Peter Dumville, B.Ed., and by the size of him as he rose to greet them, and the way he held himself, Bill guessed he was another former rugby player. His eyebrows raised a little as he took in Bill's battered appearance, and Morag's faded vest-top, old combats and Doc Martens, but was too polite to comment.

"I'm DI Bill Scathlock, and this is DC Morag Duncan, but we won't be running the enquiry into all of this," Bill swiftly said, wanting to set the record straight from the start. "A DCI will be along any minute, I wouldn't be at all surprised, to take over. We're both off duty officially, but we thought it best if we stayed with Tapio until he can be talked to formally about what happened to him."

"Ah," Peter Dumville said with the air of someone who hadn't really grasped the reality yet, but was desperately trying to stop his world from sliding into a sudden and unexpected abyss.

"Any chance of a cuppa?" Bill asked with his most disarming grin. "And I'm sure the lad could do with something sweet for the fright he's had."

Dumville blinked, then seemed to regain some focus and took in that Tapio was still standing before him. "Oh yes! Miss Flanagan, would you mind dreadfully trying to find someone who could do the honours?" he asked, and, clearly glad to be able to escape and go somewhere to scream quietly, she hurried out of the door.

"Tapio, why don't you come and sit down over here?" the head said, coming and drawing the boy over to a comfortable chair by the window and round to the other side of his desk, where he could swivel in his chair and speak directly to him without a barrier between them. It was easy to imagine that many pupils must have sat there and poured out their troubles, for to Bill's eye it was in a much more welcoming position than the chairs he and Morag sat in facing the desk. These two would be more for the parents, and any child who was there facing the head's wrath.

"Are you hurt in any way?" Dumville asked Tapio solicitously.

"No sir," the boy answered calmly.

Almost too calmly, Bill thought. He'd make a point of trying to have a word with whichever child psychologist got the job of talking the experience over with the lad.

"Are the parents on their way?" Morag asked, and was surprised to see Dumville wince, as if she'd asked a particularly tactless question. It was a perfectly reasonable question to ask in the circumstances. Nothing would quell the child's fears quicker than his mum and dad coming and whisking him back into the bosom of his family. Or was there something here which wasn't so good? Surely not divorce? Even if the parents were at loggerheads, in Morag's experience such differences would normally be put aside in the initial shock. Recriminations might follow later – especially if one had been in favour of this particular school and the other not. Stuff along the lines of 'see where *your* choice of school got us?' would be a pretty average response, but not now, not today. Today was for hugs and tears, and 'Thank God you're alright's.

Morag looked to Bill and could see by the way he'd tensed that he'd picked up on the reponse too. Did this mean that there was something dodgy about one or other of the parents? That could really set the cat amongst the pigeons, investigation-wise. She'd never been involved in a kidnapping case, but her educated guess was that potential victims were usually connected to someone with either enough money to pay up the kind of vast amounts which would attract the greedy; or were in the sort of political position where taking a member of their family would allow pressure to be brought to bear. But there was another possibility – that Tapio's family was of the criminal fraternity themselves, and was being targeted by others even more unscrupulous than themselves. God help the poor lad if that was the case! She could well imagine that the school would then have to weigh the safety of all the other pupils against his, if there was even a hint that this might happen again.

Luckily the school matron appeared, and as a fully qualified nurse, set to making sure Tapio was as fine as he said he was. This gave Bill the chance to pull Dumville to one side and ask softly,

"Is there something we should know about the parents, sir?"

Yet the head's response wasn't what either Bill or Morag expected.

"I don't actually know."

Bill frowned. "What do you mean, you don't know? Don't know if there's something suspicious about them, or don't know them well enough to tell us?"

Dumville all but winced. "Don't know, as in: don't know if they even exist."

Bill hid his reaction well, but Morag knew him well enough to know that his internal radar was instantly going full-belt towards suspicion.

"Morag, why don't you stay here with Matron while the head and I have a chat outside?" Bill suggested in such a way that the head was left in no doubt that Bill was one step short of hauling him straight down to the station for questioning.

As the door closed behind the two of them, and Dumville let them into another small office which for now was empty, Bill began with,

"Now then, are there or are there not parents who need to be informed of what just happened, Mr. Dumville? I know I'm not going to be running the greater enquiry, but the DCI isn't going to be worried that I'm pressing you on this matter. Normally the phone-call would already have been made. So why hasn't it?"

Dumville took a deep breath. "Well for a start, the people I had every reason to believe are Tapio's parents are in Finland."

Bill blinked in surprise. "Okay, that would make their turning up today a bit difficult, I grant you. So who looks after the lad? I thought you'd stopped taking in boarders at the school years ago?"

"We did. No, detective, Tapio doesn't live at the school. He lives at a house rented on his behalf with his guardian. A young woman. She seems to be something more than an au pair, but not a family member – or at least as far as I can tell."

"And what about the parents? You're surely not telling me that you take on any kid whose parents – or whoever – flash a wad of cash at you, regardless of who they are?"

Dumville frowned, clearly stung. "No we do not! We may charge fees here, but it's not all about money! We want to know something about the children we take on."

"So what did you mean when you were talking about Tapio's parents maybe not even existing? I'm sorry to have to press you on this, but if there's even a hint that something's amiss, I won't be the only policeman you have jumping up and down demanding answers. We have to get to the bottom of why someone tried to grab young Tapio today, and now we're out of his hearing, I can tell you that to my eye these weren't just random thugs thinking any kid from this school would be good for a few quid's worth of ransom. Those two bruisers meant business. So the investigating team will need to ascertain pretty quickly whether or not Tapio was the intended victim all along, or whether he was just unfortunate."

"What?" Dumville gulped. "You mean they might have grabbed just any child from the school? But I thought you said...?"

"I meant that maybe he's unlucky enough to look like the real intended victim," Bill said bluntly. "So do you see that we need to eliminate the dead ends as fast as possible, so that the team uses all their efforts to solve the real crime, instead of a bunch of random possibilities?"

Dumville sank to sit on the edge of a desk. "Bugger it!"

Bill snorted wryly, "That's one way of putting it."

The other man raised his head and managed a weak smile back. "Look, I know this is going to sound bloody daft, but believe me, it didn't feel that way when I was making the arrangements to have Tapio come to the school. I spoke several times to both a man and a woman on the phone – more often the woman. They came across as suitably concerned parents. They said that they were both employed by a small company working with high-tech stuff which is allied to the oil industry. They told me that they had a long-term contract to do work out in the Middle East. They were quite open about saying that three or four years doing this job would set them up for life, it was that lucrative, but by the same token they didn't think it was the kind of job to take Tapio with them on.

"Well that sounded reasonable enough. For a start off, they couldn't guarantee that they'd be in the one country for the whole time. So if he went with them they might be moving him every year or so, and therefore schools too, and they didn't think that was ideal at all. Also, a certain amount of the time they were going to be in Iraq, and that's not the most stable of countries, is it?"

Bill nodded. "I can see how you'd be convinced by that argument."

"Exactly. And they said that if they were going to have to leave Tapio behind, then having him close to Birmingham airport meant that he would be able to fly out pretty easily to join them if things looked safe when school holidays came around. They thought that London might be too overwhelming for him, because he'd been brought up in the country, but that we were ideally placed"

"A bit strange taking him away from the wider family and any friends he had, though?"

Dumville sighed heavily. "It didn't sound that way. They said that both sets of grandparents had died, but that there was someone whom they trusted to look after Tapio who was coming to the UK, and the UK was going to be a lot safer than where they were going. And you have to understand, detective, that we did all the usual financial checks and everything seemed completely above board and normal. The bank in Finland who forwards the fees to us is one of the major banks over there. They're not some fly-by-night unknown. And they wrote saying that the Törni family have banked with them for generations. Also, we sent letters to an address in Finland and received replies. A proper address, not just some Finnish version of a

P.O.Box. And the letters were hand-written, not typed. It all felt very personal."

"Okay, I see what you mean, but what started to arouse your suspicions?"

Dumville rubbed a hand across tired eyes. "Well it was what staff started to say to me after he'd arrived more than anything I saw myself. They said that if parents came up in the course of class discussions, Tapio seemed not to know what to say. Mr Courtauld, who takes R.E., said that it seemed very strange. Not like they'd died. We've sadly had children here to whom that's happened, and often, once the worst of the grieving's past, it can be a relief to talk about mum or dad, whoever's gone. Indeed we actively encourage them to talk as a way of keeping their memories on happier times. But Mr Courtauld said with Tapio it was as if he'd never known his parents.

"I confess to you, that I did start doing some checking of my own then. I even went so far as to drive out to the address we'd been given to make sure that that was genuine – which it was, by the way! But as far as the Finnish side of things goes, we seem to have lost contact with the parents. Now that might be quite legitimately because the house is locked up and the parents are where they said they were going to; but what I'm saying is that as far as the school's been able to check, the parents could just as easily have vanished into thin air. In the meantime, we've had no reason to ask Tapio to leave the school. He's a model pupil and the fees are always paid by the bank on time. Nor have we had any reason to contact social services. He's well fed and very healthy, if a bit on the quiet side, but you can't go around stirring up hornet's nests just because a child is a natural introvert!"

Bill was becoming more and more uneasy with every sentence. He could see Dumville's view. If there was something dodgy going on, then the school was the safest place for the lad, especially if this guardian really was doing her job and looking after him properly. Yet all his instinctive cat's whiskers were twitching like mad that there was way more to this than met the eye.

"So what *does* he say when parents come up, then?" he asked.

Dumville's answer took him completely by surprise.

"He talks about characters from Finnish myths."

"You what?"

The head's expression said he was realizing how bad this sounded. "It was one of our music teachers, Mrs Green, who first made the connection. Mr Courtauld had said to me that he was rather concerned with the way Tapio seemed to be emotionally detached from his parents, but it was only half a term later that Mrs Green decided to talk about Sibelius. She thought it would be nice for Tapio to have something familiar, and knowing that even now Sibelius is quite the national hero in Finland, she started off with 'Finlandia'. Well, it's a nicely accessible piece of music for children of that age, and she talked about the lyrics which got added to it as well. All perfectly normal stuff. Nothing untoward there. But it was when she went on to talk about his symphonic work and the references to the *Kalevala* that she got a shock."

"The *Kalevala*?"

"It's the compiled old poems of Karelia – which I've since found out, with the help of the history department, was the part of Finland which got tossed back and forth between Sweden and Russia for centuries – plus some poems from other parts ...I think! Folk legends. The kind of stuff Wagner used as the basis to create *The Ring* cycle, only it's for Finland not Germany this time. And no, I hadn't heard of it either until Mrs Green said. Apparently, as so often happened with these things, it got written down properly in Victorian times, but Mrs Green tells me that it went on to have far more significance than something like the old Icelandic epic poems. When Finland went from being under Swedish control to Russian control in the later Victorian era, they allowed the Finnish culture to re-emerge – hence the writing down – and then Finland became independent just after the First World War, so again there was this huge surge in a desire for a national identity. Mrs Green wasn't a bit surprised that Tapio would know the *Kalevala*. It's not pushed under the rug there like so many of our own folk legends are. In fact, she'd been counting on the fact that he would know it!

"But what really shook her was that when they started talking about the characters in the Kalevala, Tapio spoke as if they were real people. People he knew! She said he got very animated about two in particular. ...Hang on a moment, I can get to the files in here and give you the names."

Dumville went to one of the many large filing cabinets, and pulled out Tapio's records with such an ease that Bill just knew he'd looked at that file a lot in the last few months. He'd not had to think twice about which drawer the file was in, and the card cover bore the marks of being handled often.

"Yes, here we are, she wrote it down for us. She said he became very talkative about the roles of the various gods, but the two he spoke most about were Ilmarinen, who's the blacksmith god – forges iron into magical things and that kind of stuff – and someone called Mielikki. Now Mrs Green knew who Ilmarinen was, but she had to go and look up Mielikki, but sure enough, she was exactly what Tapio said she was – the lady of the forest, and guardian of the smaller beasts which live there. But get this; she's the wife of Tapio, who's the king of the forest and the wilderness, and the lord of the larger wild animals!"

"Bloody hell!" Bill gasped. "So he's named after one of the old gods himself?"

Dumville gave a worried nod. "We did some checking, and of itself that's not so odd. Apparently Tapio is quite a common name for boys over there. But what really gave us all the shivers was that Mr Courtauld then said that he'd spoken those two names as if they were the names of his parents. Then I went to the file, and lo-and-behold, there they are...!" And he turned the file so that Bill could see typed in the box marked 'parent's names' were Ilmarinen and Mielikki Törni. "And if it's relatively normal to have Tapio as a man's names, those two are definitely not ones which crop up regularly – and certainly not together like that!"

"Oh the DCI's going to love this one!" Bill groaned, taking the file to look at closer.

"So you can see why we began to be suspicious, but at the same time you have to understand that Finnish mythology is hardly high on any of our talents, and it was only over time that we began to wonder what on earth was going on. And I did talk to the two people I knew as Ilmarinen and Mielikki Törni. I heard their voices, and they were the same voices every time. Whoever those two were or are in truth, they had conversations as real with me as we're having now. Whether they're just who they said they were; or are some kind of slightly flaky pair of nationalists who changed their names to those; or some infinitely more peculiar variation on being our Tapio's guardians, we weren't in a position to find out."

"And you thought that at least the lad was safe over here," Bill guessed.

Dumville's sigh of relief was telling. "Yes. Yes we did! In fact given that he's a bright little lad, there was every reason to think that he might stay on until he was in the sixth form. So at least he'd be with us until he was eighteen and more able to make decisions for himself. And you have to understand, detective, that whenever we've asked for money for extracurricular activities, it's been paid without question, so I think we all hoped that if Tapio then said he wanted to go on to university over here, that there was good reason to think that that would be funded as well. We do take the care of our pupils very seriously!"

Bill smiled. "I can see that. And I do appreciate that up until today you were doing what was right for the lad, but now we're going to have to look a lot more carefully into this."

A knock came on the office door and Miss Flanagan appeared. "Sorry to interrupt, Mr Dumville, but there's another policeman outside to see you."

"That'll be the DCI," Bill guessed. "I'll come with you and break the ice for you."

Outside he was relieved to see that the DCI was Frank Watson, a sensible man only a few years older than himself. He'd been dreading that it would be one of the newer DCI's whom he classed as the bright career boys, hungry for promotion. This case, with all its potential international connotations would be pounced on as an opportunity to shine by at least one young DCI he knew, but Bill had been hoping it would be someone who would see the child in all of this and keep his needs to the fore.

"Hello Frank," he greeted him. "You've got a corker of a case here!"

"Bill! I heard you'd got yourself entangled in this already. What happened to the sick leave?"

"Officially that's what I'm on. But then this all kicked off right in front of my living room window, would you believe! Morag's in the head's office keeping an eye on the lad. Let me bring you up to speed. This is Mr Dumville, the head, by the way."

Chapter 3

Wednesday - Thursday

By the end of the day the investigation had swung into action, Bill and Morag had decamped to the station to write out their individual statements on the attempted abduction, and as far as they knew would have nothing further to do with it. At everyone else's insistence, Bill then spent an aggravating couple of hours at the local hospital getting his battered ribs checked over again, only to have confirmed what he could have told them anyway, that his bruising was going to be even more spectacular, but nothing worse.

"Bloody hell!" he growled, as he and Morag piled into a taxi to take them home, "I've been trampled in enough bloody hard tackles to know what a broken rib feels like! Why won't they take my word for it?"

"Because you're not a doctor," Morag placated him. "And they don't want you bringing some claim for damages later on. Come on, Bill, you know the form."

Incomprehensible rumblings came from the other seat, but the complaints stopped there. That was one of the many things Morag like about Bill. He wasn't one to witter on endlessly about things he couldn't change. Some of the men she'd partnered over the years would have banged on about the wait at the hospital all the way home, but not Bill. Only when they'd paid the taxi off and were walking into the courtyard which gave access to Bill's flat by the back door did he stop and declare,

"A steak! That's what I want! A bloody big juicy steak, with lots of chips! I'm starving!"

It had been a long day, and for a man like Bill, endless offers of tea and biscuits didn't do much to satisfy the inner man.

"I'll drive," offered Morag. "Where do you want to go?"

"No I'll drive. It'll take too long to go and get your car. Come on, a quick shower each and then we'll go and feed our faces out at the Talbot. I could do with that – a nice meal and then a sit out by the river."

Knowing what that meant, Morag made sure she had her fleece with her for later. Although it was a nice sunny evening, it was only May and it would be chilly later when Bill sat ruminating over what had happened today. She knew him too well. He'd not settle tonight until he'd had chance to go over and over it in his own head without distraction. Some found it disconcerting to sit with Bill and not have him speak to them for over an hour, and get seemingly grumpy with them if they tried to engage him in small-talk, but Morag found it quite relaxing not to have to talk for the sake of it.

Bill took the prized Mini Cooper with his usual enthusiasm round the bends of the twisting roads out to where the pub nestled by the side of the River Teme, although with a few accompanying 'ouch's along the way, and attacked the steak with gusto. He'd risked a pint of one of the pub's home-brews with his meal, despite his medication, but took a pint of lemonade outside with him when they'd both finished. He didn't want to risk making himself sick and losing the fine meal, and he'd always been sensible about drinking and driving, and it would be at least another hour before he'd think about driving home again anyway. As they sat beside the river watching a pair of ducks on the opposite bank rounding up their ducklings for the night, Bill was clearly deep in thought.

"What was your impression of the boy?" he suddenly

asked Morag. "You had longer to watch him than I did."

She knew what he was asking her, and what the other unspoken questions were, so took the time to think before answering.

"Nice little lad, seems really well bought-up. There were never any tantrums or showing off – and some kids finding themselves at the centre of so much attention would've made the most of it. On the other hand, his quietness could be down to him having had rather more experience of the nasty things in life than most of the other privileged kids there. Not the first time, so less of a shock, if you get my drift. He was remarkably calm about the whole thing." Bill nodded sagely but didn't interrupt.

"I reckon he could be a dreamer. The kind of kid who shuts out the world by burying his head in books. So if things have been unpleasant for him in the past, I'd say it's possible that he's transposed what he found out about these old gods onto the real people he knew. Kids find the most amazing ways of coping with the awful shit that comes their way. Doesn't explain the flaky parents, mind you. But I wouldn't be surprised if that's the way he's found to cope with them."

"That's pretty much what I was thinking," Bill agreed. "And the head has my sympathy. He did as much as he could to make sure the kid's background was kosher. I mean, they're hardly MI5 there, are they? Thank God the case went to Frank. He won't give Dumville a hard time for not being psychic and predicting problems."

"You sound as though you like him?"

"Who, Dumville? Hmm. Having only met him today I don't know him well enough to say 'like', but everything he said to me makes me think that he's nothing more than what he appears to be – a head master who took on a child and then found that if his background wasn't quite what the school had been led to believe, then at least the school was the best place for him. I think Dumville's concern is genuine, but equally that there was nothing in what he knew which would have given him any reason to expect what happened today."

"What do you make of our pair of thugs? You went down to make the formal identification. Did they give you any hint of who they are or where they're from?"

"Capstick says they're not saying much, but that they're not English," Bill informed her, referring to the duty sergeant he'd spoken to. "He thinks they might be Russian."

"*Russian?* Bloody hell, Bill! What's a pair of Russians doing trying to kidnap a kid in the middle of Worcester?"

Bill sat back and winced as he stretched to ease his stiffening muscles. "I don't know, but it worries the hell out of me. I'd have been a whole heap happier if they'd turned out to be a pair of dumb-arsed travellers who thought they were good for a few quid by grabbing a posh kid. Any kid. Or even migrant Poles. Some of those who give the rest a bad name by coming over here and doing nothing but getting drunk and causing trouble. You know the type – the ones uniform had such a game with a few years ago causing havoc down by the riverside in the city. The kind of daft bastards who might think, in their booze-filled brains, that the kid bore some passing resemblance to the child of some bigwig at home, in whatever country, who they could put the screws on. But Russians...? Where in God's name do the Russians fit in to all this?"

They sat for a bit longer in silence, each contemplating this new development and unable to untangle the mess. When it got too dark and cold, they piled back into the Mini and drove back to Bill's and continued their musings by the fire, but still getting nowhere. Morag knew it was no good telling Bill that this wasn't his case anymore. It was in his nature to care about what happened next, and she knew that he'd be making tactful enquiries as to how the case was going over the next few weeks, even if he had to find some excuse to go back into work for an hour or two while he was still supposedly off.

What neither of them expected was to have a PC at Bill's door at ten the next morning. They'd barely finished breakfast and were just contemplating what to do with the day when the doorbell rang. Muttering darkly as he forced his bruises into action to go upstairs and answer, Bill then surprised Morag by bringing someone back downstairs with him, and she was even more surprised to see it was one of the uniform lads.

"Kitchen's that way, grab yourself a coffee, we won't be a mo'," Bill told the fresh-faced PC. "Come on Morag, stir yourself! Get some proper kit on."

"Eh? What's happened?"

The PC smiled thinly at her. "Apparently the boy is refusing to talk to anyone except the DI here. The Super's not happy about it, but DCI Watson said he'd rather get your boss back in now and have the lad talk while it's all fresh in his mind, rather than arguing the toss and losing another day or more. I've been sent with a car to come and fetch you. I'm to take you out to the lad's home where DCI Watson's waiting."

Morag was too stunned to comment, but hurried to grab her bag and find some fresh clothes, grateful that yesterday she'd not had time to change into more respectable clothes, and therefore still had them clean to wear without having to go back to her own place to get some. That would have been disastrous, because she was sure that she hadn't actually been included in the invitation. She would be tagging along by Bill's choice, not the DCI's, and somewhere there was a part of her that missed being in the middle of an investigation. So for once to have the inside view without having to officially deal with her more misogynistic colleagues would be fun.

Watson clearly wanted Bill in a hurry, because the PC used his blue lights to get them clear of the city traffic at speed, and soon they were heading out into the country. They sped down the Upton road, the PC presumably taking this way to avoid getting caught up in the traffic in Malvern itself, and then turned right and began to head towards the southern end of the line of hills. When they eventually turned into a driveway, they were a bit south of Midsummer Hill with its Iron Age hill-fort, and not far away from the Victorian Gothic pile of Eastnor Castle. That no doubt helped explain the architectural quirkiness of the house, for it might almost have been described as Scottish baronial, albeit in miniature form, although it was distinctly Victorian. Presumably someone had wanted to echo the quirks of the larger estate down the road but on a more affordable scale.

"What a strange old place!" Morag breathed in awe.

"I'd have loved a place like this when I was a kid," Bill declared, turning round to look at more of it. "Look! It's even got its own little round turret! God, can you imagine the hours of fun you could have here? Your very own miniature castle to defend! Well, okay, it's not exactly a castle, but it's got that kind of look about it."

"You big kid!" Morag teased, and got a broad grin in response.

However Watson was hurrying out to greet them. "Thanks for coming, Bill. What a bloody nightmare!"

Bill scrutinized his superior and saw that the last twelve hours had obviously not gone well going by the strained expression. "Having trouble?"

Watson rolled his eyes. "Just a tad! The bad lads locked up in our cells are one all by themselves. They're not saying a word and we can't find out who the hell they are. Their fingerprints drew a blank, and that's surprising for a start for a pair of thugs like that. Immigration are saying there's no-one like them they know of who's come into the country, so however they got here, it was definitely by some sneaky back route. And the fact that someone took all that trouble to get them here and staying under our radar is worrying. That's not someone getting lucky, that's someone doing a lot of planning and having some pretty sophisticated resources to call upon. So we're reduced to sending their photos out and hoping they jog someone's memory. They're certainly not in any of the main police databases, here or in Europe."

Bill leaned in confidentially so that no-one in the house would hear his next words. "Capstick said they might be Russian? Any chance that might be true?"

Watson grimaced. "I'm praying not, but yes, they could be. Never in a million years did I think we'd be dealing with the Russian Mafia round here, but the more we eliminate, the more we're reduced to unlikely scenarios like that." He seemed to shake himself and stood a little straighter to look squarely at Bill. "Anyway, there's one problem you can help us with right now. There's a psychologist in the house with the boy, and his guardian too, but he keeps saying he wants you. Or rather he says he wants 'the big bear-man' because he trusts you. He won't talk of what happened to any of us."

Morag sniggered. It was an oddly apt description of Bill, who was only just about six feet high, but was built like a brick outhouse. And although he certainly wasn't hirsute, cropping his brown hair very short to disguise where it had begun to recede, the way he ambled along had that same air of pent up power of a bear rather than slovenliness. He could also be more than a bit growly if crossed, yet kids seemed to instantly take to him, as had clearly happened now.

"Get him to talk, will you, Bill?" Watson was almost pleading. "Time's ticking!" and Bill knew what he meant. This first day of an enquiry could make or break it. Get a good lead this early on and there was a chance of making rapid progress while the brains behind this attempt were still close enough to be got at.

"Glad to help," Bill replied, giving Watson a friendly clap on the arm. "I was going round the bend just sitting on my bum at home anyway."

"Right!" Watson said with relief, and led the way indoors.

A short hall opened into a lovely room with large French windows opening onto the garden at the back of the house. Bill guessed that there were two other main rooms downstairs of similarly generous proportions, one of which might or might not be a kitchen, because the house seemed to be L-shaped with the hall and front door in the inner angle. Both the hall and this room were wood-panelled, and although it made the hallway quite dark, with the size of the windows here in the room it simply made it feel warm and welcoming. Tapio sat on a squashy sofa at right-angles to the windows, with a woman Bill was sure must be the psychologist as she looked vaguely familiar.

She looked up at him and then stood and came to him with her hand outstretched. "Dr Chandra," she introduced herself as.

"I'm DI Bill Scathlock."

"Thank you so much for coming, you seem to have made a deep impression on Tapio."

"Hello, young man," Bill said, turning his smile onto Tapio, whose face had lit up on seeing him.

"Hello, Karhu!"

"Karhu?" Bill turned to look at the others questioningly, but his answer came from behind him.

"It means 'bear' in our language. Tapio, you must call the detective by his proper name."

"But he's Karhu!" Tapio protested.

Meanwhile Bill heard Morag's sharp intake of breath and her softly spoken "Oh, hello!" That had to mean the woman behind him was worth a second glance, and he turned to see a stunning young woman coming into the room bearing a tray with two pots on it and several cups. He made a concerted effort to close his mouth and not stand there gawping like an idiot, which was pretty much what was happening with the young constable on guard outside of the open French window. And to be fair, Bill couldn't blame him. The woman had the most incredible rich red hair, not the carrot-orange of many British redheads, but a darker colour closer to burnished bronze. It was emphasised by the same alabaster-white skin as Tapio had, but here the beautifully carved high cheekbones had adult sharpness and her eyes had a definite slant to them without being oriental. All in all she looked as though she'd just walked off the set of *The Lord of the Rings* films having been cast as an elf, the only thing missing being the pointed ears.

"DI Bill Scathlock," Bill managed to growl out and offer his hand in greeting again.

"I am Annikki Nykänen, Tapio's guardian," and Bill's handshake was returned with a calm and firm hand.

The way she looked him straight in the eye, without any guile, either made her a very professional con-woman, or just what she said she was, and Bill was inclined to go for the latter. Certainly she looked as though she was somewhere around thirty and old enough to be responsible, rather than some lass barely out of her teens, sent over to watch over him because she was cheap to employ.

"Right, Tapio, my lad," Bill said, lowering himself carefully onto the sofa to avoid his bruises. "Now then, we need you to tell us all you can about what happened yesterday so that DCI Watson here can get on with trying to find out *why* it happened." He patted the seat beside him and Tapio came and sat beside him. "So the first thing we need to know is, have you ever seen those men before?"

Tapio immediately shook his head. "No, they are total strangers to me."

"You've not seen them hanging around by the school or anything like that?"

"No, Karhu."

"Tapio!" Annikki remonstrated, but Bill waved it aside. It didn't matter what the lad called him as long as he carried on talking. Instead he looked Annikki in the eye and said,

"And I presume you've been asked the same and don't know them either?"

Her response was firm and definite. "No, I don't recognize them from the photographs, nor does Urho."

"Who's Urho?"

"He's the handyman-gardener. Urho Jäätteemmäki."

"With a name like that he has to have come with you from Finland," Bill smiled, but inviting clarification despite his casual approach.

"Oh yes!" Tapio agreed eagerly. "Urho grows all our fruit and vegetables! He used to carry me round on his shoulders when I was little, and when we came here in the autumn he picked me up so that I could help him pick the plums!"

"So you've known him a long time, then?" Bill prompted, and got a big smile and a vigorous nodding. Such a natural response had Watson scribbling in his notebook, for he'd cleared his other officers away from the room except for Morag, who'd parked herself on an elegant chair by the wall where she could watch Annikki. But Bill knew that the boy's confirmation of Urho's lengthy service would now put him to the back of the list of people to be investigated. Not ruled out, because even a faithful family servant like that wasn't above being blackmailed, but he certainly wasn't at the forefront of the enquiry for now.

"That's good, that's very good," Bill declared encouragingly. "Now then, what we need you to do, Tapio, is tell us all you can about your family." He leaned in and looked earnestly into Tapio's innocent face. "You see we need to be able to investigate who might want to hurt them too, because we think that if those men who grabbed you yesterday had succeeded, then your family would have been told about it and then some sort of demand would have been made. But until we know what they do for a living, we can't work out what that might have been or why. And if we can discover that, then it will give us more idea of who sent those two men. Do you understand me?" Tapio nodded. "Good. Then can we start with your mum and dad. Your mother and father."

He immediately heard Annikki's sharp intake of breath, and Morag saying,

"Miss Nykänen, would you mind coming outside with me for a moment?"

The young woman looked worried, but Morag was already standing over her with a guiding hand outstretched.

"It's all right, Tapio," Bill reassured him. "Nothing bad's going to happen to you without Miss Nykänen being here. We just need to make sure we get each of your stories without the other one putting words into your mouth. We need to know what *you* know, not just what Miss Nykänen knows."

"That's all right, Karhu, I trust you," Tapio declared and put his hand on Bill's. Just for a second it felt like an electric shock passed between them, and Bill instantly dismissed it as just static. He saw Dr Chandra nodding her approval from the other corner of the room, so guessed he was doing a passable job.

A thought occurred to him. "Why wouldn't you talk to DCI Watson? He's a very nice man, you know. He has children of his own." Bill wasn't going to mention that they were nearly old enough to have kids of their own, that wouldn't be helpful.

Tapio's face screwed up into earnest concentration. "If you say so, Karhu, but I don't not know if he is strong enough to stand against those who want to harm me."

Bill managed to summon a smile even though he was somewhat flummoxed by Tapio's words. "Well there are plenty of other policemen about, you know, son. He doesn't have to fight them single-handed."

"You did!"

Ah, so that was what lay at the heart of it! Bill breathed a small sigh of relief. "Tapio, I used to play a game called rugby. Have you heard of it?"

"Oh yes! We watch it on the television! Annikki is very taken with it, and I think Urho likes it too!"

This time Bill caught the smothered smiles of Dr Chandra and Frank Watson out of the corner of his eye, and fought to keep his own face straight. He could well imagine what the allure was for Annikki – all that male beefcake on the hoof pounding up and down the pitch!

"Well then you know how rough it can get." Tapio nodded. "And you've seen players tackling one another?" A second nod. "Well that's what I did to those men. I didn't fight them. I just did what I used to do on the rugby field."

"And you brought them down with a crash!"

"Yes I did. But that's not the only way to deal with men like that. There are other ways to do it which DCI Watson over there knows just as well as me. It was just that they were running with you and I did what I was used to doing."

Tapio gave another one of his serious little nods of agreement. "Yes, I don't think they play much rugby in Russia."

The tension in the room suddenly rocketed at the last word.

"Russia?" Bill asked with as much insouciance as he could muster. "Why do you say Russia, Tapio?"

"Because it's the Russians who want to kill me. That's why I'm here."

Somewhere on the Russian side of the Finnish border

The soldier gulped and did his best to straighten himself up. Why did it have to be him who had to deliver the bad news? He'd already been sick with fear twice between the communications shack and the house where the officer waited. Why did this have to come through on his watch?

With a shaking hand he rapped on the door of the house and was admitted by the sentry on duty.

"Bad news?" his comrade guessed looking at his pallor.

"A complete flop."

The sentry winced. "Rather you than me."

They shared a look of sympathy. The officer within scared the living daylights out of them all. What lay behind this mission they didn't know and they didn't want to. It had to be something underhand given that they could be no more than twenty miles from the Finnish border, and yet were in no proper army camp or border post, or even in one of the towns which lay along the shore of the huge Lake Ladoga in what had once been part of Karelia. St Petersburg lay some two hundred and fifty miles to the south – no great distance in a country as vast as Russia –

but it might just as well have been on the moon for all the contact they had with it.

All any of them knew was that the officer had come into the camp where they had been, demanded an escort, and had got them. That of itself screamed KGB. Who else would have that kind of hold over senior military men to be able to just turn up, demand, and get. The old days of the Communist regime might have gone almost exactly twenty years ago, but if anyone was fool enough to think that the KGB had had its claws cut that much they were in for a rude awakening. There was the President for a start off. He'd been one of 'them', and if the rumours were anything to go by he'd learned the lessons from the past rather too well, and would be president for a good many years to come.

The sergeant who now stood quaking in his boots at the officer's door had caught a glimpse of an official looking letter, and he could have sworn it had the president's name on it. Well if it wasn't from the Kremlin, then it was certainly what everyone else thought such a letter should look like, and that meant that it made no difference whether it was real or fake in practical terms. It would be abided by, and if that was wrong they'd probably all be dead by then and past caring anyway. Nor did he care what the grander picture was. Curiosity was the fastest way to end up being taken for a long walk in the ice and snow in just your underwear, and left for dead – suitably soused in vodka, of course, so that it looked as though you'd cracked and died while drunk. Dead drunks had no credibility, so whatever you might have passed on to others would then be disregarded, or at least it would be if your friends and comrades knew what was good for them, and didn't want to end up the same way.

The soldier passed a hand over his clammy brow and then steeling himself, knocked on the door to the room the officer was using as his own private workspace.

"Come!" a muffled voice came from within.

He walked in to be greeted by a blast of heat from the roaring fire in the grate.

"The message, sir. It's come," and he held out the printed-off sheet for the officer to take.

It was snatched from his hand, and the man immediately took a cautionary step back as the officer seized his reading glasses and scanned the printout. Seconds later the officer looked up, his face a mask of fury.

"Do you know what this says?"

The sergeant managed a terrified nod.

"Do you know what it means?"

He gave an even more terrified shake of his head.

"Ha! Get out, then!"

Without needing further prompting the soldier fled, glad to have got out in one piece. What in the name of all that was holy was it about this man that was so awful? Looking into his eyes felt like staring into the pits of hell. To the outside world the soldier had been brought up in the Communist era as a good non-religious boy, but his grandparents had remained devout Orthodox throughout, reading to him from a small bible which had been kept hidden away for safety's sake. So the soldier knew what Hell was, and the Devil too, and for some reason he couldn't shake, he was sure one of his right-hand fallen angels was right there in that room.

As he fled back to the relative safety of the freezing-cold communications shack, he noticed that the sentries had pulled back as far from the room as possible while still just about be able to see the front door. Clearly they were as fearful of the officer as he was, and if nothing else he found that encouraging simply because it meant that his fears weren't simply the product of an overactive imagination, caused by sitting out here in the wilds for too long with nothing to do but wait. From behind him he heard a spine-chilling scream of frustration come from the room, and regardless of appearances, he took to his heels and ran.

Within the room, had the soldiers been able to see, something happened which would have had them running all the way to St Petersburg without waiting for morning to come. The scream which the sergeant had heard had come not from the officer, but from the wavering form of the apparition which had appeared before him. The officer, back in the days when he'd been nothing more than human, had been a black op's man. A covert killer answerable to a very select few. But then something had entered one of that select number and had begun putting a plan of its own into place. And part of its plan had been to use others like it to control those men it would need to do the physical work on its behalf. So the officer now had a passenger sitting in the back of his mind, and it was this passenger which had informed its own chief, who was the swirling cloud of grey in vaguely human form which now screamed its fury to the world.

"What went wrong?" it demanded of its minion.

"We do not know," the other replied. "All we have so far is the message. 'Mission failed. Tapio lives. Operatives captured.' They would not risk more in a message which could be tracked or intercepted. I can only assume that it means that somehow the British police have them."

The shade swirled violently in its agitation. "The British police? Unarmed buffoons and they *caught* them? These were supposed to be men you had trained!"

Some element of the black-op's man surfaced, enough to retort, "Trained, yes! But they were hardly men like mine! You wanted men who would remain anonymous if they were caught along the way. Men who wouldn't scream 'Special Forces' just by the way they held themselves. We told you, if they get picked up the authorities will take blood samples, DNA samples, and you agreed ...*you agreed*, we should use men who were of Finnish descent to throw them off the trail. Make it look like some internal grudge killing, *you said*. So we had to go with the best we could get for the purpose.

"The British government must be one of the most paranoid in the world – it's certainly one of the hardest countries to get into if you don't want to be observed! So there was never better than a fifty percent chance of it succeeding. It's remarkable that they got close enough to get hold of the boy at all. We told you this, but would you listen? No! Why don't you go and get him yourself? You managed to walk through the walls easily enough here. It should be a walk in the park for you to do your own dirty work."

The creature gave a snarl of fury and ripped its attachment out of the officer, ripping his flesh apart in the process. As he fell to the floor, relieved that at last he could die and join his comrades rather that suffer carrying part of this foul thing an instant longer, the last strand of connection in his head caught a trailing thought.

'I can't go because he's protected. The place he's in is protected.'

Chapter 4

Thursday

Bill took the time to pour himself a cup of tea from the pot Annikki had left so that he could compose his thoughts. How to question Tapio on this? The lad seemed very certain, but equally there had been some reruns of James Bond films on TV over the last few weeks, and if he was an imaginative kid it wasn't beyond the realms of possibility that this was his way of coping with the shock.

"Did they speak to you in Russian?" he asked after taking a slurp of tea, not because he wanted it particularly, but because he wanted to seem to be asking only casually. There'd be nothing worse than Tapio saying what he thought Bill wanted to hear.

"Oh yes."

"And do you know any Russian?"

Tapio's repeated "Oh yes," was so matter of fact it clearly wasn't like some British kid bragging about it just to make himself sound ultra cool, or expand a fantasy. Then the boy added, "Sometimes we pick up Russian TV or radio at home."

"Really? Does that happen all over Finland?"

Tapio screwed his face up to think, but then shook his head. "I don't think so, but we live quite close to the border."

"Where do you live, Tapio? Can you tell me? Because I don't know anything about Finland at all. What's it like where you used to live?"

Tapio got a faraway look in his eyes as he recalled his home. "Years ago we used to live in Northern Karelia.

That's a ...um ...a province! We have many provinces in Finland. There's Northern Karelia and Southern Karelia, and once upon a time they were all part of a bigger Karelia that went all the way east to Lake Ladoga. But it was a very long time ago when the Russians took that. That was Tsar Peter."

"Is that Peter the Great as we call him?" Bill checked.

"Yes, Peter the Great. But people in Karelia still think of themselves as the same even though there is now a border between them. I think the nearest place to where we lived which you might have heard of Lieska. That's what I've heard Annikki say to people over here, anyway. But we didn't actually live there. We lived in the woods on an island in a big lake, at a place called Kääntämö. ...I suppose I'd better spell that for you?"

"It might help," Bill said with a smile. "We're not very good at spelling Finnish names."

When Tapio had explained the proper spelling, complete with umlauts on all the vowels, Bill prompted him.

"You said used to live there? So does that mean you weren't living there before you came here?"

Tapio shook his head. "No, it got too dangerous."

That made Watson and Dr Chandra sit up.

"How? What made it dangerous?" Bill asked carefully.

"We were too close to the border. I think only about twenty kilometers. And we were surrounded by forest. Not many people about. After the third time men came in the night, we knew we had to move."

That was a chunk of information all by itself! So this wasn't the first time he'd been attacked, which might explain his calm, but Bill grabbed the chance to ask,

"So who was 'we', Tapio? Who was with you then?"

"Ilmarinen and Mielikki, and Ahti and his wife Vellamo, it was their home we were at – or one of them, because they love the water. Ukko was in the north."

"And are Ilmarinen and Mielikki your father and mother?"

Tapio looked confused. "Why do you ask this, Karhu? You know that Väinämöinen was the first of us and made the world, but we are all as one another. Ilmarinen and Mielikki help to protect me now, because the danger from these men is to me, but they did not make me."

Bill was beginning to feel his head reeling, and he could see Dr Chandra giving a subtle shake of her head to indicate that it was probably best not to press Tapio on this matter, at least for now. Instead he gave Tapio's hand a pat and said,

"I don't quite get it, or why you think I should know this, but I'll take your word for it. Let's try to get back to where you were. You just said that this place...?" He looked to Watson who'd written it down.

"Errr... Kääntämö," he supplied.

"Kääntämö ...became unsafe. So where did you go to next?"

Tapio seemed less stressed at answering this, which was something. "Ah, we went to Kuhmo! That's in Kainuu, not Karelia. I had become me," and he tapped his chest very assertively at this, "by then, and it was agreed by all of us that I must go to school as other children did. That way I would be less obvious."

"So you lived in Kuhmo. In the town itself?"

"No, not quite. We lived a little way along the shore of the lake. That's when Urho came to work for us, because we needed someone to drive me in to school every day."

"And how long were you there, Tapio?"

"About five years."

Well that was something. In five years they ought to have established some kinds of records which could be traced by the Finnish police, and Bill's glance took in that

Watson was looking a little relieved at having some kind of lead to follow at last. Now, though, Bill needed to try to get some kind of handle on where the danger had come from.

"So why did you leave Kuhmo?"

"Like I told you, it became dangerous."

"Dangerous. Right. And was this danger the same kind of danger which drove you from your other home?"

Tapio sighed with such sadness it made Bill feel an utter shit for asking. "Yes, in a way. Not the same men. At Kääntämö they were soldiers. They came on skis in the winter in the long, dark nights, and they had guns. Lots of guns! We heard that they destroyed our old house. Some local people wrote to us. They said the house was full of holes and falling down. The wood was good for nothing but the fire now."

That gave Bill a sick feeling in the pit of his stomach. He was no weapons expert, but that sounded horribly like automatic gunfire, and pretty high caliber with plenty of it. That might make it the Russian army, or it might be Mafia kitted out to seem like the army – he couldn't imagine the Mafia giving a fuck if they started an international incident if they stood to gain by it. Could the two currently in custody be Russian army? Christ that would set the cat amongst pigeons! They could all end up with their jobs on the line if this got diplomatic. Not to mention the horror of professional gunmen running around this English town! Armed Mafia on the streets was enough to give anyone nightmares, and Bill knew enough to be scared shitless by the thought. Putting the teacup down so that Tapio didn't see the worried tremor in his hands Bill asked,

"And these soldiers, did they come again in Kuhmo?"

Tapio shook his head. "No, not in the town. They were more careful there. Two lots of them moved into houses as close to us as they could get. They took on houses which became empty, but there weren't that many houses like that available, so they didn't have much choice where they went. We knew there was something wrong because Mr. and Mrs. Saari, two doors away from us, came and spoke to us. Mr. Saari was very angry that we should have told our friends to ask them if they would like to move into a nice apartment in Helsinki so that they could have the house. It took Ilmarinen and Urho some time to calm him down, but eventually he believed us that we had no friends we had spoken to of coming to live by us. Then he told us he thought it was odd that we should have Russian friends like them. That was when we knew for certain that they were going to try again."

"What were they going to try again, Tapio?"

"To kill me, or take me prisoner and back with them to Russia."

It was the calmness with which this young child said those words which rattled the adults present, and Bill could see Dr Chandra shaking her head and looking very worried. She was no doubt thinking she had some very long therapy sessions ahead of her. And Bill hated what he had to ask next, but they really needed to know.

"Why you, Tapio? What is it with you specifically? Did you not think that these men would be more likely to go after the grown-ups? For Ilmarinen or Mielikki? Why not them before you?"

"Because they do not own the forests," Tapio said simply. "They want the forests, not just for the trees – which I would not let them have, anyway! – but for what lies beneath the trees. The remains of hundreds of generations of trees, that's what they want, and the ties to our souls."

It didn't make much sense to Bill, but clearly Tapio had inherited some particularly wealthy tract of land. Maybe it was up against the Russian border? Could that be it? In the context of a child owner being less likely to notice weird things going on like cross-border raids, it made more sense to think that they would want an absent child owner. But if he died and the next in line to inherit was a Russian that might make it more comprehensible, although Bill would have been the first to admit that he knew nothing about Finnish inheritance laws, and could have got that wholly wrong.

"I think we have enough to be making a start with," Frank Watson said, having had Dr Chandra whisper in his ear, no doubt with words to the effect that Tapio had had enough cross-examining for one day.

"Right, young man," Bill said, hauling himself to his feet and giving Tapio's hair a ruffle. "Thank you. You've been really helpful. That helps us a lot."

He turned, about to shake hands with Frank and Dr Chandra in farewell, when Tapio's worried voice came from behind him.

"You're not leaving, are you, Karhu? Please don't go."

Bill froze, then turned carefully towards him. "I have a home to go back to, Tapio, and I got hurt in a car crash so I'm supposed to be resting."

"But can't you rest here? The garden is very nice, and we have enough room for you. There's a big bedroom upstairs which no-one uses."

Bill bent down to put a comforting arm around the lad's small shoulders, trying manfully not to wince as several bruises got stretched or scrunched in the process. "There's no need to be frightened, Tapio. DCI Watson has men here all the time, and they'll stay here until we're sure there's no danger to you."

"But they're not *you*," protested Tapio, although without the whining any of them might have expected from a child his age.

"Why me?" Bill asked, perplexed. "What do you think I can do that four other policemen can't?"

"They are not Karhu," Tapio said as if it was the most blindingly obvious thing in the world. "They are not Karhu, you are."

By now Watson had opened the door to the hall, where Annikki stood looking very worriedly with Morag, and she heard Tapio's last words.

"It's all right," she said soothingly, hurrying to the boy's side. "We told you, this house is protected. It's safe ground."

Bill and Frank exchanged puzzled looks. What the hell was that supposed to mean?

"But I won't be able to go to school," Tapio protested.

The DCI stepped forward, "Don't you worry about that, young man. A police car will come and pick you up every morning and collect you at night. We won't be taking any chances with your safety."

Annikki smiled at that, but Tapio still looked unhappy.

Then Bill had a thought. He went down on one knee so that he could look up into Tapio's dejected face, because the lad's head had dropped and he seemed to be suddenly finding the parquet flooring very interesting.

"Listen to me, Tapio. First of all, these things don't just happen. Whoever tried to do this to you today, it took a lot of planning. And now it's failed they won't just be able to come up with something else in the next day or two. I reckon they only had those two idiots we've got locked up in this area. They won't have risked more in case they drew attention to themselves. We don't have many Russian people around here, you know. They're more Polish, and the occasional Latvian or Estonian – and you probably know better than me that those people don't have much reason to love the Russians. So they'd notice even quicker than us if a whole pile of Russians suddenly turned up and started hunting about, and since most of them want to be able to stay here and work here, they'd probably have come to the police station to tell us there was something odd going on.

"So I don't want you lying awake tonight worrying that something's going to happen again straight away. It won't! This isn't Finland where they can just walk across the border in the night. You're in the middle of England now, and we're an island and with an awful lot of people on it. There aren't the gaps where no-one sees things over here. Even the countryside is busy with farmers, and people walking and riding horses. I can tell you, we get a phone-call pretty sharp if someone just puts a tent up in a farmer's field without permission – and that'll be just someone having a bit of fun, not someone who's a danger to anyone."

On an impulse Bill gave the small boy a hug, although afterwards he couldn't have said why. He knew all the rules about not doing anything in the way of touching a child which might be misinterpreted, but there was something about Tapio which was creeping under his skin. And maybe that was why he then added,

"Listen, in the normal way of things, if I was just on my day off, my boss would want me back in work tomorrow, and doing my own work on the cases I'm responsible for. But as it happens I'm not. I'm not due in work for a couple of weeks yet. The doctor has to tell me I can go back, for one thing, and my boss has made me take some holiday on top of that. So why don't I come back over here tomorrow, eh? They won't be expecting you back in school then anyway."

"Why not?"

Bill couldn't help but smile at him. "You're being a very brave lad, Tapio, but I think they'll be thinking that you need some time to get over the shock you've had." Then as he saw that Tapio was about to protest that he was okay yet again, he added, "And I think that maybe the teachers at school might need a day or so to get over it too! They care a lot about what happens to you, you know, and it frightened them silly when the police station phoned them to say what was happening. Why don't you stay here for the next day or so? Missing Friday won't set you back that much. Then you can go back in after the weekend when everyone's had a chance to recover. Does that sound okay to you? And then I can come out and see you again tomorrow and you can show me round this lovely garden of yours."

The way Tapio brightened up at that was a relief to everyone, and as he walked outside, Bill added to Dr Chandra,

"I won't get in the way of whatever you want to do, Doctor, and I'm guessing you'll be wanting to see him on a daily basis for the immediate future?"

"Oh yes!" she sighed. "The poor boy! All that confusion, and so much repressed! I don't want to start medicating him straight away, but I do want to be on hand in case that becomes the best solution for him in the short-term. ...And thank you, detective. You're being very kind to him, offering to give up your own time like that. And I think you've got it right, too – he gets to see you, but however much he might want it, I don't think it would be healthy for you to stay overnight here. He sees you as his saviour, but it could be potentially damaging if he fixed on you too much, because as you said, soon or later you'll have to return to duty, and the wrench of separation from you then could be very painful for him."

"I'll be careful," Bill promised. "I had a bit of experience of a kid like him some years ago. It was a domestic in that instance, but I got to the scene just in time to stop the little girl from getting badly hurt by her dad so he could get at her mum. Luckily I had a good psychiatrist involved, because the kid fixed on me like a newly hatched chick! Poor little mite, she really was a mess. I bet she's still in therapy even now."

Dr Chandra looked relieved. "Ah, good! So you know the dangers – that's even better! In that case, I'll look forward to meeting you again tomorrow."

However Frank Watson wasn't done with Bill yet. "Look I'll be a bit longer here, so I'll get the car to take you back. But if you're not doing anything later on, Bill, would you come back in to the station? I'd like to have a chat with you about what we've heard so far."

"My pleasure, mate," Bill said, being familiar because he'd known Frank a good many years and there were no junior officers to hear just now, and because he knew how he'd be feeling if this had been his case.

Around five o'clock he ambled into the station, guessing that Frank's shift would officially have finished but that he would still be working on. The usual miasma of noise accosted him as he went beyond the public area. Someone in the cells was giving *O sole mio* a dreadful bending, managing to be half a key out of tune all the way and providing the aria with words it had never had before. The poor constable on cell watch wore a pained expression, and Bill didn't need to look in to know who was there. Pavarotti Pete was a well-known local drunk and pest. His habit of going down on one knee and 'serenading' every pretty girl he came across on the High Street was harmless enough, but he scared the living daylights out of the girls in question. So by the time the managers of several major retailers had had sobbing girls come in shrieking, looking for somewhere to get away from him, Pete usually ended up in the cells to sober up, at which time he became maudlin and treated the officers to his extensive alternative repertoire.

Climbing the stairs to Frank's office he tapped on the door and went in.

Frank looked up from the computer he was scowling at as the strains of *O sole mio* followed Bill in through the door. "Ah, the cat-strangling aria! Pete's in again?"

Bill chuckled. "Oh yes! Daft bugger! Shame he never got to carry on with his music. Before the booze got to him he had a good voice."

Frank sniffed. "Well I wish Pete was my problem instead of this fucking job! Christ, Bill, what a mess!" He pushed himself back from the desk and leaned back in his chair as Bill lowered himself into a second chair. "I mean, bloody hell, Russians! What in God's name am I supposed to do there? If they're just a pair of lowlife's who've somehow traipsed across Europe and ended up here, that's one thing. But what if they're connected?"

"In what sense?"

"Either! The bleeding Russian Mafia would be bad enough – that'd probably mean some smart-arse lawyer will turn up and manage to wangle them out eventually. But we can make the child harassment element stick, so they can be made to stay a long way away from Tapio. What would be worse, though, is if there's some connection to the Russian government."

Bill blinked. "Blimey, you're not suggesting the Russian government is behind this, surely?"

Frank just shrugged. "How would I know? But no, I was thinking more of them being serving members of the Russian army. Even if the buggers are deserters, that could be a diplomatic shit storm I don't need."

"Have you found anything at all about them yet?"

"Not a bloody thing! And they have to have been trained for something like this. I've never known anyone keep as silent as these two. Eventually even the toughest thug will open his gob, even if it's only to swear at you, but when I said these two were silent I meant it. The custody officers say they've not said a word to one another beyond that brief snatch Capstick heard when they first came in. I reckon that was whichever one is in charge telling the other to keep *shtum*, or it would be the worse for him when they get out. Can't even prove that, though!"

Bill's sympathy for Frank was growing. "Any luck with the Finnish police?"

"Not yet. But then it's a bit of a big ask! We wouldn't be exactly thrilled if we got a call from them asking us for information on some couple calling themselves Charles Windsor and Camilla – and no real name – somewhere in Worcestershire, would we? It's not the lad's fault, but a real name or two wouldn't half help us!"

"What about that bit he told me about the old house getting shot up? What was the reaction to that?"

"Well I didn't get to make the call myself. That got shunted upstairs pretty quickly! But what came back down to me was that the Finnish authorities were pretty worried about that. Unfortunately the place Tapio described to us is well out in the sticks. Even as the crow flies it's apparently the thick end of three hundred miles north and east of Helsinki, and a good deal more by car because it's beyond remote from anywhere civilized. So it's not like the big-city lads can just pop round in a car. It's been relayed on, but we've been told it might take a while for someone to be able to get out, find the house, and then report back, just because of where it is. I mean, we can't even give them a map reference, and the name Tapio gave us covers a pretty big area. The lads over there are cooperating; it's just such a wholly different terrain."

Bill grunted in frustration. He could see Frank's problem. Until the Finnish police could send back what they'd found it would be difficult to make a case for this assault being part of anything bigger. They only had Tapio's word for it, and Dr Chandra would almost certainly say, if asked, that the boy had a lot of psychological issues, which wouldn't help make his testimony any more credible when it came to court hearings.

"Thank God it was you and Morag who saw him being taken!" Frank said with genuine relief. "If it had been just some concerned member of the public we'd be in even more trouble! Even an assigned duty solicitor would have an easy time defending those two roughs on a civilian's word. Two officers with good records put it into a totally different ballpark at least."

"You're worried about Tapio's safety too?"

"Yes I am! I've talked to the lads who brought those two in, and seen the bruises! Whoever they are, and whoever sent them, they're two thoroughly nasty bastards, and I wouldn't be surprised at all that, if they get out, if they make another stab at the job. Tried to finish what they started. But I can't *prove* that! At the moment this case is a priority, but it won't stay that way for long if we can't make any progress. And my gut feeling won't count for much in asking for officers to stay on protection duty for the lad. That's why I'm so bloody glad you offered to go over there, Bill. You've got a few *weeks'* leave – that's more time than I fear I'll have to concentrate on this."

Bill quirked an eyebrow. "You want me to spin my leave out?"

Frank gave him a thin smile. "Oh come on, Bill, everyone here knows you're not the one for flying out for sex and booze in the sun! While the married lads are desperate to get their fortnight's leave to keep the families happy, you go off on your lonesome, yomping over the Brecon Beacons for a few days! Don't tell me you haven't got leave backed up you'll struggle to take, I know you too well. ...And I think this case is twitching your inner radar as much as it is mine."

This time Bill had to laugh. "Bugger! You know me far too well! But yes, you're right, there's something about this nagging at me. For what it's worth, I honestly think Tapio is telling us the truth – or at least the truth as he sees it. It's just going to take some unraveling. And I definitely think he's in genuine danger, whether the higher-ups choose to see it or not. I didn't want to say anything in front of the kid or his guardian, but you know I was lucky to bring those two down, Frank. They weren't expecting anything like a rugby tackle or I'd never have succeeded. They were ready to fight me off, there's no doubt about that. The one was shoving Tapio more towards the other so that he could deal with me, and I know I saw him start dropping into some weird martial arts position just before I hit him in the nuts as I went down. He wasn't expecting the dive. Wasn't expecting me to go low! That's the only advantage I had, the *only* one!"

Frank didn't say more, but thought Bill wasn't quite right on that. It took forever to get Bill angry, but he was a big man. He'd lost possibly a stone of muscle since he'd stopped playing every weekend, but even so he had to be the thick end of sixteen stone of solid bone and muscle, and despite what a few in the force misguidedly thought, there wasn't an ounce of spare fat on him. And the one thing which really got under Bill's skin was kids getting hurt – that was something he could get *very* angry about. So Frank would have bet good money on someone going down and staying down if Bill thumped them, and in the circumstances which had played out on the racecourse, Bill would have had the added justification of self-defense for laying into the pair. But it didn't alter the fact that Bill was right about the two being chillingly professional, or help with the alternatives they had.

"Will you keep going over there?" Frank asked straight out. "If you're popping in and out on a daily basis, you're likely to be the one to spot anything out of the ordinary. And God forbid, but if I have to pull the lads off watching the place, I'd feel a whole lot happier if I knew you were carrying on watching for a few weeks."

It was unorthodox, and certainly not something either of them would make known to their superiors unless something went very badly wrong again, but Bill totally agreed with what Frank was asking of him and why.

"I'll do it," he agreed, "And in the process I might even be able to get Tapio to open up a bit more about what's going on. Now switch that bloody computer off and let me buy you a pint! You won't get any more information coming in tonight, and the other lads are around if they do. If you're lucky I'll even treat you to a curry!"

However Frank's wife was evidently cooking and he made his excuses as they left. That left Bill to walk home wrapped in his own thoughts. Once inside, he dug out a large vegetable pie from his stock in the freezer and set it to defrost and cook. Then he retrieved his laptop from its case and opened it up. He had an i-phone, but found the trouble was that with fingers as big as his, he ended up hitting two apps at once, or tapping keys three at a time. So given the choice he went back to something with a more manageable keyboard. In the search he put in various spellings of what Tapio had called him, but finally got the right one in 'Karhu'. The computer spat back at him results for running shoes, skis and Finnish beer, but the bar offering images for the same search caught his eye instantly. They were all bears! Very big brown bears.

"So I'm a *big* brown bear to you, am I?" Bill muttered with a chuckle, having wondered if it was more a term for a teddy-bear. "Well that's not so bad."

A few more searches and he'd found out that the bear was the most sacred of animals in Finnish lore, and that the pre-Christian religion had been more shamanistic rather than having a rigid pantheon like the Norse gods. The little Bill knew of shamanism made that rather concerning. Had someone made Tapio ingest some trance-making substance at some point, making his imagination take what he knew of old legends and building them into something much more real for the boy? At least Karhu wasn't a god! That would have been a nightmare! The bear was revered but not worshipped, thank goodness. Bears would be thanked for a good hunt, and their skulls hung on trees so that their spirits could ascend to the heavens once more, but nothing beyond that. So that seemed to answer why Tapio would feel some affinity to the bear if the lad had been named after the god of the forest, and he had been encouraged to think of himself as being strongly linked to it. But what was that all about when Tapio had said about the trees and the trees of the past? That was still a mystery.

Chapter 5

Friday

The following morning someone should have told the weather that it was late May, not April. The sun had gone and it was lashing down, the rain bouncing off the pavements with its force. So much for a walk around the garden! Taking the Mini around the deepening puddles back out to the house made Bill feel like one of the Finnish rally drivers – the only drawback to a Mini was that if you went through a deep puddle and got splash-back through the radiator grill, the electrics would get wet and the car would cough, splutter, and die. So he spent the whole journey doing a strange sort of shimmy along the narrower roads avoiding the filling potholes, which did nothing for the aching ribs or muscles.

He turned into the drive and navigated the small waterfall which was running down its slope, noticing for the first time how overhung it was by trees. That might be very picturesque, but it was also wonderful cover for anyone who wanted to lurk unseen. As he'd made the turn, Bill had spotted the patrol car tucked into a farm gateway almost opposite, neatly out of sight from most people making the long sweep on the road, but able to see anyone coming from either direction to the house. He gave them a quick wave of his hand and saw someone gesturing back through the water sheeting down the police car's windscreen.

Today, though, no-one in their right mind would linger outside, and Bill made a dash for the door. Luckily there was a decorative stone overhang above the front door, not big enough to qualify as a porch, but enough to take shelter under while he waited to be let in after his sprint from the car. While he pressed his back to the solid old oak door to keep out of the drips, he scrutinized what he could see of the garden on this side, and was gratified to see that although the house was ringed by a dense belt of trees, around the house itself was plenty of open space.

And it was a goodly space too. Either side of the gravel drive were lawns large enough to warrant something bigger than the average Flymo – and someone certainly had a good mower, because the lawns were immaculately trimmed. That, at least, was something. If the house was invisible from the road, anyone in the cover of those trees would only be able to watch unseen. To get closer they would have to come out into the open. And if they did, then they'd be in sight of the second police car parked to the side where the front door and the drive could be seen.

The door suddenly moved at his back, nearly catapulting him into the hall. Someone grabbed his arm to steady him, and Bill found himself looking up at one of the biggest men he'd ever seen. If they ever remade *The Munsters*, this chap could play Herman without any prosthetics! He must have stood close to seven feet tall and was proportionately wide. Even on the rugby field Bill hadn't often felt dwarfed, but he did now.

"Thank you. ...DI Bill Scathlock," he said, recovering himself and making the introduction.

The giant nodded, gave what passed for a smile on his granite-like features, and said, "Urho Jäätteemmäki."

That suddenly made a lot of sense. Not just the handyman, then, but someone big enough to give attackers pause for thought. The trouble was, Bill didn't see signs of any great intelligence in those eyes. Urho might well turn out to be one of nature's gentle giants, scary only by his size, and incapable of swatting so much as a fly.

However Annikki was coming out of the door to the right and smiling in welcome.

"Detective Scathlock! Tapio will be so glad to see you. He's been getting worried you weren't coming."

The smell of something mouth-wateringly good had followed her and Bill sniffed appreciatively. She noticed and laughed again.

"I was just preparing lunch. I hope you're hungry?"

"For whatever that is? Oh yes!"

"You won't mind eating in the kitchen? We normally do."

Bill didn't have the chance to say yes to that too, though, because the door ahead flew open and Tapio tore out, skidding to a halt just inches from him, exclaiming,

"You came!"

He seemed undecided as whether he should hug Bill, shake his hand or stay where he was, but his relief was written all over his small face.

"Of course I came," Bill instantly reassured him. "If I hadn't been able to make it I would have rung to let you know."

"How?"

That stopped Bill in his tracks. "What do you mean, how? You are on the phone here, aren't you? On a land-line, not just a mobile?" Bizarre though that sounded, it occurred to him that this retreat might be so cut off as to not have had the phone put in. He hadn't looked at the folded piece of paper Frank had scribbled on, so it could just have been a mobile number. That was a bit worrying given how the signals could dip in and out round here. They might lose it just when they needed it most.

"Of course we are!" Tapio declared, with something like a normal kid's incredulity at being so technologically cut off. "But we didn't give you the number."

Bill managed a triumphant wag of his finger. "Ah! But I'm a policeman, and I can find out these things. ...Anyway Annikki gave it to DCI Watson and he gave it to me last night."

"Oh." If anything Tapio sounded a mite disappointed at such a simple solution, but in Bill's books that was no bad thing. Much better if Tapio's view of him came a bit more down to earth.

Luckily Annikki chivvied the lad in to eat, and she seemed to be used to catering for large men with healthy appetites. To Bill's eyes it was just fish stew, albeit a fish stew the like of which he'd never eaten before for flavour, but Tapio solemnly informed him that it was Kalakeitto, and different from Kalakukko – which was a different kind of fish dish. Whatever it was, the chunks of salmon and trout were done to perfection, and the potatoes somehow managed to taste better than any Bill had bought from the local supermarkets, despite knowing that Annikki must have gone to one of the ones round here. It was served with chunks of still-warm homemade rye bread, and Bill was glad to see that Urho tucked away twice the amount he managed to eat, making him feel less of a glutton.

That didn't last for long, though. Annikki brought out a blueberry pie which had Bill coming back for seconds without a thought for his waistline. If he kept eating here he was going to pile the pounds on in no time! There was also something which looked suspiciously like the rice pudding from heaven in preparation on the side, and what Annikki informed him were apple doughnuts, although they looked lighter and fluffier than the kind of doughnuts which got brought into work every so often. Mercifully she told him that this was the main meal of the day, and that the evening meal would be a vegetarian bake, with either more of the blueberry pie or the apple doughnuts for afters. There seemed to be an assumption that Bill would be staying to eat, and if this was any example of Annikki's cooking, he wouldn't be able to compete with anything he had at home – and Bill never stinted himself where food was concerned.

With the rain still lashing down outside, Urho went off to do something in the garage, and Bill was left sitting at the table with Tapio, as Annikki got on with the cooking. The question now was how to get the two of them relaxed enough in his presence to get them talking freely? The opening came when Annikki confided that she had yet to make the bread for the next day or so. She apparently cooked like this once every three days, making enough to see them through so that she had time to do the other chores in the house. That made Bill wonder what she did beside this. Commendable though it was to be making all this food from scratch, he'd had the impression from the headmaster that she'd come over to England to a job. Yet how she'd fit it in he couldn't see, and that was another inconsistency in their story.

Had she been nothing but the au pair, and Tapio's family had been around, Bill knew that Frank would have been questioning her hard about those gaps in her story. But the brutal truth was that she was the one familiar person the boy had around him at the moment, and Bill could understand why Frank was erring on the side of caution – at least until he had something more positive from the Finnish police to go on. And Urho seemed a decent sort, but not the man you'd want to leave in charge of an eleven year old boy, and Frank was pretty certainly going to be ahead of Bill in that assessment, having questioned him personally.

So when the subject of bread came up, Bill volunteered to make it. He was no chef. He made no bones about that. He loved food, but the extent of his culinary skills normally only went as far as going out to farm shops and buying up nice homemade stuff to fill his freezer with. But as one bloke living on his own, he didn't eat that much bread, and so it was an easy matter to make what he needed. And there was something very therapeutic about coming home to the peace and quiet of his flat after a wearing day, and then working out his frustrations kneading dough.

This had been going for so long that he didn't need a recipe to knock up his favourite ciabatta; or the variously flavoured versions of focaccia he'd make up to take into work in place of sandwiches – which depending on the filling, too often would dry out or curl up by the time he got to eat them. He was pleased but not surprised to find that Annikki used good quality flour, and soon had his rugby shirt sleeves shoved up and got stuck into the kneading.

Tapio's surprised, "You cook?" was at least fairly normal. Most kids only ever saw dad cook when the barbecue came out on the rare summer days it was possible to cook outside. So that suggested some semblance of a regular home-life for him in the past, and Bill was quick to build a conversation around it. Or rather, he talked a lot about his own home, and why he baked, lulling Annikki and Tapio into a false sense of security in that he wasn't firing questions at them. What he really wanted was for them to start volunteering information without him asking too obviously.

"What's your favourite bread?" got the answer, "Rye bread!" from Tapio.

However Annikki surprised him by saying how much she'd enjoyed the yellow corn bread she'd tasted one year on holiday in Croatia. A bit more gently prodding and suddenly she was saying,

"Oh it was a fabulous two weeks! I went with my girlfriends from university! We stopped on a campsite outside of Poreç. It was gorgeous! We ate so much ice-cream it was a wonder we didn't all come back five sizes bigger!"

"It's like Italian ice-cream, I'm told," Bill said innocently.

"Oh yes! ...Oh you should see the flavours! The strawberry has actual lumps of strawberry in it, and the melon sorbet was divine!"

By the time they'd talked about other flavours, and the wealth of Roman mosaics still surviving on the Istrian peninsula, any restraint had completely gone. Which allowed Bill to begin to ask seemingly innocuous questions which didn't relate to the case at all, such as, "What do the Finns think of the Romans, then? I mean, you've got no Roman remains there, so are they a bit unimportant?"

Slowly and gently, Bill got them where he wanted them, until they were happily sat around the kitchen table waiting for the next batch of bread to come out of the oven, and Bill was writing down his recipes for Annikki.

"Who made bread for you before Annikki, Tapio?" he dropped in, as though it was the most irrelevant thing. This time he'd been careful to make no mention of mothers or fathers. He wanted Tapio to answer without thinking, and he got his wish.

"Oh, Tarja did that."

"Tarja?"

"Yes, she brought it over to us. She and her husband, Arvo, lived on the next farm."

"And was it good bread? Your favourite?"

"Oh yes! Tarja made lovely rye bread!"

"Have you got the recipe? I might be able to make you some if you have."

But Tapio's mood sank. "No, I don't have the recipe. There was no point in writing it down for Ilmarinen or Mielikki."

Bill tried to keep the mood upbeat. "Well I'm sure you could write to them now. There'd be no problem with that, would there? Now you're that bit older you could write to them yourself. Tell Tarja how much you liked her bread and say a friend wants her recipe. I'm sure she'd like that. Ladies always like it when you say how much you liked their cooking." And he gave Annikki a conspiratorial wink.

Their reactions were interesting. Annikki just took the whole thing as Bill had intended. She showed no sign of suddenly drawing back from the subject, just giving a little giggle at his wink. Yet Tapio became even sadder.

"I can't," he said with such a dejected look that Bill wished he could eat his words. "I think Tarja and Arvo are dead."

"Dead?" Oddly both he and Annikki said it in surprise together – so that meant that she was less involved than he'd thought.

"What? You mean they were very old?" Bill said, feigning naivety. "What a shame. Some of those old recipes have been handed down for generations, it's such a pity when they get lost."

Now Tapio's expression changed as if he was moving more towards being angry. "No, they died because of me!"

"Woah! Hang on there, son!" Bill immediately declared, dropping his pen and putting a restraining hand on Tapio's arm as the lad rose from his seat. "Whatever happened, it wasn't your fault, all right? You're just a lad. You can't be held responsible for anything like someone dying. Who told you that you were? ...Come here," and he wrapped his arm around Tapio so that although the lad was standing, he'd been pulled into Bill's side in a hug. "I'm serious," he added gently. "Someone your age ...they can't be held responsible for what grown-ups do."

"But I'm not just a boy, am I Karhu?" Tapio said with

a heavy sadness far beyond his years. "I'm Tapio. I'm in the body of this boy, but I'm still me."

That really knitted Bill's brain. What on earth did the kid mean by that? Luckily, Dr Chandra chose that moment to pull up outside, and Bill hurried out to meet her on the others' behalf so that he could brief her on what Tapio had just said.

"I have no idea what he meant by that," Bill concluded. "Nothing we'd been talking about had led us towards such an idea. For God's sake, I was talking about the difference between ciabatta dough and focaccia only a few minutes before! And if it helps you, I don't think Annikki is encouraging him in these ideas either."

"Well that's a small blessing," the psychologist sighed. "At least it seems she's not adding to the damage that's already been done."

When she'd gone into the sitting room with Tapio, Bill drew Annikki back into the kitchen.

"Don't suppose there's such a thing as a glass of wine?" he said comfortingly. "You look like you could use one!"

Annikki shook her head, but went to a high cupboard and pulled out a bottle of good quality vodka.

"I keep this well out of Urho's sight," she said pointedly. "He's a lovely man, but the thought of him getting drunk with just Tapio and me here is a bit..."

She didn't finish the sentence, but Bill got what she meant. She must have done her share of fending off amorous men with looks like hers, and that last thing she'd need was to be stuck out here with a giant who fancied his chances when in his cups.

"Maybe a spot of disguising orange juice?" Bill suggested, and got a warm smile in response.

Well if he wasn't making headway with Tapio, at least he was gaining some ground with her.

"I'm guessing this job hasn't quite turned out the way you were expecting?" he said sympathetically, as they sat down at the big, well-scrubbed table once more.

Annikki ducked her head down and cradled it in her hands, elbows resting on the table, giving it a minute shake.

"Want to talk about it?" Bill offered. "...Not me as a policeman asking you questions. Just as one grown-up to another who understands how heavy responsibility can get?"

She looked up and gave him a weak smile. "Thank you. ...Yes. ...Yes it would be nice to talk to someone. ...I feel so alone here sometimes. Urho ...he's a nice man, but he just does as he's told, you know?"

"Doesn't take much responsibility for Tapio?"

"No, not at all. ...Sometimes it's more like I have two children here, except one of them is very big – a man with a child's mind – and the other has a child's body and an adult hiding inside his head."

That was an interesting way of putting it, but Annikki was continuing, and Bill didn't want to halt her flow.

"Sometimes with Urho, for all that he understands far more of the insides of the car than me and things like that, he doesn't understand what's happened. The other day he came home most frustrated that he'd asked for 'veres autonrengas' – new tyres – and the man at the garage hadn't understood. I tried to explain to him that he'd asked for it in Finnish, but he kept saying to me 'but that's what they are!' I couldn't get him to see that in English the words are different."

"How much English does he speak?"

"Not much, and it makes him very dependent on us. And worse, I think he's getting more and more homesick. He can't make friends here because he just can't get a grip on a new language." She sighed deeply. "I know I shouldn't say this, but I think Tapio's family were very unkind to have asked him to come here with us. He's totally out of his depth."

"And you aren't?"

Annikki laughed. "No, I love England! I came here in my year out after my degree. I'd done English literature anyway, you see, and then I decided I would like to teach English as a language to children, so I came over here for a gap year to get my English up to speed. I worked for a shop in Oxford for a while when I first came over, but that was only until the Christmas trade went. Then I managed to get some work as an au pair in London, but that was awful! So I ended up in a hotel up in Scotland over the summer. It was really hard work, but they were lovely people."

"What changed?" Bill asked. "I mean you aren't in a school now, are you? Did you find that teaching wasn't for you?"

Annikki shrugged. "A bit of that, but more, it was that I'd started taking photographs and been lucky enough to sell a few. I went back home and got a job in a school, but at every chance I'd be out taking photographs. But more than that, I got engaged and then it fell through. No-one's fault, we just weren't suited, but it meant that suddenly I wanted to get back to the 'me' I'd been when I was over here."

"And what better way to do it than coming back here?"

She laughed. "That was sort of the idea. I doubt I'd have done it if the opportunity for this job hadn't come up, though."

Bill wanted very much to ask how it had, but forced himself to just looking curious in the hope that she'd fill the silence. She did.

"My grandparents," she said simply. "They were worried about me. Well you know how it is with the older folk. They see you heading for thirty and not married and they start getting worried you've missed the boat. I can understand my grandmother. She came from a generation and a background where women didn't have the chance to earn their own living. If you didn't have a man of your own you could end up in serious financial trouble as you got older – especially if you didn't inherit a home from your parents when their time came. So they thought that if I came over here it would get the break-up out of my system – not that I needed it! Linus and I were very adult about the whole thing. There were no tantrums or plate throwing. We just decided we were happier apart, but I couldn't get that across to them.

"So anyway, they turned up the one day at my parents saying that these old friends of theirs had a member of their family whom they wanted to go to school in England, and would I go as the child's guardian? At first I said no. I'd had such an awful time as an au pair I didn't want a repeat, but they said no, I'd be my own boss this time. And my grandparents were very persuasive. They talked about how our two families had fought side by side in World War II – young men too young to be in any army, and all that, but desperate to defend their homes. All the usual stuff. But I got the idea that they actually *knew* this family. It wasn't odd that I didn't, because my dad's job moved us around a lot when I was younger, so we didn't see much of either set of grandparents except for during the school holidays."

She laughed. "I remember my older brother and his wife teasing me at that get-together, saying that the oldies were really trying to get me fixed up. That this was all a con! I'd be looking after the kid and then have his dad turn up who'd turn out to be divorced. And before I knew it I'd be filling the gap of the missing mom – in every respect!"

"I'm guessing you never saw the dad?" Bill suggested, and wasn't surprised to see her shake her head.

"No, never. Nor his mum. I know that sounds really odd, but I trusted my grandparents while also this was being set up. For a start, they made out that they knew the whole family. Said that Tapio was a nice little boy. Well he is – but I'm not sure anymore that my grandparents have ever laid eyes on him. And the pay's good. Very good! And I was told that I'd have time to go off and do my photography because Tapio would be at school like any other child of his age."

"Didn't the parents come to see him off?"

But Annikki was shaking her head again. "It didn't work like that. I was asked to come ahead and get the house sorted out while Tapio finished his school year at home. Again, you see how natural that sounded? I assumed that his parents would bring him over here, then carry on to wherever it is they were going to. Come over and spend a week settling him in with me before they left. But when I got to Heathrow airport, standing there with their names on a piece of card like an idiot, all that turned up were Tapio and Urho. There I was with this little boy in front of me saying, 'this is Urho, he's staying with us.' I mean, what could I say?

"When I rang home and told my parents, my dad was furious. He's always said my mom's mother was a bit ...how do you say that thing about the fairy folk?"

"Off with the fairies?"

Annikki laughed. "That says it quite well, but there's a special word, isn't there?"

"Oh, do you mean 'fey'?"

"Yes, that's it! And even my mom sometimes says that her mother needed to have been a bit more grounded in the real world when she was a child. It's a bit of a family joke that her mother – my great-grandmother – in turn was a hippy before they were even invented! Now, though, Dad's saying that it's one thing for Grandmother to be into all her old legends, and New Age bonding with the spirits of the land – which she talks about a lot – and quite something else to be putting her granddaughter in danger. It's not often he loses his temper, but he did over me suddenly having some random strange man sharing a house with me. It's cause quite a rift in the family, because Grandfather left all the talking to Grandmother when Mom and Dad went over there. So they were there trying to get her to see the reality of what's happened, and all she kept doing was saying that Urho was fine, but no, she's never met him, but her friends said that he was okay, so therefore he was."

"Ouch!" Bill sympathised. "And I bet your Dad will hit the roof now this has happened."

"I haven't dared ring to tell them."

He could understand that. If it had been his daughter, he'd have been on the next plane over here and getting her to pack her bags come what may. Tapio's situation was more than any au pair could be expected to handle. But he could also see how Annikki felt she was caught in a cleft stick. If she left, what on earth would happen to the boy? She was bright enough to have picked up on how concerned Dr Chandra was, and no doubt she was imagining poor Tapio being swept into care if she left.

Then another thought occurred to him. "Have you been able to make contact with the family? I'm sure DCI Watson asked you this, but I don't think he realises how badly you've been led on by them. I'm sure you've wanted to after all this."

Annikki looked at him and seemed to be wrestling with her conscience. Bill had the feeling that what swayed it was that he was here, sitting in her kitchen with her, as the only one with his hand metaphorically stretched out to help her.

"After everyone left yesterday I rang the number I have for the solicitors in charge of looking after the money and things. I was too late to catch anyone in the office, but I left a message. The thing is ...my Dad insisted on having that information from me months ago. He then tracked them down and went to see them. Well it's one thing talking to someone on the phone, it was something else having my Dad turn up, face to face, and spitting fury! But it turns out, they're just a forwarding office. They claimed client confidentiality, but told Dad that their contact was with a legal firm who represent many of the Sami people up in the north of our country. So they're used to handling people who come in to see them, then disappear off into the frozen lands for several months."

Bill felt a shiver run down his spine. "So they'd think nothing odd in not having the means to contact a client?"

"No, not at all."

"And you didn't tell DCI Watson this?"

Annikki blushed. "I gave him the solicitors in Helsinki who Dad went to. Well they're the ones best placed to deal with enquiries from the British police! Some tiny office up in Lapland won't be able to!"

"And?" Bill felt sure there was an 'and' waiting to come out.

"And I'm still hoping that now that things have gone so strange, so bad, that when a message reaches the north, Tapio's parents will finally wake up to the fact that they need to get here. I've been desperate for that phone to ring all day."

"And it hasn't, has it?"

"No."

Bill placed his big paw of a hand over hers and gave it a squeeze.

"Time to ring your Dad, I think."

"He'll be at work for the next couple of hours."

"I'm not in a rush. Let's get dinner over and done with, and Tapio settled watching TV or playing his computer games, or whatever he does. Then if you ring, I'll speak to your Dad. Explain that it would help a lot if you're still here for Tapio's sake. He'll be more reassured if I talk to him, because I can talk specifics about what the police do. He does speak English, I hope?"

"Yes! Thank you!" Annikki said, sounding much relieved.

Bill wished he felt it too. Instead, a whole new batch of alarm bells were going off in his head. And it wasn't just for Annikki's sake that he wanted to talk to her Dad. He wanted to hear from the man himself what sense he'd gotten of what was going on from those solicitors in Helsinki. If those higher up felt it warranted it, Frank would be shoved onto a plane to Helsinki, but by now the solicitors would have had plenty of warning as to what was coming, both from Annikki's phone call and from whatever calls his colleagues had made already. Mr Nykänen, on the other hand, had done what they would not be able to do – he'd taken the solicitors by surprise.

Chapter 6

Friday

By the time Bill got to make the phone call he'd already had a difficult evening. Tapio had come out of his session with Dr Chandra very stressed and angry, and Bill had seen that the doctor herself looked frazzled when she left. Clearly the session hadn't gone to plan at all! But now Bill found himself dealing with the aftermath.

"Why doesn't she believe me?" demanded Tapio, standing in the middle of the living room, small fists clenched at his side, and a grim expression on his little face.

Again Bill was struck by how much older than his age Tapio was acting. He'd expected less restraint, more emotional release and even maybe the cushions getting chucked around. But it was like watching a small older man pacing back and forth, even the body language wasn't really childlike, never mind the words coming out of his mouth.

"Tapio, you have to understand that to her eyes you're just another eleven year-old child who's been through a very traumatic experience. She's basing what she's doing with you on what's worked time and time again with other children – not just for herself, either, but what's worked for other doctors too."

His answering sigh was brim-full with frustration. "But why doesn't she believe me when I tell her that *I* don't need her help? This isn't the first time I've had to battle my enemies!"

God alone knew what that last meant. Bill really wanted to know, but had to force himself to let it go and answer the question instead. He had to get Tapio calmer so that he would answer other questions.

"She doesn't believe the words she's hearing, Tapio, not you specifically. And she does that because some very damaged children have come into her care. Children who've at first tried to push her away because they've been so badly hurt, so knocked-about that they don't trust anyone. And you might not need her help but those other children have done. She works very hard to heal them." He mentally groped for an analogy that Tapio would understand. "Listen, have you ever watched Annikki chopping up onions?"

He got a terse nod, "What have onions got to do with anything?"

"Because they're in layers, yes?"

He got an irritated shrug, but at least the lad was listening.

"Well sometimes you can cut an onion in half, and the outer layer will look fine, but then underneath one of the other layers will have gone all brown and rotten. You don't know just by giving it a squeeze, because it'll feel firm. You have to get inside it to find out."

Already Tapio's anger was visibly dissipating. The tension had gone out of his shoulders as he said, "So she thinks my mind is like that?"

"Yes she does. She thinks that you saying that you're all right is like the onion that feels okay. But from her experience, she knows that every other time she's done this there's been a nasty layer underneath that has to be..." He didn't want to say cut out. That sounded too brutal, but could only come up with, "...dealt with."

Lord this was hard work. Psychology wasn't his forte at all. He could get inside the head of the average criminal, but given the lack of brains of most of them, that wasn't saying a lot! But now he was trying to give advice to this strange child. A child whom it didn't take Dr Chandra chewing his ear off about, to work out who had a lot of issues. However odd Tapio was, however un-childlike, he was going to need all the help he could get to come out of this undamaged, and Bill very much wanted him to not suffer permanently from this.

"Tapio, please try to understand that all her experience is telling her that you have stuff you're burying inside your head that needs to be cleaned out, or it's going to poison your mind for many years to come. Don't be so angry with her. She's genuinely trying to help you, even if you can't see how."

Tapio turned and walked away, not in a childish huff, but to go and pace in front of the French windows for two or three passes until he turned back to Bill.

"Do you really advise me to see her again, Karhu?"

There it was again, that very adult way of putting things.

"Yes I do, ...please. You'll only make things a lot harder for yourself if you don't. She has the power to be able to remove you to a hospital if she thinks it warrants it, you know."

"No!" Tapio's response was positively a shriek. "I don't want to leave here! I *mustn't* leave here!"

"Okay, okay!" Bill leapt to his feet and went and caught the lad by the shoulders, totally freaked out by the sudden flash of outright panic.

"Don't let her take me away, Karhu! Promise me you won't let her take me away from here!"

"It's okay, Tapio, I didn't mean she would do that right away. I was just trying to get you to see that co-operating with her, at least for now will make everything easier. She'll only go down that route if you force her to by not talking to her. Doctors don't like doing that, they hate it! But if they think the only way to help you get better is to do that, then they will."

"But I'm not sick!"

"Then talk to her and prove it!"

The fight seemed to drain out of the lad after that, and soon afterwards he announced that he was going to bed. Since he was big enough to not need tucking in, Bill let him go off with just another hug from himself and from Annikki.

"Bloody hell, that's hard going!" Bill sighed to her when Tapio's feet had been heard receding along the landing to the room over what Bill now knew was a study – the one with the miniature turret he'd so admired when he'd first come here.

In response, Annikki went and brought the vodka bottle through from the kitchen, along with two glasses and a carton of fresh orange juice. Urho had eaten with them, but seemed to find it too hard to listen to Bill and Annikki talking in English, and had gone off to his little flatlet above the garage. Annikki had already quietly confided to Bill that she made a point of never going there unless it was to summon him to help with something specific.

"I want to keep a space between us," she'd said pointedly.

Now, though, she was quite happy to sit with Bill talking generally until they thought Tapio had had chance to settle down. They didn't want him coming back down and hearing Bill talking to Mr Nykänen and eroding what trust Bill had there. It had been difficult enough to decide when to call as it was. Finland was three hours ahead of England, and Bill didn't want to be hauling her parents out of bed and frightening them to death while still half asleep.

Mercifully it was about seven thirty when they decided that the coast was clear, and Annikki put in the call. Tapio clearly wasn't asleep, but they could hear strains of music floating down from his room which hopefully meant he was preoccupied. It didn't sound like the usual pop fare, and Annikki had said that along with Finnish artists, the usual range of British and American artists got plenty of airplay over there, so this was clearly his choice, not because he'd never heard anything else. But then nothing about Tapio fitted any usual child models.

After a lengthy and rapid exchange in Finnish between Annikki and her father, she handed the phone over to Bill.

"Mr Nykänen? I'm DI Bill Scathlock. Thank you so much for talking to me."

He made a point of repeatedly assuring Annikki's dad that his daughter was safe before moving on to the questions he had. He needed this man on their side.

"What I'm hoping you can help us with," he finally opened with as he turned the conversation, "is your reaction to the solicitors – or do you call them advocates? – when you saw them. I've no doubt that my counterparts in the Finnish police will be visiting them, but you had the advantage of taking them by surprise. Can you tell me how they seemed to you? Did they act as though what you were saying was news to them? Or did they seem to know more than they were saying?"

Mr Nykänen's response, when it came was very carefully put. "I think they knew that something was not quite as it seemed. By that I mean that I don't think they could quite understand why the advocates in Lapland would not deal with this themselves."

"But when there was an easy euro to be made they weren't going to complain?"

A wry chuckle echoed down the phone. "I think legal men are not so different the world over, eh? But I do not think that they were aware of anything beyond the thought that, if the advocates in the north wished to increase their costs, and had a client willing to pay the extra, then that was unconventional but not illegal."

"And can you tell me what you asked them? How specific were you?"

Mr Nykänen cleared his throat. "Well I was upset, you understand. My daughter tells me that she has gone to England on what seemed like an unusual job, but a legitimate one, and then I find that she has had a strange man wished on her as well as the child. If she had been in another part of Finland I would not have been happy, but it would be so much easier for her to come home if things began getting difficult. So I began by asking them if I could speak to the people who had rented the house. I told them that I wanted to know what references this man Urho had given them, and whether they had been properly checked. I thought that that was a perfectly reasonable thing to ask."

"Perfectly reasonable," Bill agreed. "What did they say?"

"That they were only responsible for the renting of the house, and for paying the fees on to the school. They said that who was responsible for the care of the child was wholly the responsibility of their colleagues in the north. I was less than happy with that."

"I can imagine!"

"I told them that I wanted the name of those solicitors. Given that they were other legal representatives, not individual citizens, I could see no reason for them to withhold the name from me."

"No, I'd agree that you had every reason to think you should be able to have that. Didn't they give it you?"

"No! Or not at first. They began by telling me that a condition of them having this contract was that they would not be referring people back to the original advocates. They told me that their clients were most insistent on their privacy. I told them that that was all very well if all they had been doing was hiring a house for a family who were going to live abroad, but that it was *my* daughter who was stuck in that house looking after their clients' child without ever having seen them, and with a strange man too. Wouldn't they be worried, I asked them? Did they not have children of their own? And how would they feel if their child had been tricked like that?"

Bill could imagine that being a pretty persuasive argument when made in person.

"Even then they were not helpful, though," Mr Nykänen was continuing. "They began to change their minds, however, when I said that I would be getting legal advice of my own, and that if I found anything amiss I would drag them up before their professional bodies. That was when I began to suspect that they had already had some doubts of their own, because all of a sudden they were more helpful."

"Hmmm. If it was all legal and above board then they could have told you to go ahead and get your legal man, knowing that it would make little difference."

"Yes! They had done their part by making it hard for me to get beyond them. But if a judge then declared that they should hand over the information, then who could blame them for doing so? They had gone through the legal process. What more could they do?"

"Interesting! So did they tell you who these people are?"

"Finally. Ollila & Canth – but it won't do you any good. I have already checked. The name has been going for a good many years. Someone keeps them on the legal lists, but if the original partners are still the ones practicing then they should be in the record books – they will both be over a hundred years old!"

"Bloody hell! There's no way that that's happening realistically!"

"No, that's what my wife and I thought. Yet someone is keeping that law firm alive, detective! We had a long talk and we decided that we should go up to where they are supposed to be. I don't know if Annikki has told you, but we live in Tampere. So we caught a flight up to Rovaniemi, hired a car and drove to Kemijärvi where these people were supposed to practice."

"Let me guess – no sign of an office anywhere?" Behind him Bill heard Annikki gasp. So her dad hadn't told her that bit. Probably he hadn't wanted to worry her any more than necessary. "What did you find?"

"Nothing. We called into the post office, but the address we had just goes into a drop box for someone to come and collect."

"And of course the staff have never taken any notice of who comes and goes."

"No. Well there was no need to. From their point of view it was a long-standing and very old contract, but there was never any trouble with it. No awkward packages which needed holding onto, only letters. And with a widespread and very rural population it's not abnormal to need such a drop-off place for mail."

"Bugger it!" Bill muttered under his breath. He was going to have to pass this straight on to Frank. He couldn't wait for that answer from Finland going on this, because it looked like the Finnish police were going to have to run their own investigation before they'd be able to be much help.

"Detective? Are you still there?"

"Yes, Mr Nykänen. I'm sorry, I was just thinking that my colleague who's waiting for a response from your police might have a long wait."

"I think he might. Having the car, we decided we would drive around a little, just to see if we could find anything, you understand. We went all the way up to

Sodankylä, back along the road to Kemijärvi, and on to Kuusampo, where we finally handed back the car and caught a flight back home. It's a good thing we had both just retired! It is very dark up there in the winter months, and several times we had to wait an extra day or two for the weather to improve. We stopped at every village we came to, asking about this strange pair of Ollila & Canth, and no-one could tell us a thing.

"My wife was getting very worried, I can tell you, and she decided that we needed to get to the bottom of this connection her parents claimed existed. It was very hard for her. Her mother is very eccentric and her father sometimes does not stand up to her as he should – does not stand up for what is sensible for her own good and that of their children, you understand – yet they love her dearly, and she them."

"Are there brothers or sisters you could call on for support in this?"

"Oh yes, Mr Scathlock. My wife's sister, Tove, has been on their mother's side, but their brother, Matti, has been most supportive. He and his wife are nearly as worried about Annikki as we are, probably because they too have children. My sister-in-law Tove lost her only child when he was a tiny boy, her marriage broke up, and she has never tried to replace what she lost. At times she can be quite reclusive, but it means she has not seen the dangers for Annikki quiet as readily as Matti and Helene.

"Having said that, though, as we sat in their parents' house explaining how worried we were, I think even Tove began to think we should have asked more questions. So at last we were able to get it out of Father that he had never met the family either! The connection is all on Mother's side! So she had to admit that the family were people whom her own mother had known, not friends of her own. She says she has met this Ilmarinen when she was younger. She is being very coy about it all, but the name makes more sense if it was one of her mother's weird friends."

That was encouraging if Annikki's father had noticed the strangeness of having all these names of gods floating about too.

"Just a moment, though. If this Ilmarinen was someone Annikki's *grand*mother met when she was a girl, how old is he? I mean, we've got an eleven year old boy here! He's not likely to be his son, is he?"

There was a very heavy sigh from the other end of the phone. "That's just what we said. It is just about possible that Tapio is his grandson – just! If this Ilmarinen had a much younger wife, or indeed his son had one. But Mother is seventy-nine! Talking about it afterwards, and putting together what we know of her early life, this Ilmarinen cannot be less than seventy himself."

"I know this might sound a bit odd," Bill said thoughtfully, "But do you think a surrogate mother might have been used? You see Tapio has said to me that Ilmarinen and Mielikki 'did not make' him. If they're a very old couple, she'd be way beyond having a kid, but he might just have managed to father one on a surrogate. It would certainly explain why Tapio's such an old fashioned little lad but also feels a bit distant from them."

There was a silence, then Annikki's father said slowly, "It's possible. I can see why you would think that ...yes. All I can say is that nothing came up in our conversations which would hint at that, but then I'm not sure what Mother knows of such things. Had that been the case, she might not have quite grasped what they were talking about, you see."

"Could you go back and ask her again?"

"Hmph! We parted on very bad terms the last time we visited. She got very angry. She told us she would never do anything which would put Annikki in danger."

"But she has, hasn't she! You can now go back and tell her that you personally have had a phone call from an English police officer. And what's more, our police have contacted the Finnish police, so she stands a chance of being questioned by them if they get to thinking she's the contact point with this missing couple. You have your leverage, Mr Nykänen, and it would be better if she comes forward now, rather than waiting to have the information dragged out of her in an official capacity."

"Aaah! I hadn't thought of it quite like that. Thank you, detective. Tomorrow I shall drive over with my wife and see what we can get out of her."

Realizing how late it was now in Finland, Bill let Mr Nykänen get off to his bed, but not before giving him both his own mobile number, and a number to reach Frank Watson on. And thinking of Frank, Bill now made his excuses and left, texting Frank to let him know that he was on his way to see him. There were still two cars guarding the house as Bill left, although the shifts had changed over to the lads who had the lates. With any luck they'd have a very boring evening, but Bill was glad they were there. Something about this case just didn't add up.

It was a conclusion Frank Watson readily agreed with by the time Bill had brought him up to speed with everything that had gone on.

"Bleedin' hell, Bill, this damned case goes from bad to worse," the DCI groaned. "Where did this bloody kid come from? Under a gooseberry bush? And we're still no closer to finding out why he was the target, either."

"Maybe not," Bill agreed, "but I'm glad that Annikki isn't implicated. The ones where the child-minder is at the back of it always get so sodding messy for the kids. I know her story has to be confirmed, but from everything I've heard she's on the level and so are her parents. Quite what's going on with the grandmother is anyone's guess."

Frank was staring off into the distance with a puzzled frown. "Why does the name Tove ring bells with me?"

"Moomins."

"Eh?"

"Moomins. The woman who wrote the Moomin stories was called Tove Jansson, and yes, she was Finnish."

"Hell's teeth, Bill, we don't need them involved as well!"

"I don't know, I was always rather fond of them as a kid. I think I identified with young Moomintroll. There was a girl who lived next-door who was as fierce as Little My – both of them used to scare the living daylights out of me!"

"Bill Scathlock as a Moomin!" Frank chortled. "That's the best thing I've heard all day!"

Bill joined in the laughter, but added, "There's a part of me that wishes we were dealing with Moomins instead of these blasted characters from the legends, you know. They'd be altogether more cozy for a lad of Tapio's age. At least Moomin Mama and Moomin Papa always turned up eventually and made everything all right. God knows what's going to come creeping out of the woodwork here – for all we know Tapio could be of Russian birth and have been taken to Finland when he was too young to know any different. And that might just mean that the Russians have every right to take him!"

Moscow

The President was a busy man. Busy enough to take no particular notice of the officer who brought in another top-secret document for him to sign, authorising a covert mission to a hostile country. It had been done before, it would be done again. The art of getting away with it lay in picking the target. A decade or two ago there had been a couple of sticky moments when questions had been asked by opposing governments. However those cases could not be avoided. Their own traitors had to be eliminated regardless of the diplomatic furore the assassinations caused.

This one was different.

"It's to do with the Finns keeping quiet about the huge oil field they're sitting on," the officer had said oh-so-persuasively. "We're still investigating. Please sign here." And the president duly signed.

He should have taken more notice of the officer. If he had he would have wondered why he never saw him about other than these times when he came with those orders. And if he'd asked his name, he would have been concerned, for who would name a child after a devil? But Koschei's whole success was in making people forget he'd ever been there. Even with a man as powerful as the Russian President, it was possible to create that small moment of blindness; to pick a point in the day when other minions were scurrying in and out, and where one more made little difference. And also to play upon that self-imposed image of total security. The President had every reason to believe that if someone walked in through his office door, that that person had already gone through several other people. No-one just walked in off the street into his office! But then Koschei hadn't come from the street, but somewhere much lower down. Straight down!

Now he slide out of the door past another official coming in, then rendering himself invisible and wrapping himself around the order so that it too disappeared from sight, he slunk down into the lower levels of the building and down into his own haunt. If the security cameras caught anything it was just a distortion, a bending of an image, as Koschei passed. To any sensors he crossed, he was no more than a passing waft of air. To modern technology, Koschei didn't exist.

Back in his lair, he allowed himself a bitter smile. If nothing had gone right with the seizing of Tapio, at least he was not out of options yet. For centuries Russian leaders had never been content with what they already had, and the current batch of power-hungry bureaucrats were no different to the tsars in that respect. Their greed made them easy to manipulate. Easier than the churchmen, that was for sure!

Koschei hated the Orthodox priests with a passion. They, more than anyone else, had weakened him over the centuries. What point was there in being a dark god, a devil as they called him, if no-one believed in you anymore? This strange faith, with its gold icons of a mother and her child, baffled him. What was it about that which had so appealed to his people? Had drawn them away so that the names of Perun, Jarilo and Morena no longer resonated as the gods to be prayed to for help and protection, and his own boss, Veles, lord of the Underworld, had all but disappeared behind this new all encompassing 'Devil'.

Well Koschei had no intention of fading away! He was going to fight back! And this time he was going to do it on his own. Veles had been a fool. That striking back against the technology these later people had created had almost done for all of them. Chernobyl had almost been wiped from the face of the earth and a fair chunk of Russian with it! What a farce, what a mistake!

So now Veles ruled over a toxic wasteland, weakened and pathetic, and bemoaning his fate with no-one to serve him. Why had Veles never grasped that? That to be a god or a devil you had to have someone to worship you? It was a symbiotic relationship, albeit with control only going the one way, but being the lord of sweet sod all was never going to mean a thing. How many other ancient gods had become nothing more than a whisper on the wind as they'd been overtaken and forgotten?

That, Koschei vowed, was not going to happen to him. And that was when he had his brilliant idea. If his own people had discarded him, he would leave them. He would find a people who still believed in the old ways. People he could turn to who would give him his due reverence. And he'd not had to look far. Finland was ripe for the picking, and for a demon whose immortal essence lay concealed beneath a mythical oak tree, all that forest filled with spirits and believers was a prize worth the taking. All he had to do was get rid of the resident gods! And the first step towards achieving that was to get someone to do his dirty work for him, for which there was no finer bait to dangle than the promise of that black gold – oil!

Chapter 7

Saturday

With so much still at stake, Bill made a point of getting to the house a little earlier the next morning. The day was drier than yesterday, and he was hoping that he could get Tapio out in the garden with Urho. If the lad translated for the big man, there was some hope he might let slip some detail that could be useful. Dr Chandra wouldn't be back until after the weekend either, so today he had Tapio to himself and hopefully a bit calmer.

Delighted to be asked to show Bill around the gardens, Tapio led him outside and round to where Urho's flat was. They found the huge man polishing the car, which was a new and expensive Saab. No money spared there, then! But why have such a car just for the chauffeur to drive the au pair to the shops and a kid to school? The only thing Bill could think of was that with the company's reputation for safety, that had been the prime consideration. And if it was that, then it meant that trouble had been expected right from the start.

"Did you choose the car, Urho?" Bill got Tapio to translate. "It's beautiful!"

Urho answered with a stream of Finnish which Tapio relayed back as, "He says no, it was waiting for us when we got here. Annikki came to fetch us from the airport in her car, but Urho doesn't like that. It's too small, and he bangs his head on the roof. My people had bought this already. So once we'd arrived Urho only had to go and collect it. He says it's a wonderful car. Goes very fast! He says he likes taking it around the Malvern Hills on the bends. That's a lot of fun."

"Does he! Well tell him to be careful with the speed bit. We don't want him getting fined!"

Bill said it with a smile and got a big belly laugh from Urho when Tapio had translated. His reply came back as,

"He knows. He says he's careful."

They managed to prise Urho away from his pride and joy and out to the gardens, where Bill got quite a surprise. The house itself was ringed by the trees, but there was an archway at the back which led out into a second part of the garden. This was much more open, giving a glorious view over the countryside, but was also laid almost exclusively to fruit and vegetables. It was like looking at a huge allotment. No wonder Urho was kept busy! Much of it looked newly planted, like the fruit bushes, but there were patches which showed signs of having already been harvested. No wonder Annikki's food tasted so good! And by this time next year, Bill guessed that they would be virtually self-sufficient.

He didn't have to fake his admiration for what Urho had done, and they spent a pleasant couple of hours with Bill asking, "What's this?" and Urho telling him via Tapio about the different kinds of cabbages and beetroots, and some which Tapio couldn't find the English names for. It certainly eased things between Bill and the big man, so that when, after lunch, Urho said that he needed to do something to Annikki's car, Bill offered to help. It sounded like an oil change, but Tapio was unable to translate, and Annikki openly admitted that she didn't know one end of an engine from the other.

Going round to the garage Bill discovered that Annikki's car was a very elderly Subaru Impretza, which made him chuckle. He could just imagine the bronze-haired Finn scaring the living daylights out of the local lads in that! She'd be the sort to have them drooling over her and wanting to show off in front of her, and then being totally deflated when she left them for dead, eating their own oily exhausts. And if it was old, it had certainly been well cared for, so working on it was a pleasure.

Yet to Bill's surprise Tapio only watched them for a few minutes and then went inside again. The lad had no interest in anything mechanical, it seemed, and yet he'd been animated and full of interest with the plants. Not what Bill would've expected from a lad of his age at all. Granted not all kids were petrol-heads, but the speed thing was usually a pull, and what was odder was that Bill couldn't figure out what *was* Tapio's thing. No games console anywhere he could see. No skateboard in the hall or kitchen. What did this kid do for fun?

With Urho it was becoming clear that his enjoyment came from making things work or grow. Whether it was seeing the new growth on the spuds and carrots, or hearing the improved rumbling of the Impretza's engine, the big man was happy if he'd made it better. And funnily enough, he and Bill managed to get by with a strange kind of sign language around the car. They both knew what needed doing, and a couple of times Bill could get into tighter spaces with his hands than Urho could. So a few gestures and Urho got the idea of what was happening and could signal back too.

When the Impretza was set to go again, Bill signalled that he was going to go and wash his hands and said "Tapio" with a mime of searching around for the lad. Urho nodded happily, shook Bill's hand and then disappeared up the steps to his flat. Whatever he got up to up there was his affair, but after this encounter, Bill was far more inclined to think it would be the usual stuff of soft porn magazines and watching Saturday afternoon sport on TV. Nothing about Urho had set his internal radar off at all. If anything he was more of Annikki's mind, that the poor bloke was lonely and ought to be sent back to his own home.

Annikki was working her way through a pile of washing and said she thought Tapio was upstairs, and so for the first time Bill ventured up to Tapio's room. He tapped on the door and got no reply, tapped again a moment later, and then tried the handle. The door opened, and Bill found himself in the oddest bedroom he'd ever seen. In fact, had it not been for the presence of a bed and wardrobe, he would never have known it was a bedroom. In his time he'd been in bedrooms so filthy you wondered how anyone had survived them; bedrooms stuffed with hard drugs and signs of them having been used; and even one or two really posh ones with some very creative sex toys, but none like this.

The entire walls were covered with photographs of what he guessed must be Finland, but there wasn't a single building to give him a clue. Nor people. Instead there were trees, lots and lots of trees. Some photos were close-up shots of branches with shoots, berries or pinecones on them. Others were landscapes – some showing glorious but stark snow-scapes with white-decked trees scattered across them, others taken deep in forests, and some with lakes surrounded by forests.

His first reaction was that he'd come into the wrong room. Annikki had said she was a photographer after all, although Bill would've thought her bedroom would be more girlie. She seemed a very feminine sort of woman, and this room was stark, far too stark for her. Had he got her totally wrong?

Then he saw a school uniform hanging from the side of the wardrobe. No, not Annikki's room then, but Tapio's as he'd first thought. But what a strange room. It clearly was Tapio's choice of decoration, since there was nothing like it elsewhere in the house, as far as he knew, but it made it even clearer that Tapio was no typical eleven year-old. If he'd come in here unprepared, Bill would have assumed it was an adult's room. There was nothing of the child here at all. He looked closer at the photos – they were beautifully shot, not a bad one amongst them, but Bill had the feeling that there were several photographers' work here. He would have been the first to admit that he was no art critic, but even to his eye there were several approaches within this collection.

And then there was the music. At first he'd not even noticed it, but as he'd come into the room and closed the door he'd become aware of it. His initial reaction was that he was hearing music which was actually being played further off, in Urho's flat maybe. But then he realised that it was closer to and just at a low volume.

He looked around and realised that the little turret area must be part of this room and behind a heavy curtain. Yes, the music was coming from behind it. It sounded at first like the kind of New Age mood music peddled at what Bill thought of as hippy shops, and in garden centres. However as he very gently eased the curtain aside it became clear that it was the genuine thing, real folk music, without electronic pan pipes and *faux* acoustics generated on a synthesiser.

What chilled him more was finding Tapio sitting, eyes closed and cross-legged on a large cushion, and clearly in a deep trance with headphones on. So that was why the music sounded so muted. For a second Bill stood still, waiting for Tapio to open his eyes and acknowledge his presence. When that didn't happen, he very carefully moved the curtain a little further so that he could see more of the alcove. The cushion on closer inspection had the kind of wear patterns associated with long use, and Bill thought it possible that it was very old. He looked at the area around the cushion too, looking for anything which might suggest drug use. Sad to say it wouldn't be the first time he'd come across a user as young as this. It all depended on the culture the child was brought up in, and he couldn't reject out of hand that if Annikki's grandmother and great-grandmother had been proto-hippies, then this mysterious Ilmarinen might have been of a similar inclination, and that might in turn mean drugs. Yet nothing leapt out at him as being drug related, and Tapio himself was positively serene and breathing slowly but perfectly regularly.

Moving away from the alcove and closing the curtains, he decided not to try and rouse the boy. He had no idea of what harm he might do him if he did. Instead he took the opportunity to thoroughly search the room, being very careful not to displace anything. The first thing which struck him was the lack of personal objects. Not so much as a teddy bear, and here if nowhere else he would have expected to find some sign of Tapio's distress at being uprooted from his home and left with strangers, such as a well-hugged toy. A child secure in its own home might have moved beyond such things by eleven, but Bill had seen enough of abuse and neglect to know how kids sometimes hung on for grim death to battered objects from a happier time.

He turned his attention to the photos and began scrutinising them. As he worked his way around the collection, he was surprised at what he saw. Yes, there were the expected acres of pine forest, but there were also other trees, and despite being varieties found in any hedgerow or field, somehow Bill didn't think those had been taken in England. Silver birches were hung with the kind of snow hardly ever seen over here, or at least not for more than a day or so. Three years ago, in 2010, for once there'd been a white Christmas, and Bill remembered going out for a walk down by the local brook and seeing the sunlight sparkling on the trees and bushes. Then it had been as though they'd been strung with Christmas tree lights. Tiny balls of snow clinging precariously to them and sometimes falling with gentle puffs onto the deeper snow on the ground. But what he was seeing here were large swathes of snow clinging to the trees. Great swags of snow which looked as though they'd been there for months.

Then he looked closer. Aside from the pines there were definitely oak trees, as well as the birches. There were some magnificent specimens, and it was the lakes in the background, the flatness of the landscape, or the wildlife in each – Bill knew that there were no bears in England – which made it clear where they must be. How homesick was Tapio? And why these images? They clearly held great significance for the lad, and if nothing else it helped explain a bit more why he kept calling Bill 'bear', since the bears were evident, but not any reindeer or domestic farm animals. No wolves or arctic foxes either, just bears, and Bill felt sure that wildlife photographers would have included these other two in their repertoire.

He was so engrossed in studying the photographs that he nearly jumped out of his skin when Tapio's voice said from behind him,

"I miss it so much."

"Home?"

"Yes. Do you not miss it too, Karhu?"

Bill shook his head, a little puzzled by the question. "No, this is my home. I've never been to Finland, Tapio."

The boy cocked his head to one side quizzically. "No? But your soul has, Karhu, your soul has. Do you feel no affinity anymore?"

That was a crippler of a question. If he answered 'no', would Tapio think Bill was deserting him? And in a weird kind of way there was something very appealing about those vast tracts of unspoilt wilderness.

"I think it's beautiful," he answered carefully. "So much unspoilt countryside – that's just gorgeous! I'm not sure I'd cope with the long winter nights, though."

"But you get the summer sun!"

Crap, but this was getting tortuous! "Yes, but it's all in one go, and the winter is so long. As I get older I kind of need my seasons a bit more broken up. My joints start creaking a bit with the cold and damp, you know." There, that would hopefully sound reasonable, and Bill had found in the last couple of winters that the bones he'd broken on the playing field were starting to make their presence more felt.

However Tapio's face was frowning in thought, clearly trying to work something out.

"Where's this?" Bill asked hurriedly to distract the lad. "Do you know this lake?"

"Oh yes! That's Lake Saimaa. Isn't it beautiful!"

"Gorgeous! And this one?"

And so they got through the afternoon, Bill desperately trying to remember the multitude of strange names so that he could look them up on a map afterwards. Luckily he managed to suggest they go and get a cup of tea before Tapio dragged him back to the more awkward questions. So much for him being the experienced questioner!

Then he managed to decline staying for dinner to Tapio's disappointment, but contrived to ask Annikki as he left,

"Those photos up in Tapio's room, are they all of one part of Finland?"

The glorious red locks got shaken in response. "No, as far as I can make out they're from all over, maybe even some bits which are in Russia now. And before you ask, no, I don't know where he got them from. He arrived with them and put them up the first night he was here."

"So none of them are your work?"

"No, although I wish some of them were!"

"Yes, even I could see that some were very good. And someone had some patience to get those shots of the bears."

Annikki gave a laugh. "Absolutely! You wouldn't catch me getting that close to wild bears – especially not the cubs! You're taking your life in your hands if mommy bear catches you!"

With a promise to return for Sunday lunch, Bill drove away, urgently wanting the peace and quiet of his own flat to think things out in. The final straw had been looking out of the bedroom window and saying to Tapio,

"But you've got some nice oak trees you can see from here. Not Finnish ones admittedly, but they're very old. They're lovely, aren't they?"

And getting the response, "Yes, they protect me. The trees are why we came to this house. That's why we chose it."

That was such a lump of information it had taken Bill a moment to assimilate it.

"Which 'we'? You and who?" he had asked, and been frustrated to receive the reply,

"Ilmarinen and Mielikki, of course. Who else would be helping me?"

At that point Bill could feel his patience slipping, and he knew he had to get out of here before he began grilling Tapio like an adult miscreant. Damn it, he wasn't trained in dealing with kids to this extent! He was running on instinct and a lot of experience, here, and that was starting to fail him. He needed to get out and talk to rational adults.

With that in mind he texted Morag and asked her if she was free for a takeaway and some beer tonight. He didn't want to go and sit in some packed restaurant or pub where he'd have to watch his words. As soon as he got in he rang Frank's phone and had a brief chat but found that nothing new had come in. That wasn't so surprising, it was the weekend after all, and if the Finnish police were working as hard on the case as Frank, nonetheless things like record offices wouldn't be likely to be open, so there'd be only so much they could do.

When Morag appeared clutching the bag of assorted dishes from the local Chinese, Bill could have hugged her out of sheer relief. They shared the dishes out between them and then went and sat to eat them looking out over the river.

"I'm absolutely at the end of my tether," Bill confided to her as he sat back and took an appreciative swig of his Mad Goose ale. "Thank Christ I'm off the painkillers and antibiotics! I really needed this!"

Morag reached over and patted his knee. "M'old mate, you've got a right corker with this one! Be glad you're not the investigating officer, be very glad!"

Bill snorted. "Phfff! And don't I know it! But I can't help but feel for poor old Frank. I mean what a bloody nightmare! Nothing about it makes any sense, Morag. If we could just get close to who this kid Tapio really is, we might be halfway to finding out why he got targeted. But the more I dig, the more complicated it gets."

Morag sat back and curled herself up against the far arm of the big sofa. "He certainly seems to believe in this stuff, doesn't he? Have we got anyone on our bit of the force who's ever done a course or something on religious cults? They might be able to give you some ideas."

Bill pulled a face. "I doubt it. I mean, this isn't exactly Texas, is it? The closest we ever get to odd religions is a few kids into Death Metal, the Malvern hippies and the odd wiccan. The Wacko siege didn't happen on our doorstep. And to be fair to Dr Chandra, she's probably a wizz' at handling kids whose dad's a dealer and whose mom's on the game, but that's not what we've got here either."

"I wonder if you went and had a word with some of those folks up at one of the Malvern alternative therapy centres, or something, if that would help? I mean they might be able to tell you more of what the significance of the oaks is. Why oaks in particular, I mean, and not beeches or ashes or horse chestnuts."

"It's a thought."

However, after Morag had gone home, Bill stood with another beer out on his small veranda and decided that aside from whatever Frank came up with, his own next move would be to ring Mr Nykänen again. If his in-laws were into their own brand of alternative culture, then maybe he could help, because surely it was rather more pertinent to ask what the oak meant in Finnish lore, rather than English?

Once again he resorted to the internet to make a start and soon found references to sacred pines – well that was pretty much as he might have expected. There was even a very early photograph of a sacred pine with a bear's skull tied to it to appease the spirit of the bear. But of the oak he found very little. In the *Kalevala* there was apparently reference to the oak as 'Pun Jumalan', which apparently translated as 'God's tree', but beyond that Bill was none the wiser. He did have a momentary shudder, though, when he discovered that Annikki was supposed to be Ilmarinen's sister.

"God save us, we can do without that in the mix!" he said rolling his eyes heavenwards. "Bloody good job our Annikki's a sensible lass. I'd bet that the spooky granny picked the damned name for her, though!" And he was very glad he'd had the chance to get to know her before he found this snippet, or it might have made him very suspicious indeed.

On he ploughed, discovering the bear had a powerful spirit which was referred to as Hongotar, and which might be the mother bear of all, and that the bear of Finland was called Otso. So 'Karhu' seemed to be a general name for a bear.

"Suppose there some blessing in the fact that the lad's not expecting me to defend the entire bloody country!" Bill grumbled to himself as he got up to ease the stiffening in his back and shoulders for a minute.

However, as he was about to give up for the night, a piece clicked into place. The Jumala of the oak's name was a name given to any god or supernatural being, but also seemed to have distinct links to the Finnish equivalent of Thor, although he never seemed to have acquired the same importance in their legends as he had in the Norse ones. And another of the gods called Ukko also seemed to have an affinity with thunder, in the way Woden did in the Norse pantheon. Moreover, early missionaries to Finland had taken the name Jumala as the name for the Christian god. So that made a bit more sense of the *Kalevala* reference – the oak was pretty much a generic holy tree, if Bill had got it right, but with a nod on the side to thunder gods.

And that made another kind of sense to Bill. Of all trees, oaks seemed to remain after being hit by lightning. Good grief, there were enough blasted oaks still standing in the hedgerows of Worcestershire to prove that! And there seemed to be some kind of World Tree legend in Finland, where a huge oak had blotted out the light and so it had been felled, only to fall across the river of life and now provided a bridge to the Otherworld, or heaven, or whatever other name they might give it.

He sat back and scruffed up his short hair. "Is that it with oaks?" he asked of no-one but himself. "They're the bridge to the other side? And they're not particularly associated with one god or another? Even in a Christian sense they seem to tick a box or two." He yawned mightily and reached over to shut the laptop off. "Is that what it is,

Tapio? You feel you've still got some kind of bridge to the spirit side of your home when you're surrounded by oaks? Bloody hell but you're a strange kid!"

Chapter 8

Sunday

"I'm not sure my employers would approve of another phone call to Finland just for me," Annikki said worriedly as Bill dialed through to her father.

"And I think that since it's them who've dropped you in the shit, they can bloody well cough up!" Bill replied firmly. "The way this investigation's going, the price of your phone calls home is going to be the least of their worries!"

He'd arrived with a pounding headache, and his mood hadn't improved at learning that the cars had been withdrawn. It didn't surprise him. There'd been no hint that a second attempt would be made to seize Tapio, and tying up two cars to guard someone who didn't seem to need it wouldn't look good when the budgets had to be balanced. He also had a sneaking suspicion that someone had let slip that he was calling in on a daily basis, and Williams was a sneaky bugger – he'd probably claim that Bill had been there officially undercover, and just doing light duties, if something kicked off. And if it didn't, Bill would remain on sick leave and unassigned to the case. None of which did anything to improve his health and temper.

"Hello, Mr Nykänen? DI Bill Scathlock again. Sorry to bother you again, but I have another question for your family. ...You were just about to go? Excellent! ...For lunch? Right, then I won't delay you. What I wanted to know was, is there some particular significance to oak trees that your mother-in-law can tell me about? ...Yes, oak trees. You see Tapio has said that he thinks the trees here protect him somehow. ...No I don't understand that either, but he's quite adamant about it. And he says that this house was specifically chosen because of the trees around it. ...Yes, most particularly.

"I know that both you and Annikki have told me that the house was already selected by the time she came over here, so someone had to have given very specific instructions. Now I can get my colleagues to ask your police to put that to the law firm in Helsinki, but that's still going to take a day or so to happen. So I'd really like to get one step ahead and find out if the fact that this house is ringed by oak trees is a reason why it would have been considered the right place? I'm thinking folk legends and the like, and as you can imagine the internet isn't the most reliable place to be looking at for that. Too much wild imaginings and not enough knowledge of the real folk lore! But your wife's mother sounds like the sort who'd know a bit about that I'm thinking."

Even Annikki, stood by the side of Bill could hear her father's laughter over that, and his reply of,

"Oh yes! She'll know. In fact she'll probably give me far more than you want!"

Thanking him, Bill let Annikki have a quick word with him and went in search of Tapio. He found the lad standing at the kitchen door, gloomily staring out across the garden.

"When was the last time you went out?" Bill asked, suddenly feeling very cooped up here. The trees were lovely, but the way they encircled the house made it rather claustrophobic.

"Out? ...You know when – to school."

Bill sighed and ruffled Tapio's hair, thinking 'poor little sod'. "No mate, I didn't mean to school. I meant out as in 'a day out'. You know, for fun."

Tapio's puzzled expression told him all he needed to know. Urho had disappeared in the big Saab, apparently to go to church, and Annikki added that technically Sunday was his day off, and he often went for long drives after church.

"Right, then we're going out for a drive, too!" Bill declared. "Will your Sunday lunch keep for another day, Annikki?"

"Well yes, but...?"

"Never mind 'but', you're both long overdue a trip out and I know just the place! Come on! In my car!"

"I think it would be better in mine," Annikki said. "Tapio needs to have a window open. He doesn't travel very well."

"Okay," Bill agreed, "But would you mind if I drove? It's easier since I know where I'm going."

Annikki looked confused but agreed with a shrug. Only when Tapio had been shooed upstairs to change did Bill tell her about the removal of the cars.

"I'm not sure it's as safe as they think," he added, "so I want to draw them – whoever they are – out, if they're outside and watching. I've done the police driving courses, and my ribs and bruises have eased enough for me to do this. I wouldn't do so well in a stand up fight, but I can certainly fling that Impreza around if needs be."

"Is that safe?"

"Look, there might not be a soul about. In fact I doubt there is. But I'd feel a whole lot happier testing it out while you're with me, than having them sneak up on you at night when you're alone."

While Annikki went and changed too, Bill used his mobile to ring into work and tell them what he was doing. He couldn't explain why, but his instincts were screaming at him that whoever was behind this was clever enough to wait until they were all lulled into a false sense of security. And that was the worst of it. He hadn't seen a damned thing which he could point to as proof if he was asked to say why. It was just his gut knotting up.

The Impreza was a joy to drive, and Bill regaled his two passengers with tales of him driving one while undercover one time. He was heading for Symonds Yat, the glorious beauty spot down on the River Wye. If Tapio liked trees he'd be in seventh heaven there! With Bill's i-pod plugged into the car's music system providing a cheerful soundtrack, they zipped down the roads past Ledbury and Ross, and down to the Wye. At the pub by the river, Bill stopped and bought them all a light lunch.

"Later in the summer this place will be crammed full," he declared, sliding into the corner table, and handing Tapio and Annikki the fruit juices they'd requested. His pint of coke would probably have him caffeined-up for hours to come, but he'd rather that than getting too relaxed.

Tapio was staring up at the great rocky outcrop with delight. "This is wonderful!"

"Thought you'd like it! And after lunch I'll drive round and we'll go for a walk up there."

"Up there? Can we?" It was the first time Bill had seen anything like real childlike enthusiasm from Tapio, but now it was painted all across his face.

When they got up to the walks nothing would do but Tapio had to go and hug a good many of the big old trees, much to passers-by's amused smiles, but Bill just kept a watchful eye and left the lad to do as he wished. It was like watching him coming to life again. By the time they got back to the car, Tapio was practically skipping despite the fact that it had started to drizzle.

"Now back to Malvern and something to eat," Bill declared, having already decided to try the Malvern Hills Hotel. The wood-panelled bar, and its site up close to the old Iron Age fort at British Camp, was another place he thought Tapio would like. It had a kind of loved feel about it and sense of permanence.

He was right, Tapio loved the place and tucked into his meal with relish, again the first time Bill had seen him eat with something like normal gusto for a hungry, growing lad. Of course, he hadn't seen Tapio before the attempted kidnapping, but it did at least feel like he'd brought the boy back to something approaching normality again. A last stroll up the path to where there was a lovely view out across the Severn valley completed the day. Tapio had even been reduced to helpless fits of the giggles by Bill's singing. Quite what it was about Bill joining in with Robert Palmer at full belt even Annikki couldn't fathom, but the lad had curled up as much as he could with his seat belt on, hugging his sides and with tears of mirth streaming down his face. At least he forgot about feeling travelsick!

It was only as they came close to the house that Bill began to feel twitchy. They'd paused to look at the pretty sunset in a farm gateway when a car had passed them. Nothing unusual in that, but the passenger had been looking about him and then did a double take when he saw them. It was a spilt second's glance that Bill caught, but then he was sure he saw the same car coming back past them just before they turned into the gate. There was also another car which passed them going in the other direction with just the driver in it, and then reappeared in Bill's mirror two car's behind. Frustratingly he never quite managed to see the license plates, but he was sure the two had been cruising around looking for them.

At the house, he took Annikki's car straight round to the garage. The big Saab was back and so he knocked on Urho's door, suggesting to Tapio that he might like to tell his friend about the day. Annikki wasn't fooled though.

"What is it?" she hissed softly to Bill, as Tapio launched into an excited volley of his own language.

"Give me your house keys. I'm sure someone was looking for us just as we got back. I want to make sure the house is okay before you two go in. If Tapio wants to come in, go into the kitchen and ask him if he wants a drink or something. I'll check there first. Don't say anything to him. I don't want to spoil today for him by getting him all worried again. I could be over reacting!"

Bill went in to the kitchen on catlike feet, not touching anything but looking hard. Everything here looked just as it had when they'd left, which was something. He prowled out into the hall and went first into the lounge. That too looked undisturbed. One of Annikki's magazine's lay carelessly open on the one sofa, and the scatter cushions still bore the imprint of Tapio's smaller body and Annikki's taller but slim frame. They certainly hadn't been moved to search behind, and Bill had the feeling that if the men hunting Tapio were of the caliber he suspected, then they would be very thorough in their searches.

Oddly, the only room downstairs he was less convinced was how it had been left was the study. Tapio's schoolbooks sat neatly stacked on the one side of the desk, but that didn't seem so odd. Tapio was a very neat little soul. Bill moved around the room looking all the time. Nothing was out of place, and then he got it! At the curtains he picked it up, a whiff of tobacco! Someone who smoked had stood very close to the heavy drapes, maybe not actually smoking in here, but in clothes sufficiently infused with cigarette smoke that it had transferred to the curtain. And with just that trace it had to have happened not too long ago or it would have dissipated. By the time Annikki or Tapio came in here tomorrow it would probably have gone.

Turning on his heels, Bill belted up the stairs, tearing into Tapio's room. The room was empty, and the first thing he did was sniff long and hard. Yes, that same faint aroma, and it was over by the turret space. Bugger it, Tapio was bound to smell it! He dashed into the hall and checked Annikki's room, the guest room and the bathroom. None of them seemed to have been investigated, or if they had, not to the same extent. He was very glad to see that they used good old-fashioned blocks of soap – he'd have been having kittens over what might have been done to bottles of liquid soap! And bless Annikki's Green principles, because instead of bottles of bubble bath and shower gel, there were a couple of nice wide-necked jars with Lush natural solid bath products in them.

"They've been here, haven't they," Tapio's voice said behind Bill, making him near jump out of his skin.

Bill felt as though he was a balloon someone had burst. So much for a lovely day out to cheer the lad up. Yet Tapio seemed to have gained something from the day beyond enjoyment. Bill looked at him hard. It was almost as though that contact with the trees had revitalised Tapio. His eyes were that bit brighter – and not with the almost feverish brightness of over-anxiety. His skin, too, looked a better colour, and he was definitely standing straighter.

"Do not worry, Karhu, they only got in here because I wasn't here. If I had been, they would have found it impossible."

"Well I'll still be sleeping here!" The words were out of Bill's mouth before he even realized it. And yet, despite mentally shaking himself for making such an instinctive reaction, Bill knew that even had he given it more thought, he would still have decided that someone ought to be in the house with Annikki and Tapio. "And I'll come in to school with you and Urho tomorrow. There are too many quiet stretches of road before you get to the main roads."

He walked over and hugged Tapio. "Get yourself ready for bed and don't worry, whoever they are, they're not getting past me!"

And he realized he meant every word. Whoever this Ilmarinen was, or Mielikki, Tapio was here and on *his* patch. That meant that someone, whoever, was going to start playing by his rules not theirs, and for the first time in a very long while, Bill wished he had a gun. Even a shotgun would have been welcome, but somehow he had the feeling the Urho wasn't the sort to take pot-shots at the local bunnies. And there wasn't a cat in hell's chance that he would be allowed to draw a firearm from the police, and especially not straight away tonight.

He needed an ally, too, and that meant Morag. She'd invested a good deal in Tapio's safety already, and being on the desk side of the job now, she wouldn't be working shifts over the weekend except if a really big job came up – and currently Tapio was the nearest thing to that. So the first call went to her.

"Morag? I need your help!"

"Bill? What's happened? Are you all right?"

"Yes, I am, but I'm with Tapio and things have suddenly turned shitty."

"Bollocks! How 'shitty' exactly?"

"Some bastard's been into the house while we were out today."

"Fuck! Where were the woodentops?"

"Pulled off as of last night I'd guess."

"Oh you are fucking joking!"

"No Mogs, I'm not, I wish I were! I'm going to put in a call to Frank as soon as I get off from you, but whatever happens, I'm staying here tonight."

"I'll join you."

"Ta, lass. But before you come tearing over here, I need you to do something for me."

"Yeah, of course, what?"

"Go to my place and get the black bag from behind the bedroom door."

"Bill!"

"Well what the fuck am I going to do if Frank can't get anyone to take this seriously? I can't let the poor little bugger get snatched for real the next time, can I?"

"No, you can't."

"And I saw one car with two in and a second car with another in, that could mean at least three men and possibly more. If they think Urho might get stroppy then they might come in mob-handed, and that means I have to have something up my sleeve. So get the bag and stick it in your car, but leave it out of sight in the boot when you get here. If I can, I'm going to try and get forensics to come out here straight away, so I don't want any questions asked. If you'd grab me my overnight bag as well, then you've got every excuse to be bringing me something, and I'll need that anyway."

"Right. The regular bag in the car and the other bag in the boot. Gotcha. See you in a bit!"

His next call to Frank caused more of a stir.

"Bleedin' hell, Bill, are you sure?" Watson groaned at the news.

"Too bloody sure, is the answer, Frank."

"Williams will have forty fits if he thinks I've dragged forensics out on a wild goose chase."

"This is no wild goose chase, Frank, I promise you. Some bastard's been in here! And the best place to look for prints will be in that study. I touched nothing but the door handle, and I don't think Urho ever goes in there, so the only traces should be of Annikki and Tapio. *Anything* else is suspect."

"Right. You're staying there?"

"Too bloody right I am! I'm not leaving them unprotected."

"Okay, okay, no need to get uppity! I'll start rounding up the lads."

111

By the time Morag arrived, the drive was starting to fill up with cars, and for the next hour or so the house was filled with SOCOs. Bill was being most insistent about having Tapio's room checked too, even though the lad was reticent to have several white-enveloped strangers tramping about him. Morag went and consoled Annikki in the kitchen and helped make tea for those who wanted it. When the house eventually went quiet again, and Bill had done a patrol to make sure that all of the windows and the front door were locked, the three of them met up in the kitchen.

"Did they find anything?" Morag asked as Bill slumped into a chair and gratefully took a mug of tea off her.

"Several partials which shouldn't have been there. It looks as though someone took gloves off to have a go at the desk and Tapio's books."

Annikki looked puzzled. "Partials?"

"Partial fingerprints," Morag elaborated. "It means not a nice full print, which is what we always hope for, but even part of a fingerprint can sometimes be enough."

"And we got something else!" Bill added with a grin. "Someone's got dandruff! They got some flakes of skin off the desk and a couple of hairs."

"Great! So maybe DNA?" Morag said hopefully.

"With any luck, yes." He turned to Annikki. "It's not quite the be-all and end-all that it's sometimes made out to be, but DNA can still be an absolute godsend. I mean, it will be a whole heap harder for someone to convince a jury that they weren't here when we have DNA which says they were. Doesn't help us tonight, though. With this evidence the patrol cars are back, but there's an awful lot of grounds around this place. Morag, will you kip upstairs in the spare room but with the door open? That way if there's any sort of kerfuffle upstairs you'll hear it."

"And where will you be?"

"Downstairs on the sofa."

"With the 'bag'?"

"With the bag!"

Annikki was looking with growing confusion at this exchange. "What bag?"

Morag sniffed. "The bag that's in my car. Bill's bag."

"And what's in the bag?"

"Don't ask," Morag said dryly. "Let's just say I'm praying he doesn't need it, because the shit that will hit the fan if he does, doesn't bear thinking about."

"Is it a gun?" Annikki asked worriedly.

"No," Morag replied, taking her by the arm and steering her towards the door while throwing Bill the keys to her car. "But it might just as well be!"

Bill rolled his eyes in dismissal, but nonetheless went and pulled the bag out, having gone and made sure that the lone PC in the car hadn't nodded off and was taking his duty seriously. Inside, Bill took the bag into the lounge and unzipped it. Inside lay a recurve archery bow and several arrows. He'd been getting into his archery over the last year or so, and if he wasn't ever going to be a great competitor, he enjoyed it. Enough to go and pay out for his own equipment, at least, and the only reason he'd not been out doing that on a Sunday of late – apart from the effects of the collision courtesy of the Thompson brothers – was that he'd got rather fed up with the club he'd been at. Too snobby by half for Bill's taste. He'd found out about another one over the course of the winter, and had been intending to join once he was fit again, especially as he'd be able to have a go at shooting a longbow too. Now, though, he was setting the bow up where he could get to it at very short notice. He wouldn't string it yet, but he put the stringer over the one end and looped the other over the bow, so it would only take a quick tug and the string would be on and ready to go. Robin Hood he wasn't, but at this close range he'd be hard pressed to miss!

"Don't let me have to use this," Bill said in supplication, looking towards the heavens. "I'll be right pissed off if I get this kit confiscated!"

He set himself up on the sofa that faced the window, rather than the one right by it, and settled down for the night. He had a rotten night, waking up at every owl hoot and rustle of the wind through the trees, but it remained otherwise quiet. In the morning Morag set off early to go into work, and the rest of the household got ready for what they hoped would be a normal school day. Annikki was getting an escort to go shopping and the cars would remain at the house. Bill rode in the back of the Saab into Worcester as Urho drove Tapio to school, then travelled back with him to collect his own car, the whole journey passing without incident.

Having made sure that the house had remained undisturbed, his first priority was to get back into town and have a word with Frank in person. He had to wait for a while as Frank was closeted with Superintendent Williams, but finally managed to get Frank alone after he'd returned with a limp looking cheese and ham sandwich, and a coffee of indeterminate origin.

"Christ, Bill, you do like to complicate my life, don't you!" Frank declared wearily, sinking into his chair and waving Bill to the other one. "Well there's good news and bad news."

"Really?"

"Yeah, well the good news is that the legal eagles think that we'll be able to get a prosecution to stick with our two cowboys downstairs. I've never know a pair whose lips have been so bloody welded shut as these two. They'd put a clam to shame! Nonetheless we're positive that they *are* Russians. And curiously, the Russian embassy isn't any too keen to claim them, so there have been no calls for extradition. Most of those negotiations are going on way over my head, but we're quietly hopeful that they'll go down for at least seven years."

"The maximum?"

"For child abduction, yes. And they might get even more if there's even a sniff that they might have intended to traffic the boy for sexual exploitation."

"I wouldn't hold your breath on that one," Bill sighed. "Bastards though they are, I don't get any sense of those sort of shenanigans. Their motives are something else altogether. So what's the bad news?"

"Tapio Törni is dead."

Chapter 9

Monday

"Dead? No!" Bill yelped, leaping to his feet and sending his chair crashing to the floor. "I only left him a couple of hours ago! He was fine. What happened? Who got into the school to get him?"

A worried fellow officer stuck his head around the door at the commotion. "Everything all right, lads?"

"Yes, yes," Frank said, making shooing waves with his hand to the man. "Shit, Bill, I'm sorry. I didn't mean it to come out like that. Your Tapio is fine. I promise! Sit down, please."

"Then what the hell did you mean?" Bill demanded brusquely, plonking the chair back upright with rather more force than necessary.

Frank sighed and for an answer thrust a computer print-off to Bill. "That came in the morning's e-mails."

It was an e-mail from the Finnish police. Bill read it with the paper held at a distance, too distraught to bother to get his glasses out. They were a new necessity, and he'd still not got used to needing them for close work, and at times like this he forgot them altogether.

"Eh?" he muttered, going back and reading it again. "So the 'real' Tapio Törni died in infancy? So what the hell does that make our Tapio?"

"I have no idea," Frank sighed wearily. "But you can see for yourself ...with the information we got from Tapio and passed on to our colleagues over there, he was the one match in their records – Finland's not *that* heavily populated. So either he's a second Törni child who's somehow slipped under the official radar, or someone used the dead boy's identity for him."

"Aaagh, bollocks," Bill groaned, burying his head in his hands as he leaned heavily on Frank's desk for a moment. "Aaagh crap, Frank, I hate this, but it makes sense of something Tapio said to me."

"You're kidding! It makes sense?"

Bill pulled a face. "Yeah, but it's shite. Tapio said to me 'by then I'd become me'. Well I didn't know what to make of that at the time. It seemed nonsensical! When would a little lad like that ever *not* have been himself? I just thought it all part of the crap someone had fed him along with all that mythological stuff."

"But if he retains some vague memory of having had the name wished on him?"

"Yeah, that's what I was thinking." Bill scrutinized the e-mail again. "This little boy died at the age of two."

Frank nodded. "And he's well-documented because the poor little mite had been in and out of hospital for most of those two years. Your heart has to go out to the parents. He was never going to live to grow up, it seems, and it must have been agonising to watch him slipping away."

"Every mum and dad's nightmare," Bill agreed sympathetically. "Christ, you can understand why they asked for him to be able to come home to die."

"And why there was no need for a post-mortem! With all the equipment they sent him home with, and the nurses who went in and out to help keep him comfortable in that last week, it was hardly a sudden or unexplained death."

Bill frowned as he read the e-mail again, still trying to take in all the information. "I know this might sound a bit weird, but do you think it would be possible to get the lads over there to talk to the undertakers?"

"Good God, Bill, whatever for?"

He scratched his nose thoughtfully. "Well I'd like to know for a start whether the lad's body was just taken briefly to the undertakers and then brought home again. You know, for a lying in, as some families do. My old gran was left in state in my auntie's front room in her coffin for a couple of days before the funeral, for everyone to come and say their goodbyes. Because I'm just wondering that if this was a very carefully prepared scam, then someone might have done things like taking hair samples so that if anyone asked for DNA..."

"...Then they'd have some which really was Tapio Törni's!"

"Exactly. You see, I can't help but think that this has been incredibly carefully planned. Whoever the lad is sitting in the school down the road, someone's gone to a huge amount of trouble to keep his real identity hidden. This has been meticulously thought through, and given the amount of time they've successfully kept it going, I reckon it was potentially in the planning for years. How long, of course, would depend on whether our Tapio was always the intended victim, or whether in reality he has older brothers or sisters who might have been kidnapped had there been a match for them. My take on this is that the real Tapio Törni was deliberately picked long before he died – maybe even when he was first diagnosed and a tiny baby. We could be looking at these folks having someone on the inside at the local hospital. Someone watching for a child who was seriously ill. This person informed them how short his life would be, and our strange 'parents' were already clued-up and ready to go at a moment's notice. Therefore, given that, it would be easy to slip our Tapio into his place while he was still too small to have become part of the mainstream of society. School records and stuff, you know?"

Frank exhaled heavily. "And before our Tapio was old enough to be in danger of giving too much away himself by doing things like answering to the wrong name. Because by your reckoning, he can't have been too far away from the real Tapio in age."

Bill nodded. "I'm more and more of the opinion that our Tapio is a very confused little lad, but utterly innocent in all of this. Do you think the Finns would forward us a copy of the real Tapio's birth certificate? It would be nice to know who our Tapio's parents are at least *supposed* to be. I could then drop the names out in conversation and see if he reacts to them at all. It's a long shot, I'll grant you, because given that a two-year-old will only think of the two most important people in his life as 'Mum' and 'Dad', he's unlikely to have known their adult names and connect them to him. But he might just have heard someone talking about them."

"Do you think the Törni family are complicit in this, then?"

"God, I hope not! That would make them a very strange bunch! No, I'm thinking more that the real parents would have been so grief-stricken that they would've been an easy target for this pair, Ilmarinen and Mielikki, to worm their way into their company. But that might mean that our missing pseudo-parents still talked of them in the early days in front of Tapio once they'd made the switch. I mean, it's not beyond the bounds of possibility that our boy was kidnapped from God-knows-who by this pair, who then forced the new identity on him. And it's not unknown for kidnappers to be careless in front of their victims, is it? Let's face it, we've still got sod-all motive for any of this to have happened to our Tapio, so we're snatching at straws here."

Frank rubbed his tired eyes. "I never thought I'd say this, but I'm wishing that this was a straightforward kidnapping. Then we could call in the specialists and hand it over to them lock, stock and barrel. But all these 'maybe's and 'might-have's are too airy-fairy for me to be able to do that. What I wouldn't give for something concrete to hang on to!"

"Oh you've got that," Bill replied dryly. "I think there's absolutely no doubt that some very dodgy people have our Tapio in their sights. But can you run with my idea amongst the others? Can you get hold of copies of the real Tapio's birth certificate and maybe even his death certificate? Then if you can copy them for me, I'll do my best to help you with what I can glean from our lad."

"I'll ask," conceded Frank. "It's not such an odd request, after all. If we ever get anyone to court for any of this, then we'll need proof that the real Tapio lived and died."

Leaving it at that, Bill went home and sorted out a rather larger overnight bag. Despite all of his best intentions, he now felt it impossible not to go and stay out at the strange old house. Somehow, Tapio had crept under his skin, and he found he cared more than was probably wise for this strange little boy and what was happening to him. He was also experienced enough to know that the feeling of ants crawling under his skin came in part from massive frustration at not being able to do more. He couldn't recall another case with such serious potential ramifications, yet where there had been so few people to question. Two villains locked up, but who were saying nothing and giving nothing away. No witnesses to question. No forensic evidence to collate. It was a case full of hints and shadows! Thank God he had no official part in this investigation, being drawn in while he was off the record was bad enough.

With enough clothes packed to see him through several more days, Bill lugged the hold-all out to the Mini and dumped it onto the back seat. Then he stood in the courtyard parking area of the flats, staring at the boot and thinking. Should he take the recurve bow again? His wiser self said to take it straight back into the flat. He knew only too well that he should never even think about using it in anger – and what the fallout might well be if he did! But the other side of him was still aware that he could be dealing with some very dangerous people. And if they did come again, he was going to be stuck out in a very rural area where his colleagues' response time might not be able to be exactly swift. Ten minutes could make a huge difference if he was fighting for his life, and Tapio's and Annikki's, against four or five very dangerous men.

With a bitter grimace, Bill left the bag where it was, locked the flat, and eased himself into the driver's seat. Driving back into town, he pulled onto the public car park not far from the cathedral, and positioned himself where he'd be able to see Urho coming past after picking Tapio up from school. Bill couldn't decide where the boy was more in danger. Here in the city? Where men disguised as local thugs could pull the car door open when Urho stopped at one of the many traffic lights. Worcester had plenty of pedestrian streets and narrow alleys where men on foot might lose pursuers, and Tapio was small enough to be thrown over someone's shoulder as they ran. Or out in the open countryside? Where there'd be few, if any, witnesses to them running Urho off the road to get to Tapio. Bill just hoped that Urho had enough sense to lock the Saab's doors the minute Tapio got in, but he had a worrying feeling that the big man wouldn't.

He managed to stay about four cars back from them all the way through the post-school traffic in the city, then pulled closer as they got out onto the country roads and gave Urho a flash of his lights and a wave to let them know he was there. He didn't see anyone suspicious on the journey, but that didn't make him feel any better.

"You're staying!" Tapio exclaimed with delight the minute Bill got out of the car.

"Yes, I'm staying," and Bill ruffled the lad's hair. "You got homework to do?"

Tapio pulled a face, but went into the house without a fuss, lugging his school bag with him.

After putting his bags in the spare bedroom, and seeing Annikki, Bill decided to go for a patrol around the grounds. It had been dark by the time the forensic team had been combing the area last night, and although Bill had no doubts that they'd searched the immediate proximity of the house thoroughly, there was still the woodland which had not been looked at. Slipping some plastic covers for his shoes into his pocket, along with plastic gloves and some evidence bags, Bill went hunting.

He decided to start at one side of the drive and work his way round the ring of woods until he came to the other side. That way he'd be sure he'd covered everywhere. Nodding to the PC on guard, Bill climbed over the rickety wooden-railed fence, which formed a nominal boundary to the wood, and went exploring along the narrow cleared corridor in front of the undergrowth, which Urho had made with a strimmer.

At first he could see nowhere where anyone could have made their way through the tangle of brambles which smothered the first three or four feet up from the ground. Even the heavy canopy of the oaks hadn't deterred the invasive thorns at the edge of the wood, and they rose too high for anyone to have been able to see over them. However, as he got round from the front of the house towards its right-hand side things changed a little. For a start, the wood edge was now facing north, so it never got direct sunlight and was too encircled to get even slanting beams from the west or east. That meant that the brambles were having a far tougher time here. Also the leafy canopy was that bit higher, and suddenly Bill found that he could see into the woods, albeit not that clearly.

Climbing onto the fence rails and hanging on to a branch for support, Bill realized that he could see something which looked like a thin track. It wasn't as grand as a footpath, but the undergrowth did seem as though it had been forced aside not too far back. Resigning himself to getting scratched to bits, Bill battled his way through the initial tangle until he got to the track. He'd deliberately come at it a bit back from where it was closest to the fence so that he didn't blunder out of the brambles and immediately trample on vital evidence.

Bending down, he scrutinised the ground. Yes, there was something which definitely looked like a partial footprint in a damp piece of ground, and that had to be recent taking into account when it had rained. He carefully laid an evidence bag over it and anchored it down with a couple of twigs. Then with great caution, he turned towards the house.

He found four more partial prints, and to his eye they weren't all the same man's. One he could believe belonged to one of the goons still locked up, who'd been part of the snatch team, because it looked older and more eroded. It was certainly big enough, but not as big as Urho's. The other was more curious. There was definitely a strange indentation pattern, as though the man put more pressure on one side of his foot. Possibly someone who suffered from a deformity, but Bill's instinct said it was more likely someone who'd been injured in the leg in the past. He couldn't see these types taking on anyone who wasn't ultra fit, so it was more likely that this was someone who was senior enough to still be useful, even when physically he wasn't so good.

Then he struck gold. There, scuffed under a bramble were several cigarette butts. With great care, Bill scooped them up into the evidence bags. If his luck held, there'd be DNA on those, and even if it only helped prove that the pair of kidnappers had been to the house, that would be something. But Bill was hoping for more – that it would tell him how many men had been standing here watching from the shadows.

He searched a little more, his nose finding a place where someone had gone to relieve themselves. Whether that would be of any use he didn't know, but what was of more help was finding a snagged piece of thread on one of the brambles. It looked like good heavy wool of the kind an army coat might be made of, certainly not the kind of stuff which could be attributed to local kids in hoodies, or cheap jackets, messing about in the woods.

By now the light was starting to fail again, and so Bill clambered back out of the wood and went to the parked PC to get him to radio in what had been found. With any luck someone would come out and take casts of those shoe-prints tomorrow, and no rain was forecast for tonight, so Bill's careful covering with bags should keep them pristine enough. Handing over the evidence bags so that they could be taken back that night, Bill went inside and was immediately assailed by glorious wafts of cooking. His stomach growled noisily, making Annikki laugh.

"We'd better feed you before you fade away!" she teased.

At the dinner table Bill kept away from the subject of what he'd found, but once Tapio was in bed, he got Annikki to come with him to talk to Urho. It wasn't the fastest conversation with everything having to be relayed through Annikki, but by the time they left, Bill was at least more confident that Urho understood the gravity of the situation and would be more cautious from now on.

However, the last revelation of the evening came in a phone-call from Mr Nykänen.

"I spoke to my wife's mother," he told Bill, as Annikki listened in via the speaker while Bill made notes. "She says that oaks have always been significant. In the pre-Christian days of our people, the Tree of Life was supposed to be an oak."

"A bit like the Norse World Tree?" Bill wondered, checking that his own research had been right.

"Yes, the same sort of thing. But the strange thing was that Mother got very shy about some parts of the legends. She says that there is a definite protection element to the oak, but it took a long time to get it out of her that Tapio, as Lord of the Forest, would have a particular association with such powerful trees. The forest was his land, she told us. Hunters who went in there had to ask for his permission to hunt, and if they upset him, he could deny them their prey and send them home empty-handed."

Bill sniffed. "Well you could see how that would be a pretty big threat back in the day when everyone had to catch their own meat."

"Yes, and of course for people like the Sami, who had no set home to farm, it stayed culturally important for much longer than it might have in countries like where you are, detective."

"Good point. So maybe we're looking for someone with cultural ties to those old ways. I'm not pointing the finger of blame at the Sami directly, you understand, but maybe someone had grandparents who filled their head with these ideas."

Mr Nykänen's grunt of agreement was audible. "Indeed. But what concerns me rather more is the way Mother was so ...cautious. So very careful about answering once I had told her why we wanted to know."

Annikki's face was a picture of surprise as she interrupted with, "Grandma? Cautious? Normally you only have to say the word 'folklore' and you can't stop her!"

"I know, Anni." Her father's voice was full of worry. "The more this goes on, the more your mother and I are becoming scared over what she's got herself mixed up in. You know what she's like! Common sense has never been her strong point."

"Oh dear," Annikki sighed. "I hope when I come home it won't be to visit her in prison."

"I hope so too," her father said, but with rather too little conviction.

Bill offered her a comforting smile. "Now then you two, that's jumping the gun a bit. She's a slightly dotty ....err ...eccentric old lady, and even if she does get called into court, the chances are she'll be seen as something more like the poor befuddled old soul who hadn't a clue what was going on."

"Sadly Mother rarely seems that feeble," Mr Nykänen sighed. "Under those circumstances she'd be just as likely to be as sharp as a knife!"

"Better make sure she has a dose of the magic mushrooms beforehand, then!" Bill joked, and finally got a laugh from the other end of the phone. That was better, he felt rotten for shoving all this worry onto the poor man. "So can I just check what you've said, then? If someone genuinely bought-in to all this folklore stuff, and they want Tapio to think that he really is – or at least has some definite affinity with – the Tapio of legend, then it's perfectly reasonable that they would have filled his head with the idea that when he's surrounded by woodland he could control, or maybe deflect, anyone hunting him?"

Mr Nykänen, cleared his throat. "Hmmm, yes detective, I think that about sums it up."

"And as we're in England and don't have your vast pine forests, a nice stand of old English oaks would be the kind of thing such people might seek out? There being oaks at least associated with Finnish lore, rather than beech woods, or ash – which is positively rampant round here."

"Yes, I suppose so."

Bill left the room then to allow Annikki some time to chat with her father in private, and went into the study where he could look out onto the trees. Did this strange couple, Ilmarinen and Mielikki, genuinely believe that Tapio would be safe here because of the trees? If that was the case, Bill could see that it would complicate any prosecution, because it would take away the element of deliberate neglect. It was one thing to be throwing the book at the pair of them for abandoning Tapio to Annikki's care, and not caring enough to check up on how the lad was. However, if they had truly believed that he was safer from any approaching harm in this old house because it was surrounded by oaks, then that made them misguided, or downright barmy, but not malicious.

And he still wanted to know just how much that pair had known of any impending attempt to kidnap Tapio. The temptation was to assume that they were the ones who'd set this whole mess up. Yet that might not be the case at all, and Bill could see that there might be a whole other reason for someone trying to grab Tapio which had nothing to do with Ilmarinen or Mielikki, and that they might even turn out to be the good guys in all of this tangle. Frank really needed to find out how specific the instruction had been to the solicitors over here to find such a house. The more care and imperative there had been on finding somewhere exactly right, the more it would look as though Tapio's vanished 'parents' had perhaps known more than they'd let on about of the dangers following Tapio's move to Annikki or the school.

Bill leaned his head against the cool glass and stared at the long shadows of trees creeping across the lawn. Who had stood here the other night? The man with the limp? And aside from his own identity, who was he with?

Somehow, that find in the woods had been the tipping point for Bill. Because why would Ilmarinen or Mielikki have needed to set men to watch the house, when they already knew what Tapio's movements would be over here? Those watchers screamed to Bill of military types, whether the real thing attached to a foreign government (and what a god-awful mess that could turn out to be!), or random paramilitary men attached to some radical group of nutters.

His thoughts were of the latter simply because they'd got careless enough to leave evidence. Of course, that equally could be due simply to scorn of what they'd seen as bumbling British coppers. Well they'd soon learn some respect if that was the case! He was getting more and more angry in that slow-burn kind of way, and if Bill didn't lose his temper very often, it was usually pretty awe-inspiring when he did – although he was too lost in the moment on those rare occasions to appreciate it himself.

Sighing, he was just turning away from the window when something made him turn back. What had that been? Just for a second he'd caught a tiny glint of light from the corner of his eye. He paused, standing just back enough from the window so that in the dim light he wouldn't be seen, and scanned the trees again. Nothing. But he'd been damned sure there had been.

Hurrying upstairs, he slipped into the spare room without turning on the light. By touch, he pulled a pair of good night-glasses out of his bag and dropped the lens caps onto the bed. He'd bought the binoculars for stargazing, but tonight it wasn't stars he was looking for. Having set up the focus, he began methodically searching the woods, taking his time.

The first time he missed seeing the actual glow, just getting the faintest hint of it from the side, but swinging the glasses back a few feet he knew he'd found something. He'd been drawn to the black patch because it had little undergrowth, for even now that night had fully fallen, with the glasses he could still distinguish foliage as it rustled in the slight breeze. And then there it was again, a slight red glow. A man taking a drag on a cigarette! Bill couldn't see the figure behind it, but he knew the watchers were back!

———— ～◦✦◦～ ————

Russia's western borders & London

In a room somewhere on the outskirts of St Petersburg, in the bowels of an unprepossessing block of local administration offices, a figure hunched over a desk speaking into a phone.

"I don't care if he does have a guard with him all the time," Koschei snarled to his minion, "you will go in there and *get* him!"

"But this man is a British policeman, not just the simple giant," the voice on the other end protested. "We've already lost Pavel and Uri. The police are holding on to them, and we can't get them out without revealing ourselves."

"To the freezing waters of the Underworld with Pavel and Uri! Forget them! They failed and now they are expendable. You must adapt. Curse your miserable souls, you're supposed to be professionals! I'm paying you enough to expect you to behave like them. Stop wasting time. You need to go in and get this boy. Can you do that? Or do I need to motivate you further?"

The reflexive swallowing was audible down the phone, as the soldier on the other end thought of the previous time his terrifying employer had demonstrated his power. It hadn't been pretty, and even for a hardened veteran of the Afghan campaigns and others, it had been a gut-churning experience clearing up afterwards.

"No sir, that won't be necessary."

"Good. Now get me that boy!"

"Yes sir. Get the boy and bring him to you. But if there's no alternative you'll want the usual solution?"

"The usual solution?" the shadowy figure hissed. Sometimes it was so cursed hard dealing with these modern humans. They seemed to talk in these strange cryptic phrases, which clearly meant something to them, but whose words actually meant very little taken at their most literal. Like now. What was a 'usual solution' for these people? In thinking too hard on that he nearly lost control of the physical manifestation by which he was using this strange telephone thing to reach so far afield – this thing called technology was both a blessing and a curse.

"Well sir, our previous 'employers' have always had what you might call a codicil to their commissions. Of course, we do everything we can to make sure that the outcome is what they desire. But most recognize that at their worst, events can move beyond our control, and in those circumstances they are willing to ...um, concede ...to a termination."

"A termination?"

The distant soldier winced and rolled his eyes in exasperation to his two colleagues standing huddled close to him in the public phone-box in London. This man had paid them very well already, and there was a promise of a very generous payment to come on completion, but aside from being the scariest nutter they'd ever been employed by, did he have no idea of conditions round here? It was common knowledge in the covert world that London was a bloody nightmare to try to work undercover in. So much CCTV coverage, so much internet scrutiny, and most importantly at this very moment, so much listening in on phone conversations both mobile and landline. The KGB might have been exemplary in terms of the amount of fear they had generated (and the senior man was a graduate of this tough school), and their knack of turning one man on his neighbour, but the old USSR had been a vast geographical unit by comparison with which London was tiny. Tiny and with a damned great government microscope trained on it!

The soldier gritted his teeth and tried to work out how the hell to say 'I presume you want us to kill the brat' without being so explicit. Because those kinds of words would have the electronic gizmos of the watchers sounding alarms the nanosecond the 'k' word was out of his mouth.

"What do you mean, 'a termination'?" the Russian end of the conversation demanded again.

Well that fucked it! One of the other men was already making winding up motions with his hands as a police patrol car cruised slowly past the three of them, and the leader could begin to feel the sweat around his collar. If any listener was unsure, that last question had confirmed what they were talking about.

"A termination sir is a contracted killing. If it proves impossible to bring the boy out, usual practice would be to kill him."

"Nooooo!" the shriek echoed down the line, nearly deafening the soldier, and sending shivers down his spine.

Before the soldier could summon the breath to query why, the voice on the other end was all but screaming at him,

"Noooo! You do not kill him! Not under any condition. Under *any* circumstances, do you understand? Fools! Idiots! You kill the boy and what's within him flies free."

Far away, the three soldiers looked at one another and shrugged in confusion. What was the lunatic on about now?

"Sir? What…"

"You do not kill him!"

131

"Very well. But should it prove impossible to extract him, what do you want us to do?"

"Leave him! The spirit of Tapio *must* remain encased within the boy! If you break the flesh the spirit will simply fly back to his homeland, and then I shall have to start tracking him down all over again. As it stands I know where he is. *What* he is. No, Tapio must remain within the boy. If you do not succeed there is still time to make another attempt. Now go! Go and get him!"

As the conversation cut off, the soldier sighed and hurried out into the fine rain with his two companions, immediately putting as much distance between himself and the phone-box as he could.

"Well do we 'do' the boy?" one of the others asked as they darted down a narrow pedestrian walkway, and then dived round several bends as they headed for the underground station.

"Seems not," the leader grunted. "He says if we fail he'll get someone else to do the job."

"Yeah, and give them the second part of our pay, I bet!" the third snorted in disgust.

"Then we'd better not fuck it up," the leader declared acidly, and limped off ahead of them.

Chapter 10

Monday night

Hurrying to the other side of the house, Bill slid into the bathroom and stood on the toilet so that he could look out of the small opening window at the top. His gaze went first to where he'd found the evidence earlier, but it was clear that he must have alerted the watchers to the fact that their hide had been found. There was no sign of movement there at all. However, that was a good thing, because it allowed him to scurry out of the back door to Urho's flat, wake him, and mime what was happening to the sleepy giant.

Beckoning him to follow, Bill led Urho into the house and then bolted the door. He found Annikki in the kitchen and then explained to her what he'd found.

"We're bolting all the doors once I've been out to the patrol outside," Bill said firmly, "but I wanted Urho here with you in case someone tries to make a dash in while I'm outside. The last thing we want is you locked in here with some nutter, while I'm stuck outside!"

Making as if he was simply strolling out to have a last word, Bill slid into the passenger seat of the police car and then proceeded to frighten the life out of the fresh-faced young constable.

"Have you got all that?" Bill demanded when he'd finished.

"Yes, sir. I'm to tell them that there are men in the woods, and that you're not calling it in yourself because you don't want them to see you talking on the radio. ...Sir? Do you really think they're watching you that much?"

"Son, if I was them I'd be watching me like a bloody hawk! If they want to try to snatch Tapio again, then who do you think is most likely to stop them? Annikki? No. And Urho's a great big bloke, but he's as slow as treacle! They could get past him in a flash. But I've already royally fucked-up their plans once, and they won't want to risk that happening again."

"Yes sir."

Bill got out of the car and began walking back across the gravel when the PC's voice called him back.

"Sir?"

Bill turned and saw the PC beckoning him. Clearly the lad didn't want to shout whatever it was across to him, and so Bill made a good show of ambling casually back to him. Leaning on the driver's side roof, and making the car tilt with his weight, he asked,

"What is it, son?"

"The radio, sir! It's dead! I can't get anything at all!"

Bill's language ought to have stripped the paint off the car. "How the fuck have they managed that?"

"I don't know, sir."

"It's all right, son. Didn't mean you." And Bill patted him on the shoulder, although with rather more force than he'd intended, making the PC wince as he tried not to show how much that had hurt. "Right, well that really sets the cat amongst the pigeons, doesn't it? I daren't walk down to the road, so you'd better drive down to the other car and let them know what's happening."

The PC gulped. "There's only me, sir."

"Fuck-me-rigid!" Bill growled, strangling the yell he wanted desperately to make. "What do you mean, there's only you?"

"Gang of lads on the Morrison's trading estate, sir. Seems they were trying to break into Halfords for car bits. Our shift's spread out all over Malvern looking for the ones who legged it."

"Little bastards! If I get them they'll be incapable of walking!" Bill snarled. Of all the lousy moments for the locals to get uppity, it didn't get much worse than this. In fact, Bill would have bet good money on there having been some dirty money changing hands to make sure that exactly this happened. Let's face it, you didn't need to be a genius to know that the lads out here away from the city force were stretched pretty thin at the best of times. So creating any sort of major ruckus was going to ensure that men had to be pulled from somewhere, and this detail was surely going to be one of them. One car or two would not seem such a compromise to a hard-pressed sergeant trying to have more men than he had in several places at once.

So what to do? The one lad on his own wasn't going to be much help. Better to send him off to where he could get some signal – and Bill had the nastiest of feelings that this wasn't just some atmospheric glitch, and that someone out there in the night was deliberately jamming the signal. At least this way, if it all did go horribly wrong, then at least Frank would know when it had all started to kick off when it came to clearing up the mess. And if the PC could contact Frank himself, he might well be able to summon men directly from Worcester given that this was really Frank Watson's case, and it wasn't just a petty burglary on Malvern's patch.

Shooing the now thoroughly worried constable off, Bill strode to the door and slammed it shut. He didn't need to make any pretence now. The watchers would have guessed already that he now knew that no help would be coming if needed. He shut the front door and shot the two bolts (top and bottom) home with angry snaps, and clicked the deadlock on. There wasn't a chain on the door, but Bill had more faith in the stout oak and the hefty steel of the bolts than he would have had in a light chain. They'd have to physically break this door down, although automatic weapons might cause it some damage. Please God they wouldn't be facing that kind of threat!

"What's wrong?"

Tapio stood in his pajamas at the top of the stairs, and had clearly seen Bill coming back in, and Urho standing in the hall with Tapio's cricket bat in his hand – although in his vast paw it looked more like a butter knife.

"Go back to your room. Try and get some sleep," Bill told him. "There's nothing here we can't handle."

He said it to try and avoid worrying Tapio, yet the lad just cocked his head on one side like a curious robin and said,

"Is it about the men outside?"

"How did you know?" Bill was aghast. He'd only found out with the aid of his binoculars. Surely Tapio hadn't been watching too?

"I can feel them," Tapio said, as if it was the most normal thing in the world. "I told you, Karho, I am safe when I'm in this house. The trees protect me."

Bill felt like screaming. On the one hand he didn't want to say what he was thinking, which was 'what a load of bollocks!' All that would do was upset Tapio, and on several levels. And on the other he was frantically thinking, 'what-the-fuck am I going to do now?' Any minute he could be facing possibly half a dozen heavily armed men storming this old house, and against them he had himself and a twenty-stone innocent, who would probably wait for too long before braining someone with that bat he was so casually holding.

"Tapio..." What on earth could he say? "Please, just go to bed. You're safer up there."

If it came to that kind of fight, Bill would hold the stairs against every man who came against him, but never in his long years of service in the police had he faced this sort of adversary. Because somewhere deep in his gut he was feeling that he could lose his life in this fight. These men wanted Tapio badly. Very, very badly. And whatever they planned for the boy, Bill had the feeling that they would be getting him far from here before they did it. Whereas he himself was just a nuisance in the way, and utterly expendable. They probably had some kind of escape route already worked out, and would be far way before the first siren was heard around here, and had no intention of facing British justice for the killing of one lone policeman.

"Do not worry, Karho," Tapio told him with far more confidence than Bill felt. He turned to Urho and said something in Finnish, which he didn't explain and Bill didn't understand, but whatever it was made Urho put down the bat and turn for the cellar.

"Urho?" Bill protested, but the big man took no notice, unbolted the cellar door and went down into the gloom.

A few moments later he emerged again, carrying in his arms a large box which he reverently carried upstairs to where Tapio was waiting.

"Oh Christ-almighty," Bill groaned with a despairing glance to Annikki, who looked as worried as he did. Whatever this unlikely pair had in mind, she was no more party to it than he was.

Together they hurried up the stairs in Urho's wake, following him into Tapio's bedroom. Urho was already springing the clips on the box, and then lifted the lid back on its hinges and stood aside for Tapio. The boy lifted something in a cloth out of the box and placed it on the bed beside the box. He made another instruction to Urho and the big man disappeared once more. He must have had to go to the cellar again going by the time he was gone, but then they heard him coming back up, this time making harder work of the ascent. When he appeared in the bedroom door Bill and Annikki could see why. He was lugging a huge tree stump.

He placed it where Tapio's pointing finger instructed, almost at the opening to the turret space. The boy then lifted the wrapped bundle that had come out of the box and took it to the stump, only revealing what it was when he shook the cloth wrapping free and set it on the stump. Bill had never seen one before, but he could make a good guess at it being a bear's skull, and a bloody big bear at that! The size of the teeth still embedded in the jaws gave him the shivers all by themselves.

Yet if he was surprised by that he had no time to recover. Tapio had brought out a reindeer skin cloak, bedecked with feathers, which he enveloped himself in before going to sit cross-legged on the old cushion where Bill had found him before. Urho clearly knew what was going to happen, because he went to the box and produced something that looked very like incense and a small saucer to burn it on. He clumsily began trying to light it until Annikki took the matches from his hands and said,

"Here, let me."

She turned her head enough to smile at Bill as she gently blew the charcoal disc into glowing life. "I had a student friend who was crazy about this stuff," she said with a wry smile. "She was always setting the fire alarms off at uni'!"

Urho handed her the incense and she expertly scattered the first of the granules onto the charcoal. It was different to Bill's experience of incense, which had primarily involved old hippies waving joss-sticks. Certainly it was a much more subtle and yet more pungent smell, and within a minute the room was filled with a strong scent of pine needles.

Annikki had slipped back to stand beside Bill.

"I don't think he got that stuff off the shelf of the nearest New Age shop," he whispered to her and got a distressed shake of her head in agreement. Whatever it was, it lacked the muskier smells he normally associated with incense. It was almost as if it was the resin of fresh pine trees of some distant age, when everything had been cleaner and fresher.

Both were so absorbed in the scent that they jumped when Tapio spoke again. "Karho, will you watch from one window, and Annikki from the other?"

Bill hurried to the one from which he expected to see the men emerging, and was appalled to see four men already climbing over the fence from the wood.

"Four men coming from the wood!" he called with more force than he'd intended, then jumped again as the deepest note he'd ever heard came from behind him. For a split second he couldn't imagine where it had come from, then realised that Urho had his eyes closed and was intoning again. Tapio, too, had his eyes closed and now began a more complex chant over the top of Urho's, which continued to roll around at a subterranean vocal level. Yet Bill had to admit that he could definitely hear actual notes. It was not just some random and undefined rumblings. This was the most magnificent *basso profundo* voice at its lowest register, and from where Urho was standing it was as if the notes were coming from the bear's skull as his voice reverberated through it.

"Sing with us!" Tapio commanded.

"What?" Bill demanded. "A prayer? What?"

Tapio had sung a few more bars but broke off to say shortly. "Anything! But make it something you believe in. Something from your heart!"

Bill glanced out of the window and saw that two more men had appeared. However, the men had paused at the lawn's edge and were looking perplexed at the house, but there was no mistaking the shapes of the automatic weapons in their hands. His mind skittered through the music he usually played at home or in the car, nothing seeming appropriate until he came to a song from a few years back. Suddenly it seemed to say everything to him, and in sheer desperation, he began singing with all his might. There was nothing else he could do. Even the recurve bow was less than useless now. He might get one or two at this range and in this light, but that wouldn't save them from the other men. As he sang about 'simple things', he wished from the bottom of his heart that life hadn't suddenly got so complicated.

The song had been enough of a hit that Annikki knew it too and began singing along with him, but neither of them expected what happened next. With their voices filling the old room, there was a sudden feeling as if something had shifted. Something had changed, and there was a definite sensation of them not being alone here, even though there was no sign of anyone else in the room.

Bill glance to the lawn and was amazed to see the six men still within sight. Granted they had taken a few paces further towards the house, but it was now as if they were wading through quicksand. He was so astonished he faltered over the next few bars of the song.

"Keep singing!" an unfamiliar voice said in his ear, and yet even without looking he knew that no-one physical was there. His gut gave a gurgle of fear and he was sure the temperature in the room had dropped several degrees. Either that or he was sickening for something and this weird experience was actually virus-induced delirium. It didn't feel quite like that, but equally he couldn't explain how he felt any rational way either.

Drawing a ragged breath, he got to the end of the song and began again, by now beginning to feel a trifle light-headed as he breathed in more and more of the pine scent.

He could see Annikki on the other side of the room, but between him and her he could have sworn he could see the ethereal shapes of three others. One looked in some vague way as if he should be a Norse smith, and one was definitely a woman, but the other was less defined. All Bill could have said was that he looked old.

Somewhere overhead there was a rumble of thunder, even though it was far from the normal season for such things and certainly hadn't been forecast. A rattle of hailstones on the window drew Bill's eyes back to the lawn and the most unbelievable sight. Afterwards he couldn't have said whether he was tripping on some narcotic in the smoke or not, but his body seemed to be on its own kind of autopilot carrying on with the song as if it was some repeating chant, while his mind took its own course. What he would have sworn was real was seeing the men being swept backwards into the trees as if by some violent storm. Dorothy had never been whisked back to Kansas as violently as those six men were hurled back into the woods, their automatic weapons left discarded and unused on the grass.

Within a minute of the men's disappearance, the storm began abating, and suddenly the air within the room began clearing. Seized with a sudden coughing fit, Bill doubled up, realizing as he straightened that the charcoal was still glowing, but the strange incense was all gone and so too were the strange visions. Annikki had sunk onto the floor and was sitting looking pale-faced and shaken, but Urho still stood where he'd begun behind the bear's skull, calm and unfazed.

"What the hell happened there?" Bill demanded, wiping his streaming eyes.

Tapio opened his eyes and gave him a beatific smile. "It's as I told you, Karho, they cannot touch me here. Did you not believe me?"

141

Bill just shook his head. Never mind whether he believed it. What in the name of all that was holy was he going to tell Frank Watson? How could he explain that six heavily armed men had come here with every intent of forcing their way in, and then had simply vanished? Shaking his head vigorously, as if coming up from the bottom of a particularly brutal tackle, Bill forced himself to start moving. Those guns were still on the lawn for the moment. He needed to get them and bring them in before they could be reclaimed; and if nothing else, they would at least prove that he'd not totally lost his mind when the reinforcements got here.

Going down the stairs he had to hold on to the handrail, his knees feeling weak, and he felt as drained as if he'd played a full match in the space of those few minutes. Pausing before opening the front door to pick up the cricket bat – just in case – he careful drew back the bolts and turned the lock. For the briefest moment he half expected to have the door kicked in in his face, but nothing happened. He cautiously peered out and switched on the outside lights. He'd left them off when he'd come in, because the last thing he'd wanted to do was make the invaders hug the darker shadows where they'd be harder to spot. Now, though, they were a welcome return to the normal world as their harsh electric light flooded the lawns.

Going round the side of the house, Bill headed out across the lawn. He knew he ought to have been shitting himself with fear. After all, there was no knowing if there were any others backing the six up who were still deep in the trees and still armed. Yet something inside him said that the danger had passed, however illogical that might be. Luckily, the stubby weapons had webbing straps attached to them, allowing Bill to pick them up without disturbing any evidence on the guns themselves.

He plodded wearily back across the now sodden lawn towards the house, laden with his spoils of war, only to be greeted by Urho blocking the door.

"Oh come on! Let me in!" Bill protested.

Annikki appeared at the big man's elbow. "Tapio says the guns mustn't come into the house," she told him, at the same time making a shrug of incomprehension in sympathy with Bill. "Apparently, because they've belonged to Tapio's enemies, if we bring them inside we effectively create an invitation for their owners to follow them in by this route."

"Jesus!" Bill muttered, but after this weird night, he hadn't the energy to protest. "All right, just get me the keys to my car then, will you?"

Annikki nodded and hurried off to the kitchen, although Bill noticed that she staggered a little and looked as drained as he felt. She came back with the keys and followed him round to the Mini.

"Would you go into the boot for me?" Bill asked. "There's a new big sheet of plastic in there. I always keep one handy in case I have to get under this old beast when I'm decently dressed. Now it'll stop the evidence getting contaminated."

Annikki nodded and retrieved the clean plastic sheeting, ripped its packet open, and spread it on the back seat. With a grunt of relief, Bill reached in to the little two-seater, deposited the guns on the seat, tipped the driver's seat back into its normal position, and then lowered himself onto it with a grunt of relief. He was then surprised to find that Annikki opened the passenger door and dropped into the other seat.

"What the hell happened in there?" he asked her wearily.

"I don't know," she answered, her voice wavering, then broke as she sobbed, "but I want to go home now!"

Shifting himself sideways so that he could wrap an arm around her without pulling at any of his battered bits, Bill let her sob on his shoulder until she'd calmed down.

"God, I'm sorry," she sniffed, helping herself to the tissues in the box down by her feet. "You didn't need a wailing woman to add to your worries."

"Don't you worry," Bill consoled her. "I wasn't that far behind you! For the life of me I can't think how I'm going to explain this to my colleagues. I mean, I'm not entirely sure what actually happened up there, are you? And as for what happened out here..." and he lifted his free hand in a gesture of disbelief with a half shrug.

"Did you think ...did you think you saw? ...oh it sounds so crazy, so weird."

"That there were others in the room with us just for a brief while?" Bill finished for her.

"Yes! Oh thank God you thought you saw them too! I thought I was going crazy!"

"Well if you were, I lost my grip on reality at the same time, lass, so we're two for a pair." That at least made her laugh, albeit shakily. "What I'm hoping Tapio will tell us is who they were ...because I have the weirdest feeling that's significant."

"I think I know who I *thought* they were," Annikki ventured hesitantly. "Or at least who I thought they were at the time. Now it just seems too unbelievable for words."

"Who?"

Annikki squirmed uncomfortably on her seat, and Bill let her wriggle so that she was out of the circle of his arm, actually rather glad to be able to move it again as he'd begun to cramp. So he was vaguely preoccupied with the tingling of returning sensation as she said,

"Well I thought the one who looked like a smith was Ilmarinen."

"You what?" Bill gasped, blinking at her in astonishment. "*That* was Ilmarinen?"

Annikki blushed. "Well that was how he was portrayed in a picture book when I was a child. Not anything like as scary, I'll admit – they didn't want us having nightmares at that age – but the general appearance, yes, it's how the smith of the gods appears."

Bill sighed. "I'm not going to argue with you. When six professional thugs can disappear into thin air, I guess anything is possible. So what about the woman?"

"The lady in green? I think that was Mielikki. The Lady of the Forest."

"And the other one."

"I don't know. I could guess, but that's so scary I don't want to say. I'd rather you asked Tapio."

"Okay," Bill said slowly. The last thing he wanted to do was scare her more than she already was, and anyway, he could hear sirens in the distance, which hopefully meant that reinforcements of a more tangible and human sort were about to arrive, and for Bill they weren't a moment too soon.

Chapter 11

Tuesday

The constable must have finally eventually raised someone on the radio, because Bill and Annikki had only just got back into the house when two patrol cars came tearing up the drive, blue lights flashing and sirens wailing. Even then the two officers in each looked a little pissed off as they got out, evidently not believing that there was much of a threat here.

"This had better be good, gov', or Williams will have your nuts served up grilled and sliced," the senior one grumbled at Bill, as the detective hobbled out to meet them. "We were this close to catching the Smith boys at last!" and he held up two fingers close together.

"Oh don't you believe it!" Bill snapped, too tired to be tactful. "Those retarded little scrotes were running a deliberate blind to get you lot chasing your tails all over Malvern! And before you say they're not that bright, they aren't. They were set up to do this. Someone with more than their couple of lonely brain-cells sloshing around in the void cooked this one up. And which particular combo' of the Smiths did you think you'd got at last, eh?" The Smiths in question were a tribe of brothers and cousins who all looked alike, and where even DNA evidence was going to be compromised given that two sisters married two brothers, making even the cousins indistinguishable. Proving which one had been where had always been a nightmare. "You didn't catch the little shits because you were never meant to. The others in that tribe were running interference right from the start, so forget them. Come and look at this lot, and then tell me I was over-reacting!"

When the four officers saw the cache of guns on Bill's back seat they all went pale.

"Fuck me rigid!" the youngest gulped. "I never thought to see those in the Hills!"

"Me neither," Bill admitted, but still feeling angry that he was being seen as scaremongering. "Now you two go and park yourselves inside the house, one at the front door, the other at the back. You other pair, you're with me."

"What are we doing?" the senior one immediately challenged, his worry written across his face.

"We're going hunting bodies," Bill told him. "I have no idea what put the shits up this bunch of charmers, but they went off into the woods like the hounds of Hell were on their tails when Tapio and Urho played some old Finnish chants at full belt at them. Don't ask me why it worked, but I've never been so bloody glad that something played on someone's deep seated nightmare, because when I saw the six of them coming out of the trees with those guns I thought my end had come."

"And you're sure they don't have back-up arms?" the other copper asked fearfully, as well he might. These weren't armed response officers, they were just the regular police who broke up disturbances and attended break-ins and traffic incidents. They weren't trained for this, but they had the intelligence to be scared stiff of coming face to face with a gun.

"I'm not planning on taking you on a fast pursuit in the dark," Bill said witheringly. "I'm not playing fucking *Rambo* in the Malvern woods! We're just checking the woods as far as we can see from this lawn. Or do you want these bastards to get sympathy at a trial because we left them lying in sight of the lawn and house with a broken leg, or concussion, and did nothing?"

Grimacing, but knowing that he was right, the two followed him as he began walking over the lawn to where he thought that at least one of the men had been thrown into the woods. Part of Bill's foul mood was in anticipation of what he might find. If they had been thrown against solid English oaks with the force he'd seen Tapio exercising, then there might be six bodies out there, and how the hell he was going to explain them was giving him a headache all by itself.

When they got to the edge of the wood, he could see the effects of the howling gale Tapio had summoned in the fallen branches and scattered leaves.

"Jesus! Look at the size of these hailstones!" one of the men said, staring at the carpet of huge white balls which they were now crunching their way over. "It's been a lovely night, but Jason said he could hear thunder when he called in. I never thought it would be like this, though, so heavy but so local. You could get brained by those things!"

They patrolled the whole perimeter, and to Bill's relief found no sign of any of the men. His private analogy with the *Wizard of Oz* when still upstairs was reinforced now. Where were they, those men who had come here? It was as if they had been picked up by a huge invisible hand and swept from this part of the world altogether. But as they got back to the cars and heard the radio, he got his clue as to where they had landed. The harassed voice on the other end was frantically calling for anyone who wasn't already at a crime scene to help tend a fatal accident at junction seven of the M5. Six men had apparently fallen to their deaths from where the road to Pershore crossed over the motorway. Drugs were suspected since they didn't smell of alcohol, but the two long-distance truckers who had been the unfortunates to hit them as they fell, had skidded their artic's and were now wedged against one another under the road bridge, meaning that the motorway was completely blocked. And because it was now a crime scene it would remain closed until all the necessary evidence had been collected, which was a headache of massive proportions building for the morning rush hour.

"You two go," Bill sighed. "I think those might be the bad lads from here. They had time to get over there if they drove like loonies. Leave me those two inside to keep an eye on the guns until we can get them locked away safely, then I'll have a word with DCI Watson and sort out a relief for them."

In truth, in the light of this new information, he was glad to see the back of them. He realised he now needed to get his story very straight indeed if he wasn't going to get some harsh questions asked of him. But what also rattled him to the core was the sudden memory of the thought popping into his head while he'd been singing and watching Tapio, that it would have been good to dispose of the Thompson brothers so easily. That these six had died just at the spot where under two weeks ago he had been being cut out of the wreckage of the patrol car following his chase of the Thompsons really freaked him out. Had his subconscious thoughts influenced where they ended up? Because in that case someone was seeing inside his head! Please God that was only a temporary thing with all that incense and chanting and stuff, because otherwise he'd be checking himself in to the nearest psychiatric clinic and fast.

Brusquely ordering the two remaining constables outside to watch the car, and to summon someone expert in firearms to deal with the guns, Bill locked the front door on them and then called Annikki and Urho into the kitchen with Tapio.

"Now listen," he said firmly. "We have to get our stories straight! I'm sorry Tapio, but telling the truth about what happened to those men is not an option. If anyone thinks that you really believe that you did what you did, you'll be whisked into a hospital faster than you can sneeze, Annikki and Urho will be deported back to Finland, and I'll lose my job."

"No!" Tapio gasped in horror. "No, that must not happen!"

"Right, then you have to accept that we have to tell everyone else – *every* last person who asks you – something which they can believe. Those six men are dead and currently being scraped off the tarmac of the M5, so we have to tell anyone who asks that the actual attack came *much* earlier than it did. We *have* to allow enough time for those men to have run off, and have gotten as far as the M5 under normal means. I don't mean them walking there, but if there's a possibility that they were driven there and then thrown off the bridge by persons unknown, that at least is more credible than a wind summoned by an eleven year-old boy throwing them there, alright?"

"Yes, Karhu," Tapio sighed, and turned to deliver a stream of rapid Finnish at Urho, who simply nodded at Bill.

"Okay, so we're going to say when asked that the attack came just after I sent the patrol car off to find help. I know it came quite quickly afterwards, but we're going to say that it happened the very moment the car left. That way it seems that they knew help was gone and attacked *immediately*." He knew he was spelling this out, but he really needed Tapio and Annikki to understand what they had to say. Since one or other of them would be translating for Urho it was less of an issue unless things got nasty, and he got taken in separately with a translator provided for him, but hopefully it wouldn't come to that.

"But it also means that there's at least some chance that we'll be believed that they had a car or cars waiting for them, which were driven like the hounds of hell were at their heels to get away from the scene of the crime. I'll say I heard a big engine being revved. With any luck that will convince people."

It wasn't long before Frank Watson appeared with SOCOs and a man from the armed response unit was said to be on his way to make the guns safe.

"God Almighty, Bill, what have we got ourselves into?" Frank groaned as Bill sat him down in the lounge with a large mug of tea to match the one he was cradling. "Guns! In Worcestershire! ...Well this bit anyway. Not exactly plunder from member of the local game shooting brigade, is it? You wouldn't go pot-shooting the neighbourhood pheasants with one of those things."

"Not unless you wanted the bloody things as mincemeat," Bill agreed. Then cunningly dropped the idea, "I reckon that's why those six got dumped off the bridge, though. If they went haring back to whoever was waiting for them and told them they'd run like kids from something little more than a folk tale, maybe their bosses thought they were useless tossers and wanted rid of them."

"Yes, that makes sense," Frank agreed, "especially having lost so much expensive hardware! You don't pick up kit like that on the black-market for a couple of quid and a box of *Beanos*, do you? But I think this all makes it more and more likely that we're dealing with some major organisation. Who else would have the cash for guns like those? Has Tapio said anything at all which might help with who this is?"

"No," Bill confessed, "but as he's not going in to school today, I intend to have serious words with him. He has to understand that for the sake of others, we can't have armed men roaming the streets. Even if he doesn't get hurt, someone else might."

"I'm sorry, but I'm going to have to sit in on this conversation," Frank replied. "It's got too serious for it to be left to just you having a chat with him. Would you go and get him please, Bill? I know it's still the depths of night, but this is too serious to wait for morning."

As he ushered Tapio down from his room where he had gone to rest, Bill urgently told the boy,

"You have to answer these questions now, Tapio. Apart from about when the attack took place and how you deflected it, you have to answer DCI Watson truthfully. If not they might feel they need to send you back to Finland and your own police. It's about protecting the ordinary people who live here too, now, can you see? If these men come with guns, and then don't get what they want, they might well decide to hide somewhere by taking some poor local person captive and holding them as prisoners in their own home."

Tapio's eyes went wide as the implications sunk in.

"I do not want anyone to get hurt, Karhu," he said earnestly.

"I know you don't, son. But to make sure that doesn't happen, we need to be able to do our jobs. So will you please talk to Frank, and in ways he'll understand – not about legend and tales of the forest? I believe you but he never will, and he's senior to me so it's his word that'll count."

Bill hated pushing the boy this hard. Whatever was going on, his instinct still screamed that Tapio was the one needing protection, and that he wasn't causing this to happen.

"Right, Tapio," Frank began firmly but gently when they were all seated in the lounge, "I need you to tell me from the start what you know of why you came to England. Take your time, but please tell me everything, even if you don't think it's important."

Tapio sat perched on the edge of the large squashy sofa, his small face set in a solemn frown. "Someone wants the land I have control over," he began. "I am not sure who this person is, but they want it very badly." He paused, and Bill knew that he was trying to work out how to say the next bit. "It's all about the forests of my homeland. I have an ...erm ...influence over how they are used, you see. About the wild parts, though, not the ones which have been manmade."

"Surely you're a bit young for that?" Frank wondered. "If you were left this land – inherited it, or whatever – wasn't there a guardian put in place until you were old enough to decide for yourself?"

"Yes!" Tapio seized on the idea with something like relief. "Yes, that is what Ilmarinen and Mielikki are! They are not just looking after me but what I ...I ...I represent. Do you see? That is why they could not come here with me but had to stay in Finland."

"Okay," Frank said cautiously, "that makes a bit more sense. But we need to get hold of this Ilmarinen and Mielikki, so can you tell us where we might find them?"

Tapio's face fell. "No I can't. They could be anywhere in the forest, watching and protecting it you see."

Frank heaved a heavy sigh. "Okay, then can you talk me through why and how you came to England, please?"

"I had been getting sick," Tapio said cautiously. "Things were being put into the water where I lived, and there were few people we could trust to help us anymore. Annikki's grandparents and her aunt were amongst the few left. They knew what was at stake. And so we had to ask for a favour. Tove's son was dying. I could do nothing to heal him." He looked anxiously at Frank and Bill. "I would have if I could, you know. I didn't want Tapio to die, and neither did Ilmarinen or Mielikki! We would never have harmed him in any way, please believe me!"

Bill hurriedly went and sat by Tapio and put an arm around him. "No-one is accusing you of hurting the original Tapio," he reassured him. "That's never been our

L. J. Hutton

thought. But are you saying that the original Tapio Törni was Annikki's *cousin*?"

Tapio nodded his head sorrowfully. "He was so small and so sick. I am older than he was, but we asked Tove if we could use his name, and all the paperwork things, for me. She and her mother, Karita, immediately said yes. Tove said she wanted some good to come out of her son's death. Her husband, though, was very angry. He cursed at Ilmarinen and Mielikki for even asking! And when he found that Tove had taken all the papers and hidden them from him, he hit her and left her. He nearly killed her, Karhu," he said in clear distress to Bill, looking up into his eyes with an expression of pain and disbelief. "Why would he do that to his wife when she was only doing good?"

"I don't know," Bill consoled him, giving him a hug. But over Tapio's head he and Frank exchanged glances. This man could be dangerous if he could be that brutal to his wife. Even the stress of a terminally ill child didn't excuse or explain what sounded like grievous bodily harm.

Frank flicked his eyes towards the kitchen where Annikki waited, and Bill knew that he meant that he intended to ask her for her uncle's details rather than ask Tapio. "Right, so now we understand why you took Tapio's name. Can you tell us what *your* name was before that?"

"I have always been Tapio. I was Tapio before I became Tapio Törni."

"Aaah." Frank again caught Bill's eye. Well that also explained why it had been so hard to get the lad to tell them who he was if the names were the same. "Okay, so your guardians, Ilmarinen and Mielikki realised you were in danger, and so they used Tapio Törni's details to give you a new identity, yes?"

"Yes."

"So what happened then?"

"Well at first we moved to a different area, like I told

154

you before. I wasn't lying, you know."

"That's okay, we understand that. No-one's saying you lied. We just couldn't understand what you were telling us, but it's getting clearer now. Carry on."

"So it got dangerous, like I said before. The men came and destroyed the house. I think Karl Törni may have told them how to find us, because we were safe for quite a while, but then we saw Karita and Tove and it was after that that the trouble started again. He may have followed them, we believe. And again I got sick. So Mielikki said that I must go away and get truly well again. That I must regain my strength. And to do that I must leave Finland, because they believed that if I left, those who hate me would not follow."

Bill sighed and looked to Frank. "So Ilmarinen and Mielikki have always acted out of good faith by the sound of it." Frank nodded, but looked back to Tapio to prompt him to continue. However, Bill had an actual question.

"Why England, Tapio? Was that a conscious decision, or just because there were available flights to here?"

"We looked at many places, Karhu. We considered Pomerania, which you now call Poland, at first. They have miles of ancient woods where I could hide. But Tove and Karita spoke to Mielikki, and said that the Russians had taken over that place so easily not so many decades ago, and that they didn't think it was safe at all."

"He means World War Two," Bill said softly to Frank, who blinked a bit, but took Bill's hint not to question the strange way of talking about time. "So where did you look at then?"

Tapio sighed. "We looked at Bohemia – your Czech Republic – but Karita and Tove said the same about that. Then Bavaria, but there are so many churches there and people have such strange ideas. I was not comfortable with living in a place where there were so many crosses with a man being tortured on them. That's a very strange thing to do, don't you think? To put all those crosses up, even on hilltops where few people go?"

Bill smiled at him. "Wouldn't be my thing either, for what that's worth, but a lot of people get comfort from the church and those images, so it's not easy to change their minds over what they see as strange or wicked in their turn."

"It was the same with France," Tapio sighed. "Beautiful forests, but too many churches and priests. When you are like me that is not a good thing."

"How did you know this stuff about France and Germany?" Frank asked, curious. "You seem to have been so isolated on the one hand, and yet so informed on the other."

Tapio nodded. "We have much to thank Tove for help with that. She made copies of things she found on the internet and sent them to us. We decided on England because Tove and Karita said it was different here, and they knew it because of Annikki coming here before. They told us that although there are no huge old forests, like in the other places, there are lots of old trees. They said that I would be safe in the countryside here. So they helped us find the right people who could find us a house. The people here in England sent us lots of photos of different houses, but when we saw this one we knew it was the one we were looking for. The man who owns it is working in South America for two years. This was his parents' house, but he didn't want it to lie empty for that long until he could come back. It was perfect for me."

Bill gave Tapio a little hug. This was exactly what they needed. Something which sounded all perfectly normal if a bit unusual.

"Well I'm glad you came here," he reassured the boy. "If you hadn't we'd have never met." And he gave the lad a wink, which raised a smile.

Frank, however, was frowning even harder. "Well thank you for that, Tapio. I can see from what you've told me now that your guardians never expected anyone to follow you here – which is at least something. Unless something comes to light which contradicts that, we won't be looking to press any charges of endangerment on them."

Bill thought it would be bloody hard to make such a charge stick, but said nothing. If it reminded Tapio that he had to make responses which would prevent that, rather than muddying the waters with tales of lost gods and the like, then that was all to the good.

"Right, well I think I'd better go and speak to Annikki now," Frank sighed, heaving himself wearily up off the sofa. "God, what I wouldn't give for an uninterrupted night's sleep!"

"You and me both!" Bill sympathised, his aching ribs and twinging bruises reminding him that he'd had no sleep at all during the night, and that now his body was reacting to it. "Tapio, you back upstairs and have a lie down on your bed. You had no more sleep than the rest of us, so try and get some now."

"What about you, Karhu?"

"I'm going to sit with Annikki while DCI Watson asks her some questions. I think she's going to need a friend with her!"

Annikki's face when Frank relayed what he'd just been told about her aunt and grandmother's involvement made it obvious that she hadn't had a clue about what was being arranged behind her back.

"Oh my God!" she began to cry as the full implications hit her. "What have they got themselves into?"

Frank was not without sympathy for her. "If it's any consolation, I think that a grieving mother – your Aunt Tove – was just trying to give some meaning to her sons' death. Can you tell me what your cousin died of, Ms Nykänen?"

"Leukaemia – but there were complications. He'd been born with only one kidney and a bone condition which all by itself would have meant that he would've been lucky to live beyond his teens." She had to pause to sob a bit more. "It was torture for us, let alone Tove and Karl! How do you cope with knowing that your only child is going to die within ten or fifteen years right from when he was born? And that the longer he lived, the more pain and suffering he was going to have? My parents said that the leukaemia was a strange blessing, because it took him before the bones warped and put him in agony, and I have to say that I thought the same. He was already on a morphine drip when he died, and they don't put children on that kind of thing unless it's terminal."

"Christ!" Frank muttered under his breath. "You don't know how lucky you are until you hear stuff like this! I can't imagine how my wife would have coped with that if it had been one of our kids."

Annikki sniffed and blew her nose, but then managed to speak a bit more calmly. "That's why the rest of the family stopped chastising Grandmother for all her hippy faith stuff, you see? It was getting Tove through the days of nursing little Tapio. If what was stopping her from falling apart was believing that the old god of the forests would come and take her son to play with him in the afterlife, who would be so cruel as to take it away from her?"

"Pretty understandable," Bill agreed. "You wouldn't, would you."

"So what happened after your Tapio died?" Frank asked.

Now Annikki's face fell again. "Oh God, that's when it all got really messy! Karl just couldn't accept it. Tove wanted all the hospital equipment gone straight away. It had taken over half of the downstairs of their house. You could hardly move in what had been the lounge for it. It was so big and there was so much of it that Tapio had had to sleep there, you see. It just wouldn't go into his little bedroom, or any other bedroom in their house for that matter. So it seemed perfectly reasonable for Tove to want it gone. And she said it was all expensive stuff and should go and help some other child.

"I think she'd done all of her mourning in those long nights when she and Grandmother sat up with him, you know. By the time the funeral came around she had no more tears to shed. But Karl went a bit mad. He had a wild shouting fit at her at the funeral, calling her a callous bitch for not crying more. He was really out of control."

"Blimey, that is a bit extreme!" Bill agreed.

"Especially as he'd hardly been able to go near Tapio when he'd been ill," Annikki said with contempt. "Three long years Tove nursed her son with only Grandmother and Grandfather living close by, and us going over when we could along with my uncle and his family. We did what we could, but we live too far away to be there every day, and neither Father nor my uncle could move jobs to be nearer. It was horrible, but that's just how it was. But you'd have thought Karl would have wanted to help care for his son. Instead he kept banging on about nursing being a woman's job, but then blaming Tove for not being good enough when it became clear that Tapio was fading."

"What a charmer!" Frank said as he scribbled frantically. "You wouldn't have got me away from my son's bed!"

"No, that's what Grandfather, Uncle Matti and Father all said. But Karl got violent when the hospital people came to get the equipment. They had to call the police to restrain him, you know. And then when it was gone, he started on Tove. I know we poke fun at Grandmother's claims at being in touch with another world and stuff, but no-one was laughing when she suddenly sat up in bed and told Grandfather that they had to drive to Tove's house right away. If they hadn't, she would have bled to death! Karl had beaten her to within an inch of her life. When my mother got the phone call saying they were on the road and had called an ambulance before they even got there, she was really angry with them, but then when we went and saw Tove in hospital, all wired up to life-support systems... Well that's why it was so hard for them to start asking Grandmother about this Tapio, do you see? She'd been right back then, so when she said that I would be okay with this job, no-one wanted to argue too hard."

Bill and Frank sat back and took in what she'd said. It explained a lot, and it was no reflection on Annikki that she hadn't made the connection between the two boys. Both Tapio and Törni were common enough names, she told them, that she had just thought it a coincidence.

"If I thought anything of it," she had said earlier, "it was that the fact that he shared my dead cousin's name which was the thing which made my grandparents so gullible where Tapio's guardians were concerned. I never dreamt that Tove would have *given* them her son's identity."

But what tweaked Bill's internal cat's whiskers was her saying,

"And this Tapio here is much younger than my cousin would have been. He died aged seven over ten years ago. My cousin would have been nearly eighteen now – seven years older than this Tapio."

So what had Tapio meant earlier when he said that he was older than the boy who had died? That didn't make sense. But Bill also had a strange feeling that the answer would be something very weird, and so he didn't make any comment to Frank about that. At least this way the Nykänen family, or whatever Annikki's grandparents' surname was, were in the clear for now. Sometime in the next day, though, Bill knew he was going to have another mind-wrenching conversation with Tapio about that in private, because if even no-one else was to know, he still needed that question answering for his own peace of mind.

London & western Russia

The man who had recruited the mercenaries was at that point having a very nerve-wracking conversation on a mobile phone he had bought solely for the purpose. Previously the team had contacted him with serious doubts about the sanity of the man who had hired them, and so when he had heard of the deaths and put two and two together, he knew that something had gone disastrously wrong. Never one to put his own life at risk, he had booked a ticket out of England by the next possible flight. His emergency bag had been grabbed, and he'd been on the next train to Heathrow as fast as he could – no taxies with chatty cabbies for him, or hire cars which could be tracked on traffic CCTV, just the anonymity of being one of thousands on the trains that day.

Only when he was outside of the airport terminal did he put the sim-card into the cheap mobile phone he had bought, and dialled the contact number.

"I don't know what you asked those men to do," he said when the creepy voice on the other end answered, "but they're dead!"

"Dead?"

"Yes! All of them!"

"All?"

"Yes!" Fucking hell, what was the matter with the man? "It was all over the news here. Six men dead on the motorway. Suspected suicide or murder – but whatever it is, the police here are all over those bodies like fleas on a cat, so don't even think about asking me to go and find out what happened. You couldn't pay me enough for that!"

In far away Russia, right by the Finnish border, Koschei ground his demonic teeth in fury. How could it keep going so wrong? What was it about this insignificant island, stuck off the coast of nowhere he'd previously heard of over the millennia, which made it such a thorn in his side?

"But did they get the boy?"

"What boy? There was no mention on the news of any boy."

The unearthly wail of frustration that came down the phone had the man whipping it away from his ear in pain. Mad! Definitely mad! His contacts had been right about that. Best to sever all ties. He didn't need the money he'd been paid *that* much. It had been a princely sum, yes, but other jobs were as lucrative and he still had contacts for those. This one would stay in the separate bank account he had opened for it in Switzerland. If it never got transferred out, there would be no trail to him, and for once sense overrode his greed for money.

"I need that boy!" the voice on the other end of the phone was screaming in Russian.

"Well you'd better come and get him yourself, then," the man said and ended the call.

The fact that he then dropped the phone down the nearest street drain and turned away saved his life. From far away, Koschei sent a streak of demon-fire along the trail of the phone signal, and as the man reached the protective safety of the air terminal's doors, a spout of flame shot up from the drain where he'd been standing. As people screamed and ran for cover, and someone called for the bomb squad, the man hurried inside. How the hell that had happened he didn't know, but thank God he'd thrown that phone away! He shot through baggage control and customs, bought himself a large coffee while he waited to board, and only began to breathe again when he saw England falling away from him, and the nice stewardess began going through the safety routine.

For Koschei, though, life had just become infinitely more difficult. Should he travel to England? Would his powers work there? And would that matter if his opponent, Tapio, was weakened from being away from his sacred Finland?

He gnawed away at the matter through that day and on into the next night, but finally he realised that it came down to a simple choice: should he linger here and accept that ultimately he would fade away, and become nothing more than one of those pathetic ghouls used by children's babushkas to get them to behave? Or should he take the risk, go to England, and fight for what he so desperately desired? Was a swift demise to whatever lay 'beyond' for creatures like himself, better than a slow one? He was determined that whatever happened he was not going to end up like his one-time lord, Veles, that was for certain.

Yet ultimately, he decided that the thing which held him back from immediate action was the need to top up his powers in a very direct way. For that he would have to return to where there were plenty of people, people he could harvest without too many questions being asked, and that meant a big city. Somewhere where there were enough outcasts living in the shadows who could disappear without a trace, or without exciting the interests of local law enforcement.

Regretfully he projected himself the relatively short distance to the city of St Petersburg, and far from the opulent palaces of the once all-powerful tsars, he found a community of homeless living under a bridge; but he also remembered that there might be one last person he could send. A last attempt to get to the boy without having to take such a risk himself. And so, having made his physical apparition as comfortable as possible in a spot in a luxury hotel, hidden from view, but where he could feast on the energy of the frantic lovers, the cocaine-hyped businessmen, and the voracious tycoons crushing their competitors, he reached out and found the one he sought.

"Hiisi, my friend," he thought, reaching out to the malevolent form of the Finnish forest-demon. "Do you still wish to aid me in taking Tapio?"

The demon was a shadow of his former self now that few people walked through the forests and got lost or stranded, but there was still a spark of wickedness in his crushed being.

"Of course! You need to ask? I sit here and listen to all those people worshipping the 'beautiful forest' – it makes me sick!" And Koschei knew he wasn't just being sarcastic. The more these modern people saw only the beauty in the forests and woods, and none of the dangers, the more Hiisi was being crushed out of existence as he was.

"Then listen carefully to me. I will assist you to get to the town he is in, but I wish for you to invade the spirit of a particular man. He will be easy pickings! His soul is already warped and twisted. But I need more control over him than I can get just by directing him. I need someone inside his head."

"Who is this man, and what's in it for me?" Hiisi might have been weak but he wasn't stupid. For a greater demon like Koschei to come creeping round to him must mean that there was a lot to be gained, and he wanted his bite of the pie.

"For a start off, when the man has brought a particular boy to where I can get to him, you can devour the man's soul, or take him to near death and revive him as many times as you like. But the ultimate reward is that Tapio will be no more, and once the lord of the forest is gone, then the lady of the forest won't be able to resist you."

Koschei had found out that Hiisi lusted after Mielikki but could never get near to her. At the moment she was too strong and could still repulse him, but if Tapio fell then it would be a different matter altogether. Already he could feel Hiisi practically salivating, if that was something a disembodied demon could do. However he was not going to tell him that the force which was the ancient Tapio lay within the same boy he was setting Hiisi after – that would be inviting the lesser demon to take Tapio and his powers for himself, and Koschei hadn't worked this hard to get those powers to share them with a nothing like Hiisi.

"Who is this man? Where is he?" Hiisi was demanding.

Koschei sniggered to himself. Truly a lesser demon was this mere Finn, so easily tempted and not of the calibre of even the lesser Russian demons.

"His name is Karl Törni, and he lives in – of all places – a town named after Ilmarinen! You will hardly have a problem finding him!"

Chapter 12

Tuesday

Back at the house nestling in the early morning light beneath the ancient Malvern Hills, Bill was dozing on the sofa in the lounge. His sleep was dreamless until suddenly a figure walked up to him, or was he drawn to it? Whatever the case, he was suddenly in a rich forest, full of life, and the figure was speaking to him.

"I am sorry, Karhu, but I had to bring you here, to my realm of dreams, for you to see me as I really am. I did not wish to invade your mind like this, but this is the only way."

"Who are you?" Bill heard his dream-self ask.

"Do you not recognise me? I am Tapio, lord of the forests."

Now that Bill's dream-self looked harder, he realised that this tall and very muscular man before him wore stag's horns, and was wreathed in garments made of oak leaves. Around his waist was a belt of acorns, but acorns like none Bill had ever seen in reality. These seemed to positively glow with life from within. And just below the magnificent rack of antlers there was a wreath-like circlet which looked very much like a crown of living sprigs. In it were pine leafs and cones, but also leaves which looked very like silver birch.

"You look like Herne the Hunter from that old Robin Hood TV series," Bill's dream-self said, and was rewarded with a laugh.

"Yes, Herne was a forest lord like me. But his power waned with the years while I have stayed strong until now. My forests are untouched. Untouched, that is, until the

Russian devil Koschei set his sights on them. These last hundred years, which are like a blink of an eye to those like me, have been hard on his kind in the land which you call Russia. They had been losing the fight against the priests with their paintings in gold for centuries, but until the great blood shedding there were still those who followed the old ways. Then these new men, these tsars who are not tsars in name but alike in all other ways, began dictating to the people. Folk were watched, folk were destroyed, folk were ground down, and the people became afraid to celebrate any god – the new one or the old ones.

"You cannot be a god, Karhu, if no-one celebrates you. I have been lucky. The folk who live in the wilds of Finland still know and respect my power. I am not a jealous god. I don't demand sacrifices or to be worshipped above all other. I just wish for men to treat my realm with respect. To not cut down the trees wantonly, or kill the beasts who live in the forests for no reason other than for the perverse pleasure of killing.

"But now I need your help, Karhu. I have been under attack for several years from one of these Russian gods who wishes to take my domain. He has poisoned the waters, he has changed the boundaries, and he has made the Russian people dig deep into the earth. They want the bones of the old trees that have lain for centuries beneath their descendents. I cannot let this happen. I cannot let them turn my lands into a frozen wasteland, into a desert.

"I came here to your land to heal and grow strong again, but my enemies have followed me. They think to destroy me while I am far from my homelands, far from the source of my power. I can use the ancient power which lies within your land, but I cannot track mortal men as you can. I am hidden in the body of a small boy, and while that has served to keep me safe, for good people have fought hard to protect this boy, it means I cannot go where a man would go. I need your help, Karhu. Help me!"

Bill woke up in a cold sweat, half-expecting to see the horned god standing in the lounge in front of him. What a strange dream! Yet as he gradually came to full waking he realised that it made a weird kind of sense of what had been happening. His rational side told him not to be so bloody stupid. How could some mythical beast, or god, or whatever, take over the soul of a child? It was ridiculous, and worse it was dangerous if that child had been groomed to think that it was the truth. And yet... Bill had to admit it did fit with what he'd seen with his own eyes.

Growling like the bear Tapio kept saying he was, Bill heaved himself to his feet and went in search of coffee. He had the state of the art coffee machine in the kitchen brewing up nicely as Annikki came in, sniffing the air appreciatively.

"Coffee I haven't had to make myself – luxury!" she declared and flopped into one of the large wooden chairs, and adjusted the thick padded cushion on the seat to make it more comfortable. She was dressed, or rather undressed, in a large pink, fluffy dressing gown, and with huge fluffy slippers in the shape of polar bears on her feet. Her rich red hair was in chaos, writhing in medusa like tangles around her head, and there were dark smudged under her eyes as tell-tales of the disturbed night. Yet Bill never for a moment thought her sexy as some men would have, but only protective of her. Just at the moment, he was thinking her father would be having forty fits if he knew what his daughter had been up against last night.

"I can't tell you how glad I am that you're staying here," she said after she had taken the first appreciative slurp of the rich coffee. "I can't imagine trying to deal with this alone."

"Oh you're welcome," Bill said, dropping into the chair across the table from her. "I've just had the weirdest dream."

"Me too!" gulped Annikki. "You didn't see Tapio as some kind of strange stag-like man, did you?"

"Yes!"

"Thank God!" they both said in unison, then laughed together, albeit rather shakily.

"I don't know what to make of it," Bill said when they had both had some more of their coffees. "In one way it made sense, but my logical self is saying that it's just my brain relieving itself of all the stress of the last few days."

"That's what I thought," Annikki admitted. "Or at least I was making myself think that until you just said you had the same dream. Two of us having the same, though, that's not just coincidence, surely? Dreams aren't that predictable!"

"Did you get the whole bit about the Russian gods wanting to take over?" Bill asked and got a worried nod of Annikki's head in confirmation. "Well we would never have come up with that by ourselves, would we?"

"No, I suppose not."

Then a thought came to Bill. "Hey, could we go and talk to Urho? I mean, he knew that old chant, didn't he? He didn't need any prompting! So that says to me that he knows a lot more about this situation than he's let on to up until now."

"But not before breakfast and I've had a *long* shower!" Annikki said firmly.

"God, no!" Bill agreed. "I was thinking after lunch, actually. Let's get let him recover too. And before we do that, I want to have a word with Tapio. I want to hear from his own mouth some of this stuff. And I want an explanation as to who he is, because you said that your cousin would have been easily seven years older than this

Tapio. So if he is this god person, whose body is he walking around in? It's one thing to be walking around with your cousin's identity; it's something else if some poor lad has been ...well the only way I can put it is expelled from his own body. I mean, that's like something out of a horror movie, isn't it?"

Yet when Bill and Annikki sat down with Tapio in the lounge, with a light smattering of rain occasionally hitting the long French window, and the reassuring lights on, the story was even stranger than Bill had imagined.

"I need to know the truth," Annikki said to Tapio firmly. "You've told the other policeman and Bill here that my aunt gave you my cousin's identity. But you, you're only eleven! So were you born like a normal child, or what? My cousin died around the time you ought to have been born, in 1998, so you aren't him."

Tapio looked at them gravely. "You understand who I am though? You saw me in your dreams?"

They both started at that. Neither of them had said anything about their dreams at breakfast, and Bill was sure that Tapio hadn't been listening at any keyholes when they had been talking.

"What? The whole..." and Bill mimed the antlers, "thing?"

"Yes."

Cagily Bill answered, "Okay, so let's say that we believe – at least for the moment – that you really are Tapio, lord of the forests. And I confess that that at least explains how you managed to send those soldiers flying all the way to their deaths on the motorway, if nothing else. But that raises a whole heap of other questions, and ones which Annikki, more than anyone, is entitled to have some answers to."

Tapio gave a small nod of compliance.

"So," Bill continued, "you really need to tell us how

you come to be in this body. The body of a small boy. And who this body *ought* to belong to! That's more important to us than you seem to realise, Tapio." He didn't dare add that whether a child's body had been taken by force might influence whether Tapio continued to have their support, but it would. Bill's morals wouldn't allow him to support a creature who had robbed another of their life. It was an appalling conundrum, and one which would tear Bill apart if he had to make the choice to send this Tapio to some mental institution, so that the one within him would remain caged for the rest of the child's life, suppressed by the use of lithium or the like, and not able to take another innocent life. But it was a decision he would not shrink from if necessary.

"My cousin, had he lived, would be much older than you now," Annikki prompted. "So this can't be his body."

"But it is!" Tapio protested. "I would not take a living soul's body! That would be...!" and he shuddered. "No! Never!"

"But you said you couldn't cure him," Annikki protested.

"No, I couldn't, not while he lived as a normal person," Tapio said sadly. "But when he died, Tove allowed Karita to bring his body into the forest. That's why Tove insisted that they go and live right on the forest's edge, you know. This was no decision made in the moment of grief. It had been planned right from the moment the doctors told her and Karita that they could not save Tapio. I waited years – at least by your measurement of time. It was no time at all for me, but I did nothing to hurry Tapio's death, either. If there was any deceit it was simply in altering your Tapio's birth certificate to read 1998 instead of 1993 – and in that I confess we were simply lucky that the end number was so easily altered. Had he been born a few months earlier or later in a different year, the subterfuge might have been all the harder, for I would have had to try and accelerate his body's growth to match what people would expect to see."

"Oh Mummo, what have you done?" Annikki sobbed, fearful of where this was leading.

"She was brave and courageous," Tapio defended her. "And I am infinitely grateful to her and Tove. I had to have the child's body within moments of his death, while the blood still flowed easily and the flesh had not begun to decay. I was able to take over the mere shell where his soul had been, and without the need to sustain it, the body was able to absorb my energy to heal. Nonetheless, it took a long time to remove all the growths, and during that time I lay in a different bed, tended by Ilmarinen and Mielikki."

He gave an incongruous pat of consolation on Annikki's hand. It was such a strangely adult act coming from a child. "We never once asked your aunt to see her child, you know. We would not be so cruel. The Tapio she had known had truly died. If I feel any guilt at all, it is that she resolutely insisted that the coffin remain shut, even when her husband wanted it opened. She was incredibly brave in the face of his violence. And in truth, had either of the three of us thought that it had been Karl's genuine fatherly desire to see his son, then I would have put this body in the coffin temporarily if it would have assuaged his grief. But we were sure beyond doubt that even back then he was under the sway of evil spirits. Ones who did not know for sure what we had done, but were aware of our presences in and around Tapio before and after he died."

"Is this what you meant about being sick and having to move house?" Bill wondered. "Were you referring to the time it took to cure Annikki's cousin of the cancer inside him?"

"Not entirely," Tapio confessed. "A year after I took over his body I had returned it to almost normal health. As a child's body it had not grown as it would have had he lived, but that would have started happening soon. That was why we were living so far from where there were any other people, you see. We couldn't afford for anyone to start asking questions about this boy who never got any older. So we lived deep in the forests, hoping that we would have the time to let me reach a stage where I could go out into the world alone, and without exciting questions."

"And that was when these others did what? Poison your water supply?" guessed Bill.

"Yes! For a terrible few days we thought that they had taken Tapio's body from us for real. Ilmarinen and Mielikki were never in such danger because they were only ever manifestations who appeared when others called on us. They didn't need the physical sustenance which my human body did."

"Which is why they moved you in a hurry," Bill realised. "The guns wouldn't harm them, but could have killed you – especially if you were trapped within Tapio's body at the time!"

Tapio winced. "Well not exactly 'killed', but I would have been expelled from Tapio with as much violence as he experienced in dying. And in that moment I would have then been extremely vulnerable to attack by others like me – attack from others who inhabit the same plane of existence as I, Ilmarinen and Mielikki do, the realm of the gods and demons."

Bill sat and swirled his tea, thinking, while Annikki got up and went to get the vodka bottle and sloshed a goodly amount into her coffee, too upset to speak. Tapio sat in silence too, watching them intently as if he was guessing that this might be the point when he found out just how far Bill was prepared to go to help him.

Finally Bill looked up and straight into Tapio's eyes. "So tell me, when you said to Frank that you didn't know who was trying to kill you, was that the truth? Or did you say that because you realised he would never believe you if you told him?"

Tapio winced. "Forgive me, Karhu, Annikki. Yes, I know who is pursuing me. He is a Russian devil called Koschei the Deathless. His soul is contained in a Russian doll of many layers, buried on the mythical island of Buyan under an equally eternal oak tree. Had he stayed within his own realm we would never have crossed paths. Unfortunately he and others like him in the place you know as Russia have long been eroded by the Church there."

"The Russian Orthodox Church?" Bill checked.

"Yes. It is old even by our standards, you understand. At first they thought it would be a fleeting thing, easily out-lasted, something they could come back from after it had passed. But it appealed to people more than a bunch of easily angered and petulant gods, and by the time they realised that they were losing ground to this new faith it was too late. Yet they still hung on until recent years in the wilder parts of the country. That was when those gods decided to start fighting back. We felt them, being so close to their borders, and we shuddered at what vengeance they brought down on their people.

"It was fighting their creations which weakened me in the first place. That place you call Chernobyl and what happened there, that would have spread across many more countries if I and others like me in neighbouring lands hadn't fought it." Then Tapio heaved a sad sigh. "And it was just misfortune that the great volcano erupted in Iceland not long afterwards, and again I was tested to my limits to save my forests. But it was feeling me become so weak which seems to have given Koschei the idea that having made a ruin of his own lands, that he could expel me and walk into mine."

Bill groaned and buried his head in his hands. "Christ,

it's like having bloody Ronnie Regan and Boris Yeltsin at one another's throats all over again, except in an immortal sphere. What a fucking nightmare!

Tapio got up and came round to put his hand on Bill's shoulder. "I did not start this, Karhu. I never wanted this to happen. And even if I gave in to Koschei, it wouldn't stop him from destroying all of my land and then looking to move on to yours when that was all waste."

Bill's huge paw of a hand covered Tapio's. "No, I'm not blaming you. I just don't see what we can do, that's all."

Yet Tapio smiled. "You have done much already! Just by keeping me alive, you have prevented Koschei from crossing the border into Finland and laying claim to my forests, and that is no small thing! What is more, I am constantly gaining in strength here. If I can reach my original level of power, I can more than fend off Koschei without your help. I will be able to return home, and unless Koschei can persuade one or more of his fellow demons to join forces with him to create another disaster with global implications, I will not be vulnerable to him."

"So it was the toxic waste on the wind, followed by the volcanic pollution which weakened you?" Bill checked. "It's not that Koschei all by himself can crush you?"

"Precisely," Tapio confirmed. "That is why I was happy to come here for a limited time. It was only ever meant to be time to heal. This was never going to be a place of exile for me, a place where I was forced to retreat to forever."

"So if we can give this Koschei a beating, or headache, or whatever you give a demon, then you can not only go home, but these attacks on my patch will stop too?" That sounded like good news to Bill. Just at the moment he would be glad to go back to just having the Smiths and the Thompsons as his only nightmares.

Tapio's smile was confirmation enough for Bill, but

Annikki still had questions of her own.

"I believe what you say about Tapio the god," she said with some bitterness, "but what about my family? You don't look much like the Tapio I remember, even allowing for the fact that he was so ill. And has my aunt seen you since her Tapio died?"

"No!" Tapio was appalled. "No, we would not do that to her!"

"But you said that Tove and my grandmother brought you information," Annikki argued savagely. "How could they have done that and not seen you?"

Tapio shook his head. "No, they did not see me. I remained hidden in another room while they were there. They only ever spoke to Ilmarinen and Mielikki, and sometimes Urho took the two of them to meet your grandmother and aunt elsewhere. They did not always come to us. Please, Annikki! We valued the gift Tove gave us beyond all others! We would do nothing to hurt her or any others of your family."

"Except put *me* in the way of a bunch of armed madmen!" Annikki snapped. "And don't even start on what that's going to do to my parents if they find that out!"

"I am truly sorry that it came to that," apologised Tapio. "We never for a moment thought that Koschei would attempt something like that on foreign soil, or we would not have asked for you to accompany me. Please believe me, we valued you greatly, I value you greatly, Annikki. I would never knowingly risk your life."

"Sometimes shit happens," Bill sighed philosophically. "I don't know about you, but I believe him. If nothing else, if they had thought he was in real danger coming to England, one girl and a chauffeur is hardly the army you'd pick to fight the bad guys off with, is it?"

That made Annikki stop before she let rip again.

"Hmmm, I suppose so. Urho's hardly commando material."

The mental image of that was enough to make Bill chuckle, and somehow that broke the tension in the room.

"Right, let's hope that we can all get a decent night's sleep tonight, and then start thinking straight tomorrow," Bill declared. "As far as I can see, it's going to take this Koschei more than a day to rally any new forces, so we have a bit of breathing time. Let's try and work out how he might try to strike at you again. And in that, Tapio, you're very much the expert. We have to rely on you telling us what to expect."

The incongruously grownup boy solemnly nodded his head, but added, "And I meant what I said when we first met, Karhu, we are safe here. This ring of trees gives me strength, and this ancient land helps me too. While I remain here, and you with me, he does not have the power to force his way in. That is not in doubt."

"Well long may it continue to be so," Bill said, raising two lots of crossed fingers as he did so.

However, when the next batch of news came it was of a wholly new kind of chaos about to descend on them. The phone rang in the mid afternoon and turned out to be Annikki's father.

"I'm so sorry," he said when he realised that Bill was there again. "If I'd have known of their plans I'd have stopped them."

"Whose plans?" Bill asked, having been frantically gestured to the phone by Annikki, who had put it onto the speaker too late for Bill to hear what had been said before.

"My mother-in-law and sister-in-law," Mr Nykänen said with some desperation in his voice.

"Oh crap, what have they done?" Bill asked.

"I'm afraid they're already on a plane for England," Mr Nykänen told him, and Bill could imagine the rolled eyes that were going with the words. "They left a note for my father-in-law, who was off on one of his fishing trips overnight, and he's only just rung us to tell us. They'd taken the connecting flight to Helsinki hours ago, and when we rang the airport they had already boarded and the flight was about to take off." His sigh was audible even on the phone. "If that pair don't get on the wrong plane when they have to change at Copenhagen, they should be with you around 17:00. But I wouldn't be surprised if they turned up in Istanbul, knowing them!"

"Oh, Papa, they're not that bad!" Annikki remonstrated, but then rather undermined her words by adding, "Or at least Tove isn't!"

"Right," Bill sighed, realising that he was echoing Mr Nykänen's sighs rather too much already – and he hadn't even met them yet! "I suppose we'd better roll out the welcome wagon, then." He looked at his watch. "If I'm going to beat the rush hour traffic and get to the airport in time to stop them wandering off on their own private crusade around the city, I'd better get going."

"I think I'd better come with you," said Annikki with a wince. "I can't possibly expect you to cope with both of them on your own."

"What about me?" Tapio asked.

"I think we don't need the shock of them seeing you in the Arrivals lounge," Bill told him sternly. "I shall ring Morag and ask her to come here straight from work, and in the meantime I'll ring Frank Watson and tell him where I'm going too. And if you want to do something really helpful, go and fetch Urho, while we get the car sorted, and between you get two more beds made up. I don't think that your 'grandmother' should be sleeping on the sofa!"

Koschei might not have been quite so smug had he taken the trouble to cast his demonic gaze Hiisi's way.

"Pompous Russ bastard!" Hiisi was chuckling as he felt Koschei's presence waning. "Think you're telling me what to do, eh? Like I don't know better!"

He had been inside Karl Törni's head for many a long year, in fact right back from when he had first been aware of Tapio's interest in the boy and his family. What kind of demon would he have been if he'd not even spotted something like that right on his own doorstep, and concerning his very personal enemies? It had been his rage that had made Karl give Tove such a beating, and in the long years since then, Hiisi had ridden in the back of Karl's mind whenever he had felt the man drawing near to his ex-wife. Indeed, he had many times prompted the man to get closer to her, even when Karl was issued with a court order to stay away. Only when Karl was thrown into prison for a few days had it sunk in with Hiisi that there was only so far he could push this matter.

However, he had not forgotten or given up. And if Karl now lived in the tiny town of Ilmarinen, between Tampere and Turku, it didn't stop him from covertly visiting Lempäälä where his ex-wife and parents now lived, and spying on her. Though Karl never knew it, Hiisi had made sure that his gambling earned him enough so that he didn't need to hold down a proper job anymore, and the forest demon had made sure that his drinking never got so out of hand that he ceased to be useful to him.

Therefore it had been a simple matter to get Karl to pack yet another bag, force him to shower and shave and make some semblance of at least looking respectable, and then drive his ancient Volvo to Lempäälä. He arrived in the small hours of the night just in time to see the two women hauling suitcases out to the waiting taxi, and had followed them to Tampere airport. Luckily something had made him grab his passport – or rather Hiisi had told him to – so he was able to board the same early morning plane to Helsinki. He kept his hat pulled well down as he shuffled past the two women to get to his seat, turning his back to them as he seemed to shuffle past another passenger trying to ram a large bag into the overhead locker. And Hiisi made sure that there was enough confusion over the seat numbers on tickets that Karl was able to sit right at the back of the plane, so that he could watch without being seen.

When he realised that they were going onwards to England, even Hiisi had a moment's panic, wondering if there was enough of this strange stuff called money – which didn't seem to exist except in some electronic form understood only by banks and whose value Hiisi had never really grasped – to allow Karl to buy the onward ticket. But luckily there was, just about, although whether Karl would ever be able to get back to Finland was a problem Hiisi would worry about later, if at all. For now it was sufficient that the watchdog was on the trail and chasing its quarry!

For Karl himself, what little remained of him which had not been twisted and tormented by Hiisi, the sight yet again of his lovely wife was the endless mixture of blessing and torture. Somewhere deep inside he still loved her dearly, and as the years passed and the loss of little Tapio receded into more normal grieving, he had become increasingly depressed that their marriage had not been able to survive the tragedy. How could someone so beautiful have had a son who was so sickly as to die? For in his own mind Karl could never quite come to terms with the fact that they had just been unlucky. How was it that his despised older brothers could both produce healthy normal sons and him not? Clearly there was nothing wrong with his family, therefore it had to be with Tove's. And when you had such a pair of eccentrics for parents as she had, maybe they had used a few too many drugs over the years? Tove was, after all, much younger than either of her siblings, so perhaps that accounted for why she had not had the children they had?

The arguments had gone round and round in his head for so long that he didn't know what he believed any longer. But now, as he watched Copenhagen appearing beneath him, and heard the announcements for passengers making onward going flights and needing to change, he made a decision. While they were away from Finland and the watching police, he was going to make one last attempt to patch things up with Tove.

Chapter 13

Tuesday evening – Wednesday

Quite what Bill had been expecting he wasn't sure, but the ravishing red-head who could not be much beyond forty was not how he'd imagined Tove.

"Blimey! Your family wasn't hit with the ugly stick!" he said without thinking, as he and Annikki stood waiting at Arrivals. They had refrained from holding up a piece of card with their names on for fear of alerting the two – after all, they weren't too sure yet why they had come.

"No, my aunt is fifteen years younger than my mother, and ten than my Uncle Matti. She's been more like my cousin than my aunt."

"Your gran' isn't exactly the witch of the north, either!" Bill pointed out, although later he was to remember those words and wonder. And indeed Karita, with her mane of silver-white long hair, and dressed in vibrant coloured ethnic clothing, was turning heads as much as her daughter. "God Almighty, Annikki, how old is she?"

"Oh... Well Mum is fifty-five, so that makes Gran seventy-seven."

Bill gave a soft whistle. "The last woman I saw who was that old and looked that good was Lauren Bacall – and I thought they'd broken the mould when they made her!"

He saw Annikki blink in surprise. No doubt when it was your own grandmother you didn't see her in that way, and Bill couldn't resist teasing her just a little.

"I think if we ever get to the awful situation of having your Gran in the dock answering questions she'll get away with murder if there are enough men on the jury. I can't imagine any red-blooded male not being swayed by her!"

"Bill!"

He laughed. "Well not everyone is going to see her as some dotty old lady, you know! With those high cheekbones and elvish eyes, she looks more like she's walked out of central casting than an old folks' home." Then a thought struck him. "What on earth is your grandfather like? Is he some eighty year-old version of Thor?"

Now Annikki joined in the laughter. "No! Although he was definitely a good-looking man when he was younger. He's quite stooped now, and he's not eighty but seventy-three. He's younger than Mummo – that's Granny in our language."

"Oh, so she was a cradle-snatcher was she?" Bill quipped with a wink. "I'd better watch my step, then!"

By now they had drawn level with Karita and Tove, who were about to move out of the cordoned off area directing people away from the main arrival gateway.

"Mummo! Tove!" Annikki called out, and hurried forward to take her grandmother's arm, adding in Finnish, "Papa called and told us you were on your way!"

Bill came up and expertly took the suitcase handles from Tove, who jumped but had no chance to protest before Annikki said,

"This is Detective Bill Scathlock. He's been protecting me and Tove!"

"Is he safe?" Karita asked urgently, but in the nicest accent Bill had heard in a long time. "Is the boy safe?"

"Yes he is, for the time being," Bill reassured her. "We're taking you to where he's staying, if that's alright?"

"It will have to be," Tove answered, her voice a little shaky. "I cannot avoid seeing him now."

"If it's too painful for you, there are several very nice hotels in Malvern, which is only just down the road from the house," Bill told her sympathetically. "I know this isn't the place to talk details, but Tapio has told me about what you did for him, so I appreciate that this is no small deal for you to see him again."

Tove was tall enough to be almost able to look Bill in the eye, and so he saw her flinch again, then take a deep breath. "No, it's alright. I will be fine."

"I have to say that your English is very good," Bill complimented them as they walked them out to the car. "I was worried that Annikki would be having to do a lot of translating."

"Oh we came to London in the sixties," Karita said with a mischievous grin. "Carnaby Street and all that. I was quite the girl about town in those days – even though I was married and with children!"

"I reckon you'd still give the youngsters a run for their money!" Bill replied before realising that this probably wasn't the most appropriate response.

Luckily, Karita simply hooted with laughter – something Bill had the strange feeling she did quite a lot. She positively oozed a love of life in a way he had rarely seen before. Then he turned and looked at Tove and realised that having a mother like this must have been sheer hell for her two daughters, and probably for Annikki's Uncle Matti too when he was younger – how on earth would you cope if all your school mates had a crush on your mom? And no doubt this wild, free spirit was a blast to be around on a night out, but he instantly grasped what Mr Nykänen and Annikki had meant when they said that she had not been the most responsible of parents. There'd probably never been a social boundary that she hadn't been able to demolish in seconds, but which her children had no doubt discovered the hard way.

"I taught English at school before I married and had Tapio," Tove said more sombrely. "I've tried to go back to teaching, but I can't face being around all those children anymore."

"That's pretty understandable," Bill sympathised, thinking he would have been more surprised if she had said she was still in schools. It would be like rubbing salt into a wound on a daily basis. "What do you do then?"

"Oh I do some translating. I work from home and get the work via an agency," she said with a faint smile. And that too made such a contrast with her mother. Tove had probably not had a good laugh since her son had died, Bill guessed. It was as though she had had the life sucked out of her, making her a beautiful but inanimate version of Karita, and Bill found himself feeling terribly sorry for her.

"Come on, let's get you back to Malvern," he said with forced cheer, unwittingly giving Karl Törni, some ten paces back, the clue he needed as to where they were going.

"We're a bit out of town, I'm afraid," Annikki told her relatives, "so if you need anything, you'd better let us know and we'll stop at the supermarket on the way."

Frantically, Karl made a note of the license plate on the big Saab they were getting into, then ran to the car hire kiosk and arranged to have the cheapest car he could for a week. Why a week he wasn't sure. The voice in his head said a week, but he had no idea why. Typing in the name into the sat' nav' he managed to find Malvern, and set out to follow them. He was beyond relieved to find that there would be many mile on a motorway when he could catch up with the Saab before they turned off and he might lose them. What he would have done if they had gone all the way on minor roads he didn't know, because by the sound of it they were heading well out of the town itself to an unknown destination.

However life got interesting when Bill pulled the big Saab off the M5. Those headlights behind him had been there for quite a while now. It might just be some businessman returning home to the Malvern area, of course. There were enough companies in the area with international connections for that to be feasible. But when they got into Malvern itself and the car was still stuck resolutely behind them, Bill decided that he needed to take evasive action.

"I don't want to worry you, ladies," he said, interrupting the rapid interchange of Finnish going on between the three of them, "But I'm going to have to thrown this car around a bit. We seem to have someone following us, and I'm not going to take him back to Tapio. Hold on!"

They did a sudden turn into what turned out to be a supermarket car-park, but the moment they got onto the car-park, Bill did a handbrake turn, spun the car through 180 degrees, and shot back out again. Yet the car behind did the same.

"Bugger!" Bill swore. "We seem to have someone who fancies himself as one of those Finnish rally drivers!"

"My ex-husband was one of those," Tove said dryly. "We went everywhere at speed. He used to scare the life out of me!"

"Well I'll try not to do that," Bill reassured her, "but he's got get lost!"

He tore out and onto the proper road again, heading towards the sub-district of Barnard's Green where he knew there was an oddly shaped roundabout where he might lose this tail.

"Annikki, take my mobile," he instructed, fishing it out of his inside pocket and handing it too her. "Now dial in this number..." When she had and put the phone onto speaker, Bill called out, "This is DI Bill Scathlock, who's that?"

"It's Martin. What's up Bill?"

"Can you send the lads to intercept me? I've just picked up a tail in Malvern. I think we've got another one who wants to take a shot at our lad."

"Fuck me, Bill, haven't you had enough excitement for one week?"

"Not me, Martin, old son. The bastards just don't know when to give up! I'm in the Saab, reg' ND14 CPU, heading towards Barnards Green, about to reach Pickersliegh Road. I'm going to take the road across the common. Tell Frank Watson, will you?"

At the said roundabout Bill shot onto it just in front of a Co-op delivery truck, which effectively blocked him from view, but to Bill's horror, as he took a chance on going straight for the Guarlford road instead of looping the roundabout, the car behind mounted the pavement and overtook the truck on the inside.

"You fucking nutter!" Bill cursed as he then flung the car right onto the road to Castlemorton Common. He held his breath as they passed the first couple of pubs, praying that no-one would come sedately out of the car-parks assuming that no-one was coming at speed down the road. His luck held, and suddenly they had open land on either side of them and no-one else on the road but them and the car behind. However, off to the right Bill could see the flashing blue lights of two patrol cars coming at speed out of Malvern the other way, and due to intercept them when he crested the next brow. And then in the rear-view mirror he saw the telltale flash of blue from behind too. Their pursuer was boxed in!

"Hold tight!" Bill yelled and slammed on the brakes.

The car behind was left with no choice but to hit them or go off the road. It shot off to the right and then came to a shuddering halt as it hit one of the many patches of boggy ground on the common. As it did, Bill was out of the car and tearing over to it, wrenching the driver's door open and reaching in intending to haul the driver out, except that he was squashed into the seat by the inflated air bags, and trapped by his seatbelt.

"You bastard!" Bill snarled. "You are under fucking arrest!"

Within seconds, the patrol cars had slid to a halt either side of the Saab, and the uniformed officers were taking charge of the other car's occupant.

"You can charge the stupid twat with dangerous driving, if nothing else!" Bill snarled to his colleagues. "The dozy cunt mounted the kerb to overtake a lorry in Barnard's Green on the pavement! It'll be on somebody's security camera, if nothing else, because I could hear a burglar alarm being set off, he was that close to the shops."

What he didn't expect was Tove's sudden cry of anguish as the man was lead away in handcuffs to the car illuminated by the Saab's headlights.

"You know this joker?" Bill asked, sticking his head inside the car.

"That's Karl, her ex-husband," Annikki answered shakily. "What's he doing *here*?"

"What? The wife beater?" Few things revolted Bill more than that. "If you'd said earlier I'd have made sure he resisted arrest and given him a few bruises of his own – unofficially, of course." Not that he'd have had much chance to do any such thing, what with the patrol cars being so close, nor would he have risked his career by doing something like that. But he'd said it loud enough for both the other officers and Karl himself to hear, and he noted that Karl was man-handled into the back seat with rather more vigour than was really required. That message would follow him back to the station anyway, but Bill made a point of additionally going to the patrol car and quietly telling the two officers who would be taking Karl away just who he was.

"If this little shit has been colluding with some unsavoury characters, it might explain why they were so easily able to follow Tapio to here," Bill told them. "DCI Watson will probably want a chat with this lad, because if he's been stalking his ex, then he may know more than he first lets on."

The other cars turned around and headed back into town, and suddenly they were on their own again.

"Right, ladies, let's see if we can get you home without any more excitement," Bill declared, but noting that suddenly Karita wasn't quite so lively. The full extent of the danger her granddaughter had been in had been dramatically brought home to her.

They arrived at the house and although Bill saw Tapio watching them from his bedroom window, the lad was in the dark and Tove didn't see him. In fact Tapio waited until the two older women were seated in the lounge, and much needed hot drinks had been provided, before he put in an appearance. With Urho behind him, Tapio walked in and stood still in the bright light of the central lamp.

"Hello, Tove, I am so sorry you have been brought into this," he apologised.

"My lord," Karita responded respectfully, which surprised Bill – he hadn't expected her to show such deference, but at least her response told him that Karita, if no-one else, had believed beyond doubt that she was helping the god of legends.

"Oooh..." Tove breathed. "You are so like him, and yet not." With tears streaming down her face she got up and walked slowly towards him until she was standing looking down at him. "I somehow expected you to have grown more. I thought I would be meeting a young man not a boy."

"The attacks by my enemies are to blame," Tapio told her solemnly. "They have made it hard for me just to maintain this life, this body, without undoing all the healing I had to do when I first took it over. I am sorry. It must be very hard for you to see me so close in size as when you last had your son."

Tove sniffed and wiped her eyes. "Yes and no. My Tapio never learned English. He didn't have time. So to hear you talking like this helps. And although you are so very like him, the way you act, the way you move, is so unlike him it's not as painful as I feared it would be. Even your face doesn't move the way his did."

Bill tactfully interrupted with, "Then let's make sure we stick to English for now, eh? Never mind whether you would be excluding me if you spoke in Finnish, and any hint that you might be planning something I might not like, if it's easier for Tove then when we're all together we stick to English." His pointed glance to Karita part the way through was intentional. Of all of them, she was the one he feared would come up with some cockeyed plan which wouldn't include him, and that could be lethal not just for Tapio but also Annikki.

Mercifully, there wasn't time for anything much more to be decided that night. Tove and Karita were tired from travelling, and the rest of them were exhausted from the long night before and were glad to disappear off to their rooms. However, Tapio did at least tell Bill that Morag had been with them all evening until she had had a call to say that Bill was almost home after the incident on the common. Apparently, Morag had an early start the next morning, so Bill forgave her for not lingering – he was just glad that she'd come.

Unfortunately the morning brought bad news. Frank Watson rang Bill and told him that they had released Karl.

"I'm sorry, Bill, but there was nothing we could legitimately hold him on. He's had his knuckles rapped over the dangerous driving, we've sent the hire car back, and we're hanging on to his driving licence until he leaves the country, but that's about it. Unfortunately he's not on camera with the driving thing, so it's just your word against his, and the CPS obviously don't want to waste time trying to get him done for dangerous driving through the courts on just that."

"What about why he's here?" Bill asked. "Did you get anything out of him about that?"

Frank's heavy sigh said it all even before he explained, "I pushed him as hard as I could with the duty solicitor sitting next to him, but got nothing useful. He just kept going on and on about how he thought he'd be able to get close enough to his ex-wife to try and make things up between them if they were out of their country. He's smart enough to know that the local cops in that place with the unpronounceable name have got his card marked, and that he'd be in every kind of shit if he went to the house and rang the bell. It makes him an idiot, Bill, but legally nothing more. And how many of our own lads have behaved like prats when it comes to ex-wives, eh? He's not exactly alone in that, is he? Like you, he worries me sick, but to everyone else he's just a fool who happens to have fallen into a nasty situation by crossing our paths at the wrong moment."

Bill groaned. He knew precisely what Frank meant. There was a world of difference between knowing in your gut that someone was the worst kind of trouble, and then being able to prove it enough to get them locked up. If instinct and experience were enough, then the police would have most of the villains in Worcestershire behind bar already, instead of preying on the populace in one way or another.

"He didn't say anything, not even a hint, about anything else?" he checked hopefully, but Frank disillusioned him.

"Sorry, mate, not a peep! For what it's worth, I agree with you. Him following the two women is just too suspicious. How the hell did he know they were leaving unless he was already stalking them? Especially at the time they must have set out – he'd hardly be going past on his way to work, would he? That all by itself bothers me. If he's not after Tapio, he could still be mentally disturbed enough to take another pop at Tove Törni, so I'm afraid you need to keep half an eye watching for her as well."

"I will. By the way, she's not Tove Törni anymore. After the divorce she went back to her maiden name, so she's Tove Mannu now. So that's what's on her passport, should you ever need to know. It's probably why we didn't make the connection to her before. She stopped using her married name over ten years ago, and she and her parents moved into the house they're in now right after Karl assaulted her. For once Karita and Väinö Mannu did the right thing and decided they weren't taking any more chances. Karita told me this morning over breakfast that while Tove was in hospital, they packed up their entire house, and all of Tove's stuff from her house, and moved – renting a house down the road from where they are now, and then buying this one after Tove's divorce went through. They aren't even in the same province anymore."

"Oh well, that's one mystery solved," Frank said wearily. "To be honest, Bill, the way trouble keeps coming to Tapio, if he'd been a grown man instead of a boy, I'd be pushing to have him sent back to Finland and let their own police take the flack. The danger of us ending up in the middle of a diplomatic incident is robbing me of what little chance I've had any chance of getting any sleep this last week or so."

"Diplomatic incident?"

"Ah, yes. Well because you aren't officially part of this investigation you don't know this, you understand..."

"Oh, I get it! Right, never heard this from you!"

"Absolutely. But those six blokes who took a dive in front of the trucks? They were all foreign nationals! Williams is having kittens up in his office, because five of them were ex-regular soldiers in the Finnish army. Every last one a bad lad kicked out with a dishonourable discharge. Given that the full-time Finnish army isn't that huge, whoever contracted this out must have scoured the place to find these five quite deliberately. All by itself that speaks of someone with serious intent. But then this morning we finally got something back on the sixth, and that really puts the shits up me!"

"I'm not going to like this, am I?"

"No. We got such a fast response because his DNA brought up a hit with our own security services. He's thought to be ex-KGB, and he's been lurking around in London for a while now. He wasn't picked up because he's been *very* careful not to do anything which could be traced back to him. However, the lads in London have told us that they had their suspicions that he was involved in recruiting mercenaries for very dodgy jobs – oh, I know 'mercenaries' and 'dodgy' are like peas in a pod, but they meant something nastier than the usual. And they said that the man who they suspected of being this bloke's boss has shown a sudden desire to get a suntan in Brazil. He was on a plane within hours of the accident."

"Bloody hell!"

"I know. Now you see what I meant. What's worse, the email said that the man who died was thought to still be in contact with his old chums, and that some of the jobs were ones with a not very well disguised trail straight back to Moscow – un-provable, of course, but you'd have to be an idiot not to know what it meant. So you see why I'm scared we'll end up in a diplomatic shit storm. We daren't send the lad back. The accusations in the press if he then came to harm don't bear thinking about, but I don't want the big boys carrying out their own private contracts on our turf either."

Bill thought for a second, then asked, "No chance that Karl Törni has any connections with any of them? National Service in the same corps as the dead men, or, God forbid, with the KGB?"

"Christ, no! He's not that bright! Apparently in his youth he was some kind of shit-hot petrol-head – won a few rallies in the frozen north, and that sort of stuff, but nothing remotely sinister. We blasted off an urgent email and got a quick response now that we know who to send the requests to. He did his twelve months' National Service when he was eighteen, of course, but then every man does. Törni apparently was mostly with the Border Guard, never fired a rifle in anger, not even at a polar bear, so he's positively inoffensive compared with the six who attacked you."

"Oh well, it was a thought. So he's a stalker and an obnoxious little shit, but nothing worse."

"Afraid so."

"Okay, thanks for that, Frank, and I'll keep in mind what you said about the others."

Going to join the others in the kitchen, where Annikki and Karita were cooking up something with the most wonderful aromatic smells, Bill told Tove,

"Your ex-husband is an idiot." That at least made her laugh. However Bill sat down beside her and said gently, "Apparently he's daft enough that he thought he'd get his chance to make things up with you once you were away from the Finnish police."

Her expression of total astonishment told Bill all he needed to know. There was no way that she had encouraged him in this.

"Don't worry," Bill reassured her. "If by some weird trick of fate he actually finds his way here on foot, Urho and I will give him a thick ear and send him packing!"

And when Tapio translated that to the big man who was in the kitchen as well, practically salivating over the coming meal, the big man grinned at Bill, indicating that it would be his pleasure too.

Chapter 14

Wednesday

When they had all had lunch Bill thought it was about time Karita told them why she had decided to come here – and in his mind he was already sure that it would have been she who had made the decision, not Tove. However, he wanted the truth, not some story made up for his benefit, and so he first of all gave them a potted version of what Frank had told him about the dangerous six, taking it steadily so that someone could translate for Urho.

"So now I have to ask you, why are you here?" Bill said bluntly. "And please don't tell me it was just because you were worried about Annikki. I've spoken enough to her father on the phone to know that the poor man is worried sick, but he still trusts the British police to keep her safe. What made you two jump on a plane and come to find us?"

Yet Karita's answer still surprised him.

"Ukko sent us," she said, as though it was the most obvious thing in the world.

"Ukko? Who's Ukko?" Bill exclaimed in frustration. "Bloody hell, there's not even more to this that you aren't telling me, is there?"

"Mummo, you have to explain things!" Annikki chastised her grandmother, as Tapio said,

"Ukko is chief of all the gods of my country. You have seen him, Karhu, he was the third one who appeared when we sang, along with Ilmarinen and Mielikki."

"I thought that was who it might have been," Annikki said in a scared voice. "He's scary!"

"No he's not, child," Karita chided her. "Or at least not if you show him proper respect."

"Oh really?" Annikki snorted. "Someone whose weapons are lightning strikes and thunder bolts? I still haven't forgotten your neighbour's house getting hit by that thunder bolt!"

Tove winced, but Karita wagged her finger and said,

"Precisely! They were wicked folk, those two, in league with Hiisi. Ukko had sent them enough signs to repent their ways, but they took no notice, and so they got what was coming to them."

Bill put his head into his hands and groaned, "Who's Hiisi?"

"Oh, he's a forest demon," Tove said, taking pity on him. "I'm so sorry, Bill, I know this is hard for you. This is the worst kind of crash course in Finnish mythology."

"Yes, Karhu," Tapio said, coming to put his arm around Bill's big shoulders. "In the normal way of things, Hiisi is a small demon who lives in the forest and tries to make things difficult for me. He is what you would call a petty crook, I think?"

Bill managed to raise a faint smile. "Probably." What such men got called behind closed doors in the station wasn't suitable for repeating here.

"And he doesn't like your sort."

"My sort? Police?"

"Bears. Karhu."

Bill couldn't hold back the groan which escaped from him. It was one thing for some kid to think he was a human bear – if not quite so inoffensive as a cuddly teddy – but it was quite another for it to be taken to this extreme.

"You have a power within you which you do not recognise," Tapio told him solemnly. "It's not just about your physical strength. You are a strong man inside too."

"I wouldn't have made Detective Inspector if I wasn't!" Bill said rather tersely. Strangely, knowing that he wasn't talking to a child meant he felt much more able to speak his mind. Then decided he needed to demonstrate that a little more forcefully. At the moment he was starting to feel that he was being led by the nose by these people, and that despite everything which had happened, that they still weren't taking things as seriously as they should. "God Almighty, people!" and he thumped the table with his fist. "Will you wake up and listen to what I'm saying? There's more at stake here now than just Tapio's life!"

"If Tapio dies then many people will suffer as a result," Karita told him with a rather prickly edge to her voice.

However, Bill was at the end of his tether. "Oh? And that would have been a consolation to some poor sod who happened to step out of a shop last night, and got run over by that useless twat Karl, would it? Tapio in any form can't bring someone back from the dead, can he? Or he'd have done it for your Tapio – unless he's just saying that as a sop to your feelings because he desperately needed the body! But there's no bloody way he'd be doing it for someone here, whichever! They'd be dead, poor bastards, whatever happened! And, might I add, so would some of my colleagues if those men who were here the other night had opened fire with those automatic weapons. I could be going to a series of funerals for men who were trying to protect you lot if things had been just a whisker different, so will you please stop patronising me with this *bullshit*!"

There was a stunned silence and then an eruption when everyone was talking at once, even Urho.

"Quiet!" Bill bellowed, giving the table another thump.

In the tense moment's silence, Tove got up and stormed out, pursued by Urho, but Karita stayed put, white-faced and eyes glinting with anger.

"How dare you say such a thing with my daughter present!"

"I bloody dare, lady, because it's my life and my colleagues' which will get sacrificed by this mess you've got us into! You may not have chosen to live in the here-and-now, but whoever your enemies are, they're taking full advantage of every string they can pull with modern armaments and technology. Did you not grasp what I just told you? Someone hired ex-KGB men to come and take a shot at Tapio, here. Fucking KGB! And that being the case, I have to tell you that whether or not Tapio can fend them off while he's holed up in this house is less of a worry for me than the chaos they might cause out on the streets when they get frustrated by that. Or don't you care that the streets of Malvern might be littered with the corpses of ordinary people who did nothing more than get in the way? I don't have the luxury of being able to think of just one person. There are over thirty thousand people living in the Malverns – how many of them have to die before you start taking this seriously?"

Karita went even more tight-lipped, making Bill think that it must have been many a long year since anyone had stood up to her like that. In the time since the person he was coming to think of as the 'real' Tapio had died, just how much had she ruled Tove's life? And was that for Tove's good, or because Karita had developed the selfishness of the elderly and taken advantage of Tove's weak spots?

Yet it was Tapio who stopped Karita's outburst.

Her, "How dare you!..." was cut off by Tapio's,

"No! He is right, Karita!"

To Bill's amazement, Karita subsided back into the chair she had started to rise from, and with less pouting than he had expected as well.

"You are right," Tapio repeated in a voice full of

sorrow. "We have been so used to fighting this battle out in the wilds of our own country we never thought about how populated yours is. I am deeply sorry, Karhu, that we did not think about that more before we came to this house. At the time we were filled with the need to find the right place for me to recover."

"And I don't have a problem with that," Bill told him. "But you yourself said that you didn't expect to be followed. Yet you have, and therefore you have to take that into consideration now."

"Indeed," Tapio conceded.

"How dare you speak to him like that, though!" Karita protested, only to be told firmly by Tapio,

"I would have been taken by my enemies a week ago, and without another hand lifted to save me, had Karhu and his friend not come to my rescue. I think that gives him a lot of right, Karita. I know you and Väinö have done much for me, but you are not the only ones, and just because Karhu has only just appeared does not make his efforts any the less worthy." As Karita subsided to sit glaring at Bill, Tapio turned back to him.

"Tell me, Karhu, who is this KGB you talk about. Who is he, and why do you think him so dangerous?"

Bill managed to man-fully squash his impatience, forcing himself to remember that if Tapio really was who he said he was, the KGB's reign of terror would have been a blink of an eye over those long years.

"It's not 'who' but 'them'," he began. "The KGB, officially, was an organisation within Russia after the tsars had been overthrown. They worked in secret, spying on people and on other countries, but they also had terrible influence over what the army did. I can give you a longer explanation if you want, but what matters now is that although the old Soviet state has collapsed, and there's a new system of government in Russia, the men who held high ranks within the KGB had enough information on an awful lot of people to make sure that they survived. And worse, they knew enough secrets that they could make sure that they now hold high positions in the government. Even the President used to be one of them!

"And if you're still wondering how this applies to you, the weapons those men brought with them the other night are very specific. You only get them through the army! Or through an arms dealer and pay a huge amount of money – money I know that ordinary kidnappers wouldn't have. The kind of men who take normal children hostage, in order to get rich parents to pay them huge sums, are looking to *earn* that sort of money. They don't have it themselves! Oh, they might have guns and knives, but they'll be the older kind of guns you can get by paying someone in the wrong parts of cities a modest price to get for you, not the kind Annikki and I carried out to my car. I'd expect to find them in a war zone, not on my streets!"

Tapio's expression told Bill that suddenly he was grasping why Bill was so worried. Therefore Bill felt he could ask again,

"So were you telling me the truth when you said that you couldn't revive the original Tapio?"

"Of course!" Tapio exclaimed in horror.

"Okay. So if I accept that all you've told me about wanting to come here and recover, you still haven't said what made this place the right one. Why did you come here, specifically? Why Malvern?"

Tapio wriggled his small body up to sit on the kitchen table beside Bill.

"To begin with it had everything to do with my current appearance. Please forgive Karita, Karhu, but she has done so much to help me that she has her own reasons to speak out. It was she and Väinö who told Ilmarinen, Mielikki and myself that a normal boy of my apparent age would have to go to a school. That meant that we had to find a school that I could arrange to attend before I even left home. We felt we could not leave it to chance that I would find the right kind of place once we got here."

"And which 'we' was that? You and Annikki?" He caught Annikki's eye and was relieved that she wasn't about to take offence at his words, and had grasped that he was trying to work round to find out when it had been decided to involve her.

"No! It was me and Urho," Tapio corrected. "Urho has been with me a very long time. He prepared the house that we took Tapio to when I first joined with him, and kept it in readiness all the time while we waited. I meant what I said, Karhu, we did not shorten Tapio's life."

"Okay, so you and Urho were going to come here – I presume that by that time you had decided on England?"

"Yes, we had. We looked at some remote schools up in Scotland, but the fees were very high. Väinö said that if I wanted to remain hidden that I would be better in a school were more ordinary people sent their children."

"To be fair, he was probably right in that," Bill admitted.

"Well we looked at a lot, but many of them were right in big cities. I need the countryside around me. When we found this school, it seemed ideal. Karita rang them and made enquiries, and was told that many of the pupils travelled into school from this area. So we looked at Malvern. The great age of the hills confirmed that it was the right kind of place, so the only thing was finding the right house.

"I told Väinö and Karita that it had to have trees around it, and we found many which were only a short walk from small woods, but this one stood out because of the ancient oaks all around it. As soon as she saw it Karita knew that it was the right house."

Bill looked at Karita, who had lost some of her glare. "So would I be right in thinking that it was you and your husband who spoke to the headmaster on the phone? Not some weird manifestation of Ilmarinen and Mielikki?"

Grudgingly she replied. "No, it was us. They couldn't have managed that."

"So why didn't your name and address come up when we tried to trace the phone number?"

Karita sniffed. "We had a second phone line installed. We told the phone company part of the truth – that we had a grown-up daughter living with us after a bad divorce. We said that she wanted some independence to hold conversations with her friends, but that because of the violence we wanted to make sure that the number remained anonymous."

Poor Tove, Bill thought. She would probably have loved such consideration, but it had taken ten years and Tapio's need before she got it, and then only second-hand. Through gritted teeth he managed to say,

"And no doubt Karl played into your hands with that because of him stalking her?"

"Yes, he did, and because there was a police record of what happened to Tove."

Now Bill felt justified in showing some of his disgust, "So didn't it occur to you two to answer the phone when the school rang you to tell you about the attempted abduction? I'm sorry, but if Tapio had been a real child I'd be thinking seriously of charging you with abandonment!"

"But Annikki was with him!" protested Karita, which stung Annikki into a riposte of her own,

"Except that you didn't tell me what was going on, did you? Thank you very much! Your own granddaughter and you don't bother checking that everything was as it ought to have been? My father asked you how you knew Urho and you couldn't tell him, could you, because you hardly knew him except that he was helping Tapio. Do you have any idea of the stress you've put my parents under? Your own daughter has been worried sick because of you!"

Karita waved an airy hand. "Well they should have listened to me, then shouldn't they! I told them you were alright."

"Oh really?" Annikki exploded. "You told them! Well that's all fine, then, isn't it! It's not like you've been known to make a proper mess of things in the past, or anything, eh? Not like accusing poor Mr Helismaa of killing wolves in his back yard when all the poor man was doing was cutting up meat for his huskies! Or Mrs Ryti who got a visit from the police because of your daft accusations, when all she'd been doing was putting down some rat poison because you put so much seed down for the birds that it was attracting the damned things, and her garden was becoming infested! And what's worse, even when the family went to see you asking about all of this, because things *had* started to go wrong, you still didn't do anything to set their minds at rest. Do you even care that when you get home that you'll be lucky if any of them ever speak to you again?"

"Oh stop making such a fuss," Karita dismissed her. "We didn't deliberately put you in harm's way. What sort of grandmother do you take me for?"

"A bloody careless one," Bill answered for her, "Because what you're still not hearing, Karita, is that we're not angry because you didn't anticipate this mess, but because when it did all go wrong that you made everything worse. We could have acted a lot more effectively if we could have spoken to you. I'm not saying that we'd have believed all the gods stuff, but you could have told the school that Tapio had a violent father who he was sent here to get away from. That would have meant that when the kidnapping attempt came we took it a lot more seriously, because my superiors were on the verge of thinking that the first pair of men who tried to grab Tapio were just opportunists until the next attack came. They were a whisker away from pulling all guards off him. And had the attackers waited that bit longer, I wouldn't have been here but back on duty."

Finally the implications seemed to sink in with Karita, making Bill add,

"And you suddenly turning up out of the blue just when it was all going to hell in a handcart looks bloody suspicious too! So I'm going to ask you again: why did you suddenly decide to get up and come here? Your granddaughter being in danger clearly wasn't the factor, so what was?"

Karita glared back at Bill and said waspishly, "And *I* told you, it was Ukko who sent us!"

"Really? So how did he do that? Send you a phone call? Can he do what Ilmarinen and Mielikki can't?"

"Karhu, please!" Tapio interrupted. "That is not necessary!"

"Isn't it?" Bill challenged him. "Did *you* send for them?"

"No, I did not, but Ukko was present when we were were attacked, if only in spirit form. He knew what was going on. There is nothing so very strange about him deciding that we needed help."

"From two women?" Bill was disbelieving. "Oh come on, Tapio! You get attacked by armed men and your senior god decided to send two middle-aged women to help you? I'm sorry, but that's hard to believe, even for a god! You say Ilmarinen is a smith – well he sounds a lot more useful in a tight spot, disembodied or otherwise."

"He wanted to send real people who could act on his behalf!" Karita snapped. "And despite your peoples' arrogant belief, not everyone speaks English – he was short of choices for that!"

Bill had to admit that that would be a consideration, whether by a god or more human agency.

"Okay, let's take that as a given for a minute, but what did *you* think you were coming here to face?"

"She thought that someone here had made a mess of things," a tired voice came from the doorway, and Tove walked back in, red-eyed and pale. "I heard her. She told Ukko that no doubt this was all some prank which had gone wrong and that she'd soon sort it out."

Her mother gave her a furious glare but didn't deny it.

"Thank you, Tove," Bill said a good deal more gently than he had spoken to Karita. "At last I think we're getting to the bottom of this. So the assumption was that you would come over, soothe some ruffled feathers, get Tapio settled back into school and then swan back home in triumph?" When no answer came from either woman, Bill shook his head. "If you had even begun to listen to what Annikki's parents had tried to tell you, you would have known even before you left home that this was all far more serious than that. But then I doubt you've ever listened that much to your children anyway, Karita."

In fury she shoved her chair back so hard that it crashed to the floor, and stormed out. However Bill went and set the chair upright and gestured Tove to it.

"Please, come and sit down with us," he said gently. "I'm sorry if my words upset you before."

"No, it's alright," she answered, hoarse from crying. "It's a question I've asked many times of her and never got an answer. But I was always told I should trust her, that she's my mother and wouldn't harm me. It took hearing a stranger asking the same thing as though it was an obvious question to make me realise that I wasn't being stupid all these years."

"Oh Tove!" Annikki gasped, appalled. "Why ever didn't you come and stay with us for a while? Get a break from her? We all thought you stayed because you wanted to, not because she was bullying you."

Tove shrugged. "At first, after my Tapio died, I did stay because I wanted to. Everything she'd told me seemed to give me something to hold onto. And I very much needed something, especially after what Karl did. But it's been in later years that I've started to look back and wonder about a lot of things."

"I hope you never thought that I killed your son," Tapio said earnestly. "Please believe me, Tove, I never did that. I respect all life, and your son's was no different."

She smiled weakly at him. "Yes, seeing and hearing you now, I can tell that. It's odd, but had I seen a healthy young man, I think it would have been worse. It would have felt as though you were enjoying the youth he never got chance to have. But to see that even so, his development has been far short of normal, is in a strange way reassuring that you have had struggle to keep even what you have alive. But will you tell me something please?" Tapio looked surprised, but nodded. "What do you intend to do with my son's body once you are well again?"

It was a question which clearly took even Tapio by surprise, and he took a moment to answer.

"I must be honest, I don't know," he confessed. "I don't think that any of us foresaw me living even as long as I have in this form. We thought that I would repair the body, escape from the attacks of my enemy and then heal. But right from the start we came under attack so often that just getting this far took all of our concentration. I have to say that I also thought that ultimately I would not be able to sustain the life in this body. What I am doing is unnatural, and we believed that would take its toll."

"So you expected that my son's body would die?"

"Yes, I think we did – still do. And the fact that I have not been able to make it grow much at all only confirms that to me."

Tove looked so surprised that Bill asked,

"Isn't that what you expected to hear?"

She shook her head, and some tears trickled down her cheeks as she added,

"She said that I must give up the idea of ever burying my son. That his body would go beyond the life of mine, and that I shouldn't be so selfish for wanting to have a proper grave to visit."

Annikki gasped and sprang up to go and throw her arms around her aunt's shoulders in sympathy, while Tapio looked shaken and Bill growled angrily.

"That's not selfish," he told her, reaching across the table and enveloping her hand in his huge paw, "that's just normal! Something your mother doesn't seem to have any grasp of! God, I'm so sorry, Tove! You poor lass, what you've been through!"

Tapio also felt the need to reassure. "I promise you, Tove, if it is at all within my power, when I am rejuvenated and can leave this body, I will bring him back to you so that you may bury him in peace. I am most heartily ashamed that I did not see the suffering I have caused you over this. I thought that you would be glad that some good had come out of the terrible loss of your son when you voluntarily handed him over to me. I am appalled that I did not think further about the attachment you would have, nevertheless, to this shell of a body. Please accept my apology and my reassurance that I will do all I can to put this right."

Tove was working her way through the box of tissues Annikki had provided, but when she had blown her nose again and could speak, she said,

"I didn't, you know."

"Didn't what?" Annikki asked for all of them.

"I didn't give him to you voluntarily. I wanted to allow my poor boy to just die after all the pain and suffering he'd been through. I wasn't convinced, you see, that the body wouldn't still feel pain even if his spirit had gone."

"Why did you do it then?" Annikki gasped, then immediately cried, "Oh no! She made you, didn't she!"

Tove nodded. "By that time I was so tired, so exhausted. All I wanted was sleep for me and him. I didn't have the strength to argue. And I thought I would feel differently when I had held his hand and felt him die. But she didn't give me chance. The moment the monitors went to blank she was unplugging him and then carrying him outside. I never even got chance to say goodbye properly."

Annikki stood up and looked at Bill. "If my father ever finds this out he's going to kill Mummo!"

"Never mind your dad! I'm thinking of saving him the trouble!"

"And I, too, am not pleased," Tapio said grimly. "This was not what I was told had happened. Not at all! It should not have happened like this."

"Well what did you think?" Karita asked acidly from the doorway. "You said you needed him with his blood still flowing in his veins. That's minutes, not hours! If this is all the thanks I'm going to get, we're on the next plane back to Finland!"

"You can, I'm staying," Tove said, reaching out and taking Annikki's hand tightly. "If there's the slightest chance that my son is going to die a second time, this time I'm going to stay with him."

─────◦◦◦◦◦─────

209

Chapter 15

Wednesday - Thursday

Karita had left them to talk after that, for which Bill was thankful. At least now he got some more out of Tove and Tapio about Ukko, and began to grasp that the central god of the Finns was too strongly tied to his country to be able to leave as Tapio had done. Therefore his only choice had been to send human emissaries. However, Tapio was quick to say that he was sure that Ukko would have intended the two women to be acting as liaisons with the school, never dreaming that they would have to satisfy the police's questions as well.

"I am becoming ever more grateful that I met you, Karhu," he said earnestly. "If there is any hand of the greater gods in this, it is that I was put in a place to cross your path. Had I gone to another school you would not have been there when I was taken, and I can only say that I find it encouraging that you should be here, given that the odds of that happening were so slim. Maybe some of your own ancient gods are in sympathy with my plight and bending events to help me?"

Bill sighed and shook his head. "I don't know who they would be, but you're right about the odds. I certainly wouldn't bet on such a coincidence, even if I was a gambling man."

Later on, they agreed that Bill would take Karita to the airport tomorrow while the others stayed with Tapio. The day had remained mercifully uneventful apart from the family arguments, and Bill had a cherished hope that they might have gained at least a week's respite from any attacks.

Surely there couldn't be another such bunch of mercenaries lurking in the area?

Yet the next morning, after he had taken Karita and made sure she went through customs to her flight, and then returned to the house, Tove came to find him alone.

"I know what I'm going to tell you will sound strange, maybe ridiculous or even fantastic, but after what I've learned here I really need to tell someone. I think I've done something terrible."

"Let's go and have a walk in the garden," Bill suggested. "We'll be less overheard there." He had a strong feeling that he wasn't going to like this, but in this instance he wanted to hear it in Tove's own words without any prompting.

Tove herself seemed glad to get out of the house and away from the others, and it was only when they were well away from the building and the chance that they might be overheard through a window, that she began speaking.

"I hope you can understand that I was terribly distressed at the time that this happened," she began tentatively. "My Tapio had been dead some three years, but for me the pain seemed to be getting worse not better."

"After what you've told me already, I'm not surprised," Bill sympathised. "Your parents never seem to have given you any time to mourn."

Tove nodded. "And moving house almost at the same time was ...was ...catastrophic! Yes ...I think catastrophic is the right word. If we had stayed living in the same area, even, I could have gone walking in those woods and maybe found a spot where I could sit and mourn. Does that make sense?"

"Yes, it does. That was the place where he died, even if he wasn't there anymore. I think that's why we have so many roadside 'shrines' these days – people don't have a place to go to as they used to with the old cemeteries when everyone got buried. But some people need time to heal, and I suspect that the more sudden and unexpected the death, the more time people need. So I don't find it odd that you would have felt the need to at least revisit the area, and probably several times. And until I met your mother, I would have been asking why you hadn't asked your parents to take you. Somehow, though, I can't imagine that request would have met with much understanding?"

Tove shook her head, making several strands of the rich red hair escape from the band she had tried to tie it back with. "No, they didn't understand at all. Or rather, Father possibly did, but he wasn't going to do anything when Mother was so adamant about everything. It was as though she thought she could make me get over the whole thing by sheer will power – and hers, not mine!

"I kept trying to tell her that I felt awful. Hollow. Like I'd been scraped out by one of those huge machines which strip coal out of the ground." She turned to look into Bill's eye and saw only sympathy there, which encouraged her. "I felt raw inside. But even a hint that I might take the train or a bus and go back to our old home by myself was enough to have Mother shrieking at me. She'd call me ungrateful. She said that I was wicked to not appreciate what had been offered me – that many a grieving mother would give everything she had to change places with me, and to be able to know that her son lived on in some form.

"And her anger was so formidable! She could keep going on about it for weeks if I brought it up just once. ...Maybe I'd have been able to resist her better if I'd been sleeping properly and hadn't been so exhausted, but I'd had so many years of just half-sleeping I couldn't go back to having a proper night's sleep."

Bill was nodding. "I can understand that too. At one point I was doing a lot of night shifts, and because of where I live it wasn't always easy to get proper sleep during the day. It played havoc with my sleep for a couple of years after I'd stopped doing it, so I get what you're talking about. You must have had years and years of sleeping with one ear alert for any change in the beeps of the machines and monitors keeping your son alive. Even if he'd died in the normal way, and you'd had the release of a funeral, it would still have taken you a couple of years or more for you to start sleeping normally. And with all your grief eating away at you I'm not surprised at what you're saying."

Tove let out a ragged sob. "Ooooh! You're the first person I've spoken to who understands that!" and she had to stop and cry for a few minutes before she could carry on. "Thank you, Bill, just to hear you say those things is a relief in itself. So maybe you'll understand the rest.

"You see I didn't have many friends left. I suppose most girls find things change when they give up work to have a family, but for teachers like I was, it's fairly easy to go back to work once you've had children because at least you have the school holidays off. But I never did go back. Tapio was ill right from the start, and if he wasn't as sick as he would eventually get, he was still a baby who needed his mother at home all the time."

"God, that made you horribly isolated, didn't it!"

"Oh yes! But I had a couple of friends from back in my university days who stayed in touch. Looking back now, I think it was significant that they were working as translators. It meant that they worked intensely for blocks of time, but then had longer breaks than my other friends had when they could come and visit. Well Minna and Hertta came to see me about three years after everyone thought I'd buried Tapio. They were genuinely worried at how I was, and I suspect that they could also see how Mother was with me. They said that they had a conference to go to help at in St Petersburg with some steel workers, and would I like to go with them?

"I was at such a low point by then I wasn't even sure, but Mother for some reason thought it was a good idea too, and so I was parcelled off with them. I can now see that it was the start of my recovery. Just being away from Mother for a fortnight was a relief, and Minna and Hertta were wonderful. They took me out to dinner at night, they took me out for visits to the theatre, and they just behaved normally. Okay, maybe Russia was hardly the best place – you can't wander around safely by yourself, and it's not as though it's somewhere you want to go shopping – but it broke my routine.

"But something else happened there, Bill. I was sitting on my own in the little coffee bar in the hotel one morning after my friends had left for work, and this man came up and sat down by me. I was surprised and frightened when he said he knew what had happened to me. How could a stranger know that? But then he started talking about Tapio not as my son, but as the forest lord my Mother talked about, and because I'd been so smothered with all of that for so many years, it seemed normal to talk like that with him.

"He said he was Koschei..."

"I've heard that name before! Tapio – he said it. Something about him being his archenemy?"

Tove nodded miserably. "The same, but please understand the state I was in. If someone had walked up and said they were King Arthur I would probably have believed them!"

"Oh I do," Bill empathised. "The human brain needs its down-time or all sorts of things seem normal."

She gave another sob of relief. "You really are the most therapeutic person to talk to!"

"Well I've been called a lot of things, but never that! I'll take it as a compliment."

"It was meant as one. But the thing was, Bill, he too seemed to understand. He said that what had been done – the taking of my child's body for another to use – was perverse and wrong. He sounded as outraged as I felt, and that was a first. I mean, I could hardly say to my girlfriends that I was having such trouble getting over my loss because my son's body still lived, but was occupied by an ancient forest god, could I? They would have had me into the nearest psychiatric ward in a heartbeat, and pretty understandably so. But it made it all the harder for me. I just couldn't talk to *anyone* about my Tapio, because as soon as I did I got into such strange territory. So I didn't talk at all, and that made the grief so much harder too."

"I'm not surprised. You couldn't even join a support group could you?"

"No. And that made the relief of finding this stranger who I could talk to, and who didn't ask me to explain the unexplainable but told me stuff I didn't know, was like a huge weight coming off my chest. I felt like I was breathing properly for the first time in seven or eight years. He said that it wasn't just my mother who was to blame, but all these second-rate gods who wanted to hang onto the past and power that was no longer theirs.

"I know it sounds daft said like that, out here in an English garden, but it made total sense at the time. And that was when he asked me for something." That made Bill prick up his ears. "He said that he had the power to make them give Tapio's body back to me. Not alive – he never promised that. He said my Tapio would still be dead, but I would be able to bury him like a normal person would. I never asked where, and I suppose I should have, because a box of stones went into the ground under my son's gravestone, so I could hardly go and dig that up. Nor could I go around depositing a boy's body in any old hole in the ground without someone asking questions – I see that all too clearly now. But I'd been too distraught for too long to think all of that out then.

"So I listened, and Koschei said that I could have my Tapio back, and that was all I was thinking of. But he said one thing was stopping him from going and challenging Tapio directly, face to face, and taking the body from him. He said that the ancient territories still had some power, so he couldn't just come into Finland – he had to be invited in! He said that even one person calling to him from the heart would be enough. It would be enough to allow him to slip through the barriers and start acting. He said that so few of our people supported the likes of Ukko, Ilmarinen and Tapio that they had far less strength than they used to have. And he knew where my Tapio was, not far from the border, but more central to what the old Finland was. So he knew he didn't have to get into the heart of modern Finland.

"Well I went home a changed woman. Someone had thrown me a lifeline, albeit a very perverse one. I asked my friends to help me get into translating work, and at home I prayed to Koschei with all my might. You'll think me foolish, but the first time Mother was contacted about things going very wrong, I never linked it to me. Still I was in my own fog of grief and insomnia even if it was starting to recede. And so we went to visit Ilmarinen and Mielikki, and that night in my bed I was so angry with them! They never once asked how I was! Everything was about this fake Tapio they had stolen from me, not about the little boy who had died, or about those who had loved him so desperately. And so I went outside that night, after they had gone, and I cried and I screamed to Koschei to come and fulfil his promise."

She stopped, looking pale and shaken, and took a couple of gulping breaths.

"The trouble is, Bill, I'm suddenly starting to wonder what I started? Oh, I carried on calling to Koschei for another year or so, but when nothing happened I just got bitter over that too. But at least in all that anger I'd somehow let a lot of other feelings out too. I could just about function normally again. I had a job, and if I had to take a few weeks off each year when we got to the anniversary of losing my boy, at least the work came on a project by project basis, and I could turn it down with the excuse of other work already elsewhere. No-one questioned why I fell to pieces for a month. I'd even managed to persuade Father into backing me, so that I could have a tiny apartment made for myself out of a couple of the upstairs rooms and an extension over the garage. Mother was still ruling my life, but I wasn't with her all day and every day.

"And that's how it's been up until this last year. I think all this talk of Annikki coming over here started giving me ideas. I had made up my mind to come and visit her this summer anyway, you know, because of course, Mother hadn't told me just who she was looking after! I only began to guess that when her parents turned up so worried and so angry, and with Matti with them and equally angry. And then Matti saying that it was bad enough that she was ruining my life, but that she had no right whatsoever to do it to Annikki. I had my suspicions then, and so when she was so determined all of a sudden to come here, I agreed, but not for the reasons she thought. I came to support Annikki however I could. I won't let her hurt my niece!

"But what really worries me now is, did I start all of this? Did my inviting Koschei in give him power he didn't have before? Is it my fault that Annikki got caught up in this? Because if I hadn't done what I did, then maybe Tapio could have renewed himself in my son and then left him? Have I started a chain of events that forced Tapio to leave Finland and bring my niece here to be put in danger?"

Bill puffed his cheeks out with a sigh as he frantically thought. "Look, I know that on the one hand I should be saying it's all a load of rubbish, that you couldn't possibly start something like that because it's all myths and legends anyway. But I've seen too much in these last few days to be able to dismiss things quite so glibly."

He reached out and pulled her to him and gave her own of his big hugs. "What I do know is that if you did start something, then you didn't start the whole thing, okay? All it would have taken was for your own mother to treat you with a bit more thought and understanding. I mean, why, once Tapio had gone into your son's body, could you not had an hour or so with him? I grasp from everything I've been told that Tapio needed a human form, and a child at that, because children are so protected. It gave him a very safe place to be. And I also get that he needed to make the transfer into that body while it was still almost alive so that the natural course of things didn't start up. I've seen enough bodies to know how quickly things deteriorate after the moment of death."

He now held her at arm's length but looking her in the eyes. "And I definitely think that even if Karl was being a knob, that there was no need to whisk you away from your home like that either. I know we'd take such an assault very seriously, and I'm sure that my counterparts in Finland did too. Your parents could have trusted them a bit more to do their jobs, but then I don't think your mother believes in anyone but herself, does she? She doesn't believe that you might have a mind of your own, and might know what's good for *you*. The more I saw of her, the more I understood why Annikki's father always sounded one step short of going and throttling her – she must be the most aggravating woman to live with!"

Tove's face broke into a smile. "I think that's an understatement! I've been saving up to move out, but I've never dared tell her that – I couldn't take the endless rows between now and the point when I actually left."

Bill nodded sagely. "And if I can say something else, I think maybe that she pushed Karl over the edge too. It sounds as though by the end he was hardly ever allowed to be alone with his son. It must have felt to him as though he had no rights, no place where he could be the father, without your mother sticking her nose in. Children dying is always rough on a marriage, but I don't think you two had a chance even before Tapio died. Maybe you would have got divorced, but I seriously doubt that it would have been under such traumatic circumstances without your mother's input." Then hurriedly added, "Not that I'm advocating a sudden reunion, mind you! I don't think Karl's squirrel-brain is something you need to deal with on top of everything else. Frank seems to think he's a few sandwiches short of the full picnic these days!"

That really gave Tove the giggles, never having heard the expression before. "I shall have to remember that when I'm translating," she laughed, then became more serious. "So you don't think I've done something terrible?"

Bill draped a friendly arm around her shoulders and turned her towards the house. "I honestly can't say about the Koschei thing. I suspect the only one who can tell us that is Tapio, but let's go and talk to him. Let me tell him. I think I can put it in a way that will make him see that you've been treated very badly by all of them, and if you have done something awful, then it was done in a state of extreme grief, not out of malice. And in truth, Koschei was very quick to use your grief for his own purposes, so he's hardly coming out of this smelling of roses either."

Inside, Bill called Annikki, Tapio and Urho into the kitchen again and told Tove's story for her. By the time he had finished Annikki had her arms wrapped around Tove and was sobbing her heart out in sympathy, while at the same time vowing that the rest of the family would hear of this, and how they would be having nothing more to do with Karita.

"She's no mother!" she sniffed, hugging Tove tightly. "You can come and get an apartment with me! I don't mind whether it's here in England or at home, but you're never going back to their house again!"

Urho was sitting hanging his great head in misery, looking for all the world like a chastised mastiff whose masters were arguing. Tapio, however, was sitting looking stunned.

"I had no idea we had caused you so much suffering," he said softly. "Whenever one of us asked Karita how you were she said you were all right, that you were going through the normal mourning process but were going to be fine. It never occurred to us that she might be lying."

"If you'll allow me to put something to you," Bill added, "I think she was, and still is, one of those mothers who enjoyed the attention she got through her daughter. You may not be aware of this, but there are some twisted mothers out there who get a peculiar pleasure out of making their children enter things like beauty contests. They have control of the child, you see. They decide what they do, where they go, what they wear, and so when a child wins it's as though it's their victory. But when it goes wrong it's the child's fault. And I have a funny feeling that there was some of that going on even when Karita came here. She was convinced that she must have set this whole thing up over here so well that it couldn't fail, and therefore something going wrong had to be Annikki's fault, or even Tove's, in some way which only makes sense in her head.

"And she got a feeling of importance out of all of this. She was the one chosen by the gods! I mean, how much of an ego boost is that? No mere churchgoing for her! She was in touch *personally* with the old gods of Finland. She, and no-one else but her, was entrusted with your safekeeping when it came to the arrangements made over here. That must have given her a sense of immense validation, of being extra special. No wonder she was hacked off when you told her I had a right to make a comment too, Tapio. I'd just unwittingly stamped all over her toes!"

Tapio visibly winced. "We never intended it to be like that."

"No, I'm sure you didn't! But it certainly explains some of the mess we've got here. And what about this thing with Koschei? Does that explain what happened for you?"

Tapio's face assumed the incongruous adult expression Bill was finally getting use to. "In a way. Tove, please don't blame yourself. Your act alone did not bring this on."

"That's a relief!" Bill said, giving Tove an encouraging squeeze from where he'd been standing behind her with a supporting hand on her shoulder. "But has it played a part?"

"Only in as much as we were mystified as to how the men Koschei sent could know where my physical presence was. And clearly they knew very specifically where I was! If we thought anything of that, it was the fear that they may have tortured some local people to find out, but we still couldn't understand how they had narrowed it down to even one province, let alone such a small area of forest. I am guardian of all forests in Finland, and they should have been barely able to distinguish me in one place more than another, but now it makes sense."

"I'm so sorry," Tove whispered.

"No," Tapio said firmly, "it is to our discredit that we not only used you badly, but put you in a position to be used by such an evil creature as Koschei. Make no mistake about that, Tove. If he had been content with his lot, or had even chosen to use what power remains to him to treat his own people better, then none of this would have happened. There are still many wandering people in this place you call Russia who look to the old spirits and natural gods such as ourselves. The churches are not everywhere. He has not wholly been driven out of his homeland. But his avarice has made him covet ours – that, and not your grief, is what started all of this."

Chapter 16

Thursday – Friday

For the rest of the day up until dinnertime it was a time for reconciliations and recovery. Tapio disappeared off with Urho for quite a while, and there was the faint, distant sound of the chants going on again, but Bill, Annikki and Tove left them to it. Whoever they were communicating with, it was best to leave them alone. There was no attack going on this time, and they didn't seem to need any help. However, Bill backed Annikki up in telling Tove that she had to tell the rest of the family what had been going on.

"Mum and Uncle Matti deserve to know," Annikki said firmly. "And I think that my grandfather should be made to explain himself too! I can't believe that he thought it was okay for Mummo to keep on bullying you like that!"

"And I wouldn't go too easy on him, either," Bill said firmly. "This wasn't an isolated incident, just a one-off. Over the years he had to know what was going on."

"Oh, he knew," Tove admitted, "but he's a weak man, always has been."

"That's no excuse," Bill insisted. "He may have been keeping quiet for his own reasons. I'm not implying anything incestuous," he hurriedly added, seeing Annikki's eyebrows shoot up and a worried look Tove's way, "but sharing Karita with someone might have been better than being stuck with her on his own, do you see? He may have fallen head over heels in love with the exotic wild thing when he was young and in his twenties, and then tripping off his head with acid as a Sixties hippy. But as the years have gone by, reality has kicked in, and the idea of old age with a selfish harridan might not be looking quite so appealing. Keeping at least one child at home to distract her might have seemed a very good idea in his shoes."

"Then he has a choice," Annikki declared resolutely. "He can leave her and come and stay with the rest of the family, or he sticks by her and puts up with her, and never sees us again. It's that simple!"

After dinner, Bill did his intercessor bit again on the phone to Annikki's family, then gratefully retreated to the garden for a walk as the emotional phone call continued without him. He was happily enjoying the peace and quiet when he heard a car coming down the road, and then slow down as if to turn into the drive. Moments later, Morag's beat up old motor appeared, with Morag waving cheerily out of the wound-down window.

"Bloody hell, am I glad to see you!" Bill said with feeling as he ambled over to meet her.

"Rough day?" Morag asked, peeling herself out of the car and leaving the windows open as a concession to the unexpected burst of summer which had turned up that morning.

"Give me a bunch of foul-mouthed old alkies any day over a family working out their problems," Bill snorted. "Come on, let's go and sit down over on the bench by the kitchen garden. I wouldn't go in the house if I was you – Tapio and Urho are chanting up a storm upstairs, and Annikki and Tove are bawling their eyes out over the phone to Finland downstairs."

"Jeez! You do live an exotic life!" Morag teased. "But funny you should say the house ...I've got something for you!"

"About the house?"

"Yep! Went digging in my lunch-hour, and found all of this," and she brandished the sheaf of papers she was still clutching in one hand.

"Morag, you little star! Come on, then, what have you found?"

She grinned smugly. "Well for a start off, if all this ancient gods bollocks is true, no wonder he feels safe here – it's sanctified ground."

"It's *what?*"

"It's sanctified ground – or at least it was for a time."

"Well I'll be buggered!"

Morag wagged a mischievous finger. "Be careful what you wish for young William, I know a few nice young men who would love to do the honours with a big bear like you!"

"Oh please, not you as well! I've had enough of the bear thing for one lifetime."

"Aaah, is Tapio still on that one?"

"'Fraid so. Apparently it's all karma, or whatever the Finnish version of that is, that I happened to cross his path." And Bill shook his head wearily, rubbing tired eyes and then leaning back on the bench with a grunt.

"Poor you," Morag sympathised. "Well let's see if I can cheer you up a bit with this lot. I went and had a chat with a mate of mine who's a real computer wiz', and he managed to go back through the letting agent's old online files. He printed this off for me, which is the original bumf which got sent out."

She handed Bill the print out and he looked with increasing curiosity at it.

"Land once owned by the Priory, eh?" he said, looking up at her. "Now that's interesting.

"Isn't it! So I took an extra hour of my flexi-time and went to have a word with your old mate, Nick Robbins. A bit of digging later in the central archive and he found these old maps. ...See? The reason why this lawn is circular is because it's the perimeter of the old graveyard, or what was intended to be. Of course there are no graves here now anyway, but the chapel which was on this site never got upgraded to the point where burials were allowed here. They all went to the Priory, because there was money to be made out of burying folks – not much different to now, if you ask me! So this place was only ever a place of worship, and not for very long either, only for about a hundred years back in the late middle ages.

"Its end came with the Dissolution of the Monasteries. It had apparently only been tottering on with a couple of brothers from the Priory, anyway, and so it got sold off to be a house. Well the first house wasn't this one. That was this farm that you can see on the second map."

Bill peered at it. "Hmm, well that explains why there are no yew trees around it."

"Really?"

"Oh yes. Yews can live for thousands of years, apparently, but the berries are very poisonous to animals. So if this was a farm for a while, then any yews the monks had planted would've had to go. And you say this isn't the original house?"

"No. The old farm got a bit dilapidated and eventually got sold off when Malvern started to become a fashionable spa town. The bloke who bought it, though, was really into all the old religious stuff. Nick found me this old newspaper cutting from the *Berrow's Journal* of the day..."

Bill took it and began reading,

> Mr Simeon Thwait has, we understand, taken over the old house known as Chapel Farm, to the great relief of local residents. He tells us that he will begin immediately removing the timber buildings which are the source of such a nuisance to other locals on account of the rats therein. His neighbour, Mr Walter

Gittins, farmer, said when asked, "We shall be glad to see the back of that place. It has been an eyesore and a threat to the health of local folk for far too long." Mr Gittins said he had lost lambs to the rats this spring, and would have demanded payment for them had there been anyone at the farm. The last owner died over a year ago and no relatives have been found, therefore Messrs Chambers, Arbuthnott and Short, solicitors for the deceased, have arranged for its sale.

We are given to understand that Mr Thwait intends to use the remaining stonework from the ancient chapel found within the farmyard, and proposes to build a suitable gentleman's residence. He is an expert on the ancient churches of this shire, and has expressed a desire to get the ground re-sanctified. It is his intent to hold occasional services in what will be the hall of the new house, and his generous bequests to the Priory Church will, we believe, mean that his requests for someone to officiate will be met with approval.

Mr Thwait said that several window frames which remain within the ruined old chapel would be used in the house. "I believe them to be very fine specimens," he told us, "and will add much to the character of the house when it is complete." It is believed that the house will be constructed in the latest baronial style seen elsewhere in the county and will add much to the ornamentation of our lovely countryside.

"Blimey," Bill muttered, "I wonder how much he paid them to have that printed? It's laying it on a bit thick, don't you think? Anyone would thing he was building a stately home here, not just some nice gent's house."

"That's pretty much what Nick's reaction was," Morag admitted. "But I'd told him roughly why I wanted to know – told him there was a kid involved with some bunch of nutters who thought the house had some significance as a sanctuary – and he said that back when it was first built as a chapel, that's what it would have been. People in those days who had been wrongly accused, and stuff, could claim sanctuary within the Church – not permanently, mind you, but for long enough to clear their names. And even though this was just a little off-shoot, so to speak, it would still have had that element about it."

"Now that is interesting," Bill said admiringly. "Thanks for that Mog'!"

The use of her old nickname made Morag remember yet again why she had loved working with Bill. He always gave credit where it was due, and she knew that if ever this information became relevant to the greater police enquiry, that Bill wouldn't hesitate to give her praise to their superiors. If she could have worked with more men like Bill she'd have been happy to stay on the operational side of things.

Now, though, Bill was looking again with interest at the old maps.

"The boundaries haven't changed much over the years, have they? And I think that's interesting. If the farm had expanded at some point, you'd have expected them to increase the land around the house with cattle pens and the like."

"Maybe it was never much of a prospect as a farm?"

"Maybe. ...But interesting that this land was re-sanctified in the 1820s. Logically you'd thing that if there was anything in that, then it should have repelled Tapio as well as the Russian and his mercenaries."

"Yes, I was thinking that. Odd, isn't it."

Bill scratched his fingers through his hair. "I don't know, Mog', what the hell have I got myself into this time? I mean it's weird – it's beyond weird! But the Finns we've got here, they seem to really believe all this stuff, and try as I might, I can't find it in me to believe that they're stringing me along. I think they genuinely believe all of this stuff and are acting in good faith, no matter how strange it seems to us."

"But the Russians?"

"Oh God, the bloody Russians! Yes, well, they seem to be on a totally different planet! Quite how someone, or something, like Koschei got ex-members of the KGB involved I doubt we'll ever find out."

They thought in silence for a while, then Morag said,

"I know this is a bit wild and woolly – but then this whole thing is! But do you think that it's relevant that this ground was sanctified with the intention of becoming a burial ground and then never got used? Do you see what I mean? In a funny way of thinking, it got purified, but then never got polluted with the sins of the dead. Could that be why Tapio finds it so safe?"

Bill puffed his cheeks out with a huge sigh. "Could be. Although I think rather than the paltry sins of a few local yokels, I think he hasn't been repelled by the place because there haven't been generations of Christian priests all doing their stuff." He thought a moment longer, then added, "And I wonder if this place is more about faith than religion?"

"What do you mean? They're the same, aren't they?"

"Not necessarily. I mean, religion is sort of the corporate side of things, isn't it? If you say you're a certain sort of thing such as a Catholic or a Protestant, then you're associating yourself with something which has..." he paused and grimaced, "well a sort of corporate identity. If you're Catholic you by default acknowledge the pope in Rome, for a start, and that he has the right – the God *given* right – to tell you how to run your life. And that you'll have to go to confession, whether you want to or not, or whether you've done anything to warrant confessing – the assumption is that you must be guilty of *something*. I've heard enough lapsed Catholics venting over that one over the years to know that it's a stumbling block for a lot of them.

"But in contrast, if you join one of the non-conformist churches, then they almost look on the pope as the anti-Christ, yet both lots call themselves Christian. And from what I've heard over the years, that's what puts a lot of modern people off going to church. They don't like the 'thou shalt not's, and the fact that so many men in the churches over recent years have been found to be less than good, and they don't like that the different branches of that faith have so many different and conflicting rules and reg's. But it doesn't stop a lot of people saying that they believe generally in the idea of Christ."

Morag wrinkled her nose. "Mmmm, see what you mean. So if this place was set up by some genuinely devout brothers from the Priory, back in the day when it had monks and all that, then there might have been a purity about the place which has never got polluted?"

"That's roughly the idea. So because no-one ever got up in a newer, fancier pulpit, built out of money wrung out of hard-pressed villagers, and started spouting on about the evils of foreign idols, and Babylon, and the like, maybe that's why it doesn't repulse Tapio? You know, quite aside from him being in the body of a child, there is something very naive about him. He was genuinely shocked when we told him of how Karita had used him to keep a hold on Tove. It had never occurred to him that Karita wouldn't tell him the truth. He never thought that even if her devotion to him was genuine, that she might not act with such good faith towards others."

"So maybe there's a ...oh, I don't know ...maybe what you'd call a purity of purpose about him?"

"Possibly. And maybe that's why he was able to call up that storm to repel those mercenaries – because one thing's for sure, *they* weren't of good intent! They came with murder in mind, and probably a good deal more as well!"

"It's a pity we don't have someone who knows about all this church stuff," Morag sighed. "I mean, we're only guessing, aren't we? We could do with someone with 'insider knowledge' to tell us if we're on the right track or barking up the wrong tree altogether."

Bill sat upright. "We do! Or rather I do. Do you remember Alf? The station sergeant back when you very first started with us?"

"Aye, I do! The chap who got called out to that horrific arson case, and was never the same again?"

"That's him. Well I still keep vaguely in touch with him, Christmas cards and the like. I know some of the younger guys scoff at what happened to him, but it was a case of the kind you hope you never get, or at least only one in your career. The only words for the parents of those kids who died are 'pure evil'. And that's what sent Alf searching for something other than a pair of handcuffs and a baton to combat them with. He took early retirement as soon as he could and then went into the Church."

"Isn't he a bit ancient to be getting involved with this sort of thing?"

Bill snorted. "Hell's teeth, Mog', he's only in his mid-sixties! And he's still fit! He helps run a hostel for derelicts and runaways up in Birmingham, so he has to use a bit of muscular Christianity on a fairly regular basis if the druggies get nasty. But we met up for a pint back at Christmas when I went up to do some present shopping, and he was telling me then that he was still surprised at how many people were downright evil. Yet there were others who looked as rough as a bear's arse and were genuinely good people who'd done nothing wrong, other than fall foul of corporate greed and other folks' avarice. I think he'd be an understanding and sympathetic ear to talk this out with."

Morag stayed for long enough to help Bill cook a meal for everyone. Annikki was too wrung out from the phone call to even think about food, but between them, Bill and Morag managed to come up with a decent lasagne, some fresh salad from the garden, and Bill's own bread with garlic butter on it. Fully stuffed and exhausted, everyone then just collapsed on the big sofas in the lounge and listened to soothing music, Morag went home, and Bill got on the phone to Frank Watson.

The DCI readily agreed that Alf was the person to talk to.

"If he can offer any ideas that will help, then I'm all for it," he told Bill, sounding even more harassed than ever.

Consequently, the next morning Bill made sure that everyone was alright to start off with, gave them strict instructions to call for help at even the slightest hint of something wrong, and set out for the city. Morag had said that she would go into work, but take some time owing and be with the others by the afternoon, which comforted Bill. He had no idea how long he might be, and even if he pushed it, he couldn't get back to them in under an hour from where he was going. He'd rung Alf's mobile before setting off and had got the 'phone switched off' automated message, but guessed that Alf might be at a hospital with someone, and therefore he might have to wait.

What he hadn't expected was to get to the hostel and be told cheerily by another of the workers,

"Oh Alf's at a church conference! He's down at Worcester."

Muttering darkly to himself, Bill turned the Mini around and headed back down the M5, stopping only at the Frankley Services to ring Morag and tell her what was happening. Yet even then fate seemed to be conspiring against him. He shot into the car park behind the college and headed for the bishop's palace where the conference was taking place, only to be told,

"Oh we've broken up for lunch and Alf's gone to say hello to his old mates at the station."

Seething, Bill retrieved the car and negotiated the one-way system around town to the central police station. To his relief he saw Alf happily chatting in the main foyer to two older detectives, one of whom was Frank.

"You're a hard man to find!" Bill greeted Alf. "Has Frank told you what we've got going on?"

However, Frank shook his head. "Alf's only just got here. I haven't had chance."

Alf looked quizzically at Bill, who explained,

"We've got a real weird one on our plates, mate. We could do with a bit of spiritual advice."

With as much economy as he could give it, Bill told Alf the gist of the story. He didn't want to say out loud in front of Frank and others the full extent of Tapio's situation, but contented himself with,

"Something about this house which we now know is hallowed ground was enough to put the heebie-jeebies up those villains – combined with Tapio's Finnish folk chants. But I could do with some pointers about what else might help. What can we play on?"

Alf took one look at Bill and gave him a surreptitious wink. He'd obviously caught on to the fact that there was more to it than that, especially given that Bill had been tearing around the Midlands trying to find him.

"Let's go and have lunch," he suggested.

Immediately Frank and the others pleaded heavy workloads and disappeared after much wishing of Alf well, leaving just him and Bill.

"I hear you're supposed to be on sick leave?" Alf said with a grin.

"Oh the ribs are still reminding me of what they went through," Bill sighed, "but this weird case has crept under my skin. Would you settle for fish and chips down by the river so that I can talk freely?"

"Gladly. And if you want, I can cry off from this afternoon's sessions. I wasn't looking forward to them, anyway. Some academic social worker from the archdiocesan office is supposed to be giving us the chat on faith as a support for those in trouble."

"Phffa! That's teaching your granny to suck eggs!" Bill sniffed. "Rather insulting really for someone like you."

"For all of us," Alf agreed. "No-one on this course is sitting behind a desk, we're all hands-on people. And we all work in multi-faith situations. Stuffing a bible in someone's face is never going to work. My best mate at the shelter is a Sikh, and the cook on most nights is a Chinese Buddhist, and we all rub along with a common purpose, where helping those poor souls in any way we can is the most important thing."

"I'm glad you said about the multi-faith thing," Bill said, steering him along the shortcut past what had been the old hospital up until a few years ago, and was now student flats. Mercifully it was deserted at this time of day except for the odd cyclist whizzing past them, and so Bill said openly, "Insane though this is going to sound, I think I've got a Finnish deity on my hands."

"Blimey, that's a bit exotic!" Alf declared. "Even I've

not had one of those!"

As they walked across the centre of Worcester, heading back towards the cathedral and the river, Bill filled Alf in, pausing only while they got the promised fish and chips. Once they were sat by the river, on a bench that was backed by the high wall which held the river back from eroding the bank beneath the cathedral, Bill asked Alf,

"So what do you think, then?"

Alf dunked a chip in the mini pot of ketchup and chomped on it thoughtfully. "I think if this lad has convinced a cynic like you that he's what he is, then that means there's something serious happening here."

"Thank you! I know it sounds bloody ridiculous on the surface of it, but I want this Tapio – whatever he is – to get safely back to Finland without causing a massacre here. And in truth, Alf, I believe him when he says that he never, ever expected to be bringing this trouble on us. I think he's genuine in that. I think he honestly thought that leaving his homeland would ensure that his enemies wouldn't follow him. But now I'm wondering what's going to come next. What else are we going to have to deal with?"

"Understandably!"

"And I think we need to plan *now* what we could do if we get another attack. Because much as Tapio has faith in that house holding his defences, I reckon this Russian demon is going to come armed and dangerous the next time. And I don't necessarily think it's going to be with guns. He's found out that they don't necessarily work, so he might come with something more... arcane?"

Alf nodded sympathetically. "That was what set me on this course. I came up against something which defied all normal courses of action." He looked around him. "You know, I know this probably sounds a bit trite, but you could claim sanctuary at the cathedral."

"Really? How is that better than where we are?"

"Well for a start off, Worcester Cathedral is old – very, very old! And in your shoes I'd be heading for the crypt."

"Isn't that ...erm, inviting the 'nasties'? Aren't crypts a bit dodgy?"

Alf brandished an admonishing chip. "You've been watching too many Hammer horrors! No, this crypt isn't one of those creepy burial places. We're talking about a lower area which is still used for services. Yes, it has burials in it, but mostly of those are men who gave their lives to the service of God long ago, and anyway, not many of those remain these days. But what I was thinking of is that the crypt is the truly ancient part of the cathedral. It's well over a thousand years old, Bill, and that makes it a very sacred space indeed. It's remained undisturbed in the sacred sense for an incredibly long time, because it goes back to before the Conquest in 1066 and to the time of the Anglo-Saxon bishops of Worcester, and if what you're telling me is right, then that makes it old enough to be giving these ancient demons a run for their money."

"Well, well, I never knew that," Bill mused.

"And for what it's worth, the copper in me is saying that it's easily defended too. There's only one way in. No-one can creep up behind you – or rather down behind you – and surprise you. And if you sprinkle some holy water at the top of the stairs leading down to it, then I think that might act as a very effective barrier."

"So where do I get this holy water from?"

"Well essentially it's water with some of the oil used for baptisms in it which has been blessed. I can do that for you. But I might ask a couple of the others at the conference to join me in saying a few prayers over it – strength in numbers, and all that. Let's allow them get to the tea break and then we'll go and nab them. By then they'll probably be glad of an excuse to get out of there!"

Chapter 17

Tuesday – Friday

Meanwhile, Karl Törni's stay in the cells over Tuesday night had done nothing to change his feelings. He had answered all of the detective's questions and had been released just in time to hear someone whom he guessed must be another policeman (although he was in civilian clothing, and with his one arm in a cast) asking,

"Is Bill back on duty yet?"

"No," another one replied, as the duty sergeant was returning Karl's possessions to him. "Officially he's on leave for another week or so after his sick note runs out, but he's got himself mixed up in this mess over at Old Court House."

"What, that kid abduction thing?" asked Clive from Traffic, having popped in to enquire about Bill to relieve the boredom of his own sick leave. "Shit, that sounded nasty! How did he get caught up in that?"

"Him and Morag were the ones who saw and stopped the first abduction attempt," he was told. "So now Bill's unofficially over at Castlemorton Common babysitting."

Clive whistled. "Never knew Castlemorton to be such a hotbed of activity – not since the unofficial rave there a few years back, anyway."

"Your mate Charlie got involved in a chase across the common last night," Karl just about heard someone else say, as the men moved further away. "That bloody nutcase over there thought he was in some Finnish rally. Still he won't be chasing them up Midsummer Hill now – he's got no car and no license!"

However, to Karl this was all still music to his ears. He had two place names now – Castlemorton and Midsummer Hill – and England wasn't such a big place to search surely? Being the rally driver that he was, Karl's first thought was to go and get a map. Therefore he asked the way to the Tourist Information office, and once there worked his charm for all he was worth on the middle-aged lady there. Perhaps she didn't get that many flatterers in there, because Karl couldn't believe how helpful she was, unaware of the fact that Hiisi was still riding along inside him, and making Karl's body give off pheromones for all it was worth.

Later in the day the woman would be telling her friends about the incredibly sexy Finn she'd had in, saying,

"He wasn't much to look at, but *phwar*! There was something about him!"

By that time, though, Karl was far away. He'd found a camping shop and picked up a sleeping bag and a rucksack, and had then headed for the bus station. A bit of puzzling over the bus routes and he'd managed to get on the main bus to Malvern, and had arrived in the centre of the small town by lunchtime. A quick trip to the nearest supermarket had stocked him up with food and drink for a couple of days, and with that he had set off. Map in hand, he had walked down the chain of hills until he could look down on Castlemorton Common.

At that point he had decided to stop and camp for the night, finding a spot in what seemed to be a long-disused quarry. He then spent Wednesday walking around the area, desperately trying to work out where this house was that his ex-wife had gone to, and without success. However, late on on Thursday he hit gold. By now he had taken to tramping across fields to look at any small blob on the map which might be a house, and it was as he was passing a coppice of oaks that he suddenly heard voices.

Stopping dead still he listened hard. He knew that

voice! That was the bastard who had made him crash the hire car!

With infinite care, Karl now slunk towards the voices, carefully avoiding the large and well-tended vegetable patch which lay open to the view across the fields. One footprint in that well-hoed soil would stand out a mile. Instead, he went around its perimeter on his hands and knees, only peering up every so often to make sure he hadn't been spotted.

At the point where he was in line with the archway in the hedge that separated a formal garden from the plot, he was able to look straight through it. There was the big grumpy cop with a woman, deep in conversation, and behind them was a house. The house! It had to be!

Almost weeping with relief, Karl continued on his crawl until he was well around the copse enough to be sure of not being seen, then sat down and took a swig from the bottle of cheap whisky he had bought. He'd been very careful with that, only buying a half-bottle and only allowing himself one swig at night, but this, he felt, called for a celebration. He had found Tove!

When his heartbeat had returned to something like normal, he got up, intending to start creeping through the woods towards the house. And that was when he saw it. Had he come from any other direction he probably wouldn't have, because the gun was wedged into a clump of brambles. The thorny tangle had wound itself around and through the simple wire fence which encircled the wood, but also disguised the fact that just along this stretch it was covering a small dip which might once have been part of a ditch.

What Karl now saw, and what had made the police miss the gun, was that someone in their haste to escape must have flung the pistol backwards into the tangle with an upward flick. It was up and under a particularly dense mass of spiny tendrils, and it had only been the lowering sun glinting on a tiny patch of the metal which had made Karl look twice. Pulling his jacket sleeve down over his hand, he carefully reached in, but still got scratched to pieces. And getting the gun out was no easy matter either.

Yet when he did, to his relief the gun was dry. Had it dropped just an inch or two lower it would have been in water. With great care he opened it up and saw that it was still fully loaded, and not a shot fired. What he couldn't know was that the man who had dropped it had been flung off his feet with such force as to not have time to get off a shot even with the gun he'd had in his hand, much less this pistol, which had been in the pocket of his long coat. It had been the spin on the former KGB man's body, as it had been rotated into the air and despatched to his death, which had shoved the pistol with such force into the brambles. But Karl didn't know that, and wouldn't have cared much either. All he knew was that he now had the means to make his wife, and that witch of a mother of hers, take proper notice of him.

Feeling happier than he had for a very long time, Karl camped out in the wood that night. It was a major frustration to find that the big cop seemed to be sleeping over at the house. Of all of them, he would be the one least intimidated by the gun. But then to Karl's joy, the cop came out in the morning, and he overheard Bill calling back at the house,

"Remember, keep the doors locked at all times until I get back! Don't open them to anyone unless you know them! I'll be back later."

So the cop was going away! Wonderful! And it seemed like he might be gone for a while, not just down to the nearest shops or the like.

Even so, Karl gave the family time to get up and about. He wanted to see just how many people were in the house before he attacked. So he saw Tove and Annikki, and assumed that Karita must be somewhere about. Urho came out and went with a pile of gardening tools to the vegetable garden, and Karl was pretty sure he would be there up until lunchtime at the earliest.

But what he hadn't expected to see was the boy. Somehow he'd never really asked himself why Annikki might be in England, and even when Hiisi had pushed the thought of 'find Tapio' into his head, he had never made a direct link with his dead son. After all, he had met many Tapios over the years. It was a common enough name in Finland. And so if he had thought anything of the name, it was that he must be Annikki's boyfriend or boss.

To see a child standing in front of the long French windows in the lounge who was the double of his late son was a shock of such magnitude as to paralyse him. She'd lied to him! The bitch had lied! Or was she so under the spell of her awful mother that she'd done as she was told? Whichever it was, Karl could feel a burning fury stirring up in his soul. After all they'd put him through, after all the heartache and misery, there was his son undoubtedly alive and well. Just at this moment he didn't care how they'd pulled this subterfuge off, nor was he rational enough to consider the apparent age discrepancy, he was just incandescently angry at being used.

He checked that the safety catch was on on the gun – he didn't want to use it unless it was truly necessary. Nothing would be worse than inadvertently shooting his son having found him again. Then, and with great care, he began working his way around to a spot where he could approach the house without being seen from any of the downstairs windows.

A short dash across the open lawn and part of the drive, and he was up against the house wall. So far so good! No cries of shock as yet.

L. J. Hutton

Carefully he began slinking along the wall, heading for those inviting French windows. By the time he got there, having had to duck under a smaller side window into the lounge, to his frustration he discovered that his son was gone. Luckily no-one else had come into the room, though, and that made him decide that he would get into the house this way anyway. That big oak front door looked too easy to shut in his face, and he couldn't guarantee who would answer it.

He took a breath and stepped out to cross in front of the first door and grasped its handle, but it resisted turning. He tried the other door's handle and found that that too wouldn't budge. Clearly both were locked, but a squint sideways showed that the key was still in the lock. Still too angry to worry about what laws he was breaking, Karl turned the gun in his hand and used the butt to break the small pane of glass closest to the lock. It must have been fairly old and brittle glass because it broke easily. A couple of additional clips with the sturdy gun-grip and he had removed any large splinters which might open a vein if he caught his wrist on them, and reaching in, he turned the key.

The handles now turned and the one door opened easily. Karl slipped inside and closed the door behind him, not wanting to leave an obvious sign to the giant Finn in the vegetable garden that the house had been breached. Luckily, the door from the lounge into the hall was shut, so no-one had heard him breaking the glass. However, it also meant that he couldn't peer through any gaps to see who was in the hall beyond.

Moving to right by the hinge end of the door, he pressed his ear to it, hoping to hear if anyone was in the hall. Either the door was so thick that it muffled everything, or there was no-one there. There was nothing for it, he would just have to take a chance.

Taking a firm grip on the pistol, Karl wiped his sweating palm on his grubby jeans and took hold of the doorknob. With care he twisted it, grateful that it turned easily without any noise, then eased the door towards him. Again the hinges had been well kept and it opened a crack without any effort or noise. There was no-one in the hall unless they were behind him at the front door, and he didn't think there was anyone there.

He slipped out into the hall and paused. Now he could hear voices, but only two. Stepping softly up to the door he realised that this one must lead into the kitchen, going by the enticing smells escaping from it as preparations for lunch got underway. One voice was female but not Tove's, and the other the higher, lighter voice of a child.

Emboldened, Karl flung the door open and brandished the pistol.

"Papa has come to take you home," he announced firmly, as Tapio turned to face him when he saw Annikki's eyes fly wide in horror.

"Karl, put that down!" she screamed. "What are you thinking?"

"I've come to take my son," he snarled. "Or did you think you could fool me forever?"

"He's not our son," Tove's voice came from behind him, making him fling himself hard against the door to prevent her from being at his back. He didn't trust her not to smack him over the head with one of the big vases he'd seen on the two hall tables.

"Oh don't try to play me for a fool!" he snapped. "The time for that is long past, Tove. And where's that witch of a mother of yours?"

"In Finland, at home," she replied wearily.

"No she's not!" he contradicted her. "I saw the two of you arriving together. So she's here! Where is she?"

Annikki had taken a couple of tentative steps forward,

and was now holding out her hand for the gun. "She went home, Karl. She really isn't here. I can understand how angry you must be over how she treated you, but Tove is telling you the truth – she isn't here. And for pity's sake put that thing down before you kill one of us!"

"I'm not the one killing *anyone*!" Karl shouted back at her, his face showing his anger rising again. "Tapio, come to me! Come to Papa!"

"No." Tapio said calmly. "I am not your son."

"Oh my boy, what have they done to you? Don't you worry! Papa is going to make it all alright."

"Mr Törni, I am not your son," Tapio said more firmly. "I know I look like him, but I am not him. Your son died just as Tove told you he did. And just because she's been trying to help me doesn't mean that she's my mother. She's here to help Annikki, not me."

"You absolute bitch!" Karl fumed, so angry now that he was starting to froth at the mouth. "So now you even deny your own son? I should never have married you! You and those parents of yours ...you're all unnatural! My poor Tapio never stood a chance with you lot around him! And I blame myself for not seeing it at the time. I should have taken him away when he first fell ill! You were poisoning him, weren't you? You and that witch Karita! She couldn't face anyone taking your attention away from her, and you were too weak to resist her! Tapio, come here!"

Yet as Tapio once again said, "No!" very firmly, the back door opened and framed Urho's huge figure.

"What's wrong?" he asked, "I heard shou..."

He never got to finish his words. Karl's finger took the safety catch off and the gun barked. One shot would have injured even a man as big as Urho, but this was a semi-automatic and it loosed off several. Worse, Karl's aim was not good, and although he had intend it to be a heart-shot, the spray started off low, put two bullets into Urho's stomach and then two more into his chest before the final one to hit him took him in the shoulder.

Both women screamed in terror and Tapio shrieked, "What have you done?" as Karl reached out to grab at him.

As Urho was thrown backwards by the force of the shots at such close range, Annikki ran to him, while Tove began grappling with Karl, but was hampered by the fact that he had already turned towards Tapio, leaving her only his back to pound at. She had nothing but his jacket to try to catch hold of and her finger kept slipping off the leather.

"You've let him in!" Tapio screamed in fury at Karl, as the demon Hiisi finally made his presence felt. "You've broken the barrier!"

As Karl tried to make another grab at his son, he felt as if something was tearing inside of him, then was even more shocked to see something apparition-like seeping out of Tapio. The two spectral beings rose out of their respective hosts and began wrestling with one another in the confines of the kitchen, causing havoc. China was thrown from the dresser, and burn marks were scorched into the ceiling and exposed walls. But Hiisi had not expected his old adversary to be so strong. The last time he had felt Tapio, Lord of the Forest, he had been crippled and weak. Now he was almost restored to his old self and as such Hiisi was no match for him. In a swirl of smoke, the forest demon was subdued and flung homewards, completely disembodied, and now little more than a wisp upon the wind.

But this had not happened instantly. While the two fought, Annikki had pulled out her mobile phone, hitting the three keys to summon the emergency services.

"Ambulance! Police!" she howled into it. "My friend's been shot! I think he's dead!"

As the dispatcher summoned all those needed, and the ambulances set out with both the ordinary police and the armed response unit, Annikki sat on the cold back step with Urko's head in her lap and wept. Tove in the meantime was flying at Karl like a woman possessed, slapping and clawing at him, the gun having kicked itself out of his hand and skittered under the kitchen table. And Karl, never having seen her like this before, was barely able to fend her off, let alone strike back. His anger had evaporated as Hiisi had left him, and with him some of the energy which had been keeping Karl going these last few days, leaving him drained and suddenly scared.

Similarly, the body of Tapio had fallen to the ground as the forest lord left him, and only when Hiisi had been fended off did the spirit of Tapio try to re-inhabit him. But it was not so easy. The aura of Tapio surrounded the boy's body, and had anyone been watching, the nearest any of them could have given as an analogy was of a large genie trying to get into a small bottle. Yet Tapio managed to get enough control of the small body back to get the blood pumping through its veins again and the heart beat to something like stable. What he couldn't do was bring the boy's body back to wakefulness again.

Only when Tove's hand had connected with the large stone pot of salt on the dresser, and she whacked Karl over the head with it, sending him into limp unconsciousness, did anyone look at Tapio. At that point her mother's instinct kicked in, and Tove tottered to him and swept the small body into her arms to sob uncontrollably over him. And that was how the emergency services found them.

Russia

Far way, Koschei became aware of the sudden eruption of energy as Tapio and Hiisi fought. He sent a thread of energy their way and was appalled at what he felt. Where had Tapio's newfound strength come from? This was not supposed to happen!

He watched with an almost morbid fascination as Hiisi was defeated and sent flying back in tatters to his homeland. And what of the creature he had sent to find the body Tapio was hiding in? Koschei searched and felt the inert nature of the body of the boy and Tapio trying to return to it, and then a faint hint of something – not exactly a scent but the supernatural equivalent of it – alerted him to Karl, lying unconscious on the floor.

Well that was no use! That wasn't how it was supposed to turn out at all! Koschei ground his metaphysical teeth in rage. Did he have to do everything himself? What was the point of being a higher demon if you had to sully your disembodied fingers with all the mundane filth? Clearly he had been misled by Hiisi's overinflated opinion of himself to think that he could deal with Tapio. He would just have to get involved. And so as the emergency services swarmed into the kitchen, men in black Kevlar body armour entering first and sweeping the kitchen with their high-powered guns, Koschei stuffed a tendril of himself into Karl.

As the leader of the team called the ambulance crew forward to try and revive Urho, another of the team retrieved and secured the pistol which Karl had used. Therefore Koschei could see that there was no point in trying to get to that. It was too far away, and by the time he had revived Karl he would be too slow. But the nearest cop in the room had a gun.

In fairness to the cop concerned, Karl himself was so clearly out cold that he was deemed to be no threat. There wasn't even a flicker of eyelids to hint that he might be coming round, and there was a fair bit of blood leaking from the split scalp where Tove had hit him. So once he had been cuffed by one hand to the curved leg of the huge kitchen table, Karl was considered to be a suspect but not dangerous.

What no-one expected was for him to rear up, still glassy-eyed and barely focusing, and try to make a grab for the policeman's gun. Luckily one of his colleagues was sharp-eyed and spotted the movement. His called warning alerted the man Karl was aiming for, and as he stepped back, the other put two bullets into Karl.

As the lead ripped through Karl's body, Koschei gave a scream of frustration and ripped himself free. What was it with these cursed humans? Why the obsession with toxic metals? And to feel it tearing through flesh like that towards the centre of Karl where he lay was unbearable. Only by fractions of a second was he able to remove himself in time to avoid contact with the metal.

As the police frantically swept the room, wondering where that unearthly yowl had come from, Koschei pulled himself in to within Russian borders and licked his wounded pride. There was nothing for it, he would have to project himself to England and deal with Tapio personally. It would take all of his strength, but the one consolation was that he had felt how much energy Tapio had expended in getting rid of Hiisi. The Finnish forest lord was not yet so healed that the encounter had not drained some of his precious energy away from him. He was still weaker than of old, although still far stronger than Koschei liked. But if Koschei struck now, there was still a good chance that Tapio would never return to Finland.

And the stakes were high. Koschei made no mistake about that. It was the key to his very survival. Get the Finnish trees and the heartland of millennia of ancient forests beneath it to harvest, and he would reign supreme for a few thousand years more. But fail, and his own existence became precarious at best. At worst he would fade from memory altogether and dissipate on the wind.

So Koschei spent a night appearing to the more susceptible folk in the dark places of St Petersburg, harvesting the energy he got from their fear and then blind panic at seeing what they had thought was no more – an ancient demon – and finally taking their life forces. He fed and he stoked his reserves, until he was sure he would have sufficient to go and come back. Then with the dawn, he drew all of his energy into himself and launched himself westwards. He would have his serfs! He would have worshippers! He would have the Finns! Tapio must die with the child he inhabited!

Chapter 18

Friday

The first Bill knew of the chaos at the house was the urgent call on his mobile just as he and Alf got back to the Bishop's Palace. As Bill was gasping "Oh God"s and "Bloody hell"s into his phone, Alf still had enough about him to know that things had got suddenly worse. Towing Bill towards a door, he left him on the phone and ran to the room where the meeting was taking place.

"Phil! Mick! I need your help right now!" he yelled into the room and ran back to Bill before the stunned course coordinator could object.

As Bill turned to him saying, "I have to go..." Alf waved him to silence.

"No! Not this very instant! Take a moment to get better prepared." At that point the two vicars he had summoned appeared. "We need holy water – lots of it!" Alf told them bluntly, and gestured to the cathedral, whose spires towered over them from beyond the ground's walls.

As the four of them turned to run towards it, a bright red car shot into the car park with Clive at the wheel, sling hanging disregarded around his neck.

"Get in!" he called.

Clive loved the big BMW he drove professionally, but his own choice of car was a top of the range Subaru Forester. Now it took the three priests in the back and Bill in the front with ease, before Clive skilfully manhandled it out into the traffic despite his injured arm, and round the short loop to the cathedral close. He and Bill sat in the car while Alf disappeared with his friends, and Bill brought Clive up to date.

"So Alf's gone for what?" Clive asked again, not sure that he was hearing right. If this had been someone other than Bill he would have been thinking this was some elaborate prank, although the way Frank Watson had gone white when the news came in of the shooting also told against it being that.

"Holy Water," Bill said with a sigh. "I asked him for help, and that's what he came up with. Not sure it'll do much, myself, but at the moment I'm out of sane options."

Moments later the back door opened and Alf piled in. "Drive!" he said.

"What? You're coming with us?" Bill was taken aback.

"You bet I am," Alf told him, looking very serious when Bill twisted in his seat to look back at him. "Now tell me, what was that phone call all about?"

Bill could feel the inner wobble starting up all over again. "Urho's dead," he told Alf, aware that for all that he'd had very little to do with the huge Finn, that he felt a terrible grief at his passing. "That stupid fuckwit, Karl, somehow got his hands on a gun! Christ knows how! And whatever it was loaded with, it ripped poor Urho apart. Five shots apparently, but the kind of ammo' that fragments rather than going clean through. Not that he'd have survived even clean shots. Two in the gut, one in the heart, one in the lungs, and the last one in his shoulder hit a major vein. I was told whoever does the post-mortem will be fishing through mincemeat to find anything."

He was suddenly angry. "Fuck it! The poor bastard only came over here out of loyalty! He was so lonely over here. No mates, no family, couldn't speak the language. He came because he thought he couldn't say no to Tapio. He certainly never deserved this!"

"That's cruel," Alf agreed. "What about the others?"

"Annikki and Tove are in Worcester Royal being treated for shock. No surprise there! One's just seen her friend cut down in cold blood by her uncle; and the other watched her husband do it, then was just leaving the room when he tried to make a grab for one of the armed response unit's guns and got shot by them. They'll need some serious counselling to get over that, I reckon. Karl's dead – no great loss there. And Tapio's in a coma. Why, no-one's said. I don't know if he's been hurt, or if he just collapsed, or if something weird kicked off."

"Definitely a good thing we have this then," Alf said, patting the large steel flask he was holding onto tightly, and which Bill guessed had previously held nothing stronger than tea or coffee. "Best go in prepared."

Clive slid to a halt outside the hospital's main entrance and let Bill and Alf get out.

"Good luck! Sounds like you're going to need it," he told them, and pulled away out of the way of a community ambulance bringing patients in for day care.

Bill and Alf hurried through the double set of glass doors and headed for the enquiries desk. Bill's warrant card soon got him the answers he wanted, and he and Alf hurried along corridors and up stairs until they got to the first ward they were seeking. The hospital was clearly having a busy time, because Annikki and Tove were on trolley beds outside the ward, but both were sedated and sleeping, their breathing easy and relaxed.

Alf took the precaution of saying a few prayers over them and anointing both of them with some of the precious water, but declared that he thought both of them were suffering from nothing more suspicious than normal shock.

"The doctors and nurses can do more for them than you or I can at the moment," he consoled Bill. "Come on, let's leave them to sleep. We can call on them later at visiting time."

They now went to the ward where Tapio was. This time it was harder to get to see him, but Bill was vehement in his need to see the boy, and given that Tapio was neither in surgery nor about to undergo it, they were let into the ward. A detective whom Bill knew was sitting on a chair by the side ward door, giving Bill some relief to know that the threat was finally being taken seriously.

"Tommy," Bill greeted him, shaking his hand. "You remember Alf, don't you?"

DC Tommy Chandler gave Alf a smile and a handshake. "You involved as well?" he asked incredulously. "I thought you went into the Church?"

"I did and I am," Alf told him, stern-faced. "This is getting nasty, Tommy, very nasty, and I'm here to give whatever help I can."

"I need to see the boy," Bill told Tommy.

"Yeah, I can understand that. Word is, you've been giving him unofficial protection," Tommy replied with a questioning look. "How come? How unofficial is 'unofficial'?"

"With Superintendant William's blessing and instruction!" Bill snapped, wiping the supercilious smirk off Tommy's face. Everyone knew he was trying too hard to move up the tree since he'd done a stint as acting-DS, and Bill had no doubt that there was a part of the DC's brain that was thinking that if Bill got kicked out for misconduct, everyone would move up a rank to fill the gap. "Now I'm going through that fucking door whether you like it or not!"

"Okay, okay, keep your hair on!" Tommy muttered, moving out of the way.

Bill and Alf went in, and Bill made a point of closing the door firmly in Tommy's curious face.

"What's up with him?" Alf asked softly.

"Too much ego," Bill grunted. "I don't know, maybe it's because he's shorter than most of the blokes and skinny with it, but he's definitely got a nasty combination of a chip on both shoulders coupled with a certainty that he's always in the right, as well. I've been told that when I go back he's coming onto my shift. Apparently I'm supposed to sort him out. I'm his last chance.."

"Ah..." Alf sighed cryptically, knowing instantly that that was why Bill had been so quick to assert his authority, and thinking that if the DC was misguided enough to think of rankling his new boss before he'd even started, that he was in for a very rude awakening. Bill might give the impression of being an amiable softie, but he was no-one's pushover, especially not where work was concerned.

Now, though, Bill was leaning over the small figure swathed in white sheets and saying ever so gently,

"Tapio. Tapio, it's me, Bill. Can you hear me?"

There was a momentary silence and then Alf nearly fainted as a smoky haze began to rise from the boy's body, but never fully leaving it.

"Karhu!" he heard a relieved voice say, although no sound broke the ward's silence. "Blessed be! I am trapped. I cannot fully re-enter Tapio, but I dare not leave him altogether either. Are the others alright? I cannot reach out and feel them. This place ...it inhibits me, it diminishes me. All these machines. They stop me from sensing anything, and what little I do is just a fuzzy noise. There are too many people around. Where am I?"

"You're in a hospital," Bill told him with far more calm than Alf was feeling. So this was the forest lord, was it? Yet Alf had to agree with Bill – he felt no evil here, however far removed this was from his ideas of any deity.

"I'm terribly sorry," Bill was saying to the apparently lifeless body. "I've got some bad news. Urho's been killed."

"Noooooo!" the unearthly wail of grief rattled Alf and had Tommy rushing in, only to have Alf yank him back to the door by a handful of his jacket, even as he recoiled by himself from the writhing smoke above the boy's bed.

"Get outside!" Bill snapped at him, "and if anyone asks what that noise was, it was just a family member in grief."

"Wh... what's that? Wh... what family member?" Tommy stammered.

"Use your head!" Bill growled unsympathetically. "I don't know ...tell 'em Alf's his granddad or something! And you saw nothing! Understand? Nothing! Now get back out on guard!"

As Tommy tottered out, pale and shaking, Bill turned once again to the Tapio apparition. "The good news is that both Annikki and Tove are okay. They're here in the hospital but just being treated for shock. They aren't hurt in any other way. You probably can't feel them because they've both been sedated. It's for their own good, Tapio. They need rest. And they're in the right place to be looked after."

The smoke-like tendrils seemed to stop writhing quite so badly, and the Tapio voice in Alf's head said, "Thank you for that, Karhu. I am much relieved to hear it. But how are we going to get me out of here?"

"I'm not sure that you are," Bill said, knowing that this wasn't what Tapio wanted to hear. "I have no authority to override the doctors when it comes to the wellbeing of Tapio's body, you see. If they want to keep you here, then I can't insist on you being taken back to the house. And in all honesty, I don't think the house is safe anymore, anyway."

"No," Tapio agreed. "I was appalled that Karl should have come in like that! And bringing in the gun of one of my enemies was bad enough. I felt the taint of one of those men the moment he came into the kitchen. But he had

Hiisi inside of him! He brought him right into my sanctuary!"

"Shit!" Bill gasped. "What? Hiisi was inside of Karl like you are in Tapio? Is that possible? I mean, you're inside the shell of a child who died long ago. There's no conflict between you and the personality of the boy he was. But Karl was alive and a grown man! Surely he would have objected to being used by something as evil as Hiisi?"

Alf cleared his throat. "If I might add something here?"

"Oh, by the way, this is my old friend, Alf," Bill introduced him. "He's a priest nowadays, but he has some ideas about how to protect you, and to be fair some of this is more his line of work than mine."

"Hello Alf," Tapio said politely, surprising Alf who'd half expected to be propelled out of the door. "If Karhu says you are to be trusted then you are welcome."

"Karhu?"

"Me," Bill explained. "Apparently it's Finnish for 'bear'."

"Suits you!" Alf chuckled. "Anyway, what I was going to say is this: that sometimes it's easier for evil to take a hold of the weak and those already on the slippery slope of badness. It's easy to promise something you never intend to give if you don't care about the damage it will do. And you can twist your promise until it looks and feels very much like something the person you want to ensnare was wanting anyway. You might have scruples and morals, Tapio, but it sounds to me like your enemies don't."

"No that is true," Tapio conceded. "It would never worry Hiisi, or his like, that they might do irreparable harm to someone in the pursuit of their goals."

Bill nodded. "It's only a rough guess, but given what Alf's just said, I'd say that Hiisi played on Karl's own feelings of wanting Tove, but also wanting revenge on her family. I doubt Karl ever really considered whether he'd done enough looking after their son to give him the right to come back into her life. He seems to me to have been someone who never grew up beyond his teens. That must have made him putty in Hiisi's hands. He was so full of his own wants, and so full of feeling sorry for himself, that he wouldn't have put up much of a fight if those things were played upon.

"So if we take it, then, that however improbably it sounds, Hiisi had no trouble riding in the back of Karl's mind and body, I hate to be the bringer of gloom and all that, but what about Koschei? We don't really believe that he's going to give up just because you've given Hiisi a pasting, do we? And the electronic haze around this place might give him as much trouble as you, but that won't stop him from using another human as his host, will it?"

"Unfortunately it will not," Tapio sighed. "But I cannot tell you how he might attack. All I can say is that Koschei is a very different being to Hiisi. Hiisi is like a spiteful child, but Koschei's attack, when it comes, will be much better thought out. For all that Hiisi's battle with me has been going on for thousands of years longer than this recent conflict with Koschei, he also lacks the application to ever truly win. Koschei, on the other hand, is fighting for his life. If he can take over my lands, with people who have had their beliefs less suppressed, he believes it will give him a new lease of life. I myself do not believe it works like that. My people have ties to me personally, and those ties cannot simply be swopped over, they need to be earned –but Koschei has never grasped that! If he had, he might still have the respect of his own people."

"Then I think we need to be prepared for just about anything," Bill sighed.

Alf stepped up to the bed. "Would you let me try something? I know you are from an ancient belief system,

257

but you're here on our turf now, and a lot of people here and now are Christian, as am I. I've got here what we call Holy Water, and I'd like to bless this space, if I may. It might just be that even though our people don't even know who you are, that simply invoking a sacred space around you will offer you some protection. Will you let me do that?"

Tapio was silent for a moment, then said, "Yes, I can see that it might work. Would you encircle me?"

"That would probably be the most effective course of action," Alf replied.

"Then if we could do it bit by bit, so that if I find it painful you can stop?" Tapio suggested.

Alf nodded. "No problem. In theory I'd make the circle first, but there's no reason why I can't do maybe the first third of a circle, say some prayers and then repeat that if you feel okay."

Just then they heard Tommy's voice starting to argue with someone outside, and Bill turned to see through the glass window of the door that Phil and Mick had turned up. Opening the door, Bill placed a firm hand on Tommy's shoulder, feeling the smaller, slimmer man positively quivering with righteous indignation as he once again snapped,

"No you bloody-well can't go in!"

"It's alright, Tommy, they're friends of Alf's," Bill said firmly. "Come on in, you two, you've arrived just in time. I think your prayers might be a lot more effective than those of an old sceptic like me."

"We got a taxi over," Phil said with a grin. "Makes a change to be doing some frontline stuff!"

"Well hold onto that thought," Bill told them with a wry grin, "because this is going to be a steep learning curve!"

When the two vicars were introduced to Tapio they both went very white. Neither had been remotely prepared to find that they were going to be praying for a spectral being.

"Think of it this way," Alf suggested. "When St Augustine came to convert the English, he had specific instructions to consecrate the worshipping places of the native pagans. That's why so many old churches have springs and natural wells by them, not to mention ancient yew trees! Very pragmatic was Pope Gregory – he knew that the quickest way to bring people into the new churches was to put them over the top of the places where folks were already going to worship. Well our oldest churches are still standing, aren't they? And Canterbury hasn't been struck down, has it? So maybe there's nothing wrong with these ancient forest spirits, or at least that they aren't evil as we would think of it?"

"St Augustine," Mick gulped. "Right!"

"Tapio's done nothing to harm anyone," Bill added. "And if he'd been intending to, don't you think he'd have picked a better body to inhabit than a rather small and under-developed eleven year-old? I mean, you're not going to be carrying out murder and mayhem when you're that size, are you?"

"True," sighed Phil. "Okay, Alf, where are we going to start then?"

"The Lord's Prayer," Alf said with certainty. "Can't beat using a prayer that's been around as long as Christianity in these isles!"

"You have a prayer that's that old?" Tapio asked in surprise.

"Well it certainly goes back a long way," said Alf. "I was told by someone who's a church warden and studying Old English at Birmingham University that there's a version in West Saxon, so that's pre-1066 and by a fair way too. Personally, I reckon that that means it goes way, way back, because it seems to have been around long before it got written down in an age when literacy was in short supply."

Mick and Phil exchanged slightly stunned expressions, then as Alf said, "Are we ready, then?" and made the first sprinkling of the water, they took a deep breath and in unison began,

"Our Father, who art in Heaven..." joined by Alf and Bill.

For an instant there was what seemed like shudder running through the Tapio apparition, but then it settled into a stiller form, subsiding down into the comatose form of the boy.

Having worked his way around the head of the bed, carefully sprinkling the Holy Water around the trailing wires of the monitors which Tapio was hooked up to, and avoiding getting any on the electrically sensitive bits, Alf paused.

"Are you alright, Tapio?"

"Yes," the voice in their heads answered, as if rather more distant. "It feels strange, but not threatening, and I can feel it working even if you can't. Please continue."

Alf gave a quick look to Phil and Mick, who had regained some of their composure once they had got into the prayers Alf was leading them in. Once beyond the Lord's Prayer, Bill had stepped back, but clearly Alf was using old prayers from the liturgy which all three knew by heart.

By the time Alf brought things to a halt, a deep sense of calm had descended on the small sideward.

"Do you know, I think I'll sleep easy tonight for the first time in over a week," Bill said as the four of them left the room. "It's a shame that the only way we can protect Tapio is by putting him in what amounts to a cage, but the fact that he went willingly tells me that it should hold against anything Koschei throws at him."

"But what are you going to do about him?" Alf asked once they were well away from Tommy Chandler's ears. Somehow Alf had the strange feeling that the young DC was not so kindly disposed towards the ethereal being as Bill was.

"Well I know this is going to sound even weirder," Bill said as they traipsed wearily outside and waited for a taxi to take them back into the city, "but that body in there has died once already. And Tapio said that he never expected to be living in it this long. I think I might be suggesting to him that he lets it die for real this time. If he can stay within it, we can arrange for the body to be flown back to Finland and him with it if he can remain anchored inside it. I'm sure that Tove and Annikki will be wanting to go home as soon as possible, so there'd be nothing strange in them wanting to accompany the body home."

"That might be best for everyone," agreed Alf. "Those two women need the love of their family around them, and maybe Tapio would benefit from the support he gets from the native folk who believe in him."

"I suppose I'd better go and speak to Frank," Bill said with a weary groan, "although how on earth I'm going to offer any logical explanation to him, I don't know."

"Then don't," was Alf's advice. "You've done as much as anyone could, Bill, and if any blame is going to get slung around because Urho got killed, then the blame is going to land neatly on the desks of those further up the tree than Frank. He could only work within the budget for manpower he was given, and from what you've said, he's time and again said that he needed more men on this job. As long as that's on record, he's covered, and so are you! Go home and get some sleep. Frank's either already marking time on the Chief Constable's carpet getting the bollocking of a lifetime, or he's gone home and someone else is getting ripped a new arsehole. But either way it's long past the point where anything you say will change things."

"Thanks Alf. Do you lads fancy a pint after all of that?"

"Thought you'd never ask!" said Mick from the heart.

"Right, time for *The Green Dragon*!" Bill decided, naming a favourite pub which would put the priests near to the station when they'd done, all three having travelled in by train.

Full of rage, Koschei arrived in England only to feel the essence of Tapio fading from his senses.

"What's happened?" he raged to himself, questing ever more furiously. Luckily he'd taken a bearing on where he had felt Tapio earlier, and so he got to the Midlands and then was able to refine his search a little more. But just as he got close, the last whiff of Tapio disappeared.

Swirling spectrally around the city of Worcester, the first clue he had that he was in the right place was the sensing of Karl's body lying in the city morgue. That hint of Hiisi could have come from nowhere else, but infuriatingly, it was the very dead body lying in the next container which oozed the only telltale traces of Tapio he could pick up. Urho had been in such close contact with Tapio for so long that he still reeked of the forest lord's presence. Of Tapio himself, though, there was no trace, and Koschei was forced to reconcile himself to tracing him through the humans.

Then he caught the faintest hint of something as Bill left the pub, wished the three priests farewell, and began walking back towards the river. This one had clearly had some contact with Tapio, although whether he would be aware of it Koschei couldn't be sure. He followed Bill as he turned right and walked down to the central police station and went inside.

Koschei had no idea what the police station was, nor did he care, but what he did grasp as he listened in was that the body which Tapio currently inhabited was in somewhere called Worcester Royal. He eavesdropped as Bill and Frank Watson walked out together, both lamenting the short-sightedness of their superiors who had refused to give Frank sufficient manpower to avert the current tragedy. So Tapio was being guarded was he? That he could do something about, but he would need people to break through that warding which the man called Alf had put around the body. Only then would he be able to get at Tapio's true essence.

He let the two men go once he saw them spilt up. They had told him all he needed, and he sensed that both of them were strong-willed enough to resist him taking them over. He needed easier puppets. Then out of the blue he heard familiar voices. Someone was speaking Russian! How had one of his own come to be in this place?

Swooping in on the speakers, Koschei found four Russian men staggering along the riverbank opposite the cathedral, all seriously drunk and looking for somewhere to sleep it off. With malevolent glee, Koschei lurked unseen behind them until they settled, then chose his first target. All four were big adult men, but the oldest one was the weakest character. It took no effort at all to slide into his consciousness. The next one he selected was the youngest, but to his surprise the man fought him off. Clearly being drunk was not sufficient for this one to relax his mental barriers that much. The other two, though, were eventually his, even though it took longer than he would have liked.

As the night wore on, Koschei managed to come up with a plan. Rummaging in their chaotic minds he realised that two of them craved drugs, and that such things existed in this hospital place. They had previously dismissed trying to get the drugs that way as being too complicated, but Koschei could see a way. All he had to do was get them there.

As the summer morning broke even his prodding wasn't going to be sufficient to keep them awake. But when they did eventually surface, grumbling, hawking and spitting into the new day, the resistant one once again came close to wrecking Koschei's plan. He would not head for the hospital, no matter what the others said, and the only way to get the others moving was to start a fight. With all of them still half-drunk (given the amount they had consumed the night before), it was an easy matter for Koschei to orchestrate a foot in the wrong place, a shove from someone else, and then the resistant man was in the river.

As he floundered and then got taken by one of the vicious currents the Severn was famous for, his friends made no attempt to rescue him, but instead turned for the road with the kind of resolute purpose they normally reserved only for the finding of more booze. None of them had a clue about catching a bus to the hospital, and no driver would have let them on, stinking as they did, but they knew enough English to read the road signs for 'A&E', and all of them were used to walking. Having arrived in the country illegally, they had been making ends meet by getting rough work on farms as they moved around the country. Therefore, although the slowness of their progress was enough to make Koschei wish that there was some demonic equivalent of alcohol to soothe his ire, he managed at least to keep their cravings suppressed enough to keep them moving in the right direction.

By the time they got to the right place, Koschei was annoyed to find that there were more of these police about the place, and his new hosts were sure of one thing more than any other – they did not want to cross these men. That would mean getting locked up, they knew, and the last thing Koschei wanted was for his new instruments of vengeance to be snatched and locked away where he couldn't use them. In their cunning brains, the three knew that it would be better to wait until it was later on. "It's Saturday night," they told him without even knowing it. "Later on the emergency entrance will get busy. No-one will notice us amongst the other drunks." And so Koschei gnawed his metaphysical fingernails and settled down to wait. What did a few hours matter if it meant that he would be able to get inside and finish Tapio off?

Chapter 19

Saturday

With the kind of good fortune which makes people say that the Devil looks after his own, that Saturday afternoon there was a fight of unusual size outside of one of the city pubs, and far earlier than such things usually kicked-off. A bunch of young thugs who had come down from Birmingham had spent the day getting progressively more and more drunk, and now wanted to round off their day at the pub by the station. Understandably, the bar staff had no intention of serving them, and in pique the young men began to pick fights with anyone passing, most of whom were locals just out doing some late shopping. By the time the same lot had tried to get into the cinema opposite and hurt innocents just coming out from a film, it was chaos, and before long there was a fleet of taxi's ferrying people to the A&E with cuts from smashed bottles and other bloody injuries.

Given that the thugs had been lashing out at people with bottles still containing beer and cider, the inside of A&E soon began smelling more like a brewery than a hospital, as drink-sodden people queued up to be attended to. Even the sober ones were reeking of booze, as they dripped it onto the floor from whatever they were wearing. Into this chaos the three Russians came, the permanent stench of alcohol that clung to them going unremarked under the circumstances, and with one of them hanging between the other two, dripping blood from where one of his companions had grabbed a dropped bottle and stabbed him with it. Koschei had no conscience at all about using the men like this. They were nothing but pawns in his greater game – if they died, so what?

"My friend!" one of them called out loudly, gesturing at a nurse.

For a second her eye flitted across them without taking much notice, then shot back to them as she realised just how badly the middle man was bleeding from around the bottle shard wedged into his belly.

"Over here!" she called to her colleagues and hurried forward with a male nurse to take him from them.

Released from their care of him, as the third Russian disappeared in a huddle of nurses, the remaining two slipped away unnoticed, and after a few wrong turns, found their way into the hospital proper. At night the staff would have been more security conscious, but this event had caught everyone on the hop. Therefore, for Koschei the day spent waiting had not been entirely in vain. He had also seen the burly man he had followed the previous night returning to the hospital's main entrance, and, curious as to what he was doing here again, he once again dogged Bill's footsteps. Through the hospital Bill went, the shade of Koschei following unseen although impotent, until he got to the side ward where Tapio lay. At that point Alf's work repelled Koschei, but he saw enough to know that he had at last found Tapio. All he needed now was for his minions to get the body out of the protection of that sacred space around the bed.

Therefore, once Koschei had got his bearings in relationship to the way he had followed Bill in, it was an easy matter for him to direct the two Russian thugs to Tapio's ward. Had Koschei known or cared, the cuts in nursing staff had made his job even easier, for the number of ward nurses was down to the bare minimum with many of them agency nurses who barely knew one another, let alone the patients. No-one remarked on the men's presence on those corridors which the public had access to anyway. They could have been visiting someone and got lost, if they were noticed at all.

The two came up to the ward and peered in. There was a man outside of the room they needed to get into, but first they had another barrier to overcome. The main door to the ward was firmly shut. To the side was a security pad, but neither had the means to get past it. Slinking back into a shadier area, they lurked in wait until a nurse went past, then grabbing her, the one knocked her out with a hefty punch while the other grabbed her pass. Shoving her limp form into a disabled toilet to cover their tracks, they locked the door with the skill of practise at being where they shouldn't.

Armed with the means to get in, they now crept back to their targeted ward and put the pass to the pad. With a click the lock opened, and plunging in, they both hit the constable on duty with force. He never knew what hit him. One minute he was struggling to keep his eyes open with the motoring magazine he was half reading, the next he was on the floor being repeatedly punched about the head by two men who were both far bigger than him.

As he went limp, they grabbed him between them and lugged him into Tapio's room. The unexpected commotion woke the presence of Tapio, but surrounded as he was he could do nothing to protect himself, and before he could act, they had seized the boy's body. One of them bundled him in a blanket and swung him into his arms, while the other one dragged the constable behind the bed to where he wouldn't be seen from the door, then held the door open for his friend as they made a dash from the ward. That was their instinct – to run – and at that point they were without Koschei's direction as he tried time and again to strike at Tapio.

Yet to Koschei's intense frustration, he was still

inhibited from acting as he wanted by the electronics surrounding everything in the hospital. Try as he might, any sort of strike against Tapio's comatose figure seemed to fragment before it could do any real harm, even though he was now beyond the encircled bed. Therefore the only thing to do was to get the body outside. There were some woods just outside the hospital, and if he could get the body into those he could act without being seen. So the two Russians took what Koschei thought was the direct route, and took the lift outside the ward to get them down to the main doors, believing that they could get out that way.

What neither they nor Koschei had realised was that Bill was still in the building. He'd had a nasty itchy feeling somewhere in his soul all day that wouldn't let him rest, and although he had gone home after visiting Tapio in the morning, he couldn't settle. Tove and Annikki had been released around midday, and Bill had come back to take them to a shared hotel room, neither able to face going back to the house. Had it only been one of them, Bill would have offered his flat and slept on the sofa himself, but unless they wanted to share the bed it wasn't an option.

So he had seen them settled, after taking them to the restaurant downstairs to make sure that they ate something, and then left to come back to the hospital. The constable on duty at that point had been worried by Bill's appearance again, quick to reassure his superior that nothing had happened at all. Yet still Bill's sixth sense was twitching like a cat's whickers over an unseen rat. Something was going to happen, he was sure of it. And so he had merely gone downstairs to get yet another cup of coffee when the Russians had struck, and was standing at the lifts on the ground floor waiting to go back up just as they came down.

He was standing back a little, aware that the lift had been called above and that someone was going to be coming out, and he didn't want to end up wearing his coffee. It was out of hours for visiting time, and so the main foyer was emptier than it normally would be in the week, but that didn't preclude someone coming out in a wheelchair, or one of the patients desperate for a smoke heading for the front doors. So there was a moment's shock on both sides when the other lift door opened which Bill could also see. As the first Russian barged out, Bill caught the most fleeting glimpse of the white face in the blanket, but that was enough to know it was Tapio. The Russian in turn registered the big man standing just to one side. Turning, intending to thump what he thought was just some visitor in his way, he was caught full in the face by Bill's coffee, just as Tapio screamed, "Karhu!"

The coffee wasn't hot enough to do real damage, but taken straight in the eyes it was still enough to let Bill get a crippling punch in without being hit back. And a hefty shove from Bill sent the man back into the one holding Tapio. The boy's body went onto the floor with a thump which made Bill wince, but before he could grab Tapio he had to disable the second man. A vicious kick to the balls which would ensure he never fathered children did the trick. Then the first man got the same treatment as he shook the coffee from his face and tried to scramble to his feet in the confines of the lift, whose automatic door was now opening and closing on both men's legs.

Satisfied that they wouldn't be running after him any time soon, Bill bent to scoop up Tapio's body. The small boy was unnaturally light, even for his size, and Bill guessed that they had very little time left until even Tapio would be unable to keep a semblance of life in this body. But while the forest lord was trapped inside, or at least inextricably attached to it, he needed to get him outside and into an area where he could draw upon what strength he had. And so Bill ran for the main doors, weaving around a couple of overweight ladies in dressing gowns puffing on cigarettes for all they were worth right outside, and a group of four men equally desperately drawing on their smokes, none of whom even bothered to look his way. Luckily he had tucked the Mini into a space few other cars would have fitted into, which was right by the entrance and he was at it within a few strides.

In the chaos he got outside faster than Koschei did, the demon having been disconnected from his target by the lift electronics, and then realising he must abandon the two Russians to whatever fate had in store for them. So the Russian demon shot out of the hospital door in a vague wisp no-one noticed, just in time to see Bill putting Tapio into the Mini. It wasn't the chunkiest car in the world, but it still had enough metal to be able to fend off Koschei, and Bill drove it off in a way which would have been Karl's envy, slaloming around the car park to avoid the barriers and getting out onto the access road where he floored the accelerator.

"What do you need?" Bill yelled at the near-corpse on the passenger seat. "Tell me Tapio! Woods? Sacred space? What?"

"I need time to unlink myself from this body," Tapio's disembodied voice told him. "I cannot save this body any longer, but I had to wind myself into it so deeply that I cannot simply leave in the way Koschei left his puppets."

"Cathedral!" Bill declared. "It's open until six o'clock – we should just make it!"

He was already weaving the Mini in and out of traffic getting some furious hoots of horns and shouted curses in his wake, but what was worrying him was who could he call upon to help him? And he feared he did need help. Not the usual members of the force that was for sure. Morag was at her sister's in Manchester for some family do, so that ruled her out. Tommy Chandler? No, his attitude was all wrong, even though he had seen Tapio's true apparitional form. Clive? No, he lived in Droitwich – he'd never get back here in time, even with his driving. Alf? In desperation, Bill frantically called up Alf's mobile number on his own phone as he slid to a halt at the traffic lights at the bottom of London Road.

"Bill? You alright?" Alf's reassuring voice came after only the second ring.

"No, I'm bloody not! Some fucking thugs just tried to take Tapio. Think they were Russians! The hospital's not safe anymore. I'm heading for the cathedral. How do I get to this damned crypt? And can you by any miracle get them to hold the door open for me if I'm not there in a couple of minutes when they close?"

Bill knew it was a tall order. Alf was hardly on the cathedral staff and probably already gearing up for a busy night at the hostel up in Birmingham. So he was utterly taken aback by Alf's response of,

"No problem! I'm at the cathedral now with Tove and Annikki. Drive up the main doors, I'll meet you there. The barrier's up because there was a concert here earlier and the orchestra has only just finished packing up."

"Oh thank God!" Bill gasped, and meaning it.

"He knows!" Alf said with a chuckle as he ended the call.

It was only a minute or so later when Bill flung the Mini in past the barrier which was normally closed, and tucked it into the farthest corner out of the way of the huge truck with the orchestra's name blazoned on its side. Sprinting round to the passenger door, he scooped Tapio up in his arms, nudged the door shut with his hip, offering up a prayer that the Mini would still be here when he got back to it. There was no way he could get round to lock it with Tapio in his arms, and if the worst happened, the Mini could always be replaced.

Striding into the huge porch, the equally large oak doors of the cathedral seemed shut fast, but as Bill got to them and called out, "Alf?" the familiar face of his friend appeared as the side door opened a crack.

"Come on in!" Alf said with a smile. "It happens that one of the vergers is a friend of mine. That's him over there," and he gave the man a wave. "The crypt's this way," and he set off across the cathedral, leading Bill around the blocks of seats which filled the nave, and round the choir with its ornate medieval stalls to where some stairs led downwards. "Tove and Annikki are already down there."

Bill said nothing until they had gone down the stairs and reached the crypt. Now painted white and not remotely spooky, it felt like a welcoming space to him. Short, stumpy columns filled the space as their ranks and rows made a lattice of arches holding up the floor above. It was like being in wood of short stone trees. However Bill noticed an 'exit' sign pointing further on along on the wall.

"I thought you said this place had only one way in?" he remonstrated with Alf.

"Well this is the main way. The other one is up a very narrow stair that bends. Don't worry, I've already done the business with that. Anyway, we're in behind these doors," and he gestured to the right.

The main space was behind a set of glass panels to make services down there more comfortable, and Alf held the glass door open for Bill to go through before closing it and saying a prayer over it.

It was far less cold than Bill had expected, but he was glad that Annikki and Tove had what looked like car rugs with them. The two women were sitting holding hands on chairs on the front row of three that face a small altar.

"Put him on the rug," Alf instructed Bill, pointing to where a tartan rug was spread out right at the foot of the altar. "I presume I'm right in thinking that the cold stone floor is hardly an issue anymore?"

At that moment Tapio's spectral self began to rise from the boy's body and confirmed Alf's assumption.

"No, I can do no more to keep this body alive." He rose into the air to form a cloud just above the body but still touching it. "Hello Annikki, Tove. Are you both unharmed?"

Bill also turned to them and noticed how both looked pale and tired. "Do they need to be here?" he wondered out loud, but Alf was quick to reply,

"Oh yes, I think they do! Not because I have any expectations of them *doing* anything, but to make sure that they, too, are protected."

Bill winced, kicking himself for not having thought that they might become targets if Koschei didn't have his way.

"Good thinking, Alf. But what are you doing here in Worcester? I was having a panic because I thought you'd be back up in Brum."

Alf gave a wry shrug. "I'm afraid there's always going to be a bit of the copper in me, and that instinct was screaming at me that I wasn't done with all this just yet. So on impulse I went and got a bed at the Premier Inn for the night after you left us yesterday. Then when you texted me to tell me that these two ladies had been released from hospital and where you were taking them, I thought I'd come down and offer to take them out for the afternoon. Nothing worse than sitting and going over and over the same things – and the concert program was some nice light stuff. I thought sitting in a peaceful, sacred space listening to some lovely music might be very good therapy. And I don't know why, but I knew I had to be near the cathedral today."

"Well whoever guided you here was bloody right," was Bill's heartfelt response. "And for what it's worth, I've been

274

all of a fidget all day, too. I had to go back to the hospital – couldn't help myself." He turned and walked over to the two women, bending down so that he was looking them in the face. "How are you both? It's been a rough twenty-four hours for you."

Annikki was more responsive than Tove, immediately nodding. "A bit better now. I still can't get over what happened, or that Urho's de... It doesn't seem right that he's gone. I keep expecting to see him walking in to fetch us home."

Bill nodded. "I know. I'm sorrier that I can tell you that it came to this. I can't imagine how Karl got hold of that gun."

"He had evil on his side," Alf said from by the altar, and that made Tove look up with more focus.

"Yes," she said, "great evil. Karl was always foolish, but he was never evil. Not until Tapio died, anyway. I've spent the day wondering whether that was what tipped the balance of his mind, you know."

"Aah, on that matter," Bill added, "Tapio says that Karl was carrying Hiisi inside of him in much the same way that he linked with your boy."

"Really?"

"Yes. So if it makes it easier for you to forgive Karl, then think on the fact that he probably wasn't in control of his own actions. He might not have been even way back when he first attacked you after the funeral."

Tove's eyes went wide and she made a soundless, "Oooh!"

"Well that would explain a lot," Annikki sighed. "No wonder he was acting weird. It wasn't Karl's real personality we were seeing, but him filtered through Hiisi. It certainly explains why he seemed to suddenly flip when Tapio died."

"Alf and Tapio think it was probably grief, mixed in

with him always being a bit of a weak character, which gave Hiisi the chance to take him over," Bill elaborated.

Tove gave a long ragged sigh, but seemed to sit a little straighter afterwards. "Yes, that is a comfort. If he wasn't his own man then I can forgive him for the bits that were him. Thank God I didn't actually see him getting shot. It was bad enough turning round and just seeing his hand flung out from around the table before the police hustled me outside. It would have finished me off if I'd seen him actually being killed. As it is I feel as though I've been ripped apart inside again."

"Well on that score," Bill said, taking her hands in his, "I'm glad you're here, because Tapio is going to have to leave your son's body altogether now. So he'll be able to have that burial you always wanted now. You'll be able to have that final closure you needed before you leave England."

Tove nodded solemnly, but with less distress than Bill had expected. Maybe she had done all her grieving already? Then a couple of tears trickled down her cheeks as she said, "It will be a relief. But where will we bury my boy?"

"Well if nothing awful happens tonight," Bill told her, mentally crossing fingers, toes and anything else which could be crossed, "I was hoping to arrange for Tapio in his current guise to be flown back to Finland." However Alf made a tactful cough. "What? Have I missed something?"

Alf walked over and pulled one of the chairs round for Bill and another for himself, so that they all sat in an arc. "Well we were thinking that was the answer when Tapio's body was still in the hospital, weren't we?"

Bill groaned and bent over to lean his head in his hands. "Oh bollocks!"

"What's wrong?" Annikki asked.

Forcing himself upright, Bill replied, "Well it would have been pretty straightforward in the hospital. They'd been monitoring Tapio's vital signs, so if he just died while there, then there would be nothing untoward about it. Although stopping to think about it now, I suppose that was always a naive thought, because he had no obvious illness, and so they would've been bound to do a post-mortem. And do we really think that Tapio would have passed that without question?" He turned to where the smoky form of Tapio hung above the body, just about touching it. "Just how many changes did you have to make to that body to enable it to survive?"

"Rather a lot," confessed Tapio.

Alf and Bill exchanged grimaces.

"Okay, so that plan was never going to work," Bill sighed, but Alf was already coming in with,

"But there's another option – and that's another reason why I wanted you two here tonight. You see, they've been doing some restoration work on some of the bishop's tombs up by at the east end, which has come to an end. Now then, tomorrow is the Church feast of Corpus Christi – most people don't know that's why we have a late bank holiday in May, but it is – and it's intended to have a bit of a re-blessing of the tombs and a symbolic sealing of them in a special service in the afternoon. However, they aren't actually sealed in the sense of lock and keys, or even of something adhesive. The one I have in mind has a heavy stone slab lid and that's always been enough.

"Now the other thing you probably won't know is that the bones in them aren't exactly as they were when they went in. Over the years, the bones of earlier bishops got chucked in with others to make room for other ...err-hem ...incumbents to be able to be buried up by the high altar. Sad to say, bishops have been no respecters of their predecessors' remains! So a few more random bones in a coffin will hardly be unusual. And what's more, the chances of those tombs being opened again in our lifetimes are remote. They've done all the archaeological work on them that they can, so unless there's a remarkable break-through in archaeology, there'll be no point in investigating them again. And they've tried to reunite the remains with their correct parts as best they can, but there are still discrepancies."

Bill was looking at Alf in surprise. "Am I hearing you right? You're suggesting we put Tapio's body in with some bishop of Worcester?"

Alf was equally surprised at Bill's disbelief. "Well it's sacred ground! And where else are you going to hide a body where it won't get found? The last thing we want is for you to be hauled up and charged with murder, surely?"

Bill went pale as he realised how this would look to outsiders. "Bloody hell! I hope the security cameras at the hospital haven't got me running out with Tapio in my arms! I mean, I dodged out while an ambulance crew were rushing someone in, come to think of it, so I think I was almost under the camera – if it's where I think it is – not in its sights ...but shit!"

"Indeed," Alf said dryly. "Not your fault, Bill. You've been running around for days now. And given what you've been coping with, it's no surprise that you haven't thought of everything. But burials are more my thing these days. And sad to say, I have experience of random, unknown men dying at the hostel, and all the paperwork that goes with that, not to mention the post-mortems – so it's a bit more in my mind than yours. We *have* to think very carefully about where we put this poor boy, not just for his sake but for yours!"

Chapter 20

Saturday

Now Alf turned to Tove and Annikki. "You are the only ones this child has of his family here at the moment, so I have to ask you, do you have any objection to the body of Tapio resting in this place? Is there anything in your family's beliefs which would find this repugnant?"

Tove straightened up with the air of a woman who had had a terrible weight lifted off her. "None at all!" she said decisively. "I can't think of anything better than him resting here in this lovely old place. He can't go into the fake grave of my son's at home without causing a whole bundle of questions to be asked, even if we could get what everyone else will think of as being a second body back there. And if I suddenly start going to that grave a lot now, people will wonder why. Even my angry parting from my mother won't satisfy everyone. And now you say it, I think it's more important for me to know that he's at rest than being able to visit the place. It was the not knowing which was killing me. But now I'll know just where he is." Then her face creased into tears as she sniffed, "And he adored music! How lovely that he'll be here with all these lovely concerts going on around him."

As she dug out a packet of tissues, Alf turned to Annikki. "And what about you?"

However Annikki gave a savage sniff. "The only person who might be in the slightest offended is Mummo – my grandmother, Karita – and given the amount of grief she's caused, if I ever see her again I shall have the greatest of pleasure in telling her that her grandson lies in an ancient

English church. Oh, not that I'd tell her which one, mind you! Just that it's been a place of Christian worship for over a thousand years ...and then watch her squirm!"

Bill's chuckle, made her blink, and then she too smiled, albeit wanly. But Bill thought he'd better add, "There's no earthly reason why Urho's body can't be flown back to Finland, by the way. His death is all very human, however horrific. I'll personally make sure that he gets treated with the greatest of respect. But I think Alf has the best solution to the problems with Tapio." He turned to the apparition. "I presume that you won't have any problems returning to your homeland once unattached?"

"No," Tapio told them, "although I may well anchor myself onto Urho and return that way. I won't have to make anything like the connections with him that I did with Tapio, because I won't be trying to use his life energy to help me heal as well."

"How are you getting on extracting yourself from the body?" Bill asked. "I don't suppose there's anything we can do to help?"

"No, but thank you for asking, Karhu. I am about halfway through doing it. This is the ideal place to be doing this, though, with its peace and security, so thank you."

"No problem, let us know when you're done."

They all sat in silence for a while until Bill thought of something.

"Alf? Do they have any security in this place? Motion sensors? Because if they do, we're going to have to be very careful moving about."

However, his old friend grinned smugly. "The Lord is clearly looking after us, young William! The organist is coming in at about eight o'clock to practise for tomorrow. While he does that he'll have to turn the alarms off, even though he'll lock the door behind him. And have you ever heard the organ here at full belt? I promise you he'd only hear us if we started up with jack-hammers in the choir!"

Bill sat back in his chair and stared up at the vaults. "You know, sometimes I think we make religion too complicated. At its most basic it's about good against evil, isn't it? About making the right choices. So what is there about Tapio for our God to object to? No-one in his homeland goes around making peoples' lives wretched in his name. No-one practises terrible rites invoking him. But Koschei, on the other hand... he's a nasty piece of work! I was looking him up on the internet at home. His big thing is capturing and raping women – a real charmer! He also takes shape as a whirlwind, apparently. And he's called Koschei the Deathless because he has an absolute terror of dying."

"That is what has driven him to try and take my lands," Tapio added, as his smoke-like form continued to twist in an intricate dance as he un-entangled himself from the body. "He thought his death would come when someone tried to steal his soul, but instead it's come from a very different direction. He never cared enough for people to watch them and to realise what progress was, so when it caught up with him it was an immense shock."

"Err, speaking of wind," Annikki said looking across to the glass doors, "can anyone else feel that draft?"

"Stay there!" Bill told them all firmly. He picked up a heavy candlestick complete with candle, and hefting it in his hand, he eased his way out through the door. Immediately he felt much more strongly the drafts Annikki had mentioned coming down the narrow stair which became the other way out of the crypt. What was more, the cathedral above seemed to be being buffeted by extremely high winds. With great care, Bill eased his way round the bend in the crypt and then up the narrow exit stairs. At the top he realised that he was right beneath the enormous pipes of the magnificent cathedral organ, and in a dark patch well out of sight of anyone curious enough to look around the place.

Somewhere a door slammed. Bill froze.

Was this Koschei come to fight?

Then he heard footsteps echoing unnaturally loud in the silence that enveloped the inside of the cathedral, even though the wind howled outside.

He looked at his watch. Nearly eight o'clock, so maybe it was the organist? It suddenly dawned on him that although the lights were on in the crypt, the rest of the cathedral was in darkness. Normally by this time of year the sun would be going down, but it would be far from dark at this hour. What was going on?

Suddenly he heard a crash of thunder right overhead, but there was no sound of rain, and he recalled that in his trawl of the internet he'd read that thunder tended to accompany Koschei. Not much doubt about it then, the Russian had worked out where they were. But he wasn't inside. These were very ordinary, normal footsteps coming down the side aisle, and he realised that what he had heard was the door from the cloister to the cathedral banging shut.

Then he heard voices.

"What a filthy night!" a man said, to be answered by another,

"I know! This wasn't on the weather forecast! I hope it dries up for tomorrow – we're due for a big congregation for the service."

They were coming closer with every step.

"Do you know the lights are on in the crypt still?" the first voice said, and from his hiding place Bill now saw that the second man was the verger Alf had pointed out.

"Yes," the verger said. "That's why I waited for you. Don't be alarmed, there are people down there. A vicar friend of mine asked if he and a policeman he used to work with could bring a family in to the sanctuary of the cathedral for the evening. It's very unusual, I know, but there are good reasons why the bishop said yes. I just didn't want you to go down and get a shock when you saw someone."

"Glad you told me," the organist said as they walked on by towards the organ loft, while Bill wondered whether the bishop had a clue as to what was happening.

He slid back down to the others and explained that the drafts, at least, had been cause by nothing worse than the organist coming in.

"Does the bishop really know we're here?" Bill asked Alf softly afterwards.

"Hardly! He's in Canterbury at the moment. Didn't seem fair to disturb him in his high-powered conference with the other bishops."

"Hmm, thought not." Bill gave Alf a wink. "So I guess the Church is like any other big organisation – the ones doing the work see a whole different world to the men at the top, and most of the time they haven't a clue about what goes on down at street level?"

"Pretty much," Alf agreed, with the same wicked grin Bill remembered from when they were dealing with the shitty end of policing, and some dignitary had wafted through the station, oblivious to the amount of scrubbing, tidying and sanitising which had gone on just for their benefit.

A moment later there was a hint of an asthmatic wheeze and then the organ burst into life above them, the noise of the pipes reverberating down into the crypt.

"Ah, the Widor *Toccata*, if I'm not mistaken," Alf said with a smile. "He's probably warming his fingers up with that – must have done it enough times at weddings to know that one by heart! He's a guest organist apparently, and I'm told that every organ is different, so you have to get to know the one you're going to play."

"That makes it sound almost human," a startled Annikki said.

"Well alive at least," Alf agreed. "Apparently the pipes respond a lot to atmospheric pressure, so no wonder the organist is sweating bullets that the weather settles. Any tuning will have already been done, so this sudden storm must be his worst nightmare."

"I don't know about his, but it could be ours," Bill grunted. "I think this is no natural storm."

"You are right, Karhu," Tapio agreed, drifting towards them. "I can feel him. Koschei is out there. This is his thunder, these are his winds."

Bill looked from the swirling vapours to the now totally separate body by the altar. "I take it you're now fully separated?"

"Yes."

"Right! Then let's get this body dealt with first! I'm still having kittens over getting caught doing this – I just hope you're right, Alf."

Gently rolling the boy's body into the blanket, Bill picked it up while Alf led the way with the two women. He said they might need to help with moving the great stone lid on the tomb he'd chosen, but Bill wondered whether in part it was that he didn't want the four of them to get separated again. If they had to make a run for it out of the cathedral, they didn't want to leave Annikki and Tove stranded in it overnight and alone.

With Tapio drifting in their wake, they went up the main crypt steps and crossed quickly behind the high altar, making their way around the east end. Once they were in what Alf informed them was the part called the Lady Chapel, Bill breathed a little more easily. They should be out of view here, and the organist had progressed onto another piece, which he was going over several times, often restarting and going over a particular passage when he wasn't satisfied with his own performance. He was obviously going to be absorbed for a while.

"This is the tomb," Alf said, pointing to one of the ornate niches set in the north wall. Although the outer edge was deckled with fine stone tracery, in the niche itself sat a more conventional rectangular stone tomb, coffin-like and with an obvious slab as its lid. "We don't need to lift it off," Alf hurriedly explained as Bill looked at him in dismay, clearly thinking that an elderly clergyman and two women were not going to be much help to him if they had. "What with Tapio being so tiny for his age, all we have to do is slide it sideways a bit. If we push it backwards it will come up against the wall and won't topple."

Bill hoped for all their sakes that this was so, but when the four of them heaved at a corner, it shifted easier than he'd expected. He was also relieved to see that there was less actually in the tomb than he'd feared. Some bones lay in the bottom, carefully arranged, but there was clearly plenty of room above them. With care they lifted Tapio's slight body and with care fed it in through the gap, Bill silently thanking his lucky stars that they were able to do this before rigor mortis set in. A stiff corpse would have been impossible to do this to.

As soon as they had got the body in and arranged it as best they could through the limited opening, they began to pull the tomb lid back.

"Now this is where we'll have to be careful to take the weight," Alf warned them. "If we drop it too hard we might crack the stone, but watch your fingers! Get a grip on this decorative lip, not the bottom!"

They inched the stone slab to within a fraction of where it needed to sit, and then with Alf and the two women supporting the corner they had moved the most, and Bill easing the lid further along towards the other outer corner, they managed to drop the lid back down. It still went with more of a thump when they gave the other side a push to settle it than either Bill or Alf wanted, and they froze, anxiously listening in case the organist had heard anything. However, he was still fretting over a particularly difficult passage and oblivious to the sounds around him. It was now that they also became more aware of the shrieking on the wind outside, and the thunder, as another clap made far more noise than ever they had.

Alf used a large handkerchief to flick away the tiny grains of stone which had been dislodged, and they crept away back down into the crypt past the back of the huge chantry tomb of Prince Arthur – the son of Henry VII who might have been king instead of Henry VIII.

"That one through there in front of the high altar is the tomb of King John," Alf whispered to Tove, giving her arm a gentle squeeze. "Your son now lies within feet of a king of England, no less! That's an honour you could never have expected, eh? A little Finnish boy keeping company with a medieval king and a renaissance prince!"

Tove blinked owlishly, then her face broke into the first genuine smile of the day, making Bill glad that they had managed to do this. It wasn't what she might have wanted when her son first died, but now it must be a reassurance that his resting place would never be desecrated, and it meant that she could always return here as a tourist without anyone wondering why.

"So what are we going to do now?" Bill asked the apparitional Tapio when they got back downstairs. "Dare we go outside? Or will Koschei be waiting for us?"

"I fear he will be circling this building waiting for one of you to appear," Tapio replied regretfully. "He knows that you are a weakness to me because I would not wish to see any of you harmed."

"Right, so that means that you have to confront him before we can leave, presumably?" checked Bill, and got a regretful,

"Yes."

"Can you do that? Are you strong enough now?"

"Yes, Karhu, I think I am. It helps that he is weaker here. He is far from his sources of strength, and he has expended much since being here. I sense that he used more energy than he realises in controlling those men he sent after me, you know, whereas you have helped me of your own volition without me needing to coerce you. That makes a huge difference."

"Then if I can make a plea as someone who has to police this city," said Bill, "it would be good if you could have your battle in the early hours of the morning. Saturday night is always a bit lively, but with this lousy weather Koschei has worked up, the late-night revellers will be running for taxis, not lingering about the town. About three in the morning would be good. People living in the city will assume any noise is the last of those out on the town, which they won't do if it's much later. Can we hang on that long?"

Tapio's swirling shape shimmered and they heard a ghostly laugh. "Oh yes, we can wait. Koschei will only have drained himself further by then! As long as he believes we are still in here he won't go away."

"Then we'd better give him some encouragement," Bill declared. "At some point, if he looks like faltering, I think we should show ourselves. Make some show as if we are trying to make a break for it, even though we know we won't be."

However, the next thing which happened was that the organist finished, and they heard Alf's friendly verger coming back to escort him out. But the verger came to see them after that, asking,

"Are you going to be here all night, Alf? Because I'm not happy about leaving the cathedral with the alarms off."

"Could we go into the cloister?" Bill asked. "Then you could lock the main body of the cathedral up."

"That would be better," admitted the verger, "but you'll need to stay away from the gift shop area. That's alarmed too."

"Look, could you leave me the key to just one door?" Alf asked him. "I know it's a big ask, but these two women are in great danger of violence being done to them if we don't protect them."

"Why can't you take them to the police station?" the verger asked, prompting Bill to think fast and come up with,

"If we do, then there'll be record of them there, and the blokes who are a danger to them have got a very sharp lawyer! They'll come and ask why we're holding them. We can hardly say we're going to lock them up for their own good without any legal representation of their own – do you see? Once they're in the nick they become part of the system, and the trouble is, we don't have the kind of concrete proof which will stand up to that. In the morning I can take them to Birmingham Airport and they can fly back to Finland and safety, and without anyone asking awkward questions. But if these blokes get their hands on them, they could move them to somewhere it will take ages for us to find. And I don't want to be on that murder case."

It did the trick. Just the mention of murder had the verger looking anxiously at Tove and Annikki.

"Alright then, Alf. The keys to the cloister door, but you'd better come with me so that I can show you how to set the remaining alarm. And I want those keys back first thing in the morning!"

"You'll have them, I promise," Alf reassured him. "I'll bring them round first thing, if I haven't already dropped them in through your letterbox by the time you get up. I'll take full responsibility for this should the bishop ever find out, don't worry. I'll make out that I pushed you very hard and presumed on our friendship to the extent of making it seem like blackmail – if that's what it takes. But I have no reason at all to believe it will come to that."

"Let's gather up the rugs and things," Bill told the two women. "We'll take them up to the cloister and sit up by the chapterhouse and the loos. I don't suppose you can leave the loos unlocked, could you verger? It would make things a lot more comfortable for us."

The verger rolled his eyes, but could see the sense in that, and promptly bustled Alf off to show him the alarm system. However, Bill had another reason for asking for the toilets to be left accessible.

"Water," he told Annikki and Tove cryptically.

"Water?" Tove echoed, puzzled.

"Yes. If Alf can bless it, then we've found that it slows Koschei down. It won't stop him. It's not that powerful. What would make it have that kind of *oomph* I'm not sure, but I suspect it would be something like nine priests and a bishop all blessing it – and that we don't have, unfortunately. But we do have Alf and he's a lot better than nothing, so if we can get to a ready supply of water, then at least we have something."

He was being very careful not to address Tapio, who had drifted up to the dark patches in the ceiling, while the verger was around. The poor man would probably have a heart attack on the spot at find a speaking spectre in his crypt! But Bill was definitely looking around the place and working out means of defence, and ways to help Tapio. He'd half thought of taking the solidly made cross from off the altar in the crypt. If he threw that into the swirling mass of whatever it was which made up Koschei in this form, who knew what it might do? But he also recognised that if the cross got damaged then it would bring a world of trouble down on both Alf and the verger, and Bill thought they were helping them enough already without getting them into trouble as well.

However, he did appropriate an armful of cushions from the chairs in the crypt – they would be needed against the chill of the stone seats in the cloister, which were hardly more than ledges carved into the walls.

"Here, put a couple of these under you," he told the two women as he helped them settled down on a wide seat on the side of the cloister furthest from the cathedral. He would have liked to sit with his back to the holy place, but there was a ramp to allow disabled access along that wall, and that would have been even more uncomfortable than this ledge. As it was he managed to make a reasonable seat so that Annikki and Tove could sit with their legs tucked up and out of the drafts, each of them wrapped up warmly with a couple of the car rugs.

A clunk of the cloister door down the far passage told of the verger leaving, and moments later Alf reappeared.

"All sorted?" Bill asked and got a nod. "So Tapio, how much prodding do you think we're going to have to give Koschei?"

Chapter 21

Sunday

"Not much," Tapio answered, becoming more visible again now that the verger was gone. "He has a lot of anger to work his way through!"

For a while they then sat in silence except for Alf, who began praying. Bill wished he had Alf's faith to fall back on, but organised religion had never been his thing. Instead he took to doing a prowl around the cloisters, like a bobby back on his beat. The old, familiar rhythm of that way of walking soothed him, and he found that his mind gradually cleared.

With fresh eyes he looked again at the neat garden contained within the cloister. It had no access from the outside world. It was a self-contained little patch, surrounded on all sides by the cathedral buildings, and that gave Bill an idea. If Tapio was going to fight Koschei anywhere, then this ought to be the place.

On his next circuit he stopped at the glass double doors which were the only way into the garden, and had a good look at the lock on them. These weren't meant to deter those determined to break in – the alarms within the buildings were there for that – and the only way someone would get to these doors was either over the roofs or through the alarmed doors. He stared hard at the lock again, and thought that with a bit of luck he could pick this one, or if not, then given that they opened outwards, a bit of heavy leaning on the doors might do the trick. But whichever it was, he wanted access to that garden.

He was concentrating so hard on the lock that when Tapio spoke from behind him it made him jump.

"Karhu, what are you doing?"

"I want to get these doors open. If you're going to fight Koschei anywhere, I think it ought to be here."

"Hmmm," Tapio's disembodied voice mused. "Yes I can see that it would a good place to ensure that no-one strayed into Koschei's grasp."

Bill gave a thin grin. "Bit more to it than that, actually. You aren't affected by the sacred space, but Koschei is. I was thinking that this might tip the balance a bit more your way."

"Oh!"

"Yes... Well we want to make this as hard for him as possible, don't we? So let's use everything at our disposal."

Tapio swirled in front of Bill, and then a tendril of himself slid into the tiny lock opening and a second later Bill heard the lock click open.

"Now that's impressive!" Bill chuckled. "Just don't take to a life of crime, will you? We'd never find anywhere which would hold you! ...Right, let's go and get Alf to do his thing again."

Once Bill had explained that he wanted Alf to make a circuit of the cloisters, sprinkling them with sacred water, they began to see what he was aiming for.

"You need to stay low," Bill explained to Tapio. "Stay down below the roofline within the cloisters. With any luck that will force Koschei to come down here too, and he'll have dropped into the trap before he even realises it's here."

With relish, Alf set about anointing the cloisters, sprinkling the water around at windowsill level so that only the glass remained as a barrier between it and the garden, rather than the thick, stone walls, and praying as he went. He paid particular attention to the glass doors.

"We don't want him thinking that this is a way out," he told Bill, "because after what we've found out, I think he could be in so much pain that he'll lash out randomly, and that could put us four in danger."

"When we start," Bill told Annikki and Tove, "I want you two to go and shut yourselves in the loos. Shut the outer door – it looks like good solid oak, so it should hold up for a while – and don't come out until one of us two comes to get you! No way are you staying in the cloisters. I'd be a whole heap happier if you could go back into the cathedral, but that's not going to happen, so we'll have to make do with what we've got."

A little after midnight, there seemed to be a lull in the wind, the thunder having already disappeared a few minutes earlier. Bill couldn't be absolutely sure, but he thought that the thunder had been getting weaker as well, rather than simply more distant as natural thunder might have done. Tapio assured them that Koschei was still out there, but silent and stationary, making Bill say,

"That's no good! We need him to wear himself out even more! Right, time to poke him a bit! Ladies: into the loo with you, this might get messy!"

Taking the flask off Alf, which had been replenished with holy water, he walked purposefully to the garden door. They hadn't got any of the chrism oil which Alf had added to the water he'd used at the hospital, but Alf had given the water in the flask every blessing he could think of, so Bill could only hope it would be up to the task. He opened the door and stuck his head out, looking up at the night sky as if searching for Koschei. Seeing nothing, Bill acted as though he thought that the coast was clear and stepped out into the garden, walking across on the path which cut the garden into half and then quarters. His actions seemed nonchalant enough, but he was actually dribbling some of the holy water onto the path as he walked.

However Koschei didn't notice that. All he saw was the hated man who had done so much to foil his every plan.

With a shriek of demonic delight he rose from behind the cathedral tower above the crossing, and plunged downwards like a hawk stooping on a vole. But as he descended in a dark cloud laced with lightning and fire, Bill turned on his heels and sprinted for the door. The last two yards he took as if making a flying tackle, but purposely aiming to roll upon contact with the ground rather than hitting it flat.

Even so, his hands had barely hit the stone flags of the cloister floor to break his fall, when he felt something entwine around his ankle and bring him down. Koschei made a vicious tug at Bill, but Bill had been pulled out of many a collapsed scrum and this was no new experience.

"Oh no you don't!" he snarled. "Think I'm some soft southerner, do you? Well I'm not!" He gave the tendril a fierce punch. "Bloody League and Union trained, me!"

Yet something else kicked in as well as his rugby training. With a fierce roar, Bill reared up and grasped at the tendril, twisting it in his grip as if to wring it out like an old towel.

This unexpected fighting back by a human shocked Koschei. He'd had no experience of a mortal who wasn't frightened of him, but more than that, there was something else visible to him and Tapio which Alf (as the only human watcher) didn't see. There was something more than human here. Something furry and brown, angry and feral. Something bear-like. Not quite like the huge brown bears he had encountered in his homeland, but also not the smaller, spiritually crushed specimens he had sense in captivity in the west, nor even the bears he was aware of in Tapio's territories.

Where had he felt this before? Long ago. Long, long ago.

As he writhed, unable to get the better of this thrashing body but unable to get free either, a memory surfaced. A memory of big men in furs coming in boats down the rivers of his homeland. Men who came from the north-western territories on the ocean's edge. Men who did not worship the gods of the local people. Men who had founded settlements which had turned into cities like Kiev. Vikings! Men who worshipped the red mist of battle rage when they felt the spirit of the bear take them. Men in bearskin shirts or tunics or coats. Berserkers!

But here? Now? How was this possible? Where had this man come from? What bloodline had made this possible?

Blind to this, Bill was in the grip of sheer rage. How dare this bloody thing come and invade his patch? His manor? By heck he'd show him what is was to take on a northern lad, even if he didn't sound like it these days. He wrung the tendril a bit harder, and in the process – had he known it – summoning every ounce of his ancient Norse DNA in the effort. Then he heard Alf calling his name and regained focus enough to remember the back-up plan.

Loosing with one hand, he reached back and felt Alf thrust the handle of the cleaner's bucket into his hands as he made a rapid dash into the garden, before running back to the cover of the cloister. But Bill was already swinging the bucket now filled with what was as near to holy water as they could make it, and flung it into the heart of the swirling mass that was Koschei.

The screams of rage turned to ones of pain and Bill was dropped like a stone, luckily not far, and as he rolled to safety, Tapio swooped out of the doors on the attack. As Koschei writhed in agony to shake off the droplets of the burning water, Tapio wrapped himself around him and squeezed, forcing Koschei inwards to encase the water, not lose it. Round and round the cloister garden they spun, a whirlwind churning up plants and grass. Koschei kept trying to rise up, but Tapio kept pulling him down, making for a tumbling motion in their intertwined spirit forms as each got the ascendancy briefly.

Bill scrambled to the safety of the cloister and was helped to his feet by Alf. Together they stood watching the tornado going on outside, and unable to tell whether Tapio was holding his own or not.

"What do we do if he doesn't win?" Alf asked worriedly.

"Bugger all!" Bill snorted. "We just have to hope Koschei sods off back to Russia when he's got what he wanted."

But something was definitely happening out there. With human eyes at first it had been impossible to tell which bit of the swirling cloud was who, but the outside one was now rapidly coalescing into a still sphere and beginning to glow paler and paler from gold towards white, while the heart of the mass was going darker and writhing ever more frantically.

"Would a few prayers help?" Bill asked Alf.

"Let's give it a go," his old friend suggested. "Let's start with the Lord's Prayer again."

Together the two of them stood in the doorway, right on the boundary between the interior sacred space and the garden, and recited the ancient prayer. As they began, the form which they guessed was Tapio started forcing Koschei downwards, until as they got to the last line, he pushed Koschei onto the path. In a quick flick, the portion of himself which had been containing Koschei beneath slipped out of the way, and the demon was squashed onto the flagstones. But it wasn't simply the stones which had an effect. The flask which Bill had been using to dribble the holy water from had been dropped by him as he fled at the centre point, and its contents had now puddle out onto the stone slabs, which was what Koschei was now brought into contact with.

Screaming in agony at being crushed between his ancient enemy and this new threat, Koschei's writhing became frantic and tortured, and there were glints of something sparking within him, like some electrical fault on a grand scale. The gold miniature lightning flashes within his dark-cloud form began increasing, as though he was being stabbed with needles of pure light. Then suddenly he exploded with an enormous bang and a huge and intense flash of light, as if the tiny flashes had all joined together for one catastrophic instant.

The explosion took Bill and Alf off their feet and threw them backwards into the cloister, fetching up hard against the stone wall. When they had clambered to their feet again, blinking with eyes which were still seeing bright flashes, and struggling to hear much of anything, it was to see that the rather nice stone urn which had been in the centre of the garden had disintegrated. Some of its shards had gone through panes of the leaded cloister windows, but considering the force of the blast, there was remarkably little damage done. The central flagstones, though, looked as though they had been melted, and were warped rather than fragmented.

"I hope the bishop thinks this was a lightning strike," Bill told Alf. "If necessary I'll buy a new vase-thingy for the garden."

However Alf was smiling. "I think the bishop and the trustees of the cathedral will think we got off rather lightly for a strike in the heart of the cloisters. With any luck they'll think that the Lord was looking after his own, and that's why there isn't any more damage."

Then Bill suddenly realised that the silence wasn't just about his slight deafness, and ran out into the garden. "Tapio? Tapio, where are you?"

There was no response and the garden remained empty.

"Oh crap, I hope he's okay," Bill said worriedly, scan the rooflines and sky. "I know I probably shouldn't be concerned for a pagan deity, given where we are, but I've got rather fond of him. I'd hate it if in getting rid of an evil bastard like Koshcei he was killed – or whatever happens to minor spectres."

"I think we'd better get out of here first," Alf said firmly. "If that's woken the verger or anyone else on the cathedral staff, and they come to check that the old place is alright, it wouldn't do for them to find us here. If Tapio's still around he can find us a lot easier than we can find him."

"True," Bill agreed, and they hurried to retrieve Annikki and Tove.

It was way too late for the women to get back into their hotel, and so Bill led them across the river bridge and up the road to his flat. The Mini wasn't an option because the barricade was down and Alf didn't have a key for that. So it was walk or nothing.

Once inside he made hot drinks for everyone, and they sat on the big squashy sofa where he and Morag had sat before all this had started. They had a lovely view out across the river towards the far side of the city, and as far as they could tell, the place was quiet. There were no strange clouds about, and mercifully no sounds of urgent sirens either, which might have meant that further damage had happened to the cathedral. In fact the city was unusually quiet for the early hours of a Sunday morning, and none of them were sure whether that was a good thing or not.

After a nap in Bill's armchair, Alf excused himself around six-thirty, saying that he would walk back and drop the keys through the verger's letterbox, then check out of his hotel room.

"I don't think you'll be needing me anymore," he told Bill, as they warmly shook hands at Bill's front door. "It'll seem positively tranquil going back to just a few human wrecks tomorrow!"

"I'll come up and see you soon," Bill promised, already mentally putting a bottle of Alf's favourite malt whisky onto his shopping list as a thank you gift. "The least I can do after this is give you a few nights of my time."

However Alf laughed. "And you're expecting nights off when you get back to work? No, it's okay, Bill, I know what the job's like. Just come up and see me when you can, and bring me all the gossip. I can't wait to find out how you get on with young Chandler! That's got to be worth a few stories over some pints."

"Well I can't tell you how glad I am that you were around," Bill said from the heart. "I never thought I'd be needing the help of a man of the cloth, but I don't like to think how this would've ended if I'd been on my own, or with someone like Morag. We'd have been right out of our depths."

Alf grinned again. "I'm not going to say go to church, because I know that's not you – and anyway with the hours you work a chance would be a fine thing. But try offering up a prayer every so often, for my sake if not your own, eh?"

"If more of the vicars I met were like you there might be more chance of me making time to get to church," Bill confessed. "And I do realise it's a bit cheeky ignoring the Big Fella and then screaming for help when I need it. But he needs to have a change of staff on the earthly side if he wants folks like me to turn up regularly. They don't do him any great service, I'm afraid. If I'd turned to the local ones I know, they'd have either turned their backs on Tapio, or seen him as so much of a threat that they'd not even have realised the danger from Koschei until it was too late. So I'm beyond grateful that you were around."

Alf nodded, then just as he was going out of the door turned back and said, "Who knows, maybe the Lord has his uses for creatures like Tapio, and that's why I was sent to help you?"

Bill watched him go and thought that the world needed more Alfs, but that it would still be a while before he became a regular churchgoer. And he stepped out and gave the skies another scan. Was Tapio alright? Was he just gone, maybe back home, or was he terribly injured somewhere? And what of Koschei? Was he sent to wherever such thing went to when they did the equivalent of dying, or was he likely to come back? Bill closed the door and went back to where Annikki and Tove were snoozing on the sofa, but he knew he'd be worrying for months to come.

⚜

Far away in the frozen depths of Russia, the fragmented remains of Koschei began coalescing in the uninhabited wasteland that was his home. Stripped of so much of his power that he barely continued to exist at all, there was little he could do except to try and recreate himself and lick his wounds. It would be many long years before he would be strong enough to venture beyond his natural boundaries again, and he had been dealt a frightening blow. For whereas Tapio had been aware of the power of the other faith but untouched by it, for Koschei it had been a terrible discovery of just how much such beliefs had replaced the ones he relied upon, and the tangible effects they could have on him. The pain he had suffered had been beyond anything he'd encountered in thousands of years, and had been all the worse for being completely unexpected. Everything he had expected of an actual fight between himself and Tapio had been as nothing compared to that.

As his awareness swirled around in the icy winds of the north, he vowed over and over that once he was a coherent force once again, that he would make it his priority to attack such faith. Who were these men, with their golden icons, to come and rob him of all that had once been his? And yet as he felt around him, for the first time he realised that there was a vast emptiness where the others like him had once existed and filled with their energy. Maybe they were still around in isolated pockets of the world, but the vast interlaced web he had known in his heyday had gone without a trace. Were they really such a dying breed? How could they have become so forgotten?

As for those men over whom he had had such a personal hold, they found themselves waking to the new days with the feeling that they had experienced a dreadful nightmare, but one which they could not remember. A clerk in the Kremlin looked down at his desk and wondered why on earth he had a strange memo on his desk. Why would the president ask for such a thing? It didn't seem to relate to anything of importance. And with the impatience of a man who barely had enough time in the day to deal with the larger matters at hand, he screwed the paper into a ball and launched it into a bin. Then when a strange email of a similar nature was found on his computer from a couple of days previously, he had no hesitation in deleting that too. What on earth was all this nonsense about? Russia had bigger things to worry about than some kid in Finland!

In much the same way, the middle-ranking army officer looked at the request to send covert troops into

Finland to seize someone, and similarly decided that this was just a joke some idiot had thought to play on him. Well it wasn't funny, and he wasn't going to play! Who'd risk an international incident like that!

It was only when he went back further through his documents some months later, trying to find a totally unrelated order, that he found that there had been a previous request. And God help him, but it looked as though in some moment of insanity he had granted it! In a controlled panic he rapidly went through all his files deleting and burning anything which might hint that he had ever done such a thing, although his griping gut warned him that those who spied on everyone might know nonetheless. He found himself in church later on, kneeling before the beautiful little icon of the Madonna and Child, praying with all his might that no-one ever asked what had happened to that covert team he had seemingly sent across the border, because they had vanished without a trace! No complaints from the Finns, no reports of bodies, nothing! They had just vanished off the earth as though they had never existed. But if ever their families dared to ask questions, it would be better that he'd never been born than try to answer to a higher authority as to why their sons had never come home.

And as for the scientist who had produced the report of vast oilfields beneath Karelia and stretching westwards into Finland, he simply sat and stared in disbelief at it when he found it again. How could he have done this thing? It made no sense. It didn't fit with any of his research, and what was worse, he had no memory of ever having written the damned thing. Fearing that he might have had such a breakdown as to present this absolute rubbish to a colleague, he was walking on eggshells for the next year, fearing that at any time someone would come up to him and say, "Alexi, what were you thinking?" but it never happened. He offered up heartfelt thanks when he realised that he had almost presented the results at a conference, but mercifully he had stuck to his long-standing research instead. That could have derailed his career permanently! Although had he known that his report had mysteriously only ever had one other reader and the president at that, he might not have been quite so relieved.

Therefore, with the kind of luck which that same president would have derided, the mischief which Koschei had caused managed to find itself swept under mats and into dark corners, never to see the light of day again. And if Tapio's counterparts who now survived only amongst the shamanistic tribes folks were not as strong as they had once been, they nevertheless patted themselves on their metaphysical backs and gave thanks for a disaster averted. Perun, Jarilo and Morena thought that things had worked out remarkably well given that they were hardly the most powerful demi-gods left in the world. Koschei himself they could not stop completely, but once alerted to what he was up to, they could at least set his plans back by a few centuries.

So a natural balance returned to the world once again, and the lives of men continued in ignorance of what had so very nearly come to pass.

Chapter 22

Sunday to Friday

As soon as Bill thought it would be unremarkable for the two women to return to the hotel, he walked them back across the river, and then joined them for a hearty breakfast at the hotel. Then leaving them to get more rest, he took himself off and wandered round to the central police station.

When he got there he found Frank Watson in and nearly tearing his hair out.

"God Almighty, Bill! What a massive cock-up!" he fumed. "I've PC Denton off sick after being beaten up by some bloody Russian derelicts at the hospital. The boy has vanished altogether. The Finnish consulate is asking what we've done with two of their citizens, because the two women have gone walkabout. And to put the tin hat on our miseries, someone put a call in last night about a bomb going off in the cathedral! The lads have been running round like demented fleas all night!"

"Have a coffee," Bill said soothingly, putting a cardboard cup of Frank's favourite from Costa's down on the desk. "I presume the bomb was just an overreaction? I heard nothing."

Frank subsided and took a grateful slurp of the coffee. "That at least was nothing odder than a thunderbolt earthing itself in the cloisters, thank God – although I don't think the cathedral authorities are quite as pleased with Him over that. The glazing bill is going to be a bit steep, apparently."

"Then let me set your mind at rest over Tove and Annikki," Bill added. "I've just walked them back to their hotel. They just got the jitters being there alone and came over to my place. They've been doing nothing more exciting than drinking decaff and eating my homemade scones. I'm sorry if that gave you a fright. I had no idea you were intending to keep them under surveillance now that Karl's dead. But I'm worried sick by what you're saying about Tapio. Has no-one seen him?"

Frank's face relaxed visibly over the news about the two women, but creased back into a frown at the mention of Tapio. "No. Not a bloody thing! We can't get a sensible word out of the Russians who got caught in the hospital. Denton has positively identified them as the two who attacked him, and some of the hospital staff have confirmed that they got inside by bringing a third man in who was badly wounded. He's critical and unlikely to make it, having lost too much blood, but the other two are no better. We've had to leave them in the hospital, because it's like their brains got fried, or something! Truly, Bill, they're suddenly dribbling idiots, the pair of them. It's not just that they're not speaking English. We've had a native Russian speaker try to talk to them, and even he says they're just babbling about some demon or other."

Bill could feel his donation to the cathedral getting bigger in thanks for that escape. They at least wouldn't be saying a word about seeing him.

"Was there nothing on CCTV? No sign of anyone running from the place?"

"A glimpse of a shoulder and a hospital blanket!" Frank snorted in disgust. "Two fat biddies puffing away so bloody hard on their fags it's like a steam-train going past has obscured the rest. Christ, who goes into hospital and then stands outside tarmacing their lungs? And the daft pair say they saw nothing! The bloody world could have come

305

to an end and they'd not notice as long as they had their fix. Nor are the blokes who were outside any better. Apparently they were having an argument over who was better, Aston Villa or Wolves – forget a kid being kidnapped, that was far more important!"

"Shit, what a break!" Bill declared, hoping he sounded suitable disgusted instead of intensely relieved, as he felt.

"The worst of it is," Frank continued, "the doctors say we are almost certainly looking for a corpse. They're absolutely certain that Tapio had suffered some kind of fatal stroke when he got brought in. I'm told that they'd already been wondering just how soon they would be turning the life-support off. They are convinced he was brain dead, but they'd been hanging on until his parents could be informed. You know, just in case he was a member of one of those faiths where burial has to take place within so many hours of death. They were just giving us the chance to fly someone in from Finland. Well that's never going to happen now, is it?"

"No," admitted Bill. "But on the bright side, you'd been moving heaven and earth to try and find the kid's family for over a week already. So if you haven't got anywhere by now, it's hardly likely that the authorities are going to accuse you of not trying. I reckon the Super' will bounce this back, saying that we've given the Finnish authorities every possible help we can in finding the family, and that if their own can't trace them, there's little chance that we're going to. After all, as far as we know, the family might be in Dubai or bloody Iran from what we were told at the start. It could even be them who came and took Tapio."

Frank sighed. "Thank you for that Bill. It's put it into perspective for me. Yes, you're right, we've hardly been sitting on our hands over this." He heaved himself up and went to look out of the window of his small office. "We've had dog teams out all over the woods around the hospital, you know. Not a shred of evidence. Someone took him in a car I reckon. And if his feet never even touched the ground the dogs have no scent to track even close by the hospital. Even the damned car-park CCTV went on the fritz, would you believe? Right up to that point when – as best we can tell – Tapio left the building, it's fine, then the next thing is it goes to snow and the circuits go pop. The technicians say it's like they got some kind of electrical overload – going to cost a fortune to reinstall, apparently, because the electronics are so fried they're coming out of the cameras in lumps. I've never known a case dogged by such bloody bad luck."

"Pray to the god of dog walkers," Bill chuckled, referring to the way it always seemed to be some poor unfortunate out walking their beloved Fido who found a body when all else had failed.

Frank gave him a baleful glare. "Well without wishing to sound callous – given that the poor little bugger was probably dead the moment they disconnected him from the life-support – but I hope his corpse turns up on someone else's patch. I'll happily go back to trying to trace the movements of that drunken sod who assaulted his wife three weeks ago. Finding him seems like a piece of cake in comparison!"

Bill didn't linger much longer. He wasn't sure how long he could keep that act of ignorance up for. Instead he went and retrieved the Mini from behind the barrier at the cathedral where it had been locked in. To his amazement it was still there and undamaged. He'd been expecting to find it at least propped up on four piles of bricks and the wheels gone. With a few enquiries he managed to find the verger Alf knew and offered to make a hefty donation.

"You saw and heard nothing?" the verger enquired suspiciously.

"No," Bill lied smoothly, hoping that this wouldn't count as a black mark against him, especially as they were standing in the cathedral chapterhouse at the time. "It got to midnight and the women were getting terribly cold. You forget how chilly these old places can get, even like now in the summer. I didn't see any point in saving them just to make them ill. I'd put off taking them to my flat earlier on, you see, in case the men who were after them followed us. In the crowds of people around earlier in the evening it would've been next to impossible to tell if someone was following us until it was too late. But in the depths of night, and with that filthy storm making it unlikely that many would be out and about, we decided to risk it.

"Alf had locked up and we were on the way to the bridge when we heard that enormous bang. We knew it had hit something close to the cathedral, or even the old place itself, but looking back we couldn't see any damage from where we were out on the street. We even stopped to look in case we could see any smoke rising, because we'd obviously have called the fire brigade then, but there was no sign of anything. It's a good job we weren't still in the cloister, isn't it? We could have been hit too."

The verger seemed taken in by the story. "Well you'd have been all right inside," he said with a rather superior sniff. "It's the garden which took the hit. Some say it was a thunderbolt, but it could equally have been a lightning strike. There are scorch marks on the stone whichever it was."

"Well look, have this cheque," Bill said in his smoothest tones. "It should mean that you can start to put the garden to rights at least, and I presume that insurance will take care of any damage to the building?" He was very careful not to say the windows. That would imply that he knew more than he should, even though Frank had told him of the damage too.

"Oh, that's very generous of you!" the verger declared, instantly mollified by the size of the amount.

"Well Alf and I very much appreciated what you did to help us," Bill replied, desperately trying not to sound too oily. He didn't want the verger to later on start wondering why a detective was being such a creep towards him. "Don't worry, we won't be asking for any other favours like that. I've not had another case like that in all the years I've been on the force, and I hope I don't get another!" That at least was the truth and very much heartfelt.

It certainly rang true with the verger, and he came and ensured that Bill could get the Mini out, waving him off before turning back to the cathedral and the preparations for the coming service. With any luck, Bill thought, he could come back and take Tove and Annikki to the service, which would seal things nicely for them.

He'd not been back home for long, though, before Annikki rang him. The Finnish authorities had been on to them.

"I hope we did the right thing," she said, "but we stuck to the story we worked out with you last night. We said that the hotel room had started to feel like a cage, so we went out for a walk, then couldn't face going back. We told the irritating little man who questioned us that we had your phone number and rang you to come and fetch us. I told him that we could hardly go back to the house when it was a crime scene."

"Quite right!" Bill praised her.

"Funnily enough, your colleagues were far nicer about us not being in the hotel room than he was. They agreed with us when we said that with Tapio being in hospital, and with Karl dead, there didn't seem to be any danger to us that we were aware of. It was only that self-important consulate man who seemed to think that we should be telling the police of our every move, and I did point out that given that it's still only Sunday, we were hardly likely to be going to inquests or anything."

"Good girl," Bill chuckled, thinking that the consulate man must have got off the phone with Annikki's voice singeing his ears. "Look, I've one more week off work before I'm due back. I can come with you to the house to get your things when you're allowed back, if you like. And I'll certainly be called to give evidence at the inquest into Urho's death, so you won't be going into that alone, either, in case you were worried about that at all."

"Thank you!" Annikki said warmly, her tone telling Bill that going back to the house was going to be a terrible ordeal for them both.

They accepted his invitation to go to the cathedral as ordinary members of the congregation, though, and later that afternoon the three of them sat quietly at the back of the cluster of people who had come for the service as the tombs were once again blessed.

Coming outside afterwards to a glorious English summer afternoon, Tove turned to Bill and smiled.

"That was lovely," she sighed. "Just what I needed. I can go home now at peace inside. And it makes such a difference to know that if I want to, I can come here just as an anonymous tourist and visit the grave of my boy. I can't tell you how that's changed things for me. It's like the last hold my parents had over me has been broken, as well. I'll be glad to go home and move close to my sister and Annikki, and to see Matti and his family more often."

"I'm really glad for you," Bill said, feeling that if nothing else some real good had come out of this for her. Even Karl's violent death was tempered by her knowing that he'd not been in control of himself, and not responsible for his actions.

Two days later the women were allowed to be escorted back to the house by Bill to pack their things, having been let in by Frank. The house's owner was proving to be as elusive to trace as Tapio's mythical parents, but the letting agents were being very understanding over the damage done to the house, in part by Frank carefully painting Karl's break-in as the act of a drug-crazed stranger. No-one could be asked to anticipate such a thing, and the agents accepted that neither Annikki or Urho had done anything to invite him there.

When they were alone, Bill thanked Frank for his tactful handling of the matter, and was told,

"To be honest, Bill, I just couldn't face them getting shitty over compensation if we told them that Karl was Annikki's ex-uncle. I told 'them upstairs' that given that we hardly excelled ourselves in protecting them from Karl, especially as we had him in custody then thought of him as so little of a threat that we let him go free, that we'd be opening up a whole can of worms if we told the precise truth. I don't think they were keen to be portrayed as unable to keep some violent foreigner from toting a gun around the shire and then using it to lethal effect."

"Not exactly the stuff the PR people would love," Bill agreed. "It's uphill work at the best of times without handing them a nightmare like that to smooth over. But I'm curious that the owner is so hard to track down. We never considered him or her to be tied up in all of this because everything went through a letting agent, but my own curiosity would love to know who the hell they are."

"Not my priority, my old son," Frank told him with such emphasis that Bill knew better than to press the matter. Privately, though, he wondered whether the place had been on some spooky kind of radar for a long time. Tapio had been most emphatic that it had been the right place, and that had always bothered Bill. How had some pagan nature spirits from over a thousand miles away known anything at all about a house in the middle of England, beyond what they'd been sent on paper?

"Give it up, Bill," he told himself firmly after leaving Frank. "That's something you'll probably never get to know."

Instead, once back inside the house, he helped Tove down with her one suitcase and put it in the Mini, then helped Annikki to pack all of her things into the Subaru. Having been living here for longer she had much more to pack, but going back upstairs, Bill had to ask her what she wanted to do about Tapio's things.

"I mean, I doubt Tove will want them, will she?" he asked. "It's not like they're her Tapio's stuff. Do you want me to pack them up for you?"

"Would you?" Annikki said gratefully. "Even knowing now just what he was, when I look at his stuff I still see the little boy I looked after for all those months. I can't separate the two."

So the next day Bill went back and began the task of packing things away. Luckily there were some large trunks in the basement which were what things had been shipped over in. He left the packing of Urho's belongings to others. That was still too raw for him, because Urho was very much a flesh and blood man who had lost his life for no good reason, but luckily Morag came over and did that for him once the forensic team had done with Urho's flat. That left Bill with the bigger task of packing up the house.

Mercifully the agents had come up with the inventory for the house, and Bill was relieved to find that almost everything belonged with it except for the obviously personal things. Tapio's clothes he quickly packed up to be sent to a charity shop, and the school stuff he sent back too. But harder to deal with were the more esoteric objects. In Tapio's rooms were shaman's rattles, some rather odd musical instruments which Bill guessed a Sami might know how to play, but few others would, and goodly number of pieces of wood which looked as though they had been handled a lot.

And of course there were all of the photos. Those at least Bill decided he would keep for himself. Once off the walls they made a fairly compact pile which he could store in a folder. Also the big ethnic cushions and throws, which looked as though they too were of folk origin, would cost quite a bit to ship back because of their size, but would fit in Bill's flat. So his living room went from being fairly bland, with the magnolia walls and minimal furniture, to having a much warmer look as the rich colours and weaves brightened it. And once they were in Bill felt as though Tapio would be happy with the fact that he had them.

However he had to ask Annikki what to do with the shaman's instruments and paraphernalia. What on earth to do with a bear's skull for instance? However Annikki was also at a loss.

"The only person who would want them is Mummo, and I think she's forfeited any right to have anything of Tapio's," she told Bill. "After what's happened I don't think my parents would want any of it, not even in the basement, and neither will Uncle Matti. If you can find someone who wants such a thing, let them have it, and the rest of the stuff."

That said, there was a part of Bill which felt that handing objects which had been used with such reverence over to mere collectors, or in the case of the drums, to people who would play around with them and then discard them, was just plain wrong. So in the end he packed them up and added them to the collection in the basement room beneath his lounge. He'd have to make a decision about them before the winter set in, because the room was meant more as a garden store and accessed from the outside via a simple wooden door. It would be just as wrong to let them get damp and mildewed, but at least it gave him time to think. The blocks of wood, on the other hand, Bill guessed Tapio had brought with him to remind him of the trees he had left behind, and so Bill made a little arrangement of them at the bottom of the stairs down from his back door. It was high enough so that even when the Severn flooded they wouldn't get swept away, and nature could take its course with them.

Words must have been exchanged at a high level, because Urho's inquest was fitted in at the end of the week, allowing Bill to get that out of the way before his return to duty. It was a traumatic affair for both Annikki and Tove as they had to recount what they had seen and heard, and even Bill found it hard to be as detached as he normally would be when telling what he knew of Urho. However, it had a welcome outcome, because with Karl being beyond any trial, there was no reason not to allow Urho's body to be shipped back to Finland immediately.

"The case is closed until they can find Tapio's body, we've been told," Annikki told Bill when they sat having a coffee afterwards with Tove. "We're free to go home whenever we like, so we'll be taking the plane home on Tuesday."

"Well I hope this won't put you off coming back for a visit," Bill said hopefully, suddenly realising that despite the short time they had known one another, that he would miss Annikki terribly.

Luckily she smiled and said, "No, I've other happy memories of England, so I'll be fine about coming back for a holiday. But maybe not for a while."

"No, I can understand that."

"And we have a lot of family sorting out to do as well," Tove added. "I'd love to think it'll be as simple as me renting a place with Annikki near the rest of the family, but I fear my mother will do her best to make things awkward."

"I wish I could say I'll run you to the airport," Bill said, "but I know that the moment I walk in through that door on Monday, a whole heap of work will fall into my lap."

"That's alright," Annikki reassured him. "We have a car coming to take us, apparently. I think the consulate want us out of their way as fast as possible! But why don't you come and visit us some time? Wouldn't you like to come and see some of our forests?"

Chapter 23

Aftermath

Bill's return to work was as chaotic as he'd anticipated, and in one way he was glad to get back to a much more normal routine. It was strangely good to get back to dealing with flesh and blood criminals. Yet when he got back to the flat at night, the presence of Tapios' things, and the lingering faint smell of the incense he had burned still clinging to them, kept reminding Bill that he knew nothing of Tapio's fate.

He'd had a phone-call off Annikki to say that she and Tove were back home with her parents after an uneventful flight, then another to say that no-one had been able to find any family for Urho. That had made Bill half wonder whether to try and fly out there just for the day of the funeral, but it turned out to be impossible. Instead he rang the Nykänen home on the evening of the funeral, and was told that at least Annikki's family had made up for the lack. But Annikki had other news which she had to text to Bill.

'Couldn't say this in front of family,' she wrote, 'but think Tapio came! Was standing outside church when I saw a cloud lower than the others. Think I'm the only one who saw, but for a second it went into the shape of a bear! Maybe he's ok after all?'

'Hope so. Sounds like something he'd do!' Bill texted back, and really hoped that this had been a sign.

What he did manage to do was to organise a trip to Finland for just into the new year. Once the mayhem of the Christmas and New Year revelries had passed, it was as good a time as any to take some leave, and it was hardly a time of year when his colleagues were queuing up to take holidays.

"You're going where?" DC Chandler said with the sneer Bill was becoming wearily accustomed to. "You must be mad! Why not go somewhere nice and hot?"

"Because 'nice and hot' is filled with tossers like you!" for once Bill bit back, and was gratified to see Chandler subside. Well it wasn't far from the truth. The dangers of traipsing off to one of the Costas or one of the Spanish islands, as far as Bill was concerned, was that they tended to be filled with very much the same kinds of people he ended up dealing with as part of the job. Not wholly, he conceded, but with enough of a random sample behaving as badly away as they did at home, it wasn't the kind of holiday he wanted. The frozen north, on the other hand, sounded wonderfully peaceful!

So on Twelfth Night, Morag took Bill to the airport and waved him off, having received strict instructions to check up on the woodpile and make sure that the neighbours didn't disturb the hedgehogs who had made a winter home there. That would please Tapio, Bill knew, that some English woodland creatures were making use of his Finnish woods. There had also been progress on the bear's skull. Morag had a contact who was a florist, and with some encouragement from Morag, she had taken the skull and then brought it back artistically decorated with pinecones and other dried materials. And now that it didn't look so stark, Bill was delighted to have it as the centrepiece on a small table in the flat's hallway.

"Being such a big old place," he told the Nykänens when they came to pick him up, "and with me being downstairs, there's still quite a big hall space where the stairs come down from my front door. I've had the table there for ages, just because it makes the place look a bit less empty, but the skull looks really good on it. It's got dried grasses round the back of it and all sorts of things in it, like acorns and chestnuts. Very arty it looks!"

"I don't think I could have it out on view," Annikki's mum said with a bit of a shiver.

"No, I know what you mean," Bill confessed, "but I somehow couldn't just throw it away. I asked the local vets down the road from me if they wanted it, but all they did was offer to incinerate it for me, and that didn't seem right either. That's why I'm so glad that Morag's friend was able to do something with it to make it less creepy. I hope Tapio would approve."

However talking about Tapio seemed to bring a chill over the family, and so Bill found that he could only get to ask about things once he was alone with Annikki and Tove. Luckily they had just rented a flat a mile down the road from Annili and Nils, Annikki's parents, and so Bill went there under the excuse of helping them move a few things around.

"So how did it go?" he was finally able to ask Tove.

"Oh, my mother did as we predicted. Threw a real tantrum and called me ungrateful and selfish. Luckily Annili and Matti stuck by me and told her exactly what they thought of her."

"And what about your father?"

Tove smiled at Bill. "Well I think you were right about him. As soon as it sank in that I was moving away and had no intention of ever coming back, he was suggesting that they put the house on the market. I'm not sure that he's had the courage to tell her that they won't be living together anymore once the sale has gone through, but for the last few Saturdays he's been taking Matti out with him to his cabin in the woods, and they seem to be having manly conversations. Matti's told us all that Grandfather's desperately sorry that things have worked out the way they have, and he says he didn't realise how unhappy I was."

"And you believe him?" Bill thought that was pushing it a bit for the old man not to have noticed anything over so many years. However Tove was more convinced.

"Actually I can see why. My mother was so wearing to be around that if I was working I would only come into the kitchen to eat with them. Then I'd escape to my own flat in the evenings. And of course if I was working odd hours, she was around in the day to see me, whereas he's only retired a few years ago. Then at weekends he'd disappear off fishing or whatever." She sighed sadly. "It wasn't until you said about him escaping that I realised that that was why he was never around on Saturdays and Sundays – he was quite literally heading for the woods and some peace and quiet!

"And it seems that he's owned a little cabin about three hours' drive out of town for many years now." She laughed bitterly. "One thing you can say about Mother, she left him to sort the money out as he saw fit – she didn't soil her hands with mundane matter like that! So he was free to siphon some off to get his cabin nicely set up without her questioning him about it. Matti says it's rather nice, apparently."

Annikki was nodding. "It seems, in honour of you being here, we're all invited out there this weekend. To be frank, I think he feels he owes you one, Bill. He may be weak, but he's not stupid, and I think he's rapidly realised just how bad things could have got over Mummo making me take the au pair job with Tapio. Uncle Matti came and told us that the first time they went out and talked that he was in tears at the thought that I might have come to harm or even been killed."

Bill sniffed. "A bit late in the day for such regrets, but I suppose better late than never. I must confess I expected you to say that he was staying with Karita, even if he was as miserable as sin with her. Some men do stick it out even under the most horrendous conditions, and God knows, I've seen enough to know!"

He was certainly wary when they all drove up there in a convoy of three cars at the weekend. It was going to be hard if his experience told him that Väinö Mannu was a lying bastard, who was twisting his family around his finger just as much as his wife had done, even if it was in a different way. Tove was probably not the best person to ask about his actions if you wanted an objective response!

Mercifully Väinö turned out to be a very nice older man, just with not much determination as best Bill could see. Väinö repeatedly thanked Bill for what he had done for the family, but not in a way as to make Bill wonder whether excessive breast beating was being done to try and cover something up. If anything the poor bloke just seemed worn down by years of being henpecked by Karita, and for that he had Bill's sympathy.

"You have come at just the right time of year!" Väinö enthused to Bill as the brief winter daylight began to fade again. "The Northern Lights have been wonderful these last few nights! Have you ever seen them?"

"Not for real," Bill replied. "And I suspect that however good a photograph might be, it would never do them justice."

"Then you must stay the night!" Väinö insisted. "There isn't room for everyone, but I can bring you back to Nils and Annili's tomorrow. Please, stay! It's the only way I have of being able to give you something back."

Bill saw that the rest of the family were just smiling faintly, probably because they weren't as keen on the wilds as Väinö was, but no-one was looking remotely concerned. And there was something in the older man's manner which made Bill think that he wanted to tell him something. All the years of being on the force had given Bill a good instinct for when someone was about to cough up a confession.

"Okay, I'll stay," he agreed. "I've always wanted to see the Lights. It'll be one of those once in a lifetime things for me."

The others departed soon afterwards, but Matti and Nils both warned Bill on the quiet,

"Don't let him get you on his homemade vodka! It's lethal stuff!" With Matti adding,

"Heaven knows where he hides his illicit still, but there always seems to be a ready supply of it! Maybe that's what's addled his brain so much that he couldn't see what my mother had become. But if he offers you it, make sure you dilute it well."

When the taillights of their cars had disappeared, Väinö ushered Bill back inside.

"We've got an hour or two to go yet before the display will be really visible. Make yourself comfortable and I'll go and get us a drink."

Immediately Bill asked, "Could we maybe have a coffee too? Just so that I stay awake long enough to see the Lights?"

"Sure," Väinö replied with a smile, and moments later Bill smelled the wonderful aroma of proper coffee being put on to brew.

When Väinö returned it was with two mugs of very good coffee, and a bottle of something tucked under his arm.

"My son and son-in-law don't drink much," he said with a sigh, "so they don't appreciate this. One sip of anything stronger than beer and they're wrinkling their noses in disgust. Now have a try of this and tell me what you think."

321

Bill had a sip from the simple little glass which Väinö handed him, then gasped in pleasure as the taste slipped over his tongue.

"Bloody hell, that's good!" he gasped, taking another sip. "That's as good as some of the single grape grappas we've started to get coming into England. What's the flavouring in this?"

"Herbs I gather from the forest," Väinö told him, beaming with pleasure. "I knew you would be a man who would appreciate it!"

"My God, you could market this and make a fortune!" Bill complimented him. "Have you ever tried to sell the recipe to one of the big distillers?"

However Väinö shook his head with a wry smile. "I did that with a previous recipe of mine. It was wonderful for the first batch, then they started cutting corners, and by the time the year was out it was a sad shadow of the original. No, I give the recipe and the herbs to friends nowadays. I was a pharmacist, you see. Not the major chemical company kind. I made herbal cures for a moderately large company who just sell in this country. We got on well. They paid me what they could, which was not a poor wage even if I could have earned more elsewhere, and I got the satisfaction of working for a company who had some moral backbone and an ethical conscience."

He sank into the chair opposite and became serious. "I'm sure you think that sounds strange from a man who in your eyes must look like someone who didn't care enough to argue with his own wife about his children. But let me tell you, it wasn't that simple." He leaned back in his chair and seemed to be staring back into the past. "When I met Karita I thought that she was the most beautiful, the most alive person I had ever met."

"I can believe that," Bill encouraged him softly. "She still turns a few heads, I can tell you. She walked through Birmingham airport like she owned the place."

Väinö nodded sadly. "When she was younger she didn't have that arrogance. That came from a man she had a long-running affair with."

"An affair? You knew?"

"Oh yes. I don't know why I thought I would be able to keep a woman like that. When every man notices her there were bound to be a few who would try their chances with her. What I didn't expect was for her to be quite so willing to respond. We'd married in a hurry, you see. Two young folk madly in love and not willing to wait. But the trouble was, I needed to have a good job, because it became clear that although Karita got work as a model here in Finland, she didn't have the right look to make it internationally. So I gritted my teeth and took a job with an international pharmaceutical company.

"She didn't like that, not one bit! Said that I had 'sold out' to 'the man', but what could I do, we had to eat. And once it became clear that her career was going nowhere, all she wanted was to have a family. But even there I failed her."

Bill felt himself go cold. He could see what was coming even before Väinö said,

"We tried and tried, and then I had some tests. Turns out I could never father children. I was too close to some tests when I was doing my military service, if you understand? Not enough to make me sick, but enough to make me sterile.

"That was when Karita started taking lovers whenever I was out of town on business. And I was just about to leave her when she announced that she was pregnant. I got back from a trip to Stockholm to find that she had already told not only her family but mine as well. I was trapped!"

323

"Jeez!" Bill breathed in sympathy. "So you couldn't ditch her without looking a right bastard and having even your own family calling you every name under the sun."

"Exactly. So I stayed and tried to go through the motions. I tried so hard. I prayed every night that the feelings I would have had for my own child would come for this other child. And Annili was a dear child, always smiling. But there was something missing.

"But then it got worse because everyone, my own parents included, kept saying that we should have another child as company for Annili. I tried to say that it didn't matter that she would be an only child, but I was still travelling a lot, and I got back to find that Karita was pregnant again." He sighed deeply. "We had the most bitter row. I asked her how she was going to explain if this child looked nothing like Annili, but she laughed in my face. She said that it was the same man. He couldn't leave his wife because she also had a child and that child wasn't quite right."

He leaned in towards Bill. "I am telling you this because that child was Urho."

"Christ Almighty!"

Väinö nodded sadly. "It is a tangled web Karita has woven. It didn't take me long to work out who the couple were, and I felt very sorry for Urho. He wasn't as bad as they tried to make out when he was a boy, just a bit slow. But he never got any support from his father. I may not have been the ideal father, Bill, but I was a good deal better than that!

"Well I gave up my job with the big corporation and took the job with the local firm I stayed with right up until I retired. I hoped that with me being at home almost every night that it would put a stop to Karita's affair. It did, but it was as though she hated me for it. I could not do anything right. And then her lover left the area, and left his wife and

Urho behind, which Karita blamed me for. She said that if he had still been able to come to her he would have stayed and Urho would have had a father to defend him from the school bullies."

"Not likely, though," Bill sympathised. "Sounds to me like he was a man who would have done whatever he wanted anyway."

"Yes, I thought that. I think he had tired of Karita and wanted someone younger and without two children around her skirts all the time, but she never saw it that way. But he was the man who got her into all the old legends and stories. At first when he'd gone, I saw her obsession with those as being her way of coping with the rejection. The only time I protested was on those times when she came close to neglecting Annili and Matti, when she got so focused on some aspect of them that she could see nothing else. On those times I was glad that I now came home every day, because sometimes it was me who cooked their meals and washed their school uniform."

"That must have been hard."

"It was. And I am honest enough to confess to you that I often resented them. These were not even my children! But at night, when I got home tired from a full day's work, I had to start again looking after them because my wife wouldn't. And the worst of it was that all our neighbours and families thought I was so lucky to have Karita. When I asked my sisters for help they just laughed, Karita was that good at taking people in."

Bill's heart went out to the man. What a wretched life he'd had, and by the sound of it he'd done his best to try and make a go of things. "And what about Tove? Who was her father?" He half wondered whether he should ask, but Väinö seemed to be getting some relief out of finally telling someone the whole truth.

"Oh, by then Karita had found others who were as obsessed as she was. I think – but I can't be sure – that Tove's father was a right con artist, making out that he was a Sami shaman. He certainly seemed to linger about our home at the time. And he was quick enough to run when Karita began proclaiming to the world that she was having a third child."

"Forgive me asking this, but by then Annili was in her teens, and Matti was old enough to be taking notice. Is that why there seems to have been a distance between the two of them and Tove? If this bloke was hanging around like you say, they would surely have been aware of him?"

Väinö nodded. "I think they did. Of course to the outside world if they were a bit distant it was easily explained by the huge gap in ages, but Annili certainly never wanted to take on changing the new baby or feeding her. And she's been a good enough mother to Annikki for me to have seen that she's not lacking in motherly feelings."

"Thank you for telling me this. It makes a lot of sense of why Annili and Matti didn't get so involved when Tove was struggling with young Tapio."

"Yes, they felt very sorry for her, but there wasn't that bond between them which would have had them at her side all the way. And I'm afraid that it cut me to the heart too, because try as I might, I could find nothing in my cures which would even help that poor boy's pain. I wasn't such a vain man as to think I could cure him, but I did have a desperate desire to ease the terrible pain he suffered. But nothing worked. Nothing at all. And in the end it all got too much for me. I had a breakdown. Probably not the best time, and I know Tove was angry that I cracked up when she too was almost at her wits' end, but it wasn't the right time or place to tell her what I'd been putting up with for years before she ever had Tapio."

"God, I can understand that," Bill sympathised. "Look, do you want me to tell the family this? It's a lot easier for me, and I'm not without experience of telling folks stuff they don't want to hear. If it comes from me it'll be a lot easier than from you."

The enormous sigh of relief which came from Väinö told Bill that he'd been trying to summon up the courage to ask Bill to do just that.

"Thank you! I have wanted to tell them so many times, but until they fully saw through Karita there just didn't seem to be any point. And I couldn't believe it when Karita came in and presented Urho to me as the man who would be going to England with Annikki. But now I want my granddaughter to understand that even though I didn't exactly *know* Urho, that I had been keeping an eye on him all the time he was growing up. I even gave his mother some money once or twice, and bought him some clothes on a few occasions – I don't think his real father ever bothered to come back and see if they were alright."

"Ah, on the subject of Urho – what about his family? Annikki told me that no family could be traced?"

Väinö shrugged. "If his father is alive I've no idea where. It's been twenty years since he was last in the area. I saw him only briefly then, and that was in the city. He was just coming out of a bank with a young girl half his age hanging on his arm. He was probably spinning her some tale, but I'd already had enough of his leavings to deal with for me to be worrying about another of his soon to be cast-offs. As for Urho's mother, she died long ago, worn out by having to look after a son who remained a child long after he should have done. It was me who got him a place as an apprentice mechanic, you know. He started off just sweeping the floors and making the tea, but it turned out he had a talent for something after all. I'm just so desperately sorry that he got dragged into Karita's crazy world."

"So there really was no-one left to mourn him?"

"No. But I got in touch with the undertakers; there'll be a proper headstone put on his grave. And that's another thing. It's going to be put in place on Tuesday, would you like to be there?"

"Very much so! And please, let me pay something towards that. It seems to me that you've spent your life picking up Karita's breakages. Well this time it happened on my patch, and I've been feeling guilty ever since then that we didn't protect him better. It would salve my conscience if you'd let me pay half – after all, you're on a pension and I'm still earning."

Väinö accepted Bill's offer graciously, but then a strange light flickered in through the un-curtained window.

"The Lights!" Väinö exclaimed with a smile. "Now, let's go and enjoy the best show on earth!"

Chapter 24

January, Finland

Going outside, Bill gasped in amazement as the sky became shot with glorious shades of green tinged with blues. Väinö had loaned him a thick jacket against the cold, and if Bill's larger size meant that it wouldn't do up, he was too entranced to worry about getting cold.

"That's amazing!" he gasped as the lights shifted and formed a new pattern across the sky.

"I never get tired of looking at this," Väinö admitted. "When it all got too much for me, I'd come out here and just watch. In the summer it's glorious too, but I love the winter because of this."

"I can understand why the ancient people who lived up here thought there were gods in the forest and skies," Bill sighed. "Even though we know more about what causes them, it takes nothing away from seeing these for real. I love the way it changes colours!"

"If we're lucky we might get some reds in there too. They're always shifting. Look over there! They're reflecting on the snow covering the lake."

As Bill lowered his gaze to look at the wonderful patterns playing across the pristine snow of the lake, he saw something moving. Then ambling out of the edge of the trees came a bear!

"My God, I thought they hibernated!" Bill gasped as the bear sat back on its haunches, almost like a human sitting down to look up at the sky. The bear was big too, and Bill had a sudden tingle of fear as he remembered seeing wildlife programmes which showed just how fast these big bears could move if they wanted to. Luckily this one seemed quite happy to just sit and watch the lights.

"He must have woken up. It happens sometimes," Väinö said softly. "Don't worry, we've got plenty of time to get back into the cabin if he looks like taking an interest in us."

"Tapio used to call me Karhu, you know."

"Really?"

"Yes. At first it just amused me, but I've always felt a bit of an affinity with bears. All of my mates laughed when I told them what he called me; they said it suits me. I'm told that my family are Yorkshire through and through, although they'd moved to the Midlands by the time I was born. There's a bit of Viking blood in there if you ask me, because all of us men end up with red beards if we grow one, even though we're not particularly red haired. Must be a bit of the old berserker in there somewhere! I've still got the bear's skull that Tapio and Urho brought over to England, you know."

Väinö positively jumped at that. "You do?"

"Yes. Why, do you want it?"

Väinö seemed too disconcerted to decide. "It was my grandfather who shot that bear, you know. He was Sami." He gave a bitter laugh. "Isn't it ironic – I'm the one with Sami grandparents, not Karita! My family lived in the far north. My mother's father was the first of his family to settle down, and he brought his family south during the Second World War because he was frightened of the Russians taking them if they'd stayed where they used to roam. And my father's grandfather was also Sami. But it was my mother's father who shot the bear. He treasured that skull. He said it was the last time he asked for the blessing for a hunt so that he would have food to bring his family on the long walk to safety."

"Isn't that what Tapio does, give his blessing to a hunt?"

"Yes."

"But how did Urho come to have it?"

"Because I gave it to him. Matti had found it and it frightened him. He had nightmares for weeks afterwards, and Karita demanded I got rid of it. I was taking it out to the car, intending to bring it somewhere up here and bury it – it was before I had this cabin – and Urho saw me. He was absolutely fascinated with it, so I gave it to him. I had no idea that he still had it."

"Had it and valued it from what I saw," Bill told him. "When the Russians made their first attempt to break in, Tapio and Urho began making some old chants, and that skull was put on what I took to be an altar with a candle inside it."

"Really? Well, I'm amazed! I never would have guessed."

"Would you like me to pack it up and send it back to you? It sound like it's really yours anyway."

"Thank you. Yes please, I would really like that. It would be something to remember Urho by."

Then the unearthly call of the bear in the distance made them look again at the lake and then the skies. There in the sky, quite clearly, the lights had shifted to make the shape of a bear. A large red bear against a green background. And Bill thought he heard a familiar voice calling "Karhu!"

Unable to stop himself from grinning Bill said to Väinö, "I think Tapio made it home."

They stayed there, entranced as the best show of lights even Väinö had ever seen were displayed for them. Only when they finally turned for the cabin cold but delighted, did they realise quite how long they had been out there. Yet even as Väinö led the way in, Bill heard something and looked back. Against the white of the snow he was sure he saw three figures in misty shades, and the middle one was waving at him. Yes, Tapio had definitely made it home!

Before we get to the notes which give you some back ground on the story, thank you for taking the time to read this book.

I hope you would like to read other books like this, and the fastest way to do that is to sign up to my mailing list. I promise I won't bombard you with endless emails, but I would like to be able to let you know when any new books come out, or of any special offers I have on the existing ones.

Go to ljhutton.com to find the link

If you sign up, I will send the first in a fantasy series for free, but also other free goodies, some of which you won't get anywhere else!

Also, if you've enjoyed this book you personally (yes, *you*) can make a big difference to what happens next.

Reviews are one of the best ways to get other people to discover my books. I'm an independent author, so I don't have a publisher paying big bucks to spread the word or arrange huge promos in bookstore chains, there's just me and my computer.

But I have something that's actually better than all that corporate money – it's you, enthusiastic readers. Honest reviews help bring them to the attention of other readers (although if you think something needs fixing I would really like you to tell me first!). So if you've enjoyed this book, it would mean a great deal to me if you would spend a couple of minutes posting a review on the site where you purchased it.

Author's Notes

Finnish mythology is a fascinating subject, not least because it really only gets recorded in modern times. The native people who travelled around as many of the modern Sami do would have had little use or space for books. So most of what we know of their world mythology comes from the *Kalevala*, the definitive version being the one written down by Elias Lönnrot in 1835, although it was first written down almost a century earlier. It was to become key in defining Finnish identity in the struggle for Finnish independence from Russia at the time of the First World War. It remains in print today.

The history of Finland is interlinked with Russia. As early as the Middle Ages, the region known as Karelia was ceded to Russia, while the rest of Finland came under Swedish rule. In the 1808-9 war between Russia and Sweden, Russia conquered Finland, and in 1812 the capital was moved from Turku, where it had been throughout Swedish rule, to Helsinki. It was against this background of imposed Russian rule that Lönnrot's *Kalevala* became so important in establishing a separate Finnish identity.

It then becomes understandable that when the Soviet Union signed a non-aggression pact with Germany, and wanted to build military bases in Finland, that the Finns objected. In the Winter War of 1939-40 the Finns' resistance to the Russians became legendary, as with small numbers of troops compared to the Russians, they nonetheless inflicted heavy casualties on the larger army. They fought in small groups, making skirmishes against the Russians in Karelia and Lapland with deadly effect. There are historical accounts of this war if anyone wants to learn more.

The school which Tapio atttends only bears a resemblance to the real schools near the river in Worcester in terms of similar location. The staff and policies of the school in this novel are all fictional and should not be confused with any real school in the city. Nor has anybody has ever been kidnapped from any of the Worcester schools!

Worcester Cathedral is worth a visit, but there is no tomb of a bishop of Worcester in the spot in the north wall of the cathedral as I have described here. However, the crypt in its present form is definitely early Norman, but there was almost certainly an even earlier one on the same site. Certainly there was a cathedral here in Anglo-Saxon times, with its last bishop being the famous Bishop Wulfstan (c.1008-1095), who was one of the very few Anglo-Saxons to remain in office after the Norman Conquest; and it was Wulfstan who ordered the rebuilding of the cathedral of which only the crypt now remains after several later alterations.

Also by L. J. Hutton:

Time's Bloodied Gold
The first Bill Scathlock novel

Standing stones built into an ancient church, a lost undercover detective and a dangerous gang trading treasures from the past. Can Bill Scathlock save his friend's life before his cover gets blown?

DI Bill Scathlock thought he'd seen the last of his troubled DS, Danny Sawaski, but he wasn't expecting him to disappear altogether! The Polish gang Danny was infiltrating are trafficking people to bring ancient artefacts to them, but those people aren't the usual victims, and neither is where they're coming from. With archaeologist friend Nick Robbins helping, Bill investigates, but why do people only appear at the old church, and who is the mad priest seen with the gang? With Danny's predicament getting ever more dangerous, the clock is ticking if Bill is to save him before hc gets killed by the gang ...or arrested by his old colleagues!

The Rune House

A detective haunted by a past case, a house with a sinister secret, and a missing little girl! Can DI Ric Drake rescue her and find redemption along the way?

When DS Merlin 'Robbie' Roberts hears he's got a new colleague it's the last thing he wants, and especially when it's Ric Drake – infamous, recovering from a heart attack and refusing retirement. But when a modern missing child case links to one from Ric's past, and to a mysterious old house on the Welsh borders, they find a common cause. Do the ancient bodies discovered under a modern one hold the clue to both girls' fate, and does the house itself hold the key? As the links to the past keep getting stronger, Robbie and Drake must find a way to break the strange link before more children fall prey to Weord Manor's ancient lure.

Printed in Great Britain
by Amazon